Second in the Series:
And Also Some Women

# The Sin
## of the
# Mother

Sherri Sechrist

1

For information contact:
Sherri Sechrist
P.O. Box 1172
Burleson, TX 76028

Dedicated to my beautiful and loving family:

Parents who have modeled the best of
Christian love, Ernie and Mary Ann;

Children who are the pride and light of my life,
Lauren and Doug;

My husband, best friend, and inspiration,
Steve;

Dedicated to the joyous life and memory of our son,
Christopher Augustus Sechrist.

*The man who does the will of God lives forever.*
*Adapted from I John 2:17*

*After this, Jesus traveled about from one town and village to another, proclaiming the good news of the Kingdom of God. The Twelve were with him, and also some women…*
*Luke 8:1 – 2a NIV*

# CHAPTER 1

"Oof!"

The unexpected impact thrust her in a teeter, wobbling between an upright dignity and a humiliating sprawl in the dirt.

Her skinny arm grabbed for the heavy basket on her head, her first reaction being to safeguard the purchases it contained.

Too late, she realized she was falling. Her other arm flailed wildly, clawing at air... but to no avail. Her stagger lurched into a full blown tumble. There would be no graceful recovery for this gangly, awkward girl.

Her big feet tangled up in her frayed robe and she collapsed into a clumsy heap, inhaling a mouthful of dirt for good measure. The basket rolled on its side, its contents scattered on the dusty street of Shiloh.

Who had she run into as she rushed around the corner from the market?

"Ma... Ma... Marah!"

Marah closed her eyes. Please, no. Not him. Anyone but Benjamin.

"Daughter, Daughter, such a sight! You should walk, not run!"

At the sound of the second voice, she squeezed her eyes shut tight. Please, not him, too. Please, anyone but Benjamin and her father.

"Oh, Benjamin, look at the way my daughter rushes to her work! My Marah is so smart in the market, so accomplished at running our little inn." The round little man with his scant beard turned to Benjamin, a wide smile on his bobbing face. "I don't know what I would do without her, but soon enough she will leave me for marriage, it's true, is it not?"

Marriage. Marah's eyes popped open, the bright sun blocked by a face looking down at her. Even with the shadow of the sunshine behind him, Marah could see the pockmarks on Benjamin's face as he ogled her, his Adam's apple bobbing up and down with nerves.

Her father Naaman leaned over her too, a broad grin stretched from ear to ear as he thundered her name. "Marah! Isn't this something? You ran into Benjamin! Benjamin, it's my daughter, Marah!"

As if the slack-jawed, bug-eyed teenager was so stupid he would not recognize the girl he had known since they were both young, the same girl who had just stood in his father's shop. Only a few moments ago – an eternity now – she had haggled with Benjamin's father over onions while Benjamin hovered nearby, unable to rid himself of a foolish smirk or to meet Marah's obstinate eye.

He gawked at her now, though, his mouth hanging open as he stared at her. "Sss… Sss… Sor… Sorry, Mmm… Mmm… Ma-Marah."

Marah nodded at the stuttered apology even as the lump in her own throat welled up. She could not have whispered a single word if her life depended on it.

It was a mystery to everyone – especially Marah – that her quick mind with its sharp retorts to the Shiloh shopkeepers, to her six older sisters and even to her father was silent as a stone before everyone else. She could not form a single word in the presence of others beyond that intimate circle.

She'd been that way all her life, ever since that terrible day ten years before.

Benjamin stuck out the offer of a hand. Marah shook it off and scrambled to her feet. She was not prone to familiar gestures like arms slung over shoulders, tight hugs of laughter or even a helping hand to pull one up from the dust. The touch of another was alien to her.

She was a towering, skinny jumble of sharp knees and bony

8

elbows topped by a long nose in a thin face, a face with a fierce stare under straight black eyebrows that long ago settled into a frown. The girl was without a single redeeming mark of beauty… unless she smiled.

When Marah smiled, white even teeth were the perfect foil for two deep dimples that crinkled up her somber black eyes and smoothed the wrinkles from her brow. When Marah smiled, she was transformed into a striking young woman.

But Marah rarely smiled.

She bent to pick up her purchases, a red-flushed scowl on her sweating face.

Emboldened by their encounter – perhaps thinking Marah weakened by pain or embarrassment – Benjamin found some shred of bravado to continue.

"I sss… sss… saw you at our shop t… t… today." He bent to help her, but Marah kept her eyes on the dirt, her lips pressed together, secure in her silence.

Neither stuttering nor speechlessness deterred Naaman. "Yes, Benjamin, that was my Marah at the market! I am blessed, seven daughters, all married but Marah. And my Marah, such a good girl! She can read and write and cook. She runs the inn, not me! What a worker! She is all one could want in a daughter. She is all one could want in a wife, a good wife, young Benjamin."

A wife! Marah scrambled to gather the rest of her things, hurrying to escape her father's cheerful ramble, Benjamin's nods of agreement and the knowing stares of both men.

"Yes, my daughter will make a fine wife, a fine wife indeed. 'I am blessed when I go in and when I go out,' says my brother Moses. 'I am blessed in the day and blessed in the night.'"

*"Oh, yes, such a blessing, homely, hideous Marah sprawled out in the dirt. What a fine bride she will be. Run, Benjamin, run!"*

The constant companion Marah so reviled whispered its jeer in her ear. It was all she needed. Marah hefted the basket to her head and gathered a shred of courage.

"Father," she croaked, a quiet note of desperation in her voice. Such an effort for a single word.

But Naaman understood.

"Yes, my Marah, you may go. I know you are anxious to get to work, there is much to do. Many will come, many will go, all on the road to Passover. What would I do without you, my daughter?"

Marah had no idea what he would do and did not plan to stay and find out. She nodded her farewell at two dusty pairs of feet and turned, fleeing to the safety of the ancient inn a few doors away, the place Marah and her father called home.

Voices continued behind her, but Marah didn't hear her father's words of praise or the stammered replies of the gawky Benjamin. She heard only one thing.

*"A bride? I don't think so. You're not a beauty like your sisters. You're the girl no one wants, an ugly, silent stick of a girl. Mangy Marah, that's you."*

No matter how fast she ran, Marah could not outrun the whisper in her head.

ଔ

Marah stomped the last hundred paces to the inn, no minor feat considering she did not slacken her swift pace with the basket of now jumbled purchases balanced on her head.

One old man sat in the courtyard of the inn, waiting for Naaman and an idle conversation in the warmth of the sun. Naaman was not as busy as Marah in the hectic days that marked the coming of Passover.

"Marah." The ancient voice was a familiar, kind croak.

She nodded but did not answer, her steps a trot until she stole into the privacy of the small storeroom with its tidy shelves and ordered supplies. Her sanctuary. No one would bother her here.

She set the heavy basket on the floor and turned to press her forehead against the rough wattle of the mud wall, a lump in her throat. Bitter thoughts swirled through her mind like Samson's foxes with the knotted tails.

Marah knew she was an oddity. At fourteen, she was a spinster by the standards of the neighboring wags. Something terrible was going to happen to her and soon. No matter how much she argued, cajoled or pouted, her father would soon marry her to Benjamin or some other dolt just like him.

She saw Benjamin in her mind's eye, with his stutter and blemish-scarred face and gaze that could not hold her own. Marah did not dislike him. She just could not marry him. How in the world could she spend the rest of her life with him?

*"He spits like a snake and you are silent as a stone. Seems like a*

*perfect match to me."*

She shook away the maddening whisper that taunted her at every turn.

Marry Benjamin? Impossible.

But what could she do?

*"You can't do anything. Anything right, anyway."*

She slid to the floor, willing her mind and the whisper to be still. There was much to do and only Marah to do it. She took a deep breath, the familiar mental litany of her chores calming her. Supplies to store in their rightful places. Guest rooms to ready. Water to carry. An evening meal to prepare, visitors to receive, animals to bed in the stable. Much to do.

Passover Week began in two nights. Every room in their inn would soon be full with well-to-do visitors making their way to Jerusalem, families who would leave in the morning to be replaced by others later that day. The next two days would be busy.

Marah seldom went to Passover in Jerusalem, leaving her father to make that journey with his old cronies. Someone needed to stay at the inn, after all. Shiloh was a routine stop for the faithful making their pilgrimage to the Holy City of David. Marah knew most of the travelers by name, guests who returned year after year.

Occupancy took three forms: empty, one or two visitors with their choice of the narrow ten rooms, or so full they turned people away. Marah remembered the time she bedded down an entire family in the hay with the travelers' donkeys, not a single room available at their inn. They were so grateful, but sleeping with donkeys!

The family was large and very poor, just like Marah's. She vowed on the spot she would never, ever sleep in a stable – even though their stable was her most favorite place in the world. Still, who would want the humiliation of sleeping in one?

*"Remember how happy they were, the father and all those children. Oh, and remember their mother, how much everyone loved her?"*

She shook her head, relentless in the pursuit of uninterrupted thoughts. If only she could live alone in her own head.

Her father would leave for Jerusalem in two days, staying here as long as possible to help with the rush of Passover business at the inn. Or to catch up with old friends, Marah snickered. She could not stay angry with her beloved father… only cross.

"Why does my father bring up marriage to horrible

11

Benjamin now, when I am so busy?" Her voice seemed overly loud in the tiny room.

Marah doubted Naaman had any idea how much she loathed Benjamin. Naaman was oblivious to the daily details of his youngest daughter's life.

"Why can't I just accept the fate of my sisters?"

But Marah knew why.

Marah's six sisters were short and curvy with curly hair, dimples and sparkling brown eyes. They were famed far and wide for their beauty and good humor. Save the eldest, they were opinionated and meddling and free with their unwanted advice for Marah.

For the first eight years of her short life, the motherless Marah had been ordered around by one or another of her sisters. Only Miriam, with the de facto role of motherhood thrust upon her eight-year-old shoulders, won little Marah's affection. Miri was the closest thing to a mother Marah ever knew.

One by one, Naaman's six beautiful daughters married and moved into their own Shiloh homes, Miriam's betrothal and wedding to a teacher of the law the most celebrated marriage of all. Only homely Marah was left behind with Naaman.

Her sisters had no interest in the inn. Marah did not want their lives or marriages or children anyway. She wanted the life she had right now, her and her father and the inn.

As each bossy sister left, Marah's responsibilities and freedom grew. With no mother to guide her and with the pleased encouragement of the lonely widower, Marah followed her father about like a shadow. He responded to every question the little girl asked, and to his surprised delight, the girl was quick to learn the answers.

"Too smart for a girl!" Marah could not count the times she'd overheard the comment. Marah didn't care. She loved her life, alone with her father at the inn.

Everyday, she used her head to solve problems, taking care of things before her father even knew anything was wrong.

If an unexpected group of guests arrived late, Marah would prepare a quick and hearty meal, enough to satisfy every guest, from her well-stocked storeroom.

After the guests left, Marah alone set each room to right, each room soon pristine and ready for the next weary traveler.

She shopped for all the supplies; the merchants claimed it

was easier to squeeze water from a stone than to get one extra copper coin from Marah.

Two years ago, she started helping her father keep his simple record of guests, noting with painstaking, careful entries on the worn leather hide who had paid, who owed money and who might stop on a return trip. Today, that chore was left to Marah.

If a shutter hung on its hinge or a crack appeared in a wall, before the day was out Marah would make the repair herself. She was a girl unafraid of hard work. Indeed, work was her only friend. There wasn't time for the silly girls of tiny Shiloh. She only cared about her inn and her father.

"I am as smart as my father," Marah thought. "Why must every decision about me be made by him? Why can't I have some say in the matter?"

*"You should have been born a man, Marah. Then you could do whatever you wanted. Your sisters were right. You're a skinny girl who looks like a boy, flat-chested with muscles in all the wrong places. You're a terrible girl. You should have been a boy, the little brother your sisters really wanted."*

Marah shook her head at the memory of her sisters' taunts and the cruel barb of the whisper.

True, she was as good as any man, but she was, after all, still a woman. She just did not want to be married off to the first available Jewish boy from Shiloh.

*"The first? Try the fifth."*

Marah scowled but the whisper always spoke truth. Benjamin was not her father's first recommendation for a husband. Marah resolutely vetoed the four suggestions before him.

And though her father often spoke of finding her a husband, he had not pushed to marry off his last daughter. Marah knew why, and it was not because he needed her help, or because she was so talented at running the inn, or because she didn't like the husbands he previously offered to his youngest daughter.

No, there was only one reason Naaman had not yet married off Marah.

He loved her. More than any of his daughters, Naaman wanted his youngest girl to be happy. His wife dead these long fourteen years, this youngest daughter had been at his side almost since she was born, and certainly every moment the last ten years.

What would happen when Marah left her father for the life a Jewish girl was called to lead?

13

Marah knew.

Without her, Naaman would be a lonely old man in an inn falling into disrepair and neglect.

She couldn't leave her father or the inn.

When she married, who would help aged Naaman?

No one, thought Marah. There is no one but me.

"Why must I give up my life for marriage to someone like Benjamin? He is not even bright enough to tie the laces on his sandals!"

Not even the whisper answered her.

She could not imagine spending the rest of her life with Benjamin, to work with him, worship with him, live with him... to have children with him. She shuddered. With six sisters who gabbed to each about everything, Marah knew what that entailed.

She had never even spoken ten words to Benjamin!

Of course, if one compiled a list of the young men to whom Marah had ever spoken ten words, it would be a short list indeed. A non-existent list, really. Except to bicker over a price at the market, Marah could not find the courage to speak to anyone outside of her family.

Marah snorted. If this were not so serious, she would be amused.

If only she had someone to confide in, someone to talk to about her dreams, her hopes, her questions. But Marah's only friend was her oldest sister Miri. Right now Miri was busy with a husband about to leave for Jerusalem, with her three children and with a belly great with her fourth child.

Marah despised the company of her other sisters. All they ever talked about was the need for Marah to get married, alternating between ridicule to embarrassment to sympathy for her pathetic spinster state.

Even Miriam was starting to annoy Marah. Miri was firm that Marah's destiny was to be married, the sooner the better. "Don't worry about father and the inn! You must get married and soon!" Marah could hear the scolding tone.

Of course, it was easy for Miriam to be so flippant about Marah's marriage. After all, didn't Miriam have a marriage that was still the talk of Shiloh?

Asa was been a young man with a bright future. He studied for months at a time in Jerusalem. He was a young teacher of the law, working in their little synagogue school and even serving in the Holy Temple for four weeks each year! A young man with promise.

To everyone's surprise, this studious, bearded, quiet young man fell in love with the oldest daughter of an impoverished innkeeper, the beautiful, smiling, curly-haired Miriam. It was an unheard of match for the rising star that was Asa and dowerless daughter of Naaman. Ten years later, Asa still taught in the Shiloh school, was still was a man of promise rather than accomplishments, and still adored his beautiful wife and growing family.

If Miriam, who was married so well and so happily to Asa, told Naaman his youngest must marry, that would be the end of it. Naaman might ignore the chattering of his other five daughters, but he listened to Miriam.

No one was on Marah's side in the distasteful subject of marriage.

But married to Benjamin?

Ugh.

*"That's probably exactly what Benjamin thinks about marrying you, Marah. Ugh."*

If her only company was going to be the whisper, she might as well get busy. The whisper would offer its opinion if she were busy or idle, that much she knew.

*"You have other company besides me, you know. You could always pray to your father's Jehovah…"* The scorn was unmistakable.

Marah refused to admit what the whisper knew. Long ago she stopped wasting the time it took to kneel in prayer. Her days were so full of chores and hard work and worry. Who had time to pray?

Anyway, in all these years, God never spoke to Marah.

Still, I could use a little divine intervention, Marah thought. It would be about time, too.

She closed her eyes and pressed her forehead against the rough wall, as though willing God to hear her thoughts, to hear her prayer, to know the fears in her heart.

"Lord, I know your path for me cannot be the path my father has chosen. As Moses said to you, 'In the morning I will see the glory of the Lord, because you have heard my grumbling.'"

Naaman quoted his beloved Moses from dawn to sunset. This was one of her father's favorite quotes from the patriarch of old, or one of the few that Marah could remember, anyway. Naaman often directed it toward his youngest daughter when he thought she was being a mite too tetchy with the patriarch of their household of two.

She forced her father out of her mind. He was the cause of this dilemma anyway.

"What is your glory, Lord? What is my path to be? I hate to grumble, but I know my life is not to be shared with Benjamin. I know you would not choose that for me, Lord. I know it. So what is my path, Lord? What?"

She waited in the silence of her workroom, eyes squeezed shut, jaw clenched, waiting and listening, trying not to think of the work waiting for her, trying to hear the mysterious voice of the God her father worshipped.

Silence.

She opened her eyes.

*"Perhaps if you were not always grumbling against God, perhaps if you were just once obedient instead of such a smug know-it-all, perhaps you would hear what God has to say."*

Of course. There was the only answer Marah ever got to her prayers. A soft, sarcastic whisper mocking her, making fun of her, taunting her, speaking truths she could not bear to utter herself.

"Fine." The word was loud and belligerent, the better for God to hear.

Her father was old and weary. There was much to do today and only Marah to do it. It was time to work, not to worry or pray.

But she spoke aloud again, giving Jehovah one last chance.

"If you would just show me something, Lord, anything… I would do my best not to grumble anymore."

Nothing.

"Fine. Well, just to be clear, Lord, I do not intend to marry Benjamin."

Marah left the storeroom, the work of her inn waiting, the business of her unanswered prayers complete.

# CHAPTER 2

Naaman sat in the warm sunshine with an old crony from his past, reminiscing about their youth, the two beautiful women they called their wives, their children, their grandchildren and whatever else crossed their idle minds.

"I remember the day you become betrothed, my friend. Oh, you were the envy of all us, to take a bride of such great beauty. And she loved you, too. An added blessing from Jehovah. It was such a tragedy that you lost her when your youngest daughter was born."

Naaman grunted, the pain still raw after all these years. "A sad day. Your wife was lovely, too. And you had such a long marriage."

Their shared silence spoke loudly to the recent burial of one man's wife and the death of the other's fourteen long years ago.

"And our children."

"Yes, all our children."

"I will never know why God burdened you with such a house so full of women, my friend. I do not understand it. Not one son in the mix!"

"Ah."

"Why did God's favor turn against you, to send you daughter after daughter, first one and then another?"

"Yes, at one point I cried out to Jehovah like the Moses to Jehovah: "'I have become a foreigner in a foreign land', for I was the lone man in house full of females!"

The two men laughed, the sun warming their frail bones.

"Friend, I will always be grateful for the exceeding bounty of Jehovah."

"Eh?"

"What would I have been after my wife died if not for my seven daughters? Just a lonely, bitter old man. Instead, my life was full of noise and laughter and chaos! Only because of my beautiful daughters."

"But no son, my friend..."

"No son, but six fine sons-in-law. And all my daughters are married save one. All are nearby to watch over their father in his old age."

"Ah."

"Every day I seem to have another grandchild. Miriam and Asa will add one more at any time now. There are so many, I can hardly think of their names, except for the two boys named Naaman."

"Two boys named Naaman!"

"But you'd better believe those curly-haired toddlers know their Grandfather! Whenever I turn around, there's always one or more hanging from my knees or my back or my beard. As Moses said to the Lord, 'What I have done to displease you, that you put the burden of all these people on me?'"

"The burden of all these people?"

"There's always a daughter or a grandchild underfoot, and sometimes I look up and here they all sit in my courtyard! Six of my seven girls have married and moved, yet my house is still noisy and messy and full of children."

"It's a good life, my friend."

"A very good life, indeed."

"All married save one?"

"All but my Marah. I am almost finished with the duties of a father, the responsibilities to my girls as commanded by the precepts of our Almighty Lord God and the laws of Moses."

"Almost finished."

"Almost finished, yes, I am almost finished with my work as a father."

The two old men basked in the warmth, Naaman's chin drooping on his chest, his breathing even and steady.

"Perhaps you won't want to marry off that youngest girl, Naaman."

Naaman's head jerked up.

His friend continued. "Look how hard she works here at the inn. You have no sons. Who will help you here if she marries and leaves?"

Naaman was silent. He did not know his problem was that apparent to others, even if it was an old friend who had shared this bench with him for many years.

"What will you do when she leaves?"

Naaman sat without speaking.

"Sometimes I think it would have been easier to care for thousands of complaining Israelites than to be a poor man with seven beautiful daughters. But you have done well in the eyes of Jehovah, my friend. You will do the right thing for your daughter Marah."

Naaman nodded. He turned to his friend. "I am grateful to Yahweh for all He has done. But I wonder… I am a faithful Jew, a loving father… Why do you suppose the All-Knowing, Almighty Jehovah has made this last paternal duty so infernally difficult? Why is Marah so difficult? She has rejected every husband I have offered!

"I have found a husband that is a good fit. She is so shy, she doesn't even know him! But it is a good fit, she would be as big a help to him and his family as she has been to me. But I am afraid she will talk me out of it again!"

"Spare the rod, old friend, spare the rod."

Naaman could not imagine using the rod on any of his daughters or grandchildren, but especially not on Marah. Her young life had already been so hard, motherless since the moment she drew breath and wailed her newborn cry.

He had no intention of using the rod at this point in his life.

"Be bold, my friend. You are the father. Just tell her what she must do. The father always knows what is best."

Easy advice from a man who never had any daughters, much less one like Marah, Naaman thought. He closed his eyes to silence his old friend and soon his pretense of a nap gave way to the real thing.

ം

Only three rooms were left to clean. The inn was almost ready for the next wave of guests. Marah found herself humming, pleased with her hard work.

"Marah."

"Hello, Father! Did you enjoy your afternoon nap?"

Naaman bristled. "I was not sleeping, I was visiting. Can a man not rest his eyes against the glare of God's sun?"

Marah laughed. She'd overheard the comfortable snores of the two men, but her good mood overcame her inclination to contradict. Naaman could nap all he wanted; it freed Marah to structure her day as she wanted.

"Marah, I want to talk with you. I have something to tell you."

"Yes, Father?"

"Marah, stop. I have something important to tell you. Very important."

Marah turned. Her father was an open book, and she knew at once this was news he did not want to share with Marah. He looked as nervous as a plover near her nest.

Naaman lowered himself to the low pallet and crossed slow arthritic knees with a sigh. "Ah, that's better. Sit, Marah."

"Father, I have much to do yet." Could she escape with the excuse of her work?

"Sit. I have something of great significance to tell you. Very, very important."

She sat at the far corner of the bed, chin high, her back as straight as a board, every muscle taut. Naaman had started a conversation with just those words, in just this manner, on four other occasions. She stared straight ahead.

"Marah, Benjamin's father and I have agreed that the two of you should enter into a betrothal."

It could not be true.

"He is a good man of a good family, Marah. It is a good match."

She had not thought the conversation about marriage to Benjamin would come up this soon. Marah did not quite have her arguments ready.

"No. I will not marry Benjamin."

Naaman never argued with Miriam, the wise rock of his family. His five other daughters, with their dimples and tearful pouts and sweet talk could amuse but never sway him. But Marah… Marah would argue, reason, make her case for so long that soon he could not remember which side he started on.

But not this time.

"You will marry Benjamin. It is done. This will not be an argument, Marah. I am your father and it is my duty to see you wed."

Marah crossed her arms, a mutinous look on her face.

"He is a good boy, Marah. He is from a good family."

She heard the pleading tone in his voice and pounced on it.

"Of course he is a good boy from a good family." She forced herself to sound agreeable.

"Don't pretend to be sweet with me, Marah! You are as prickly as a thistle. I will not be fooled while you try to talk your way out of this one. You will be married to Benjamin. I will enter into a betrothal contract after Passover."

"Father. I cannot marry Benjamin."

"Why not? He is from a good family." Naaman did not know why he felt compelled to repeat this. Marah had already agreed with him. "It is a good match!"

Marah saw his reddening face and chose her words carefully. "But I do not like Benjamin. Yes, he is from a good family and will someday grow up to be a good man. He will make some woman a good husband." Marah's pleasant smile did not mask the condescending tone in her voice. "Some other woman. Not me."

"Not some other woman, Marah, you! You, my stiff-necked daughter, descendant of the mighty Moses! And you do not even know Benjamin. You will grow to love him!"

Marah opened her mouth but he held his hand up to silence her.

"It is a very good match, he is the oldest son of a shopkeeper, a shop that he will someday own. He will not have to labor at the whisper or whim of another man who is his master."

Marah shrugged but inside her stomach was rolling. Her father sounded different this time. Had he already started a process she might not be able to stop?

"And you, Marah, you are the last daughter of a poor innkeeper, with no real dower. And this young man, this Benjamin, he wants to marry you. This is a good match, Marah."

"No. I cannot."

"You can and you will marry Benjamin. His father sees how

smart you are. You can help to run their shop, help in ways that Benjamin cannot."

Marah pounced on the argument. "Benjamin cannot run his father's shop because he is a dolt! Slow of speech and tongue, as your Moses would say. I would add a meandering mind to his attributes. I cannot marry him."

Naaman scrambled to his feet, grunting at the stiffness of his joints. "Marah, Marah! This time, you will do as I say. You must. As it says in the Book of Moses: 'Why do you quarrel with me? Why do you put your father to the test?' Marah, I am your father!" The pitch of his voice rose higher until the last word father was almost a squeak. He coughed. "Honor thy father, Marah!"

Marah stood too, a disadvantage for Naaman. His youngest daughter was easily a head taller than he. He flinched at the set of her jaw, the steel in her eyes.

"Honor thy father, Marah." But Naaman's brief spurt of anger was weakening. He loved the daughter who loved him best too much, and she knew it.

At the look on her father's face, Marah knew at once she had her edge.

"Father, Father… I love you so!" She looked down at him, a wide smile showing off her rare dimples. She'd heard it from her sisters for years: 'You are so pretty when you smile.' Perhaps Naaman would be swayed by what he so rarely saw: his youngest daughter smiling.

"Father, I believe Moses said 'Why do you put the Lord to the test?' I do not wish to test you, Father. You are right. Young Benjamin is very nice. He will make some woman a fine husband. Just not me." She spoke as though she was talking to a child, an imbecile child, slowly and deliberately, the smile never leaving her face.

She picked up the broom and began sweeping the wood floor of the guest room, talking as she worked, as though this were an ordinary conversation.

"Father, I will stay here with you until I die. I will work for you at the inn. Who else is there to help you? I will dedicate myself to you and, like the great prophetesses Huldah and Noadiah, dedicate myself to our Almighty God." She turned to face him. "I cannot, however, dedicate myself to Benjamin, Father. It is not God's destiny for me."

She tucked the broom under her arm, picked up the soiled towels and walked to the door.

"But thank you, Father. I know you mean well."

"Marah, Marah, my lovely, fierce Marah."

*"Lovely? Lovely Marah?"*

She couldn't argue with both of them.

Marah, tall, skinny and towering an easy eight inches taller over her short, round father, leaned down to kiss him on the forehead.

"I love you, Father."

She turned to leave but paused at her father's soft reply.

"'Since I am slow of speech and tongue, why would Marah listen to me?' So says the Book of Moses."

She did not turn around. She won a brief reprieve. She knew it. He knew it.

*"But he doesn't know you know it. You can use that to your advantage, Marah."*

Sometimes, just sometimes, the whisper was very wise.

Marah walked out with a wide smile, a pretty dimpled face for no one to see.

# CHAPTER 3

Marah sat at the door of her courtyard, deftly mending a tear in one of Naaman's threadbare robes, waiting for the last guest of the day, one who stopped without fail on his trips to the Holy City. A room was always set aside for this traveler.

She looked up at the shadow standing in the door.

"Jarius, at last! Finally you have arrived!"

Marah craned her neck at the tall man before them, but it was Naaman who greeted their guest. Marah and her father had set aside their mid-day quarrel in the afternoon flurry of arriving guests and their mutual discomfort at having argued. There would be plenty of time to continue the battle another day far too soon.

"Master Naaman." Jarius laid a hand on Naaman's stooped shoulder, towering over the old man. He nodded at Marah, who turned red and bent down to scribble his arrival on the old sheepskin in her lap, lest he initiate a conversation with her. While she knew this man well, she had not spoken to him in ten years.

"And how is my old friend these days? How is your father, Jarius?"

Jarius shook his head. "Worse, I am afraid. He struggles for breath and his pain is... some days, his pain is terrible to see."

"I am sad to hear it. I miss your father. Please, Jarius, sit with me. Let us catch up." Naaman motioned to the bench. Jarius was a favorite of Naaman's, the only son of his lifelong friend from Capernaum, a man who now lay ill with a disease no one could cure.

"I was afraid you would miss our evening meal. Marah has prepared your room for you."

"Thank you, Naaman. I will be glad to see that room this evening. It has been a long day."

Jarius had stayed in the same room at the inn for years, a room twice the size of any other, the only accommodation that commanded an income of any significance.

"It's your room, Jarius! Where your father stayed, where you have always stayed, the room where you and your bride Deborah once stayed, too. Ah, Jarius, we have seen too much, haven't we, my son? I'm so glad to see you. Sit with me."

Jarius fumbled with the pouch on his belt, answering in a low voice. "First allow me to wash off the dust of my travel, Naaman. Perhaps Asa can join us, too?"

"Ah, Asa." Naaman smiled at the mention of his son-in-law.

Jarius bowed in respect to the older man but handed several coins to his daughter. "Marah, I leave for Jerusalem before first light tomorrow. You won't need to prepare any food for me in the morning. I will return in one week but pay you now for both nights' lodging, if I may."

Marah took the coins, a red flush flooding her face at the direct address from Jarius.

Naaman answered on her behalf. "Jarius, you are always welcome. I would be offended if you did not come to see us when you passed through! Marah will see to your donkey, and dinner will be ready in only a short time. We will send word to Asa."

Jarius nodded and left without speaking. Marah was careful to not look up, noting his advance payment on the worn cowhide. Stretched taut over a wooden frame, it had been used and reused so many times you could almost see through it. Still, it served its purpose, allowing Marah to make her tidy marks as to money collected for rooms and food during such a busy time.

But the moment Jarius was out of ear shot, she spoke.

"Father! Why must you speak of Jarius's sick father? Didn't you see how that upset him?"

Her father cocked his head at his daughter, silent.

"And why did you bring up Deborah? Didn't you see how sad Master Jarius looked when you said her name?"

She pressed her lips together in frustration, not wanting to scold her father. One argument with her father in a day was already more than she could bear.

A sad smile pulled at Naaman's face. "But Marah, he loves his father. It's good to ask others about the people they love. Jarius still grieves for his Deborah. Even though she and their baby son have gone to be with Jehovah, it is a comfort to know that others remember those we love who are with the Lord."

"I just don't think you should make him sad the minute he walks in."

"To remember is not to be sad, Marah. If your family and friends do not remember the ones we have loved and lost, who will? Someday you will understand, Marah. After all, I still love your mother after all these years…"

At the mention of his beloved wife, the usual tears welled up in the old man's eyes.

Marah could not stand one more bout of emotion with her father, and most of all she could not discuss her mother with him. She jumped to her feet, a forced gaiety in her voice.

"Our rooms are full at last, Father."

Naaman nodded, wiping his eyes.

She pressed on with her cheerful tone. "I will take care of Master Jarius's donkey and send for Asa. It will only take a moment, and then you and the guests can eat. Everything is ready. All right?"

Naaman nodded, dabbing at his tears.

Marah turned to leave.

"I love you, daughter."

Marah did not stop to answer the old man. She did not like to argue with her father, but even more, she could not bear that she was the cause of his fourteen years of sorrow.

ॐ

Strong as an ox, Marah was still weary with the day's work. After the morning guests departed, she set their rooms to right and then turned around to situate the new arrivals. The aroma of Marah's dinner for three dozen people filled the courtyard, but there was still much to do in Marah's day.

She found her oldest nephew sitting in the courtyard, watching the milling guests and their children. Under her watchful eye, he took the guests' donkeys two by two to the well for water. The animals were bedded down in the stable for the night. He sat quiet as a mouse, waiting for his next task.

"Good job," she whispered to the boy. "You are my best helper." His black eyes shone at Marah's approval. He was the oldest of the twenty nephews and nieces that adored their Auntie Marah as much as they loved their Grandfather Naaman.

"Now run home and tell your father that Master Jarius has arrived. Asa is waiting to see him. And take care of your mother! Any day now you will have a baby brother or sister to take care of, too."

"Do you want me to take the last donkey to the stable?"

"No, just run and fetch your father."

The eight-year-old sprinted from the courtyard.

Marah undid the reins of Jarius's donkey herself and pulled him into the stable. She ignored the welcome bray of their family donkey, by far the oldest animal in the assembly of animals.

Ah! Just as she'd asked, her nephew left a full bucket of water in anticipation of the latecomer.

Marah led the sleek donkey into the last stall and removed his blanket. She stopped to stroke his gray nose. He stared at her with unblinking brown eyes, a solemn agreement to Marah's own persistent thoughts.

"Yes, Mistress Marah, you must not marry Benjamin."

Marah laughed to herself. She was in sad shape if the only affirmation she could find was from a donkey, and someone else's donkey at that.

For as long as she could remember, Jarius had been a guest at their inn, first with his father, then alone when his father fell ill, and then with a new wife, a confident, beautiful woman with her rich robes, silken voice and laughter like the chime of a small silver bell.

Once, a much-younger Jarius teased and chased her sisters. Later, her sisters whispered and giggled about his strong build and handsome good looks.

However, except for the love-smitten Asa, men like Jarius did not marry the daughters of poor innkeepers, even if the innkeeper and the young man's father were life-long friends. Jarius was the son of a ruler, the man in charge of the Capernaum synagogue. He was the only heir in a wealthy and influential family. Men like Jarius married women like Deborah.

The first meeting with Deborah so awed five of Marah's older sisters, they became as mute as the mum Marah.

All but one.

While Deborah dazzled Naaman and the five sisters and their husbands and every guest of the humble inn, only Marah noticed the single cool reception.

"An arranged marriage," Miriam sniffed to Marah. "Not a marriage of substance."

Only Marah noticed the slightest edge of condescension in Deborah's greeting to Miriam, the equally lovely wife of her husband's good friend Asa.

Marah often noticed things that other missed. But she never shared her observations with anyone but the whisper in her head.

Engaged in their own laughter, Asa and Jarius missed any reserve between the two women at the first meeting and the future meals they shared.

Miriam never spoke a word about Deborah again. Only Marah senses the tension in her sister whenever Jarius and his bride stopped at the inn in Shiloh.

But now, Deborah was gone, lost in childbirth along with their first-born son. A shadow would pass across Miriam's face whenever Deborah's name was mentioned.

Jarius always knew what his destiny would be, Marah thought.

*"But not every destiny turns out the way it was planned, does it?"*

Jarius's wife and son were dead. His father was old and sick and would not rule much longer. Jarius would soon take over his father's role, years before his appointed time.

No matter how much people planned for their destiny… destinies sometimes changed themselves.

*"You could change your destiny, too…"*

"Marah!" She jumped at her father's bellow from the inn's courtyard. "As Moses said, 'We are waiting, give us meat to eat!' Time to serve our meal!"

It was her father's standard call whenever the guests appeared to be ready to eat – or he was hungry. Naaman was convinced Moses possessed the wisdom and word for every situation.

But for once her father was right. It was time to serve dinner and there was still much work for Marah to do.

Marah rushed from the stable. Let the donkeys ponder the destiny of Jarius.

The evening meal over, the guests meandered to the benches in the courtyard, chatting in the cool night air as they warmed themselves around the large fire pit. The flames leapt high, the fire roaring. Marah started it as soon as she finished serving dinner to her guests.

While her guests ate, Marah rushed from room to room, emptying the dirty water bowls and pouring fresh water in each of the ten bowls. Her guests would have fresh water to wash away dinner and to refresh themselves in the morning.

It was a great deal of extra work, something few inns would offer. After all, the well was only a few paces down the street. But there was a reason that people stayed at Naaman's little inn year after year, and that newcomers came bearing the names of friends who told them to break their travels in Shiloh.

In the courtyard, men sat warming themselves by the fire, their low voices discussing everything from the Romans to the Torah to local and Temple politics. Women clustered in small groups, laughing while watchful eyes followed children chasing round the fire. One by one, guests and families began to retire to their rooms, satisfied by their meal, weary from their travels.

Marah was still working. The dishes were already washed and stowed. Her broom made short work of the dinner crumbs left behind by the younger children. She stood alone at her workbench, wrapping food in clean towels for the morning travelers.

"All is ready, my daughter?" Marah looked at the stooped frame of Naaman. He looks tired, she thought.

"Yes, Father. I baked bread with dried fruit for families to take with them. Several families have already purchased bread for their trip on the road. Here is some extra cheese I made two days ago. I can sell that, too."

Naaman nodded, pleased with her efforts.

"A good week for our little inn, yes?"

Naaman nodded. In his old age, it was a great comfort to know there was someone he could trust to manage his little inn. If only that person were a son and not his youngest daughter.

"Yes, a good week. Do you need any help?"

Her father never helped her; he only got in Marah's way. "No, Father. Go and sit with Asa and Master Jarius, visit a little. It has been a long day for you."

"Will you bring a little more wine for us, Marah? The cold is seeping into my bones."

She smiled at last. If anyone deserved a little company and wine, it was her father.

*"He's getting old. Soon he won't be around to tell you what to do anymore. Or to marry you off to some buffoon..."*

Asinine whisper.

"Marah, when I return from Passover, you and I must talk." He laid his gnarled hand on her shoulder. "We must talk of your marriage to Benjamin."

Marah's good mood disappeared like smoke in the wind. "Father, you know I have been far too busy to think of that today." She hesitated. She knew her father's one frailty. He loved his children too much, especially her.

*"Say something now, Marah. You know when your father is feeling weak."*

The duplicitous whisper was right. Now was the time to get rid of Benjamin once and for all.

The irritation left her voice, replaced with a kinder, more persuasive tone. "Father, Benjamin is not a good match for me. I would not be happy. I am happiest here with you. Look how hard I have worked for you today, and what a good day we have had."

She sat on a low stool. Looking up at him was much more persuasive than towering over him.

"Marah, I wish you could stay with me forever. You are such a good girl, such a great help to me."

"Here with you, this is my life. It is what I must do. This is my destiny, Father."

"It cannot be, daughter, it cannot be. I do not know what your destiny is, but it cannot be to run our little inn until the end of your days."

Marah's gaze was unwavering. The hardness between them brought tears to her father's eyes again.

She felt a catch in her own throat. She knew it hurt him to be stern with her.

Marah bit back her harsh answer and broke the mood with a small laugh, standing to hug her short, sweet father.

"I did not mean to make you cry, Father!" She used the hem of her loose veil to wipe his eyes.

Naaman laughed a little, too, and put his arms around her. "As it is written in the Book of Moses, 'We will wait to find out what the Lord commands concerning you.' God will speak to me about your destiny, Marah. He will speak to me and to you."

They stood in silence for a moment.

I'm listening, thought Marah.

"*I don't hear anything, do you, Marah?*" The whisper was laughing.

Marah shook her head. She didn't have time to stand around like this. God apparently had nothing to say to Marah, and she had things yet to do.

She took her father's arm, interrupting his reverie with God. "Go. Sit with Jarius and Asa. I will bring some wine."

He nodded and slowly shuffled to the dying fire, confident in the promise of God's destiny for his daughter.

ભ

Marah made one last tour of the inn, checking the stable, the courtyard, the gate. The inn was quiet; her long day was finally over. Only three people remained in the courtyard huddled around the dying fire: Asa, Jarius and her father.

She started to ask if anyone wanted more wine, but paused in the shadows, startled by the sound of weeping. Jarius was crying.

"She died with the baby, a perfect boy! I only held him for a moment…"

His words were slurred with wine. Marah had heard it many times before at the inn, but never once with Jarius or his father.

"I turned to look at Deborah. She had a look of terror on her face, pain and terrible fear, something I can never forget. It haunts my dreams! I remember her maids pulling me from the room, the shrieks of the mid-wife, the screams of my wife. And the blood, oh, the blood was everywhere."

He was sobbing. Marah heard the murmur of Asa's voice, his words unintelligible.

"I know, Asa! But I am angry. I have no one else to talk to, I cannot speak of this in Capernaum. I cannot understand why Jehovah took them both from me. We were only been married a year! I cannot understand…"

"It is a hard thing, Jarius." Naaman's reached an arm out to

Jarius as he spoke. "It feels like yesterday that I too lost my wife of so many years, lost her in childbirth just like Deborah. Such a hard thing."

A spasm of pain shot through Marah's head.

*"Deborah died in childbirth like your mother."*

"We are blessed, Jarius."

"Blessed! How so, Naaman, how so?" Marah heard the anguish in Jarius's voice.

"When God sends a glorious spring full of new life, are you not thankful? Do you not remember the budding leaves, the bright flowers, the green grass long after the blooms are gone and the grass has turned gray? God gave us wives we loved, and we will always be thankful and remember them as God's gifts to us!"

*"Your father will never forget your mother."*

She wanted to leave, but her feet were rooted in the shadows.

"You are young, you will marry again."

"Never."

She heard but could not understand Asa's response.

"And now my father is dying." Jarius's face was distorted by pain and odd shadows from the fire. "If it were not for my father, I would leave Capernaum at once. I would move to Jerusalem, Caesarea on the Sea, anywhere to be away from these terrible memories!"

"As it says in the Book of Moses, 'The Lord has given you a despairing heart.'"

"My father will be dead. I will be alone in Capernaum. How can I bear it?" His voice rose. "I only want to be rid of that city. It is nothing but agony to me!

"You are the only one who can care for your father. You will stay." Her father's voice was sharp. "But when he dies, you must stay in Capernaum for another, even more important reason."

"What reason is that, Naaman?" Jarius sounded defeated.

"Why, you are to be the ruler, Jarius! Remember? Your father has worked for years to secure this destiny for you. Those from Capernaum speak highly of you. You are all we hope our rulers would be. You and Asa, you are the next generation to lead the Jews. Why would you want to leave Capernaum now, Jarius?'

Marah could hear Jarius sigh all the way into the shadows. "My grief is too great for me to lead others on the path of Yahweh,

Naaman."

"Jarius, your father's heart would be as broken as your own if you turned away from this. Even Moses doubted, you know. You are bound to Capernaum. Your father is dying. You must rule the synagogue. To leave would dishonor the memory of your father. It is your destiny."

Jarius sighed again. "It is a destiny I do not want."

"We take the destiny that God has given us, my son."

The fire crackled in the silence.

Naaman broke the silence. "I will never see my old friend again."

More silence.

"Jarius, there is something else. You must marry again, and soon."

Jarius, Asa and the hidden Marah all stared at Naaman.

"Naaman, I cannot think of marriage again. Not now. Maybe never."

"You must. If only to keep away the many determined and devious mothers who will want their own daughters to marry the rich young ruler of the Capernaum synagogue... and for reasons that will not help you."

Jarius snorted, something between laugher and derision.

"Don't laugh. You don't need some misguided wags using the old spurned woman trick against you in the politics of a synagogue. Face these facts, my son: You have an important father who is sick and dying. You are lost in grief for your wife and son. You have a demanding public life filled with private sorrow. You have no one to help you. It is too much for anyone to bear. You must marry, not for love. You must marry for a helpmate."

"I don't need any help."

"You are strong, Jarius, your father raised you that way."

Like me, thought Marah. That's how you raised me, Father.

"But you need help."

*"Not like you, Marah. You don't need anyone's help."*

"Jarius, you must continue in the role God has given you. You will rule the synagogue in Capernaum. The people will elect you, and you must accept it."

"How? After all that has happened, with all that is happening right now, how can God place this on me?"

"Who knows? Who knows? But you must do God's will! As

it is written in the Book of Moses, 'The Lord God has made your spirit stubborn and his heart obstinate!' But you must accept. You must!"

Asa spoke a bit louder to his father-in-law, defending his friend with careful tone. "Naaman, Moses was talking about the obstinate heart of some wicked foreign king. Not about someone like Jarius, with his broken heart and grief."

Asa only has the kindest words for people, thought Marah. Miri is so lucky. She heard her father grunt, followed by silence. As far as her father was concerned, Moses had the final word for everything. Even through the darkness that separated them, she could almost hear her father thinking, his thoughts were so loud.

Finally he responded, "As it is written in the Book of Moses, son-in-law, 'You need only be still.'"

Marah heard Jarius chuckle, and soon Asa and Naaman joined him. The men stood. Marah pulled further back into the shadows, but watched Jarius embrace her father.

"Naaman, you are like a father to me." He swayed slightly in the darkness.

Asa grabbed his arm to steady him. "Jarius, let me help you to your room. Naaman, I will see you early in the morning. Tomorrow we make our way to the Holy City."

"Tomorrow... I can claim my destiny tomorrow." Jarius's voice was a slur. "I'm sorry, the wine. There is nowhere I can act freely in Capernaum or Jerusalem. Forgive me, my friends."

"There is nothing to forgive, brother." Asa slung his arm around Jarius's shoulders, staggering slightly under the considerable height of Jarius. The two men turned to Jarius's room across the courtyard.

Marah waited a few moments till they entered the room where Jarius was staying. She slunk up the stairs to the second floor of the inn, following her father at a safe distance to their rooms at the end of the building.

She slipped into the small room she called her own, only a bit bigger than her pallet of a bed, plain and sparsely furnished. She had slept there almost every night since she was a young child, right next to her father's room, alone ever since the age of four.

Naaman once suggested she move into a bigger room. Even at a young age, however, Marah wisely pointed out a larger room brought a much better rent than her minute closet would. Anyway, she liked her miniscule sanctuary with its window to the courtyard.

She heard her father moving about and finally settling on to his own low pallet. She knew he would soon be fast asleep.

But he never went to sleep without uttering four words. And until Marah heard them, she could not sleep, either.

First his prayers.

"Thank you Jehovah, for another day in my old age. Be with poor Jarius in his sorrow. Care for my Miriam as she soon bears me another grandchild. Keep me safe on my journey to Jerusalem.

"Be with my Marah."

Marah winced.

"Help me to know what is best for her, the daughter of my heart. Help her to be happy and to know your will, Lord."

*"At least someone is praying to Jehovah for you, Marah."*

Hush!

"El-Shaddai, we wait patiently for the long promised Messiah.

"Make your face to shine upon me, Lord, and be gentle to your old servant Naaman. Thank you for your many gracious blessings. Amen, Jehovah, amen and amen."

Silence.

And at last, the words she longed to hear. Marah's day was not complete until she heard those words.

"God keep you, wife."

Silence filled the inn.

Marah's voice was a whisper. "God keep you, Mother."

Soft, muffled snores told Marah her father slept. But sleep would not come to Marah.

Deborah was a beautiful woman, the wife of a synagogue ruler with a fine home and servants. Deborah had a destiny: an honored place in the community, a privileged life of wealth and opportunities, mother of a first born son. Stolen by the ultimate destiny, death.

*"What sin was hidden inside Deborah, that Almighty God snatched her life away as her punishment? And the life of her son, too? It must have been a very great sin indeed."*

She did not die for any sin, Marah thought. She died in childbirth. Not for her sin.

Why would any father want his daughter to get married? So often women died bearing their children, leaving behind a widower

35

and those same children without a mother. Marah shivered. She did not want to marry some shopkeeper's son and die giving birth to a baby she would never know.

*"Like your mother died giving birth to you."*

"Do not speak to me of my mother!" Startled, Marah realized she spoke out loud. The whisper scuttled away to some dark recess of her mind, waiting.

No matter how good Marah was, no matter how hard she worked, soon her father would force her to marry someone she did not love. Nothing but a husband, a house and children as her future.

*"Poor, poor Marah. Don't we feel sorry for you? For you have to do what every Jewish girl has to do, get married. Oh, poor Marah."*

I should not have to marry some man just because he wants me for a wife, she thought fiercely. Unthinking, she spoke aloud again. "What about what I want?"

Her outburst startled her. It wasn't supposed to be about what one wanted, it was supposed to be about God's destiny for your life.

Jarius did not want his destiny, but it was his anyway, shaped by the death of his wife, his son, and soon, his father.

*"Isn't God cruel? Why would anyone pray to him about their destiny?"*

Her father was obediently following Jehovah's will, too, with a single-minded determination to marry off his youngest daughter.

*"That's your destiny. Marriage to stuttering, stupid Benjamin. Maybe you shouldn't have vetoed the other four."*

Or was it her destiny? Marah couldn't figure it out, and God certainly wasn't telling her. Hadn't God prepared her for so many other things all these years? Hadn't he made her a woman who could read and write and make repairs and do things that most men couldn't even do?

God must have more in store for me, or he would not have made me the way I am, she thought. It was a fervent beat in her heart. God made me this way, God made me this way.

She heard the sarcastic response. *"What God forgot to do was make you a man."*

Marah rolled over and shut out the snide whisper, suddenly weary at this harsh truth.

God made her a woman, a woman who would marry the man her father chose. It appeared that man would be Benjamin.

*"Welcome to your destiny, Marah."*

# CHAPTER 4

As was her habit, Marah woke up well before any guests or her father, whose loud snores assured her that he still slept.

No such luck for Marah. No matter how hard she worked the day before, no matter how restless her sleep, how much the whisper tormented her, she was always awake long before the sun cracked the dark horizon of dawn.

She washed her face, braided her long hair in a tight plait, threw on her robe and paused at the door of her room. No time for prayers today.

No one knew she skipped this ritual, anyway.

Careful not to disturb any guests, she slipped down to the courtyard without a sound.

Brrr! At once she added wood to the fire, stirring the buried embers to life. There was a distinct chill in the air this morning.

She turned at the sound of footsteps behind her. So early, she thought. Who could be stirring at the inn at this hour?

"Why, Master Jarius!" Surprised, she spoke without thinking and then bowed her head, self-conscious at her words.

Jarius nodded at her. "Sorry, Marah, I did not mean to startle you. I meant to leave without waking anyone. I didn't know you would start your day before the sun came up."

Jarius looked no worse for wear after the cups of wine and difficult conversation around last night's fire. But Marah's memory of his tears moved her to an impulsive speech.

"Master Jarius, I am sorry about Deborah and your son. She was... a beautiful woman. And now, your father is so sick, too. I am sorry."

A sudden flush covered Marah's face. Why was she talking to Master Jarius!

"Just a moment, Master..." In her embarrassment, she rushed into her workroom and picked up several items on the table. She ran back to the courtyard.

"Here, for your journey." Marah shoved a loaf of bread and several of the fruit pastries into his hands. She would not even charge him for the bread.

"Thank you, Marah." Jarius smiled the saddest smile she'd ever seen. She was sorry she brought up his dead wife and dying father. She had scolded Naaman for the very same thing only yesterday.

Humiliated she had opened her mouth, Marah sought a way to send Master Jarius on his way as soon as possible. Her face flooded with heat. She forced the words from her lips, anything to get rid of him. "We will see you in a week? When you return?"

"Yes, I will return to Capernaum as soon as Holy Week ends. As you said, my father... my father needs me as soon as I can return. He is... quite ill."

The silence stretched between them. Marah did not have the courage or a single word to add to the conversation.

Jarius rescued her. With a smile, he nodded, took the bread and left Marah alone with her morning chores and her speechless mortification.

ભ

All her guests were gone at last.

Marah had already packed Naaman's provisions, robes and money. Tomorrow morning he would clamber up on their aged old Donkey to make the long day's trip to Jerusalem. He would travel with an old Shiloh friend at a slow and steady pace, populated with stories and reminiscing and laughter.

Marah wished he would go today. She worried about the rigors of the trip on her father. He seemed so tired, lately. The thought of Jarius's ill father came to mind, but she pushed it away.

38

Naaman was in good health, everyone said so. Naaman would not leave until he saw the last guest on their way to Jerusalem. "To help you, Daughter," is how he framed it.

She stood alone in her storeroom and smiled, both at her father and the task that lay before her.

Marah favorite chore was to count what supplies remained on the orderly shelves, figure out what was needed, and then barter at the market for the best prices to once again stock her shelves. The organized rows and neat stacks somehow brought a sense of order to her mind, too.

A nearly full sack of dried figs. Marah nodded in approval.

She found herself humming and smiled to herself.

"Marah."

The shadow of a vastly pregnant Miriam stood in the door of the small storeroom.

"Miri! What in the world are you doing here?"

"I can still walk, Sister! Having a baby is not the hardest thing in the world, you know. I'm not confined to my bed yet. Since the guests are gone, and I knew you would be working, I came to see you."

"I'm so glad you are here." Marah could not help but think of the work waiting for her. She didn't have time for an idle chat, but she pulled her lips back into a smile. "It's been a busy week, hasn't it, Miri?" She did not stop her mental counting. Six pomegranates.

She could not hide her thoughts from Miriam. "I know you have much to do, Marah. I will not keep you long. Stop working for just a moment."

Miriam was holding a low stool. She set it in the middle of the doorway and then lowered herself carefully, propping her swollen feet out in front of her.

Two was a crowd in the storeroom, especially when one was as tall as Goliath and the other, her belly great with child, blocked the doorway.

Like she doesn't want me to escape, thought Marah.

"Miri, we can go somewhere more comfortable."

"No one will bother us here, Marah. I need to visit with you alone for a few minutes."

Marah turned back to her shelves, staring straight ahead, already on her guard.

Only four onions. Where had they all gone?

"I must to speak to you about something very important."

This was the same way yesterday's terrible conversation with her father began.

"I have been talking to Father about your betrothal to Benjamin."

Marah froze. For Miriam to bring up the subject of Benjamin did not bode well for Marah. She did not answer, staring straight ahead at the four onions on the shelf, dirt clinging to their roots.

"Marah, Father told me what you said. It cannot be. You must marry. It is unheard of for anything else to happen."

Marah was silent. The bag of wheat was nearly gone.

"Benjamin is a good match for you."

Marah did not look at her sister, but she shook her head stubbornly, her lips set, the wrinkle between her eyes deep and defiant.

They needed olives, both to eat and to press for oil.

"Marah, listen to me. I suggested young Benjamin to Father."

This got Marah's attention. She looked at Miriam, disbelief on her face.

"Benjamin is an only son. Soon he will own the shop of his father. You will help him run it, just as you help Father run this inn. It is a good fit for you, the wife of a shopkeeper. There would be much for you to do until your family came."

Benjamin, who jumped with nervousness at the sight of a girl? Benjamin, who couldn't utter more than one sentence before he collapsed in embarrassment? Benjamin, as dull as an unsharpened axe? Impossible!

As if to read her mind, Miriam continued. "He is a good choice for you. Benjamin is quiet, like you. He will soon own a business. But he does not have the common sense, the gumption to run it. You think he is not the brightest of young men. And you are right."

Marah felt her face grow red at her sister's unflattering assessment of the young man she thought a suitable husband for Marah.

"But you are smart, Marah. Under your guidance, the shop would be successful. Everyone knows this."

Everyone? Who was everyone?

"Even Benjamin's father sees this, and is glad. You would have the same freedom that you have here, except you would be a wife instead of a daughter. And Benjamin's father will gladly let you help Father run the inn, if you want. We all know how much you love this place. "

"But I would be a wife to Benjamin, Miri!" The desperate words burst from Marah's lips.

"Yes, yes, yes. You would be a wife. So what? That is as it should be. No matter that it is Benjamin. The life he would give you would be a good life. Marah, I know you like no one else does. It would be a life you would like, my little Marah, my precious sister."

She reached up to tug on Marah's robe. "Father does not want to push you, but soon, now, Marah… You must do what all Jewish women must do. You must marry."

Miriam yanked on her robe again, trying to pull the resolute Marah closer, a smile on her face. "And Marah, no matter what you might tell our father, you and I both know you will never become the next Noadiah or Huldah. My sister, my sister, to be so disrespectful to God!" Her laughter softened the scolding words.

Marah flushed an even deeper red, ashamed the faithful Miriam knew about her careless, cavalier comments. Did Father tell her sister everything?

"When Father returns from the Passover, he will enter into negotiations with Benjamin's father. I know his mother well. It is a good family and Benjamin is a good and obedient son."

She reached out a hand to Marah. "Help me, sister."

Marah pulled her lumbering sister to her feet. She wanted Miriam out of there as soon as possible, the close space of her sanctuary now unbearable.

But Miriam put her arms around sister, the embrace awkward between a short round woman with soft curves and a great belly and a tall skinny girl with a stiff stance of bony shoulders and sharp elbows.

"Marah, my beloved sister, my most precious gift from God! I love you so, we all do. I know you do not want to marry. But when you are a wife, when you have a home and a husband and children of your own, you will feel differently. I know this. This time, you must do what Father tells you to do. No arguing with him, it saddens him so. I know you do not want to, but just this once, trust me. Trust your oldest sister." She stood on tiptoe to give Marah a loud, noisy

41

kiss on the cheek.

"Marah, I love you. Please trust me. This is your destiny." Miriam smiled, picked up the stool and paused in the door. "Trust me! Haven't I been a mother to you since the day you were born?"

Marah watched her lumber away.

*"Yes, Miri's been the only mother you have, Marah. And everyone knows whose fault that is."*

&#x2603;

The skinny little girl peeked around the corner with somber eyes, careful to stay hidden from the five little girls huddled together with their whispers.

Only four years old, Marah already sensed she was different. How she wished she was like them, with their curly hair and round faces, laughter and dimples, friendship and secrets. Something set Marah apart from all her sisters, but little Marah did not know what it was.

She hung back, watching, wondering what they were plotting. Her father was nowhere to be seen. Miri was probably somewhere in the inn working.

How she wanted to join that circle of dark-haired conspirators muttering under their breath, sneaking quick glances over petite shoulders, giggling. But she hung back, unsure of the welcome she might receive.

They were a lot older than her, the next closest in age just celebrating her ninth birthday. The twins were ten, and her other sisters numbered eleven and twelve. Then there was then beloved Miri at thirteen. She was already a woman, some said.

Marah didn't know why Father waited so long for her to join their family. If only Marah were older, she could be friends with her sisters, too. Not just the baby sister someone always watched over.

The disposition of Marah's five sisters toward the baby of the family seesawed between a spoiled pampering to merciless teasing and leaving her behind.

Already as tall as the twins, one of the two might whisper in her ear: "Skinny little Goliath! Nothing but bones and knobby knees!"

But the other would sit down and braid her hair with the best of her ribbons.

One sister would laugh at her boney shoulders and pinch her long muscled legs. "Like a boy! You should have been our little brother, Marah!"

Then a twin would scoop her up so she could reach into the stall to stroke their beloved Donkey's nose.

If Miri was not watching, a sister might force little Marah do some of her work. Another day, one would do little Marah's easy chores so the littlest sister could play with the baby goats.

Her sisters never let Marah catch them on purpose when they played. "Come on, Marah, run faster! You are such a baby!"

But from an early age, the leggy Marah could soon capture any teasing sister and topple her to the ground. She would hold a shrieking sister down until Miriam, always the disciplinarian, pulled them apart.

The tears Miri might wipe away were never Marah's.

"Miri! Make Marah stop!" Marah heard it all day long from one sister or another for as long as she could remember. She followed them everywhere, mirroring their actions, mimicking their every word. "Stop it, Marah! Stop it! …Miriam!"

But what were her sisters doing now? She would watch and see before she risked their teasing, or worse, their rejection.

The oldest stood, looked around and then slipped into the stable amidst the giggles of the other four sisters. She walked out a moment later, triumphantly tugging on a reluctant Donkey.

Donkey! They were going to ride Donkey!

"Me, too!" Marah ran right into the middle of the circle of sisters. The chance to ride Donkey filled her with the courage she needed to interrupt her five older sisters.

"Marah!" The chorus was loud and unanimous. "You are too little! Go away! Leave us alone, Marah!"

"No! Me, too!"

"You can't!"

"Marah, you will ruin it for all of us!"

"Go away!"

"Me too, me too!"

At the ruckus of so many female voices, Donkey brayed long and loud and plopped his hindquarters in the dirt.

"Now look what you have done, Marah!"

"He's too heavy! Stand up, Donkey!"

"Help me push him!"

"Someone pull his bridle!"

Donkey did not budge, wide brown eyes staring resolutely at six sets of brown eyes. As one, five pairs swiveled to glare at Marah.

"This is your fault, Marah!"

"Yeah, this is your fault, Marah! You scared him!"

"You ruin everything!"

"Girls, girls, girls."

Five pairs of eyes swiveled to look up at the balding round man that was their father. Little Marah stared at Donkey, her face a black frown under a straight line of eyebrows. She wanted to ride Donkey, too.

Naaman strode over and took the reins of the beleaguered animal. At the sight of his master, Donkey scrambled up from his haunches and turned to face the stable gate, his tail swishing a farewell, eager to escape the familiar horde plotting an afternoon on his old back.

"Daughters, I have told you many times, you cannot ride Donkey without me! He is not for play, he is for work! He is our only donkey and he is very old! We cannot afford a new donkey!"

It always took a bit for Naaman to work up his anger, but word by word he was working into his fatherly rhythm of ersatz rage.

"Now you girls find something to do, or I will find something for you! And you won't like what I find!"

His attempt at anger was building as he struggled for an apt punishment. "Aha! Now, not one of you will get any dinner tonight! Not one of you! Naughty girls! Tonight, only bread and water!"

Their howls went up as one.

"No crying! Or the next thing will be a spanking! For everyone one of you! You should be watching your little sister, not getting into trouble! Yes, a spanking for everyone but Marah!"

Naaman never spanked his girls. Bur empty threat or not, five daughters looked up at him with trembling lower lips and tears welling up in their eyes. There! That did it!

Satisfied with his threat of punishment and eager to escape the weepy sentiments of this flock of females, he shook his finger at the lot.

"Yes, you are all bad girls today! Now, shoo! Go on, and take Marah with you! Watch over your baby sister! And stay out of trouble, or I will show you what real trouble is!"

He pushed Donkey into the stable, slammed the gate and

strode away.

As one, the five older girls turned on Marah.

"You're always Father's favorite, Marah!"

"It's not fair."

"This is your fault, Marah."

"Father wouldn't be mad at us if it weren't for you."

A familiar anger welled up in Marah. She only wanted to be with her sisters, to do what they were doing, too. Why did they always leave her out? She crossed her arms, her bottom lip jutted out.

"She ruins everything." One of the twins started to cry in earnest.

"Stop it." The older gave the younger twin a push.

"No, you stop it. She does ruin everything. She ruined our lives."

"She did ruin our lives, and Miriam's too."

"I did not!" Marah stomped her foot.

"Oh, yeah? You did so!"

"Take it back!"

"Will not! You ruined everything!"

"Did not, did not!"

"Yes, you did! You ruined our lives!"

"Hush! Don't say anything else!"

"I will! Everything is Marah's fault!" She turned toward Marah with a fresh rage. "It's all your fault, ever since you were born. You killed our mother! Murderer! Murderer!"

Five pairs of round eyes stared at the youngest twin, aghast at the words no one had ever spoken to little Marah.

"Well…" The twin was horror-stricken at what she had blurted out. "Well, she did… It's not my fault… it's hers…" She burst into tears.

No one heard the quick steps behind them.

Miriam grabbed the twin by her hair and, right there in the dirt of the street, turned her over her knee, spanking her as hard as she could.

"No one leaves." She shouted the words to the other five watching in horrified fear. "No one leaves! You apologize! Apologize! No one leaves! I am spanking all of you. Everyone but Marah! No one leaves!"

Miriam's face was a raging storm, her arm beating a sister now screaming in pain and, even more, in fear at the eldest's rare rage.

"Stay here! No… One… Dare… To… Leave!"
No one dared save one.

*"You murdered your mother. You killed her. You ruined everything."*
Little Marah hid behind a basket in the little storeroom with its untidy shelves of figs and onions and flour. No one ever came in this messy, cluttered room. No one would find her here.
*"You murdered your mother. You killed your mother. Murderer. You ruined everyone's life."*
Marah squeezed her eyes shut and covered her ears, but she could not stop the strange and fearsome whisper that swirled round and round in her head.
*"You killed her!"*
"But how?" Marah whispered to the alien whisper. Little Marah never even met her mother. Miri was her mother and her sister. How had Marah killed her own mother? Who was her mother? Just a woman her father talked about, no one Marah knew.
*"Murderer. You ruin everything."*
At last Miriam found Marah. The little girl was rolled into the smallest ball behind a large basket. She was not crying, but stared at Miriam with wide, fearful eyes.
Miriam crawled on the floor beside her and pulled the little girl into her lap. They sat on the floor for an hour, Miriam whispering, consoling, humming, holding Marah tight.
But Marah would not speak, her lips pressed together in fear at the voice slithering through her head.
*"You killed your mother."*
Miri rocked her to and fro, words of comfort. "Mother died when you were born, Marah. Sometimes that happens to women. It is never the baby's fault! Babies are a gift from God!"
*"It was your fault. You murdered your mother."*
"I remember Mother was so excited to have you, you were her last baby, Mother always said. 'I'm saving the best for last!' she said.
"She died to give you life, and she was glad you were alive.
"She heard you cry, and she named you right then. 'Her name is Marah,' she said. I know, Marah, I was there. This is what

46

Mother said: 'Her name is Marah. It means bitter water, and how bitter is my sorrow, that this beloved baby will grow up without me.' She was holding you when she died, Marah, and she loved you. I was there with her and Father. I was there! 'My Marah,' Mother said. 'Watch over my little Marah.'"

*"You ruin everything."*

"Talk to me, Marah."

Little Marah buried her head on Miriam's lap, but no matter how much Miri begged her, she would not utter a single word to her sister.

*"Murderer, murderer, murderer…"*

She was too busy trying to silence the alien whisper in her head.

ଔ

In her heart, Marah knew she stopped being a child that week. She wasn't a woman, of course. But she was no longer a child, either. For only a few days later, little Marah learned her first lesson about betrothal and marriage.

Miriam was marrying that man they called Asa. What was worse, Miriam marrying Asa meant Miri was moving away. Miri was leaving Marah.

Miriam found Marah hiding in the stables, crying as though her heart was broken.

"Why, Marah, sweet girl, why are you crying?" Miriam picked her up, alarmed. Little Marah rarely cried, and since that terrible day, had barely spoken a dozen words.

Miriam hugged her tight. "What is wrong, Marah?"

"Don't leave me!" The words burst out of the little girl, punctuated by sobs. "Why must you go, Miri? Don't get married and go away."

"Why, Marah, it is what Jewish women do!" Miriam laughed in surprise at Marah's distress. She feared far worse when she found the somber little girl crying.

"Marah, Jewish girls marry and have families of their own. I am happy and want you to be happy for me! Anyway, I am only moving a few houses away, you will still see me all the time."

"It's not the same!"

"Marah, I will be here every day to help Father with the inn, help him with you and your sisters."

"You have to be here! No one loves me like you do, Miri! Not any of my sisters. Don't leave me. I don't want to be alone."

*"You won't be alone. I will always be here with you."*

Don't leave me with this horrible whisper I do not understand and cannot silence, Marah thought. Don't leave me, Miri.

Miriam smiled and pulled little Marah into her arms. "Oh, my little sister, I love you more than anything. We all love you, little Marah!"

*"Not everyone. You ruined everything. You murdered your mother."*

Marah shook away the whisper that scared her so. She could not confess to anyone the terrible things the whisper said, not even to Miri.

She forced herself to listen to her sister instead.

"I will always be here for you, no matter what! But to be a wife is my destiny, and it is time. I am happy, and so fortunate to be marrying Asa. I love him."

Asa, the synagogue teacher with a bright future: quiet, bearded and completely smitten with the beautiful, lovely Miriam, stealing Miri away from Marah.

"I hate Asa."

Miri chuckled. "No, you don't, little sister. I know you love him, and he loves you as well. She squeezed Marah's shoulder. "I want you to be happy for me, my Marah."

Red-faced, Marah shook her head violently, stomped her foot in anger and ran away, slamming the stable gate behind her.

Who would be on her side once Miriam was gone? Not her sisters, they teased her without end or mercy. Sometimes they were mean to her. She ruined their lives, after all.

Not her mother, she was dead, and that was Marah's fault.

There was only one person left. Father.

At once, Marah knew what to do.

Marah would help her father, work for him, do all the things Miri did for him all these years. She would not be like her sisters, giggling and complaining and lazy. She would work for her father, stay with him always, make up for the trouble she caused him by being alive.

*"You owe him that. Your mother was his wife. He loved her. He still talks about her. And you killed her."*

If she worked hard enough, her father would never regret

that Marah lived and her mother died. Maybe he would forget that it was Marah's fault his wife was gone.

Marah would make him love her.

"I will never leave my father. Never."

*"Never?"*

"Never!" But there was no one to hear her shouted promise but the whisper in her head.

# CHAPTER 5

Marah strode from task to task that morning, her mind as busy as her hands setting the now-empty inn in order.

She could not really say when the idea first found its way into her mind. At first, she laughed at her own absurdity. Ludicrous. Hilarious, really. Absolutely unsuitable. Completely, totally, utterly impossible.

But yet… why not?

Because the poor and the wealthy don't mix. Because the unschooled and the educated don't mingle. Because a handsome, well-liked man wouldn't even consider the company of a shy, somber, unattractive woman.

Because he is old and you are young.

*"Not that old. And definitely not that young."*

Marah seldom admitted the whisper was right, but it was true. She probably should have been married long ago.

And he wasn't that old. She knew a girl from the synagogue who just married a much-older widow, and now she was raising some other woman's children to boot. At least he had no children.

A twinge of guilt poked between her boney shoulder blades, but she dismissed it at once.

Marah was stung by the reasons Miriam considered Benjamin a good match for her: he wanted to marry her, he was submissive, he had a shop for Marah to run, and worst of all, he was not very bright. Her own sister, the sister Marah loved, thought she needed a dolt of a husband to boss around.

*"Well, it's true, isn't it?"* She scowled at the relentless whisper in her head. *"Does anyone tell you what to do now? Miriam knows your destiny, to be one of those bossy, domineering wives with their poor, trembling husbands hovering behind. The kind of wife everyone laughs about behind their backs. Miri knows you, she sees how selfish you are."*

No!

The whisper fell silent. Marah would marry someone. Just not Benjamin, that's all. Even though she was only fourteen, she knew marriage to Benjamin was impossible. Even if her father and Miri and her nosy, pushy sisters did not.

*"I wonder if God thinks it's impossible?"*

So let's ask him, Marah thought impatiently. God was always on the lips of Naaman and Asa and Miriam but never stepped out of the shadows for Marah, always lurking in the background, never offering any advice she could use, not even a single word.

But this was big. For a plan of this magnitude…

*"Of such great sin…"*

She pushed the whisper away. Surely God could weigh in just once for a plan of this magnitude.

Standing alone in the hall of the second floor, she closed her eyes and bowed her head. She couldn't fold her hands, they were full of dirty linens.

"Almighty Jehovah, you know my mind. You know my heart. You know my problem. What is your answer?"

Nothing.

She opened one eye and looked around, as though God might be standing right down the hallway, not wanting interrupt her while she stood there with her eyes closed.

Still nothing.

Marah had things to do. If God had something to say, he needed to speak up and make it snappy. She closed her eyes again and counted to ten.

Not a single word.

Marah did not have the patience or time one apparently needed to stand around and wait for an answer from God.

She returned to her own much more productive thoughts.

The idea was so outlandish, she dared not speak of it to anyone. Her father would be appalled and ashamed at her audacity.

Her sisters would cry she was leaving and then be shocked and jealous, claiming she had always been a presumptuous know-it-all.

They would say bad things about her, all except for Miriam. She alone would be glad for the good fortune of her clever, hardworking baby sister. Only Miriam might be on her side. After all, hadn't Miriam married an esteemed synagogue teacher in the making?

*"But Asa picked Miriam, not the other way around,"* the whisper laughed. Marah dismissed it at once.

Except for Miri, everyone would oppose the idea. They all would think she was insane.

*"Especially your intended,"* said the whisper.

She knew the whisper spoke the truth again.

But this was her destiny, she knew it in her heart. No, God did not speak to her, at least that she could hear. But didn't God Himself place this opportunity in front of her?

Marah would not marry Benjamin.

Instead, Marah would marry Jarius.

Yes! Marah would marry Jarius. She could care for his sick father and manage his large household. A dinner for thirty people was no problem for Marah. No one could outsmart her at the market. She had never managed servants, but how hard could that be? She knew how to keep the inn with its many demands. She could read and write and keep records. She knew her synagogue prayers, mostly. When she wasn't working, she would brush up on the sacred writings, as befitted a ruler's wife. She would even have his children and be a good mother to them, like Miriam was to her children.

Marah dumped her load of other people's dirty towels in a basket. She clenched her hands and then looked at them as though they belonged to someone else. They were calloused with broken nails, a large red welt on the back of one hand where she burnt it while cooking, blisters on the other from mucking out the stable just that morning. Were those freckles from the sun? These were not the hands of a lady. Rough and plain as Marah was, Jarius would be repulsed at the thought of her as his wife.

Marah knew she was not pretty. She never really cared until now. Everything about her was lean and strong. She was thin and muscular and tall, towering over her short, round father, her sisters and almost everyone else. Her hair was straight, her face was long with a thin long nose in the middle. She already carried a small but unfortunate wrinkle between her eyebrows, a mark of the preoccupied frown she wore from the moment she awoke until she fell into bed at night.

Marah pulled her lips back into a grimace and felt her face. She screwed up her lips again, more broadly, showing her teeth. There! When she smiled, her two deep dimples popped out to frame white and even teeth. Smiling was her only physical attribute; at least, that's what her sisters claimed as they badgered her for ten long years. Smile, Marah, smile!

She'd just have to smile so wide her face hurt whenever she saw Jarius.

*"Like a crazy person, grinning like a hyena."*

What about clothing? Jarius needed to see her in something other than the garb of a servant. All she had were the everyday tunics she worked in, with her only nicer robe being a hand-me-down from her last sister. It showed its wear, but who had time to spin thread or stitch together a new tunic?

Still, it would not do.

She ran to her room, threw her faded Sabbath best over her arm and went to look for her father.

He was right where she expected, sitting in the courtyard sun and talking with the old man, his travel partner to Jerusalem.

"Ah, Marah, there you are!" Her father smiled with genuine delight. "I see you have been hard at work this morning."

"Not really, Father, just the usual chores." Marah hugged her father, making sure to give him a big smile so he could see her dimples.

"I do not know how I would get along without Marah." Her father leaned towards the old man, as though letting him in on a little-known secret. Or perhaps he was deaf. "There is nothing my daughter cannot do, nothing! She is God's blessing to me in my old age. All she needs now is a husband."

Her father's old companion looked at her with interest, nodding in approval. Marah remembered the old man was a widower for many years. Perhaps he thought Marah's father was making him an offer.

Naaman must have thought so too, for he changed the subject. "Marah, why do you have your good Sabbath robe?"

"Everyone has left," Marah made a point to ignore the old man beside her father, even though he was a paying guest. "I have a few free hours before the next guests get here. This old thing needs mending again! But even though it's kind of threadbare, I love it. It was Miriam's, remember?"

She knew her father would not remember.

"Miriam's? This was Miriam's tunic?"

"Until she married, yes, father, then it was passed on to two of my other two sisters and then to me. I treasure it."

The tunic did not originate with Miriam, Marah's oldest sister. If that were true, the tunic would be so old and ragged it would be indecent. But there was not a chance her father knew this.

"Oh, Marah, you never ask for anything for yourself." Naaman shook his head.

That actually was true. Marah never asked for or spent any income from the inn on herself.

Her father grabbed the edge of the tunic and ran his hand over the nubby, worn fabric. He turned to his old companion. "She never asks for anything, anything! Does it not say in the Book of Moses, do not be hard-hearted or tight fisted toward your daughter?"

Naaman's companion scratched his head, trying to remember exactly when Moses said that.

"This week, Marah, take a little extra money to the market and buy new fabric for your own tunic. Not a hand-me-down from a sister! Something new, worn only by you. Don't weave your own cloth, either! You don't have time for spinning or weaving. And someone who will soon be betrothed needs a new gown."

The old companion nodded again, confirming that Naaman's hard-working daughter really did need a new tunic. He looked at Marah hopefully, as though she might want to show him her new clothing when he returned, or better yet, consider him as a possible betrothal prospect. Marah refused to look him in the eye.

"Father! That is too generous, I can just mend this. I have had it for years, it is dear to me."

"No, no, I insist. And this week, while you take care of the inn, let Miriam sew you a new tunic. She is too pregnant to do much else, anyway. I will tell her."

Marah stood up. Her father might not remember the tunic was only a few years old, but Miri most certainly would. Even though Marah really did need a new robe, Miriam could spot a white lie a mile away. Marah did not want her sister wondering about anything.

"Don't bother, Father, I will ask her. You are too good to me! Thank you!"

Mission accomplished, Marah directed the conversation into safer waters. "When are you leaving for Jerusalem, Father?"

"Within the hour. We will travel together again, right my friend?" His old companion nodded in agreement and smiled a toothy smile at Marah. Since he was missing several teeth, this was particularly unattractive.

"I will get Donkey ready for you right now, then." Marah bent to give her father another hug. She hoped ancient Donkey was up for the long journey to Jerusalem. "Don't worry Miriam about the tunic, I will take care of it." She avoided his eyes and nodded respectfully to Naaman's old companion, as one would to an aged and infirm elder, careful not to smile and unintentionally encourage any matrimonial thoughts the conversation might have planted.

She left the courtyard. Out of sight from her father and his friend, both dimples were in full view as Marah smiled broadly to herself.

&#x25cb;&#x298;

Marah held the garment up to the dim light of the lamp in her room. The fabric was exquisite, probably more expensive than what her father would have allowed. Marah hated to spend that much, too. But she was in charge of their finances and knew they could afford this one-time extravagance. Instead of the cheapest wool, Marah purchased a smooth cotton, not as expensive as linen, but a luxury. The color was a mossy green, with soft yellow stripes along the edge. She wondered if it would be a good color on her. Marah did not usually ponder questions about her appearance.

Best of all, the seller reduced his price four times and in the end even gave her the yellow braid she added for trim.

"Marah, Marah," he said with a mock sigh. "I am glad your usual purchases are from the oil presser and the flour grinder and not from me. I would be out of business."

Marah smiled, but did not bother to tell him she pressed her own oil and ground her own flour. She was far too thrifty to pay for such lazy indulgences as those.

"Something special for a betrothal, eh?"

So startled was Marah by the shopkeeper's words, she nearly forgot the yellow braid in her haste to leave.

Now, Marah was finished with her tunic and with her plan.

Her father arrived home tomorrow. Jarius would arrive the following day. She could not speak of her intentions to her father, who would certainly punish her - albeit for the first time ever - at the mere suggestion.

She could not approach Jarius, who, after he got over his shock at the silent Marah speaking to him a second time in one week, would laugh her out of the room. Or, he might humiliate her before her father. Or tell his good friend Asa, who would most certainly tell his wife Miriam.

If only Marah could talk to Jarius, explain why this idea made so much sense! But their morning conversation a few days ago was a first between Marah and Jarius. Everything Marah knew about this man she learned second-hand.

*"That's right, Marah. You learned everything about Jarius from your father. Hasn't your father taught you everything?"*

Marah did not want to think about her father, not right now.

Marah was not a businessman, but she was a businesswoman. A good businessman acted on an opportunity before the moment was lost. Just because she was a woman didn't mean she would not act. God had presented this opportunity to Marah. Circumstances dictated the means, the way one might best benefit from an unexpected opportunity. To ignore an opportunity was careless and wasteful.

Jarius wouldn't recognize this good opportunity unless Marah created circumstances he would not be able to ignore. A situation that would force Jarius to see things her way.

I am the solution to Jarius's problems, Marah thought. I'm what my father told Jarius he needed. I can make things easy for him.

*"Be careful, Marah."* She could not silence the hissing whisper in her head. *"Do you really know as much as you think you know, more than your father or a future ruler? Is this for the benefit of Jarius or so poor Marah doesn't have to marry Benjamin? Be careful, so very careful."*

She was risking much: an outright refusal from Jarius, the public shame of her family, the ruin of her reputation in their small town. Or worse, if Jarius chose to make it so.

If it didn't work, she would be ruined in more ways than one. No one would ever marry her then. She would be left here to run the inn, even after her father was gone. Her sisters would share in the income, and she would be free labor living in a closet no one else would want, the family slave. She wouldn't have to marry

Benjamin or any other of the town idiots.

I win either way, she thought. It's a risk I'm willing to take.

*"Unless they stone you,"* said the sly whisper. *"It could happen, you know. You could be stoned."*

Not all the men of Shiloh loved women the way her Father did. As a future ruler, Jarius probably didn't love women either. Her destiny might be public humiliation and death at the hands of good and faithful Jewish men. Men like her father.

She could hear her father's voice. "As it says in the Book of Moses, this daughter of ours is stubborn and rebellious; all the men of the town shall stone her to death!"

Marah refused to acknowledge that terrible possibility. It happened, supposedly, but not here in little Shiloh. She would not let it happen to her.

It wasn't her destiny to live an ordinary life, to marry Benjamin, to have some dolt tell her what to do for the rest of my life.

*"Your way is not the destiny your father would want for his baby daughter..."*

With a wrench, Marah realized the great pain her plan would cause her father, no matter the end results. If he ever found out what she planned to do, he would be heartbroken. She was defying everything he believed in.

But this is my destiny, Marah thought grimly. God opened this door for me, a door I will never see again. It would be a greater sin to turn my back on this opportunity.

Everything would be all right. Marah was a savvy businesswoman who knew how to get things done. She would take advantage of this opportunity and she would make certain that everything would turn out right, too. She would do what she had to do to create the destiny she knew was really hers.

# CHAPTER 6

Once again, Marah's inn was full.

Most of the guests arrived early, tired from their long week in Jerusalem. Jarius returned that afternoon, too. Marah had plenty of time to prepare dinner and to replace the water in each guest room, as was her own particular practice. Each detail was as it should be, all her evening preparations complete.

No one noticed when she slipped away with her basket, not even her father, reliving the busy week of fellowship and worship in Jerusalem with his many guests. The basket was heavy with its treasure of warm bread and a pot of Marah's savory stew for Miriam and her children. A small bag was tucked inside; too, holding an old clean tunic, a towel, the rough soap she herself made, her comb and some little-used fragrance Miri gave her years ago.

Miriam was surprised and happy to see her. "Marah! You are too busy to worry about me today. But I am glad to see you!" Miriam was so close to the arrival of her fourth child. She was anxious to see her husband home in case this baby decided to make an early arrival.

"Poor Miri. You look tired." Marah refused to think about what happened to some women in childbirth. "With only a few days till this baby comes, I imagine all you can think about are your swollen feet, aching back and a good meal! I just came to bring you and Asa some dinner. I know you are too tired too cook."

"Oh, Marah." She reached out to hug Marah but wrinkled

her nose instead. "You smell, Marah! Have you been working the stables again? That is a man's work, silly!"

"Yes, I have," Marah said stiffly. "Someone has to do it. But I'm on my way to the baths right now."

"Well, you have earned it! Sit in a hot bath for an hour! Come here and hug me anyway. How did you know I would want something hot for dinner tonight, my sweet little sister?"

"Just guessing someone about to have a baby would want to eat something she didn't have to cook." She gave her sister a hug, already forgiving her for speaking the truth even Marah could smell.

"Miriam, I must go. I'm running to the baths, but just for a few minutes, not an hour. All our rooms are full tonight. How are you feeling?" Marah knew the answer but asked it anyway.

"Of course, I am fine. Asa is home, finally. He ran to the synagogue and will be right back for dinner, a fine dinner thanks to you! I missed him."

"Father mentioned wanting Asa for a bit tonight, is that all right?"

"Of course! I want to see him and then I want to sleep! But why?"

"I don't know, really. I was too busy to talk with Father; he just mentioned it in passing. I thought I would ask you first, Father forgets how much you need Asa right now, I think."

"Marah, we are so lucky, the way you care for our Father, for me, for my family. For everything..."

Marah nodded, a sudden lump in her throat.

"Thanks for dinner, Marah. I'll say something to Asa."

She nodded again and walked out the door.

*"What will Miri think of you tomorrow?"*

If her plan was successful, Miri would be happy, excited at her little sister's good fortune. If it was not, Marah would be a shameful outcast, the name her nieces and nephews were forbidden to mention.

Marah ran to the public baths. It was deserted in the dying heat of late afternoon. Any travelers who stopped here earlier were safely ensconced in Marah's inn.

She sank neck-deep into the water of the rough stone vat, realizing with embarrassment that she did smell. She worked hard today, cleaning stuffy rooms, working over the hot ovens and bedding down animals in the stable. She had earned the sweat she could smell, which only made her more nervous about her plan.

*"Not sure you can pull it off, are you? Quite ambitious for a smelly stable hand…"*

What a delight it would have been to soak in the hot water at leisure! Instead, she spent the few minutes in a vigorous scrub with the harsh soap, paying special attention to her fingernails and toes. She jumped out of the water and toweled her just-washed hair with a brisk force till it was almost dry and her head hurt. She combed her hair and plaited it into a neat braid; she would undo it at home. She dressed in the ragged clean tunic and scrubbed her teeth with eucalyptus. Although worn out by a hard day of work, the hot bath and her hasty ablutions, Marah was ready.

Marah hurried back to the inn.

"Ah, here you are Marah! Where have you been? As Moses would say, 'give us meat to eat!'" Her father grabbed her into a tight hug. "Oh, daughter, how good it is to be home. But I missed you this week! Thank you for all you do for me, thank you, and thank you."

Marah squirmed to get away, hoping her father wouldn't notice her damp hair. "I'm glad you are back, Father. But you are right; it's time to feed everyone." She practically sprinted away, past the people milling about or sitting in the courtyard around the fire. Evenings at the inn were always a social hour for men, women and children.

She grabbed her oldest nephew, called into service the moment he and his father returned from Jerusalem. "Go tell your father to come see Jarius and your Grandfather after dinner."

"But…"

"No buts. As soon as he is done eating, have him come back to the inn." After the meal Marah just delivered, Miriam would gladly do without Asa for one more night.

Marah hauled out the giant pot of stew and lined up the bread in a neat row. Naaman shooed the guests toward the waiting food. It only took a single invitation for the hungry guests to line up. The aroma of her stew and hot bread was incredible, if she did say so herself.

Dinner was interminable, all the guests talking, laughing, and reliving their week in Jerusalem. Would they never finish eating? Jarius sat with several other men, quiet. He never even glanced in Marah's direction, even when she served him his food. However, Marah found herself looking at him again and again. She couldn't stop.

A few minutes later, Marah pulled her father into the work room. "Father, there's a problem. Don't say anything, promise me."

"What is it?"

"Promise you won't say anything." It was hard for Naaman to keep secrets.

"Yes, Daughter. What's wrong?"

"I overheard Master Jarius tell someone what a terrible week this has been without his father along. He seemed so… sad, so lonely."

"What?"

Jarius had said no such thing, at least that Marah overheard.

"Yes. He mentioned how glad he is to have you and Asa in his life."

"He did?"

"Yes. It was so sad. Don't tell Jarius, but I sent for Asa. Perhaps the two of you could spend a little time with Jarius before he leaves for Capernaum."

"Ah, yes. Jarius is dreading his return home for so many reasons."

"He is?" Marah was all innocence, betraying nothing.

"Never mind that, daughter. Thank you for telling me, I will sit with him now and wait for the other guests to go to their rooms. When we are alone, will you bring us some wine?"

"Of course. Remember; don't tell Master Jarius I said anything."

Naaman hugged her again. "Such a good daughter, such a fine young woman. Always worrying about others! I hope Benjamin realizes how lucky he will be to get you for a wife."

Marah whirled around to face her father. "Do not speak to me of Benjamin!"

"Marah…" She heard the hurt in his voice.

"Sorry, Father, sorry. Please, do not talk to me right now about Benjamin. We can talk about that tomorrow, I promise."

Naaman stared at her for a moment. "Of course, my daughter, of course." He sighed and turned away.

He seemed small and tired to Marah.

*"After tonight, he won't ever have to worry about Benjamin again!"*

At last, her guests started retiring from the courtyard, Marah picking up the plates of those who were finished and even a few who might have still been eating. After Passover Week, people were far less inclined to visit into the late hours than before the week began.

Asa came strolling in as she lugged an armful of plates to her work room. "Marah, thanks for the dinner! You made my wife very happy, and I was pretty happy myself!" He reached out to hug her, but changed his mind at the sight of Marah with so many dishes teetering in her arms.

Why did everyone want to hug her tonight?

"You sent for me?"

Marah whispered the same story she told Naaman, with an added embellishment that Naaman wished aloud, "If only Asa were here."

"Don't tell him, Asa! He knows you should be with Miriam tonight. And don't tell Master Jarius, I'm ashamed I overhead his conversation! I know you are friends."

"I'm glad to be here, Marah. It was right of you to send for me."

She smiled a rare smile at Asa, her dimples in their finest form.

"Let me get you some wine."

&#x2683;

Marah added more wood to the fire, poking the charred logs into new flames. As she had hoped, the three men were still talking, the flask of wine before them almost empty.

Marah nodded respectfully to Jarius, and at the last minute she remembered to smile, which seemed completely out of place in the moment. Flustered, she turned to her father who saved his awkward daughter.

"Marah, we are fine. Why don't you go to bed? You have worked so hard today. We will soon turn in, too, won't we, my sons?"

Asa nodded his approval to Marah, as though there really was a need for him other than her whispered fabrication.

"Thank you, Marah." She jumped at Jarius's voice.

She smirked her idiotic grin and bent into something like a curtsy.

Across the courtyard, up the stairs, down the hall… Marah did not stop running from the three men until she reached the safety of her room.

In her room, Marah took off the old clean tunic. She had her own fresh water and towel, just like every guest in the inn. She rinsed off the sweat of the evening's labor and let the night air cool her skin.

She held up her new tunic in the dim light of the single candle. She had never owned a garment that was not a hand-me-down, ever. She pulled it over her head, the crisp cotton an alien touch to her bare skin.

She unbound her hair from its tight braid. It fanned out over her shoulders, hanging straight and heavy almost to her waist. Not even the dampness from the warm baths raised a curled ringlet on her long satin sheen of black hair.

She sighed, and sat on her bed in the darkness, waiting, waiting for the start of her new future to begin.

Every detail of her plan had fallen perfectly into place; luck was with her today.

*"Luck? Or maybe it's God's hand?"*

She flushed. She didn't think God would approve of what she so carefully and painstakingly planned.

But then again, who was she to say what God would or would not approve? Hadn't other great women created their own circumstances to get things done when God faltered?

Didn't Sarah guard the safety of her only son Isaac by sending Hagar and Ishmael off to meet their death in the desert? Didn't Tamar disguise herself as a prostitute to make sure her offspring would inherit their rightful place in the house of Judah? Didn't Esther wait until King Xerxes was totally beguiled with her beauty and charm to tell him she was actually a despised Jew, saving her people from certain massacre? Would any of those things have happened if the women just sat around waiting for their circumstances to change?

"No," Marah whispered. "Those women created their own destinies. I can do it, too."

*"Is there anything you can't do, Marah?"*

With nothing but a relentless whisper to answer her, Marah did the only thing she could think of to silence her unwanted guest:

She stuck her fingers in her ears.

℘

The creak of her father's footstep on an ancient floorboard announced his arrival into his room next to Marah's. She peeked out her narrow window into the courtyard. Empty. Asa and Jarius were gone as well. She listened for Naaman's mumbled prayers and the final words she so missed this week, the soft and reassuring mumble.

"God keep you, wife."

"God keep you, mother," she whispered. Her life would be so different if her mother had lived. Surely Marah would not be sitting here in the dark plotting a future no one else could imagine for her.

Marah felt sick to her stomach. She forgot to eat in this dogged regimen of a day. She hadn't taken a bite since noon, and then only a bit of bread and cheese. She was tired, too. Marah woke up every day long before dawn, and today had been no different.

*"Are you sure this plan is from God, Marah? Are you absolutely sure? Did God TELL you to do this? If you do it, there is no turning back, you know."*

At the sound of the whisper, Marah's knees grew weak. Her hands were shaking.

She shook them hard, bringing some circulation to her entire body.

"Can you never speak comfort or encouragement to me!" Her words were a hiss in the darkness.

The whisper sighed. *"Hmm, comfort, comfort. How about this, Marah? And the Lord said to Moses, tell that stubborn Israelite Marah to turn back! Turn back! So says your father's beloved Moses. How about that for comfort?"*

Marah had no answer, and stomped her foot in an angry, wordless response.

But it was a half-hearted stomp, careful not to startle the sleeping inn. Her plan was about to begin. There wasn't time to argue with the whisper right now.

# CHAPTER 7

The inn and the whisper had been silent an hour, both waiting for Marah to act. It was time.

Marah stood, stiff from a motionless vigil perched on the edge of her low bed and numb from rehearsing every word, every detail of her scheme in her head over and over again.

She listened intently for a sign of life in her inn. Anyone moving around now would be creeping about just like her. If she met someone in the dark, she could say she was still finishing her evening chores. No one would know the difference.

Only her father might notice she was wearing her new tunic, and Marah could hear the indisputable proof that he was sound asleep next door.

Marah pushed open the door of her room and looked both directions into the darkness. She heard a cough a few doors down, the snort of a snore, a child's high sneeze somewhere, the familiar rustle of an inn at rest. She pulled the door closed behind her. Her bare feet made no noise on the ancient wooden risers as she crept down the steps. If Marah knew one thing, it was how to move through this building without making a sound. She had done so at dawn for many years.

On the first floor, she paused and looked at the six doors

that faced the courtyard. Master Jarius was on the far end in the room he always rented, far away from the nook where her father lay sleeping above. She stood in the silence, gazing at the closed doors, wondering what was about to happen to her.

Marah wanted to pray. But she could not. She prayed for years only to be answered by silence. How could she even think of praying now, just before she was to commit such a great sin?

She wondered if Rebekah prayed as she cooked the stew and covered her son Jacob with goatskins to better deceive her old, blind husband Isaac. Did King David kneel in prayer before he sent poor loyal Uriah, Bathsheba's trusting and faithful husband, off to fight in a battle and face his certain death? Did Deborah, mighty Judge of the Israelites, feel remorse when her army slaughtered 10,000 Canaanites and the shattered head of the ruler Sisera was presented to her in victory?

Sometimes God's people took action that might require God's forgiveness. It happened over and over again. God forgave sinners. It's not like she was murdering anyone.

*"You already murdered someone."*

Marah's knees weakened even as her resolve strengthened. Surely God will forgive me for this sin! Anyway, this is not my fault, Marah thought bitterly. It's God's. He made me the way I am.

*"He made you just the way you are. You had nothing to do with it."*

She was weary of her own self-aggravation and the maddening whisper. Time to act, not stand here thinking about old deceived Isaac, poor murdered Uriah, or the head of Sisera with skewered tent peg driven through it.

Marah took a deep breath and glided toward the room where Jarius, weary from travel, worn down by sorrow and sedated with wine, lay in a certain sound sleep.

At the last door, Marah stopped and listened for a full minute. She heard nothing. She took the key she carried and turned it once in the lock. The single click seemed to echo through the dark courtyard like the twang of a taut bow. She stood waiting, but silence was the only answer. She lifted the latch with a careful, deliberate hand. The door swung open, silent on the hinges Marah herself oiled only yesterday.

The lantern was turned down and the room dark, but Marah's eyes were used to the blackness. She could see Jarius in the dim light; he was lying on the mattress at the far wall, his face turned

66

away from hers. A twitching convulsion at the sight of his bare back caused her to shudder.

The whisper coiled around her, its sneering hiss an odd comfort. *"Perfect, Marah, perfect. Just as you planned, everything is perfect. He hasn't heard you. He lays there unsuspecting his fate. It's not too late to run away, though, before you throw your life away on your perfect plan. Run away, Marah, run away…"*

I will not run away, she thought. This is my destiny. I must do what I must do.

*"Of course. You must do what you must do. Who knows better than you, after all?"*

Marah ignored the question and stepped up to the bed without a sound. She slipped her new tunic off and let it fall to the ground; she wore nothing beneath it.

She knew how this worked. The idle, intimate and endless chatter of six older, long-married sisters served her well. Long ago Miriam told her about the joys of the marriage bed and in no uncertain terms the danger it held for the unmarried maiden.

"Sorry, Miri," she whispered with a stab of guilt at the thought of her sister.

She knelt on the floor by the mattress, and with slow, deliberate motions, crawled under the blanket next to Jarius. His even breathing did not stop. Marah shook at the realization that she lay next to the body of a man for the first time in her life, and that man was unclothed under his blanket just like her, as naked as a newborn.

*"Why wouldn't he be naked, Marah? After all, he was alone in his own bed in a locked room until you showed up."*

Marah lay there for just a moment, then slipped her hand so close to Jarius's mouth, she could feel his even breathing on her rough hand.

As she pressed her naked body against his, she tightly clamped her hand over his mouth. She felt him inhale sharply and then hold his breath, frozen in silence. He did not move. She pressed against him again; she was so tall it was no effort to whisper in his ear.

"Do not cry out. I have been sent to comfort you in your sorrow. Do not cry out, Master." The long exhale of his breath was hot against her hand. She inhaled the sharp sour smell of the many glasses of wine she herself had served him.

He did not move, except for that soft exhale and the fall of his chest.

But only for a moment. In one motion, he rolled over and forced her on her back. His eyes were squeezed shut, his lips set in an angry line. She was shocked at his unmasked ferocity, at the brute strength of his body against hers. She could not have moved if she wanted to. But she did not want to. This was the plan. She was afraid, but she would not move.

Jarius never opened his eyes, burying his face in her long hair, his body taut against hers, a spittle of controlled outrage fierce in her ear.

She froze at the words of rage he whispered.

"Deborah, Deborah!" It was a wild, mindless chant repeated over and over again. "Deborah. Deborah. Deborah…"

Deborah! Marah never once thought Jarius would cry out for Deborah.

Then, even more quickly than Marah had imagined, the sound of another woman's name in her ear, Jarius took her as a husband takes a wife, deadened by the deep stupor of sleep and wine, blind with a rekindled passion for another woman, uncontrolled with an animal rage, never once raising his head from her shoulder.

Then… it was over. He lay on her panting as though in a terrible pain, and then rolled away to face the wall, no longer touching her. Marah lay on her back, half on the pallet and half on the floor, too afraid to move. She had been compliant and silent, her lips pressed together against the cries of pain that struggled within her. It hurt her, something she didn't expect.

Her body started to shake with pain from the act, his cries for another woman, his rage, and her creeping apprehension that the painstaking plot she so carefully constructed was slipping away.

As she laid there listening to the ragged breath of a man who was a stranger, a stark realization dawned.

What was her plan again? What was she going to do now?

She could not remember.

The magnitude of what just happened welled up within her, a scream against her lips in the silence. She gave herself to a man who was not her husband. A man who would not want her. She clamped her mouth shut against a rising panic. She slithered off the bed, the dirt floor on her back. What had she done?

What now, God, what now? Help me, God, she thought.

For the first time, God did not answer her with silence.

Deep gasping breaths broke the stillness, ragged with a brutal pain.

Jarius was crying.

Marah was jolted from her confused stupor. He wept with loud wrenching sobs, nothing like the weeping in the courtyard with Asa and Naaman. Marah was faint with fear. Someone would hear him. How could she silence him?

Oh, what had she done?

She could barely understand his wine-slurred words, but when she did, her heart stopped. "Why did you die, Deborah? Why? O God, why did you take Debora away from me? I love her, God. Why did you take her and my son, too, God? Take me, Lord, take me too. O God! Do not torment me with these dreams of Deborah any longer!"

He was shouting.

Frightened, Marah was certain the guests in the adjoining room would hear. With one swift movement, she scrambled over and clamped her hand over his mouth a second time. This time, however, Jarius was not dead asleep. At her touch, Jarius sat up like a deer startled by a wolf.

"What!" He looked at her with wide glassy eyes, horrified. "Who?" He grabbed the blanket and jumped up from the bed, covering himself as he ran to the other side of the room. A look of horrified disbelief spread across his face as he realized who lay in his bed.

"Marah?" The loud question hung in the air between them. "Marah?"

"Master Jarius, you must be quiet! The other guests will hear you." She sat up, grabbed her new tunic and clutched it to her chest. She hissed the words, urgent and beseeching. "Please be quiet!"

He looked at her and then, as though his legs would not hold him, he slumped down to a sitting position, leaning against the wall.

"I thought you were a dream," he whispered. "A dream. What does this mean?"

He looked at her, huddled on his bed. His face screwed up, as though he looked upon something repugnant. Like a rotted carcass, thought Marah, mortified.

"I thought you were a dream." He continued to stare at her as though he had never seen anything so vile in his life. Watching him, Marah could almost see his feelings as he realized what had

69

happened. He would not be silent.

"Marah, what have you done?" His disgust was replaced by a look of dread. "O God, what have we done? What have we done!" His voice was loud again, this time with a note of hysterical panic. "Oh Yahweh, O Mighty God, I have sinned! Such a sin! What have we done?"

Marah realized she needed to act before Jarius lost control. He didn't know it was her, a real, live, breathing person, she realized. He thought she was the ghost of his wife, some lovely vision come to him in a dream. Not the devil disguised as the sinful, shameless daughter of an innkeeper.

"Master Jarius." She spoke in a whisper. Jarius looked at her, anger spreading across his face. His fists clenched the blanket, his knuckles white. As though he wants to strike me, she thought.

"Master Jarius, you must not speak out loud," her whisper was urgent. "The others will hear you."

"Marah, what have you done, to come to my room at night? To creep into my bed? To, to…" She heard the edge of a scantly controlled rage in his voice. He could not speak the words of what just happened between them.

What if he dragged her into the hall right now, to share her sin with anyone who could hear?

*"Speak, Marah! Speak the words you said over and over in your storeroom, the stable, the dirty rooms of others. Speak!"*

"I came to you as a wife comes to her husband, Master Jarius," she whispered. Ah. Here were the words she practiced until she could say them with confidence, speak them as though she believed them. But the hands that held the tunic to her were shaking so hard she could not still them.

She had agonized about what to say, rehearsed her painstaking speech many times. Prompted by her faithful whisper, her careful plan with its deliberately chosen words started to come back. She could not lose control now, not when she had just risked everything.

"I come to you as the wife you need, to manage your household, to help you with your sick father, to help you when you become the new synagogue ruler, to bear you many children, to be the helper my father says you need."

"Your father? Naaman knows you are here?"

"My father? No!" If Jarius interrupted her, Marah would

70

forget her practiced discourse and all would be lost. She would be mute, dumb Marah once more. She forced her mind away from any thought of her father, back to the speech she practiced over and over.

"Master Jarius, I have the skills you need in a wife. All you need. God has sent me to you, sent me to help you."

He looked at her in complete disbelief. His whisper was a hiss. "God? God sent you to me? God bids you come to me at night while I sleep, come with deceit and falseness? You come to me in such a way that forever shames me and ruins you! God has no part in this, Marah! I will have no part of this, either!"

He looked away from her. "Leave me at once. Never speak to me again."

Marah sat for a moment. She would not give up. Not yet. Much was at stake in this dark room.

*"I wonder if this is how Sarah felt, sending Abraham's son Ishmael out to die in the desert, as she betrayed Hagar, the servant girl who trusted and loved her?"*

Marah would not acknowledge the whisper, not right now. She pulled her tunic over her head, trying to hide her nakedness from him, sensing the irony in her perceived modesty.

She stood and crossed the room, not to the door but to the lantern in its alcove. She turned up the wick and a dim light filled the room. She walked back across the room to where Jarius still sat on the floor, close so that he would hear her deliberate whispered words.

"Master Jarius, I will not leave. You must marry me. I am to become your wife."

He looked at her in disbelief. He spoke out loud, with certainty. "That is impossible."

Marah refused to acknowledge the fear rising within her. Speak, Marah, you must speak the words you chose so carefully, or all this has been for nothing!

*"All for nothing, all for nothing, all for nothing!"* How could she endure this silent taunting?

But her soft syllables were measured and controlled, gentle yet strong as iron. She rehearsed this conversation many times this past week. "It is not impossible at all. You are a widower. I am of the age to be married. I know you think I am not good enough for you, Master Jarius. But I am to be your wife."

"Impossible." He shook his head, but his voice was less

confident.

"It is not impossible, Master Jarius, it is destiny. Yours and mine."

Something in her voice made Jarius look at her with a fearful suspicion.

*"Who is this shameful woman speaking like this to kind Master Jarius, Marah? Shameful!"*

The words she knew she had to speak were suddenly loathsome to her, but she continued in an even, quiet voice. "You must marry me. For if you do not agree, Master Jarius, I will go right now to my Father's room and tell him what happened here this evening."

Jarius stared at her, his mouth open.

"What?" Jarius wore the oddest expression. "What?"

"Listen to reason, Master Jarius. You will marry me."

He must, she thought. He will marry me.

*"Only because you will threaten to destroy him,"* the whisper taunted.

She plowed on. "Yes, I will run to my father - who loves and trusts me - and tell him what happened here tonight. That as I finished my last chores of caring for the guests here tonight, you met me in the hall. That you called to me, whispering for me to bring water to your room. Calling me as you would call a servant." Marah's careful plan was returning to her, word for word.

"I will tell my father that when I entered your room, you covered my mouth so I could not scream - no, Father, I could not even breathe! I will tell him how you, in a drunken, mindless rage for your wife, forced yourself upon me. I will tell him how you took your sorrow out on me, a girl who only came to serve you. Me, the daughter of a man who is a friend of your dying father. The daughter of a man who counts you as a friend, as a son, even. Yes, Master Jarius, I will leave this room if you command it. I shall leave it, and run screaming for my father."

Marah took a deep breath. She had never spoken so many words to someone outside her family in her entire life. But her composure was returning.

"Think how shocked my father will be at the shame you have inflicted on me. The disgrace you have wreaked on your father's old friend Naaman. And such a dishonor for your friend Asa, a teacher of the law. Think what the guests will say, how they will talk here and when they leave."

She'd never seen a look like the one she saw on Jarius's face. He did not speak, move, or even blink, a man carved of stone.

I have paralyzed him, Marah thought. What if he died of a seizure right now in her inn? She forced herself to continue speaking.

"It would be a shocking affair. To refuse me in marriage would be to shame me. My family would be devastated and shunned forever by my actions. This would break my father's heart, perhaps even kill him. Any future for your friend Asa would be over. And you? You have the power to ruin me, perhaps even to have me stoned to my death."

Still Jarius sat unmoving, his head tilted back to look up at her, his mouth open like a fish.

"But the deed is done. You have taken me. I have known no other man. The blood on your bed will speak to this. You too will bear this shame. You would not be stoned, but you would be forbidden to read or speak at the synagogue until you at last atoned for your sin. And such a scandal! Your chance to be the ruler of your synagogue would no longer exist.

"I know how these things work, I have heard my father talk about the council and the ruler here in Shiloh. Your future will die with your father. And your father will die with a heart broken by the lust of his son, the widower who ravaged the daughter of a friend."

"Marah." Jarius's voice was a whisper. "Why are you doing this to me, Marah? I barely know you. What have I ever done to deserve this from you?"

"You have done nothing, Master Jarius. I do this because I must. This is my destiny, our destiny. My father wants me to marry someone, anyone, just as long as I marry. I cannot marry just anyone! I can read, I can write, I can run this inn. I can add up numbers and barter goods at the market. I am smart! I have been told so all my life. I cannot just be the wife of some dolt here in our village!" Marah's voice did not rise above a whisper, but there was no mistaking the intensity of her emotions.

"I know you grieve for Deborah. But Father told you what you need now. A helpmate, someone to handle your household and its demands. I can do it, Master Jarius. I am the wife you need. I can care for your house and your father. I can manage your servants, your shopping, your animals and money, everything. These things I can do, I know."

Unexpectedly, Marah sensed tears were close. She was horrified. If there was one thing Marah never did, it was cry. Not since she was a little girl, not since she learned she was a murderer, not since Miriam had left her alone so many years ago, had she cried. She blinked hard. Jarius must not see her tears.

"I came to you like this because I must. You would never, ever consider a girl like me. But I am the woman who is best for your future. I know this to be true, for I can take care of you. And so… you must marry me."

The room was silent for a long time. Finally, Jarius stood up from the floor with slow and painful motions, as though he was crippled. He leaned against the wall, looking as though he would fall over without its support.

Marah realized her knees were shaking so hard, she might fall over herself. She must not show weakness to Jarius! She walked across the room and sat down on the low bed, straightening out the crumpled sheet to give her trembling hands something to do.

They stayed like that for some time, Jarius hunched against the wall, Marah mindlessly smoothing the bedclothes over and over. For an eternity, thought Marah.

Be silent, Marah, she commanded herself. Silence is the art of good negotiation in the market. Be still!

*"Isn't that how you always get your best deals at the market, Marah? Let them make the offer! What are you buying and selling today? What's your best price, Marah?"*

She pressed her lips together, ignoring the whisper. She would wait for Jarius to speak.

"Impossible. Impossible." Jarius turned from her and rested his forehead against the wall, stricken, his arms spread out wide, hands clutching the faded blanket, pressing himself into the clay wall, his knuckles white.

She opened her mouth to speak but was silenced by the soft sounds coming from Jarius. He was crying.

Marah did not know how to negotiate against this raw, untouchable emotion.

The whisper she so wished to banish hissed in her ear. *"Oh, yes, Marah, you did what you had to do. Wise, wise Marah, with her careful, conniving evil plan."* She wished desperately the whisper would drown out the sound of Jarius's crying. *"You are as wise as vindictive Sarah! As wise as devious, deceitful Rebekah! As wise as the murdering, adulterous King*

*David! So what happens now, wise, wise Marah? What do you have planned next for poor Jarius? Murder? That would shut him up…"*

The sound of Jarius's sobs and the whisper won. The enormity of what she had done rose up around her. In her exceptionally ridiculous plan, she imagined Jarius would realize at once he had only one choice, to marry her. And he would even be thankful that God had put the gift of Marah in his path.

How laughable that would be, except for the fact she had just ruined her life.

*"And Jarius,"* said the whisper. *"Don't forget you ruined poor, grieving Jarius's life, too."*

Her actions had shamed this righteous man beyond repair and ruined herself, solely for her own gain.

All these years, she thought she was so smart. Her father told everyone who would listen how clever and wise his youngest daughter was. Yet in truth, she was the dullest, most witless person she knew.

"O God, what have I done?" Marah whispered. Jarius did not hear her.

*"God? God doesn't know what you have done, Marah. He doesn't hear you. He never has. All those times you stood there shouting, 'Answer me, God!' He has never, ever listened to you, and after tonight, he never will…"*

Jarius pushed himself away from the wall. He pulled the blanket tight around himself and knelt on the floor, his back to her, his face to the dirt floor. He began speaking in a low tone. Marah strained to hear.

He was praying!

"For the sake of your name, O Lord, forgive my iniquity, though it is great. My eyes are ever on the Lord. Only he will release my feet from the snare. Turn to me, O Lord. Be gracious to me. I am lonely and afflicted. The troubles of my heart have multiplied…" Jarius was silent for a moment.

"The troubles of my heart have multiplied. Free me from my anguish."

Marah had heard these words before. A psalm. She did not know which one. She crept over to Jarius and knelt beside him, facing the wall, her head bowed low to the ground also. She needed to hear this prayer to God. Although she desperately wanted to see Jarius's face, she forced herself not to look at him.

Jarius's low voice continued. "Look upon my affliction and

my distress. Take away all my sins. See how my enemies have increased, how fiercely they hate me!"

I am the enemy, Marah thought. I am the enemy, the affliction and distress. She could smell the dirt of the floor, dusty and grimy and never clean no matter what she did.

Jarius continued. "Guard my life, O Yahweh. Rescue me. Let me not be put to shame."

Marah listened silently. His shame was at her hand.

"I take refuge in you. May integrity and uprightness protect me. My hope is in you. My hope is in you. My hope is in you."

He stayed with his face on the floor. She heard him whisper, "Deborah." Then after a long silence, she heard her name. "Marah. Oh, Marah."

Jarius stood up, looming over Marah, who stayed huddled on the floor at his feet.

She had changed her mind. She was afraid to look at the face of this man who so earnestly beseeched God in prayer. Did God answer Jarius? What would God have him do to her? How would God rescue Jarius, save him from the terrible shame of Marah?

Perhaps God could murder her right now, put her out of her misery…

*"Murder a murderer… Where do murderers go when they are dead?"*

Marah wanted out of this room. She had most definitely changed her mind.

Jarius reached down and touched her shoulder. "Stand up, Marah." She jumped at the gentleness of his touch and his voice.

She stood with the sudden realization she was every bit as tall as he was. They stood eye to eye as he spoke.

"Marah, I… I do not know what to do. I ask you this: Please leave me, leave me alone to my prayers and to my God. I will look for you in the morning and we will talk. Please, Marah, please do not…" he stopped, searching for words.

"Speak to my father?"

Relief spread across his face.

Why did she say that? Her plan was to force Jarius to act at once. If Jarius thought for a moment that she would not tell her father, there was no threat. He would not marry her unless she made him.

*"Act now, Marah! You have him right where you want him,"* the whisper sneered.

76

But she knew she would not wake her father. She would tell him nothing. To tell such a great lie to her father after what she did… surely the God of Jarius and Naaman would strike her dead on the spot.

Jarius looked down. "Yes, thank you, Marah, please do not speak to your father tonight. I do not…. I do not know what to do. You are right. Had you or even your father asked me, I would not have considered a marriage to you, not for a moment. We are not a good match. There are many differences between us. And now, there will be great anger and many problems between us. I do not… I do not know how to live a life of anger…"

Marah wanted to somehow assure Jarius, to defend herself. But her earlier words, "God has sent me to you, sent me to help you," sounded crazy even to her.

"But Marah, you and I have both sinned tonight, sinned together, sinned greatly in the eyes of God. Our families will be shamed by your actions and by mine, also, by this terrible thing I have done."

The whisper was contemptuous. *"Remind him what really happened, Marah. He didn't sin, you did! Tell him the blame is yours and yours alone. You know it's the right thing to do. Don't you want to do the right thing, Marah?"*

To tell him the fault was hers would defeat her plan, jeopardize all she that risked. But still, it took every bit of her willpower to remain silent, to not blurt out her guilt, even as her shame deepened.

"I do not know what to do." Jarius turned away from her.

Marah waited for only a moment. She could not dishonor herself anymore than she already had. There was no turning back. She took a deep breath. Now more than ever, the outcome of this night was important.

"I know what you must do, Master Jarius. Marry me. You will not be sorry."

He looked at her, an odd expression on his face. "I am already sorry, Marah. More sorry than you could ever know." He shook his head sadly, his voice soft. "I do not love you."

Marah hung her head. She knew this. Love was never a part of her plan, not even for a moment. But to hear the bald statement that she was not loved, even from a stranger she set out to destroy, hurt in a way she did not expect.

Miriam was right. Who could ever love Marah except for stupid, simple, dim-witted Benjamin? No one else would have her.

Of course Jarius did not love her.

He would never love her, ever.

At once, she needed to escape.

Jarius loved Deborah, and he would never love Marah. She could not blame him.

*"Love!"* The whisper was laughing now, relentless in its disdain of Marah. *"Love! Jarius loves Deborah! Asa loves Miri! Your father loves your mother, dead for fourteen years! But you don't need love, you said so yourself. Remember? Good thing, for Jarius will never, ever love you. Never ever never ever never ever…"*

She thought Jarius would hear the demon in her head, the whisper seemed so loud. Oh, what had she done in this room tonight?

"It will soon be dawn, I must leave you." Marah stood, tightening the belt of her tunic around her. She wore no shoes or undergarments, carried no comb or veil. She needed to get to her room right now. Anyone who saw her would be scandalized by her appearance.

She paused at the door, straightened her back and looked directly at Jarius. Her words were formal, as though she spoke to a guest she barely knew.

"Thank you, Master Jarius." Her head held high, she opened the door only a crack, slipped out and closed the door with a gentle click behind her.

*"Oh, thank you, Master Jarius, thank you! Thank you for not dragging Marah out to her public humiliation at once! Thank you thank you thank you!"*

Thank you? Why did that pop out? Mortified at her last words, her face flushed red.

*"After what just happened, after all the things you just did, you are embarrassed you thanked Master Jarius? Now isn't that ironic?"*

Marah looked about, nervous that someone might be up. But the inn was silent. She pushed open the door to her room. The soft snores of her father greeted her through the thin wall. Her father who loved her still slept his peaceful sleep.

He was unaware that his beloved youngest daughter had just destroyed all he held precious and sacred. When people found out about this scandal, Naaman would be ruined. What kind of man raised a monster like Marah?

Jarius was alone in his room. He did not love her. Perhaps he would rather throw away his right to rule than to be married to someone like her.

*"A fallen woman! Will he cast you out into the street for the punishment you deserve?"*

Marah put a hand on each cheek, pulling her face so tightly it hurt. She would not listen to the whisper, she would not.

She heard her father cough. He could not marry her to Benjamin now. She was no longer a virgin. Her father would never look at her again the way he had for all of her life, with pride and respect and love. Miriam would turn from her, shamed. Asa, a respected Jewish teacher of the law, would forbid his children, his family, even the entire synagogue to ever speak to Marah again.

Marah had risked everything for a different life and lost. All she loved would be taken from her. She threw everything away for an arrogant, misbegotten whim, a fit of selfish pride.

Perhaps she should just leave, run away. Yes, run away!

But to where?

*"Who cares to where, Marah? If you must run away then you must run away. You must do what you must do, right?"*

She squeezed her eyes shut, willing the hateful whisper to leave her.

*"Good thing you didn't just sit around waiting for your circumstances to change! Good thing you created your own destiny! Good thing God gave you this opportunity to ruin your own life! Ruined, alone and unwanted! It's your destiny, Marah, your destiny to ruin everything! No need to run away, it's time to face your destiny!"*

She had no answer for the dreadful, mocking whisper in her head.

# CHAPTER 8

Marah woke up with a start, bewildered at the gray light stealing into her room.

Only a few hours passed since she slipped into her bed, but her habit of waking early did not fail her. Memories of the night flooded her mind. Was it all a dream?

No, it was the worst nightmare ever, one of her own making. Oh, Marah!

To lie in bed would arouse the suspicions of her father, familiar with her early morning habits. Marah's practice of rising before the first light of dawn was learned firsthand from a man who greeted the sunrise with a smile whether the inn was empty or full.

Marah stood up, sore in a way she did not recognize. When she realized the reason, she closed her eyes in shame. She could not dare to try to pray today. God would not want to hear from her ever again. He never answered her anyway.

She dressed, pulling her hair into such a tight, stern braid it hurt. She scrubbed her face and hands until they were red. Despite yesterday's trip to the baths, every part of her felt dirty, as though she'd spent the day in the hot stable mucking soiled straw. She dressed in her oldest, most tattered tunic. Dirty, filthy, smelly Marah, worthy only of rags and ruin.

Marah went to the courtyard to prepare the morning food for the departing guests, the motions second nature to her. She added wood to the fire to chase away the last of the evening's chill. She set out bread, fruit and cheese, along with goat's milk for the children and whole loaves of bread for purchase by the guests. She retrieved the water jars and set them on the table along with a row of assorted clay dippers. Soon the guests would leave. Jarius would leave, too.

That she had expected the future ruler of a synagogue to marry her was ludicrous. What in the world was wrong with her? Jarius would leave without a word to anyone, most of all to her.

But wait; she threatened to make their sinful actions public if he did not marry her. She planned to falsely accuse him of the most heinous and evil of actions. He couldn't just leave, not with Marah's horrific threats hanging over him like a black cloud. Who knew what a mad woman like Marah might do next?

The first guests filtered down to the courtyard, men, women and children trickling over to the table laden with food. All had a friendly word or smile for Marah, the shy daughter of the beloved innkeeper Naaman. Marah wanted to burst into tears whenever anyone spoke to her.

Naaman tiptoed up with a quick hug. "How's my favorite daughter this morning?"

Marah nearly jumped out of her skin at his touch. "Fine!"

Naaman jumped nearly as high at her screech. "Marah! What is wrong?"

She covered her face with her hands. "Nothing! Father, don't sneak up on me like that!"

"But I…"

"You just startled me. I'm sorry!"

Marah saw his puzzled look and knew she was about to be barraged by questions she could not begin to answer.

"Marah…"

"Nothing! Nothing is wrong!"

"Um, all right…" Naaman scratched his beard at these uncharacteristic outbursts from his habitually stoic daughter. "Well… soon you will begin getting the rooms ready, yes?"

"Father, I am selling bread!"

"Ah, yes… Well… I wanted to tell you I spoke to Jarius this morning."

Marah dropped the loaf of bread she was holding. Father and daughter watched it roll up to the calloused big toe in Naaman's sandal.

"He spoke to you? What did he…?" Marah's voice was a whisper.

Naaman picked up the bread. "Oh dear. I guess the birds will feast on this Marah! Or should we save it for ourselves? We can cut off the crust…"

"Father… You spoke to Master Jarius?" Marah thought she might faint.

"Yes, he came looking for me." Naaman was still contemplating the bread.

"Father…" Her voice was the faintest breath.

"What? Oh, yes. He said do not clean his room. He doesn't want his things disturbed. He will return later, he said. Jarius was in a great rush, up as early as my hardworking daughter Marah!"

Marah shook her head. It felt sacrilegious to mention the names Jarius and Marah in a single breath. "Where did he go? What did he want? Why did he speak to you?"

"Why did he speak to… He told me not to clean his room. He's coming back later." Naaman looked at her oddly. "Goodness, Marah, what is wrong with you this morning?"

She could not face his questions. "Father, I must go."

"Go?"

"Yes, I need to go work on the guest rooms."

"The rooms? But Marah, people are just now coming down for food!"

Marah's mind raced. Where had Master Jarius gone? Why was he returning? Marah was as grateful to hear that Master Jarius had left as she was to hear he would return. Now that she had done this terrible thing, she needed to know what would happen next.

*"You might not like what happens next, Marah…"*

Marah scowled at the whisper's interruption. "I must go, Father!"

"But what about the bread?"

Marah thought she might choke. She turned to the work table and picked up as many loaves as she could hold in the crook of one arm. "Here!" She thrust the pile into Naaman's hands. "You sell the bread!"

"Me?"

"Yes! I must go to…" Marah couldn't think of anywhere she needed to be. "To… to… the market!"

"The market?" The market was hours from opening.

"Yes! No, I mean, not the market. I must go to the stables!"

"The stables?"

"Just sell the bread, Father!"

"Of course, of course. People and animals, animals and people, they all want something from us, don't they Marah?" Naaman laughed.

Marah ran. If any guests wanted to purchase any bread for the road, they'd have to get it from Naaman. She could not face him for another moment. Surely he knew her agitation was only a mask for her disgrace and her sin.

Marah fled to the quiet second floor, where several of the guest rooms were already empty. The doors stood open, giant blank eyes accusing her. She shook her head impatiently and busied herself at once cleaning the rooms. Naaman did not call her for help. She hoped he wasn't just giving the bread away.

Why do you care about that, she scolded herself. Seems to me you have far greater things to worry about than the price of your foolish bread.

*"Far greater things than bread, Marah. Like Master Jarius."*

Master Jarius! She could not face him either.

Marah no longer wished to marry Master Jarius, or be his helpmate or even talk with him. She had a change of heart. She now wanted what he wanted, that he would never lay eyes on her again.

With each step she took, her weariness grew, seeping into her very bones. By the time she finished the third room, she could not take another step. She was tired in a way she had never known, not in her body but in her heart, in her aching, broken heart.

Perhaps she should lie down, just for a moment. She slipped down the hall to her small room and fell to her bed, the buzz of laughing chatter from the busy courtyard drifting up.

Although the morning was already warm, she pulled her blanket up to her chin. The unfamiliar touch of a single hot tear slipped down her face. "Stop crying, Marah! Just stop!" Her voice was testy. "Just get some rest and get back to work. You can figure out what to do later."

*"What to do, what to do…"*

Her tears and the whisper could not be silenced.

After Jarius got over the shock of seeing her, the first thing he did was pray to God. She heard the echo of Jarius's voice in her head. "Forgive my iniquity, God, though it is great. Rescue me."

Oh, that God would forgive her. Oh, that he would rescue her. If he would not forgive her or rescue her, please, just this once, couldn't God please speak to her, tell her what to do?

*"Do you really want to hear what God has to say to you today, Marah? Really?"*

Squeezing her eyes shut, she shrieked a silent shout at the whisper. Quiet! Quiet, quiet, quiet!

Like her frenzied thoughts, the whisper slithered away. At last, Marah fell asleep.

ରଷ

Marah opened her eyes, confused at the bright sun streaming through her window. Why was she sleeping? Why was she in bed?

Oh, yes, yes, yes.

She sat up with a jerk. There was much to do. Another round of guests would arrive this afternoon. The last of the Passover guests were headed to their homes. There wasn't time to lie in bed and wrestle with her ugly thoughts.

She jumped up, galvanized by the urgency of the work to be done and the notion that her father would find her sleeping in the middle of the day. What would he think?

She looked at the sky above the courtyard. It was not yet mid-morning. No harm done. She hurried back to clean the remaining rooms on the second floor.

Marah's routine settled her jittery nerves. She always did everything the same way, first straightening the blankets on the low beds. She carried down the dirty water and, because she expected guests again this evening, returned to refill each bowl with fresh water. Clean towels were laid out and the lamps refilled, their wicks neatly trimmed. Finally, Marah swept the worn wood floors of the second floor until they were spotless. Not a speck of dust remained. She would mop the creaky floors after this last wave of guests were gone.

She lugged a huge pile of soiled towels to the closet next to the stables. Tomorrow would be a hard day of laundry at the stream. Marah liked the demanding physical work of washing. She wished she could escape to the stream right now.

But it was time to clean the first floor rooms. She started with the room as far away from Master Jarius's as possible. How could she even enter that room, the room of her great sin and stupidity?

In short order, Marah finished the first five rooms. She did not open the door to Jarius's room, even though he would need fresh water. He said to leave the room undisturbed, and that was fine with her.

The courtyard was deserted. She covered her eyes, feeling the callous palms against her cheeks. What should she do now?

The growl of her sour stomach interrupted the silent courtyard. How ladylike, she thought, cross. The idea of food made her both ravenous and queasy.

The last time she ate was yesterday's meager noon meal of bread and a bite of cheese. Maybe food would help her settle her mind. The kitchen would be empty at this time of day.

She rushed across the courtyard to the kitchen. Just as she crossed the threshold, she spied her father sitting on a low stool, carefully wrapping the leftover bread she'd thrust upon him earlier in a worn cloth.

She took a quick step backward but too late: Naaman looked up at the sound of Marah's light step.

"Ah, there you are, Marah. I have not seen you all morning! You have been getting the rooms ready for the next guests, yes?" Her father smiled up at her as though she were the most beautiful thing on the face of the earth, his earlier confusion at her morning agitation forgotten. Marah could not look at him.

"Yes, we are ready." Realizing this fact gave her no reason to leave, she shook her head to correct herself. "I mean, no. There is still some work to do. Let me go finish, Father."

"Ah. Poor Marah, always working."

Her father looked so weary, his feet crossed under the bench, his shoulders slumped. Passover in Jerusalem was not an easy trek for Naaman.

Poor Naaman. She turned to leave.

"Marah, wait a moment. Come here." He held a hand out, beckoning her. She could not deny his smile. He grasped her sweaty hand in his.

He squeezed her hand hard as he gazed up at her. "I know it will be hard for you to marry and leave the inn. You do such a good job, you are an amazing girl. Everyone says so."

Marah wanted to hide from her father's words. Soon he

would know what she really was.

"You are so smart, and I am so proud of you. I know you hate to leave the inn, but we will figure something out, don't you worry. What I do know is you will make the shop of young Benjamin's family very successful. You will be such a good wife to him."

*"Benjamin! That's right, you're marrying Benjamin!"* The whisper sneered. *"Benjamin will be a great husband! You can fool him into marrying you, Marah. He won't even notice what you've already given away. After all, your own sister said he's not that bright!"*

"Your mother would have been so proud of you. I wish she could see you now."

Between her father and the whisper, Marah was on the brink of a scream that would scare both of them away.

"I must work, Father!" She snatched a loaf of bread from the counter and tore off a large chunk with a jerk, shoving it in her pocket.

"Okay, Marah," her father called as she fled. She wouldn't have to leave the inn, she'd be living here the rest of her life, shamed and hidden in her tiny bedroom in the inn. Her inn.

A terrible thought came to Marah. When people learned of this, as they surely would, the news would most certainly hurt their business. When people learned that the daughter of the innkeeper crawled into bed with a respected man who was not her husband or even her betrothed, they would stay away in droves. She worked so hard to make this a clean, well-kept inn with good food and good beds, safe and respectable, a friendly place where families would come again and again. She felt wretched. She had thrown everything away.

She not only ruined her life, but that of her father, too. Her sisters would bear the mark of her shame. She could not imagine what Asa, a learned and respected teacher of the Jewish law, would think of his promiscuous, sinful sister-in-law. "Stone her, it is the law!"

She could not even bear to think about beloved Miri.

Marah sat down hard on a step and tried to eat the bread, but found it was impossible to swallow even the smallest bite. She crammed the bread back in her pocket and walked across the courtyard to the stable. No one would look for her there.

She lifted the latch of the heavy wooden gate and pulled it

open. It slammed into place behind her, shielding her from the bright sunshine and horrible world outside. She looked at the dark, shadowy stable.

This was one of her favorite places, a haven visited only by Marah and her oldest nephew, quiet and peaceful. Her father only came in here with a treat for his beloved Donkey; guests never did.

Marah liked the strenuous labor of the stable, carrying the buckets of oats, brushing the donkeys, mucking the straw. The familiar smell greeted her.

Jarius's tall, handsome donkey stood in the first stall, eyeing her with suspicion. Even his donkey is mad at me, thought Marah. Wherever Master Jarius was, he went there on foot.

The only other resident in the stable would be her family's sway-backed old donkey. But where was he? She walked past the now-empty stalls. There he was, lying on his side in the last pen, his eyes closed. Donkey was so old.

"Donkey?" He opened a long-lashed, brown eye at the sound of her voice, but didn't raise his head.

To care for little Donkey was one of Marah's favorite tasks. She reached for his brush and sat down in the hay beside him. As she ran it over his coarse hide, he closed his eyes and lay completely still. Only his ears gave away his enjoyment, twitching his appreciation of the scratchy bristles. She would not think about herself and her troubles any more. She would not.

"Has it been a long week for you, Donkey?" Marah spoke out loud as she brushed him with steady, even strokes. "All the way to Jerusalem carrying little Naaman on your back? A scary week in a strange stable with lots of donkeys you didn't know?"

Donkey let out a long sigh. "No one understands me like you do, Marah." If Donkey could talk, Marah knew that was precisely what Donkey just said.

"Did you have to share the street with a big fierce horse?" Marah remembered the great horses of the Romans. "They scare me, too. Were you frightened by all the noise?"

Donkey nickered to confirm what a trying week he just endured. "I know, little Donkey. I have not had the best week either."

That was the understatement of her life. If only she could get on Donkey's back and ride away, never to return to this big mess she had made.

She stopped brushing Donkey and lay down beside him, scratching his long ears. He was a soft gray color, but his head and shoulders were snow white. "How old are you, Donkey?"

No one knew how old Donkey was. Her father bought the fully-grown Donkey long before she was born. Some of her earliest, happiest memories were of Donkey, she and her crowd of sisters riding the long-suffering beast, one shrieking girl after another. Donkey would patiently abide pulled ears and kicks to his side from seven laughing passengers of all ages. With much coaxing and an occasional treat, they would jar him into a gentle trot on the dusty streets of Shiloh. That is, until he tired of them. Then he would stop, and no amount of persuasion would make him move.

Her father would come and rescue poor Donkey, hollering empty threats at his rambunctious female rabble.

Donkey was her earliest memory. Donkey and the day the whisper came to live in her head.

"I had good days with you, Donkey," Marah whispered.

Now, when Marah needed Donkey to carry large parcels from the market, he swayed behind her with plodding steps. How he carried Naaman all the way to Jerusalem and back was a mystery to Marah.

He was such a good little donkey.

"Are you tired, little Donkey?" Her voice was a whisper.

Donkey did not answer her. Of course he was tired. He was old. He worked hard all of his life and still did his work as best as he could, never complaining, only asking for the occasional scratch of his ears. And he was still the best of company for a bereft and grieving soul.

Her father was old, too. He worked hard all of his life. A widower with seven daughters! He loved and cared for each one, and when they needed something, he did everything he could to get it for them. He was the best father anyone could want. He pretended to complain but in truth never spoke a cross word to anyone. He greeted each day with a smile and a prayer of thanksgiving to God for blessing him with such a life, for the time he shared with his beloved wife, for his wonderful daughters and, most of all, for his Marah.

All he wanted was for her to be happy.

Her father taught her to read and do sums, to repair gates, to doctor Donkey's hoof, to patch the roof. Anything she asked about, he showed her. As if any Jewish girl would be treated so!

He could have married her several times over. But he didn't, because they were young men Marah did not know or approve or like. As if any Jewish girl was allowed to have a say in such things!

Marah was crying.

Donkey was old. Someday, she would come in here and his brown eyes would not open.

Her father was old. He did not deserve the pain Marah would soon cause him. As if any Jewish girl would so brazenly defy her father and abandon all he held sacred. Perhaps such grief would be the end of Naaman, too.

*"Murderer. Mother and Father. Murderer."*

Marah could even not measure the enormity of how she had betrayed her father. What kind of daughter, what kind of woman was she? Not a good Jewish girl. A wretched daughter. A worthless woman. Unworthy and despicable. A worm. That's what she was. A worm.

But I love him, Marah thought miserably, I love Father more than anything.

*"Not as much as you love yourself,"* the whisper reminded her.

She did not have the strength to argue with that terrible truth.

❦

"Marah!" The stable door flung open, echoing as it slammed against the wall. "Marah!" he shouted again. "Marah, I have been looking all over for you! Come, come quickly!" Although he was only a few feet from her, Naaman was still shouting. "Marah!"

He was immediately silenced by her appearance. He looked at her with shock as she sat up slowly, wiping her swollen eyes. Marah was crying!

"Marah, Marah, are you all right? Are you hurt?" Naaman was truly worried. Five of Marah's older sisters still cried at the slightest whim or imagined hurt. Not since she was four years old, however, had Naaman seen Marah cry. "What is wrong, daughter? Marah, what is wrong?"

Marah heard the alarm in his voice. She stood up, tall and narrow as a willow sapling. For years, she towered over him.

"I am fine, Father, do not worry." Her voice cracked.

"Oh! But… But… But what is wrong, Marah? What?"

She rubbed her face with a frayed sleeve. "I am fine, Father." She would not lift her eyes to meet his.

She sounded so weary and defeated. Naaman opened his mouth, but Marah shook her head. Her voice was stronger this time. "Please, do not ask."

Having raised a houseful of girls whose moods changed faster than the flap of a crow's wing, Naaman decided to obey his daughter's request. Just because he didn't see Marah cry did not mean she did not shed the same tears his other daughters so freely shared with anyone in sight. Marah's tears took the edge off his excitement.

But only for a moment.

"Marah, come with me now!" He grabbed his daughter's hand and pulled, twitching with excitement.

Why does he need me now, thought Marah. Can I not have a moment's peace? Soon enough I will never have peace again, and neither will he. "What is it, Father? What is wrong?"

"Nothing is wrong, Marah, nothing!" He was yanking her hand, pulling her towards the door. "But I must speak with you. You must come with me right now!"

Marah heard his urgent words and pulled her hand away. This is it, she thought. He knows. Father knows.

"Come, Marah, come at once!" Naaman nearly ran from the stable, turned back and grabbed his statue of a daughter by the hand. Marah followed, her long arm stretched out as Naaman drug her along.

"Hurry, Marah! Come on!"

He knows what I have done, Marah thought. What will happen now? What's going to happen to me? Oh, what have I done?

Her father started talking, he could not be quiet. "Oh, Marah, our lives are about to change. In a moment, you will see, you will see. When all our neighbors hear this, they will shout for joy and fall face down, so says the Book of Moses!"

Shout for joy? At those words, Marah halted, almost pulling Naaman over in the process. She stared, looking at him for the first time since he startled her in the stables. He did not seem angry or upset or heartbroken. He was excited, a wide smile plastered on his face.

He was as animated as she had seen him for months, perhaps years, grinning from ear to ear, almost dancing on his toes in a delirious elation.

How long did she hide in the stables, scratching Donkey's ears? Something had happened to make her father happy, very happy. What happened?

They stood in the courtyard, the arch to the great room where guests gathered a few feet away.

Her father took Marah by the shoulders and looked up at her, trying not to grin.

"Marah, I know you do not want to get married, even yesterday we discussed it, but it is time! This is a great blessing for you, you will be happy! I am so happy! So happy!" He could not help himself, he was beaming.

At once, Marah knew what had happened. Her father went this morning to see the father of Benjamin. They must have agreed upon a marriage contract. Benjamin and his parents stood in that room.

Her destiny awaited her. Benjamin.

She could not marry him, not now. She could not even face Benjamin, not after what happened last night. Not ever.

"Father, I must speak to you, I cannot…"

"No, Marah, I will not hear any argument from you, you must come."

"No, no, Father!" Her mind scrambled for an excuse. She had to escape! "I must change, I've been in the stables, please let me take off this robe, please let me…"

Before Marah could finish, her father physically shoved her through the door.

Miriam sat on the low bench, Asa standing beside her. Despite the great girth of her pregnancy, she jumped up to hug Marah, her smile wide, tears in her eyes. She opened her mouth to speak, but a discreet cough from Asa silenced her. She smoothed Marah's hair, and arm in arm, they faced the man standing alone by the wall.

It was not Benjamin.

It was Jarius.

"Marah, Master Jarius came to me this morning to ask a most important question, and I am so happy to have told him yes. However, you are my youngest daughter and I wanted to talk with you and Jarius together, if I may. Please sit down." Naaman motioned to another bench. Marah plopped down just as her knees gave way.

91

"Please, Jarius, please, perhaps…." Her father was fluttering in a nervous half-circle, his hands waving in the air. He turned to Miriam. "Perhaps I should get some wine?"

Marah's heart started racing, beating as though it would fly out of her chest. Her father and sister and brother-in-law would not glance at her with wide smiles and jovial nods if they knew what happened. Miri would not be standing next to Asa glowing with happiness.

No, if Miriam knew what Marah did last night, she would be crying, great gulping sobs like when Asa's mother died. Asa's face would be carved from a cold stone, no comfort for his wife, the sister of a fallen, sinful woman.

Her father would be crying, praying, mumbling words from the Book of Moses.

Marah could not breathe. Could it be?

"Please, Father, say what you have to say." Her voice was faint.

Naaman sat down heavily on the bench next to his youngest daughter. He was out of breath. "Marah, Master Jarius, well, I do not know how to begin. It is such good news, I was surprised, Miriam and Asa were surprised, and daughter, oh my daughter, I know you will be pleased.

"Just a few days ago, Jarius and I were talking about what he will need in his next wife, and here he is taking my advice! But I never dreamt such a fine young man would listen to my wisdom! Was that only seven days ago? Or longer?

"As it says in the Book of Moses, 'We will take the choice fruit from the trees, and palm fronds, leafy branches and poplars, and rejoice before the Lord your God for seven days. We will rejoice with my son and my daughters and my menservants and my maidservants…'

Marah closed her eyes. They did not have any servants and the closest palm tree was miles away. Her father was more befuddled by the moment.

"Now, where should I begin…" Naaman sprang to his feet again, agitated.

Jarius bowed respectfully. "Master Naaman, if I may."

Her father nodded so hard his thinning beard flapped, relieved to be rescued from this quagmire of emotions that choked rational words from his head. He flopped back on the bench, exhausted.

"Marah, I have asked your father if I might enter into a betrothal contract for marriage with you. If this is agreeable to you." His tone even and unemotional, his eyes two unreadable orbs.

"But I do not love you," he said last night.

*"And he never will, Marah. Never, ever, ever! He will never love you, not after what you did."*

Miriam ran to the seated Marah, the ample belly nearly smothering her as she engulfed her youngest sister in a tight hug. Her father's short legs bounded across the room in two steps. He reached out and shook Jarius's hand, laughing out loud, thanking Jarius in a babble of words, welcoming him to the family. Asa joined the two men, pounding Jarius's back in celebration.

Marah pushed her sister away and stood up. She looked at Jarius, with Naaman pumping his hand for dear life, Asa's hand clapping his shoulder.

"Father."

Her father turned to look at her, his smile stretched from ear to ear.

"Father, I wish to speak to Master Jarius alone." She wished her voice did not sound so terse.

Naaman, Asa and Miriam stared at Marah, surprised these measured words were her first response to the proposal of Jarius. As though they were struck dumb, she thought.

Naaman narrowed his eyes, on his guard at once. Marah had argued with her father too many times for him to be fooled, especially when it came to the subject of marriage.

"And why do you want to speak with Jarius alone, Marah?" His voice was like iron, each word as harsh as a plow against a stone. It was a strange, unfamiliar sound from the little man known far and wide for his spirited good cheer.

"Father, I just want to speak with Master Jarius alone."

Naaman flushed a beet red. There was real anger on his face, something Marah had never before seen.

"Surely you cannot find any fault with this proposal, Marah!"

Miriam jumped; Naaman was shouting, his hands clenched at his side. "You cannot live here forever! It is time you understood your place as a daughter! Why are you so difficult?"

Everyone stared at Naaman, stunned by his outburst.

Naaman pulled himself up to his full height, strode across

the room and, still inches shorter than his daughter, stood on his toes to thrust his face into hers. "Is this not good news, daughter? Is this not good news? As Moses said, 'Is this the way you repay your father, O foolish, unwise daughter?' Is it? Is it?" Naaman looked as though he were about to explode.

*"Yes, is this how you repay your father, Marah? After all, this is just exactly what you wanted. The man you destroyed wants to marry you!"*

She forced herself to smile, ignoring the taunting whisper. "It is the best of news, Father. I only wish to speak with Master Jarius alone, for just a moment." The forced gentleness in her voice sounded as false as it was.

*"Yes, Marah, speak with him alone, as you spoke to him last night."*

Against her will, her face flushed red with shame. She wanted to look away but forced herself to stare calmly down at her father's flushed face.

Naaman looked at her with distrust. His daughter had manipulated him far too many times. He had allowed her too much freedom too many times.

His anger got the best of him.

"Fine! Fine! But if you do not want to marry Jarius, I will marry you off to Benjamin, who even I think is an ass!"

"Father!" Miriam face was aghast at the public pronouncement before her husband's friend Jarius.

"Hush, Miriam!" With each syllable, Naaman's voice increased in volume and pitch. "Marah, you listen to me! I will marry you to Benjamin if I wish! I will marry you to the old man who was here last week, the one who doesn't have a tooth in his head! I'll marry you to anyone I wish! I will not be burdened one more moment by such an ungrateful, stiff-necked daughter as you! Not even for one more day! Not one... more... day!"

The last word was almost a squeak.

"Naaman, Naaman." Asa put his arm around his father-in-law's shoulder. "Naaman, it's all right. Marah and Jarius have never shared a moment alone. Come, all will be fine."

"Yes, Father, come," Miriam added, but she cast a warning look at her youngest sister. Marah's stubborn streak was well-known to her as well.

Marah looked at her feet. As hard as she tried, she could not pull her stiff lips into a smile. Those dreadful tears were so close. Another angry word from her father, one word of rebuke from

Miriam, and all hope was lost for Marah.

"Please, Father…"

"Fine! Fine, Marah! Jarius, I leave you with my plague of a daughter! I leave to pray, as Moses prayed!" Naaman shook off Asa's arm and started waving his own. "I leave to pray, Jarius. To pray that, that… that your house…"

So great was his distress, he could barely stutter the last words, stumbling over the well-worn words of his beloved patriarch. "I pray… like Moses… I pray that your house will be rid of frogs!"

Naaman's eyes grew round in a desperate plea for deliverance from his own tongue.

"Yes! No! I said… I meant I will pray about plagues, not frogs! Like Moses! Not frogs! Not frogs!"

There was a short pause in the room as the enormity of what just happened struck Marah's father.

Moses had failed him.

"Frogs! Aaaaaaaaah!" Naaman's short legs sprinted to the door, but he turned to shout a final rebuke at his impossible daughter: "So says the Book of Moses!"

Waving his arms in the air, his face as red as a beet, his mortification complete, Naaman ran out of sight.

Her mouth a round circle of surprise, Miriam followed him from the room with eyebrows arched all the way into her thick brown hair.

Asa caught Jarius's eye and shrugged, bemused.

In the sudden silence, Marah and Jarius stared straight ahead at the departing backs.

Frogs? What on earth possessed her father to blurt out 'frogs?' Oh, Father, thought Marah. She could not help it, she started smiling. How she loved her father.

She heard the voice beside her. "May your house be rid of frogs? Is this how your father blessed the marriages of your six sisters?"

Marah could not look at him. She was afraid if she did she would burst into laughter. She searched for something dignified to say.

"My father is upset. But he is seldom truly angry. He just could not find the… appropriate words to express his irritation with me. Or words for his blessing." She could not look at Jarius, her chin high, her straight profile pulled into its stern stare. She would not allow him to belittle her father, no matter how ridiculous Naaman might be.

Even though, for as long as she lived, she would never forget the crestfallen look on her father's face after he bellowed that one word: "Frogs!"

Marah heard some muffled sounds beside her. She turned to look at Jarius in disbelief as he sat down heavily on her father's bench. Jarius was laughing.

Marah looked at him for a long minute, and then sat down, too.

Jarius laughed until he cried, wiping tears on his sleeve. A small smile its way to Marah. The only man Marah ever saw laugh like that was her father.

"Ah, Marah, I have always loved your father. Always smiling, always happy, all these years in love with his daughters and his life. But that's not the only reason I laugh. I laugh from a lack of sleep, a lack of food, a lack of peace. I have no peace today, Marah."

At those words, the smile froze on Marah's face. No matter how much her father made them laugh, they could not forget the dreadfulness of what had transpired between them, the magnitude of what she had done. She had not only ruined her life but his too.

"Master Jarius." She could not think of anything else to say.

"Marah, I have not slept since you left me last night. I have thought about what happened and all you said to me. I spent my morning at the synagogue in prayer. But I do not have any answers. God feels… far from me."

That's my fault, thought Marah bleakly.

"We are not suited for each other in any way except that you will make a good manager of my house. But there is more to being a wife than this, Marah. I only need hire a household manager. As for a wife, I see that the kind of marriage I had for such a brief time I will never have again." He dropped his chin to his chest and said in a low voice, "I am truly heartbroken by what happened last night, Marah. For I loved Deborah and my son with all my heart. I still miss them every day."

Jarius cleared his throat. "I do not love you. I do not even know you. I hoped someday I would find someone like Deborah, someone I would love. I am sad for the marriage we will have, a marriage without love. Impossible."

Marah was numb. But the words "the marriage we will have"

echoed over and over in her mind.

"However, just as you feel you deserve more than what has been offered to you by your father and your life, I do not deserve to have all the things my father and I have worked for these many years to be taken from me. What is clear to me today is this: I do want to be the synagogue ruler. I did not know this for certain until I realized how easily it could be taken away from me. Taken away from me by you." Jarius narrowed his eyes, the accusation clear.

"I believe that I will be a fair and good ruler. I have studied the law in Jerusalem with the best teachers. I have served in the synagogue now for ten years. I have worked hard to build my alliances. And certainly I know about the world and the terrible trouble it brings to people who do not deserve it."

Marah knew this trouble was not the death of his wife and son. The terrible trouble he referred to was her.

"Still, one thing has become apparent to me. It will actually be better for me to bring an unknown wife from far away to Capernaum. It will save me from the difficulty I might encounter as different families squabble over whose daughter might marry the synagogue ruler, even more so one whose family holds lands and possessions and wealth. I would not trust their motives any more than I trust you. And, my beautiful Deborah was well-liked and known to every Jew and Gentile in Capernaum. Everyone loved her. To marry a friend of my wife's would be unthinkable to me."

Marah cringed at the words "my beautiful Deborah." He would never say those words about her. Deborah was the wife he loved.

"You were right about something else, after all. My father is ill, and I am deeply concerned for him and his care. I do need someone who can run my household. I cannot be burdened by a thirteen-year-old girl who knows nothing, nor do I wish to marry a widow with children. Yet, the demands of my father's illness, my family's wealth, my position in the Capernaum synagogue and Capernaum… it is all too important, too overwhelming for me to remain unmarried." He turned away from her.

"I want to be the ruler in Capernaum, and I need a wife who can help me."

Jarius spun around to glare at her, his voice angry. "The sin of ambition is in my heart! I did not know this until you left me last night. It is a sin to want something so much. I want to be the ruler of

97

the Capernaum synagogue! I want it! I now want what my father has wanted for me these many years! I confess my sin to you, Marah, because you showed my sin to me! Speak of this to no one. For you are no stranger to the sin of ambition yourself."

Marah was shamed at the truth of his words. Her greedy ambition was the only reason Jarius stood before her now.

"I do not wish to be disgraced, to have what I have worked for be taken away by my sin with a village girl. Even more than that, I do not want anything to hurt or shame my father in these final months of his life.

"You have left me with no choice but to marry you. And so we shall. We shall marry." He sighed. "I only wish, Marah, that I loved you."

*"You did it, Marah! Jarius will marry you. You'll share a marriage bound by the same sins – ambition and shame. You have your whole life to make this man love you! After all, you can do anything, can't you?"*

Marah did not know what to say to Jarius. Her ludicrous, bizarre plan worked. But she felt hollow, as though there was a place in her that could never again be filled. Her wonderful plan would ruin this marriage before it ever began and haunt her all her life.

*"Of course the marriage is ruined. You ruin everything…"*

There was no respite from the ridicule that welled up inside her.

Jarius broke the silence. "Marah, if we are to marry, I have certain conditions, things you must vow to me on pain of death before I agree to marry you. Your father is fond of the words of Moses, and I quote them now to you: 'Every pledge by which she has obligated herself must stand.' Will you make these vows before me and before God in the house of your father?"

Marah nodded, frightened. To vow before the stranger that was Jarius, and before that silent, unspeaking God was one thing. It was quite another to make a vow in the house of her beloved father.

"First, you must never tell anyone about what happened last night. No one. Ever. If you do, I shall divorce you, no matter what the recriminations will be to me. Last night will be our private shame forever. Tell no one, not your father or Miriam and Asa or your sisters or friends! No one will ever know of our sin. We will never speak of it, ever." She heard the anger in his voice. "Do you promise?"

Her face flushed. She wanted to tell him she didn't have any

98

friends, tell him that it was her greatest fear that her father or Miri would learn what she had done. She would die before she ever told anyone about last night.

She already made this vow to herself. She nodded at Jarius, her eyes wide.

"Say it, Marah."

"I promise." Her voice shook.

"Your actions show you to be untrustworthy. I do not know if I can share much of my life with you. But you will see and hear things that you are never to discuss, never to repeat with anyone. Ever. If you must ask a question, ask me and me alone, and only in private. You are a quiet girl, not one who talks mindlessly to anyone near her. That is a good asset for me. Do you promise to keep my affairs private?"

She nodded again.

"Speak the words, Marah!"

"I promise." Her voice was soft, but firmer.

"Since Deborah has died and you are now to be my wife, you will do just what you offered last night: manage my household. I will have far greater time to pursue my own responsibilities at the synagogue without having to cater to a young wife. This too is an advantage for me. Do not expect me to entertain you, Marah. Instead, you will do whatever you must to maintain my household in a way that befits me, my family and my position. Do you promise?"

This was almost word-for-word the bold idea Marah suggested to Jarius. But her heart dropped. Would they ever share private conversations and quiet laughter like Miriam and Asa, giggling hugs like her sisters and their husbands, an undying love like Naaman still carried for the mother Marah never met?

*"Are you insane?"*

"I promise."

"The last thing is very important to me. My father is ill, much worse than most people know. In his last days, you will care for him as though he was your own father who I know you love. You will attend to his needs, make sure he is as comfortable as possible every moment. You will serve the foods he likes and oversee the care he receives from the servants and the physicians. I want someone to watch over him as keenly as an eagle seeks its prey."

"Before Father dies, I want him to know that I will fulfill his dreams for me, and that I am married to a good Jewish wife who will do whatever she must to make me successful. He will never know or even suspect the sin that has happened between us. Father will die with a happy and peaceful heart. You will make sure this happens.

"Do you promise?"

Jarius loved two people. His wife Deborah and his father.

*"But soon the only one left will be you, Marah."*

"I promise." This time her voice was loud.

"Before God, in the house of your father, do you promise to honor these vows you have made to me today?"

She took a deep breath. "I promise."

*"Then we shall be married."*

Marah nodded. There was a long silence between them.

Her voice was hesitant when she spoke at last. "Master Jarius, I realize now, too late, that what I did was wrong. I am sorry." She hung her head, her cheeks scarlet. Marah could not think of anything else to say about last night. Her apology sounded lame even to her. Jarius did not even acknowledge her regret. He thinks I ruined his life, she thought.

*"Haven't you?"*

But Marah wanted Jarius to hear something. She spoke a little louder, trying to sound convincing.

"I know you loved your wife. And I am so sorry Deborah died, and sorry for your son too. It is… was a terrible thing." Jarius looked at his lap, his only answer an imperceptible nod. She saw the tears spring to his eyes.

He's like my father, Marah thought. So tender-hearted, emotions so close to the surface. She forced herself to return to her own words.

"But Master Jarius, you will not have to love me to appreciate me. I will be all you could ever want for a wife. You do not love me, I understand. But you will find me useful every day of your life. You will not be sorry you married me. I promise."

Jarius did not look at Marah as he spoke.

"We're not even married yet, Marah, and I am already sorry."

# CHAPTER 9

The law required a betrothal of one year, but Jarius was a man of considerable influence.

Jarius met with the synagogue ruler in Shiloh and explained the illness of his father, his probable role in Capernaum as a fellow ruler, and his need for a wife to help him with his many responsibilities as soon as possible, sooner than the Law would typically allow even for a widower. His father was dying, after all.

A betrothal of only six weeks was agreed upon immediately. Jarius needed the help of the innkeeper's daughter at once. Someday soon, Jarius would be a very important man in Capernaum, a far greater city than dusty Shiloh. That a Shiloh girl was marrying a wealthy man from Capernaum was amazing enough, much less one who would soon be a ruler. To think that skinny, towering stick of a girl could snag a polished, handsome, rich man like Jarius…

No one in Shiloh could believe the good fortune of Naaman.

Marah didn't think her father even read the marriage contract, so great was his excitement. Jarius departed for Capernaum and his father, but left a generous dowry to be used for Marah's bridal attire and new robes befitting a new bride and the future wife of a ruler.

No sooner did Jarius leave than Miriam delivered her fourth child, a baby girl that only a few days later gurgled and smiled, clutching Marah's little finger as tightly as Miriam gripped her youngest sister's hand.

"Look," Miriam whispered to Marah. "She has your dimples, dimples like our mother." Marah had not even known her mother had dimples.

Any thoughts Miriam had about Marah's marriage to Benjamin were long forgotten, replaced with a mixture of happiness and dread. "Marah, you are going so far away. What will I do without you?"

Much to Marah's surprise, no one was prouder of her marriage than Asa. Lifelong friends, Asa and Jarius once studied together in Jerusalem. That Jarius would marry his sister-in-law was an astonishing surprise. His future brother-in-law would be a synagogue ruler, and in an influential outpost like Capernaum!

Asa loved Miriam, but neither one ever spoke what they both knew: Asa did not make a politically strategic marriage when he took beautiful Miriam for a bride. He loved the small, smiling, curly-haired woman even more now than when they married, sacrificing a future as a teacher in the Holy City, reconciled to a life of relative obscurity in Shiloh.

Now, he could not believe his good fortune. After all, family relationships were as critical to success as one's own efforts and his future brother-in-law was not only a friend but family.

"Perhaps Jerusalem," he whispered to Miriam at night. "Perhaps I might someday teach in the Holy Temple in Jerusalem."

Miriam smiled at Asa, new baby at her breast. She did not voice her opinions about the great distance between Jerusalem and Shiloh, much less Jerusalem and the far outpost on the Galilee, Capernaum.

Marah's five sisters were ecstatic at the opportunity to sew and embroider such fine cloth into beautiful garments for their littlest sister, whose good fortune could not be believed. Much to Marah's surprise, their general consensus was not that Marah was lucky but that she deserved this. God was blessing their little sister for her faithful service to their father.

"Oh, Marah, he's lucky to have you!"

"Who has worked harder than you these last ten years?"

"You will be the perfect wife!"

"No other woman is as smart as our sister!"

"No one."

Her sisters agreed with one noisy voice that Marah deserved

this marriage. Too much time with her five sisters voicing the sentiment over and over gave Marah a headache.

Marah's worry over the fate of the inn proved to be ill-placed. Her third sister was married to a second son, a jovial young man who in Marah's estimation wasn't much brighter than Benjamin. The young couple would help Naaman, care for him and the inn. It was a good opportunity for her brother-in-law.

Marah got the feeling they had been waiting for her to marry someone and leave.

She spent long hours with them, a quiet litany of storeroom supply quantities, chores before and after the guests, recipes to feed large gathering, caring for the stable, the laundry, the ovens...

Marah's sister murmured her surprise to the entire family at how hard it must have been for Marah to do so much work at their father's inn by herself.

My inn, Marah thought. This was my inn.

Two weeks after Jarius left, for once alone in the quiet sanctuary of her storeroom, Marah said a perfunctory prayer of thanksgiving to no one in particular that she was not with child. She prayed only as an obligation. She was, after all, extraordinarily thankful that she was not pregnant. One sister or another proved every year that Naaman's clan was indeed an exceptionally fruitful clan.

*"But you said you would even have his children, Marah. Too bad you couldn't surprise Jarius with an early wedding present, a baby obviously conceived during betrothal. What a nice surprise that would have been!"*

Yes, Marah was certainly thankful.

Marah's singular prayer of thanksgiving was the only thing she could think of to say to God. What else was there for someone like her to say to the Almighty? "I'm sorry?" The magnitude of her sin seemed too big, too unforgivable to put into words.

*"Liar, fornicator, murderer... Big sins, Marah. Too big to be forgiven."*

Naaman walked about telling anyone who would listen of the upcoming marriage of his daughter. His smart, amazing Marah would wed a future synagogue ruler! When Naaman came to the part about her moving to Capernaum, his eyes would fill with tears, and the oddest sentiments from his beloved Moses would pop out. "My feet did not swell for forty years!" he might proclaim, or "I will bring locusts into your country tomorrow!"

No one seemed more startled by these pronouncements than

Naaman, who would then end the conversation with a fervent farewell: "Thus says the Book of Moses!" His listeners would stare at his departing backside and scratch their gray beards in confusion at such incomprehensible wisdom.

When he came upon Marah at her work, he would look at her with mournful eyes, intoning a new lament: "As it says in the Book of Moses, I will never appear before you again," or "How will anyone know that you are pleased with me, Moses asked of the Lord?"

"Enough of Moses, already!" Between her sisters and their sewing, question after question from her brother-in-law about the inn, and Naaman's doleful proclamations, Marah was at her wit's end. "I've listened to Moses more than the poor Israelites did for forty years!"

But this did not silence Naaman, who had waited fourteen years for this moment, the day when his youngest daughter would marry. Never did he imagine that his little girl's husband, his last son-in-law, would be someone so important! A synagogue ruler, one who was wealthy, respected, and most of all, exceedingly kind. A nice person who would be good to his daughter, someone known to Naaman since the man was a boy, the only son of a dear friend. Yet, Naaman did not rejoice over Marah's good fortune like the rest of her family.

For Naaman was broken-hearted his youngest daughter was about to leave him.

ఴ

Sooner than she could have imagined, Marah, her father, four sisters, assorted brothers-in-law and Asa traveled to Capernaum for the wedding. One sister was too pregnant to make the trip, and Miriam would not travel so soon after giving birth to her fourth child.

Marah was bitterly disappointed. More than anyone else, Marah desperately wanted Miriam at her side as she stepped into this new life. But Marah had made her bed alone, and she alone would lay in it.

The carts Jarius hired were loaded with her few possessions and her large family. The last sound she heard over her sisters' chatter was the sad bray of Donkey. Her sisters would not let her run in and hug him one last time.

"Marah! You'll stink like the stable!"
"You'll smell like Donkey!"
"Time to act like a bride, Marah!"
"A synagogue ruler's wife!"
"Pee-ye-ew, Marah!"

As the carts rolled on towards Capernaum, Marah stared at the inn until it was hidden from her sight. She could not turn to face the new life ahead of her, choosing instead to gaze as long as possible at her old life fading away. How she would miss that life, Miri, her inn, even her sisters. Her father. How she would miss her father.

Still, traveling by cart took her mind off both the old and the new life. Marah's family never traveled anywhere except on foot. "Follow me, children!" her father would proclaim. "God will make us wander in the desert, so says the Book of Moses!"

She forgot about her old life a little bit more when confronted with the sight of beautiful Capernaum, its buildings sitting like whitewashed stones by the sparkling jewel blue Sea of Galilee. They passed by the huge Roman garrison; her father told her over one hundred soldiers were stationed there. A century of soldiers, Naaman called it. She'd seen soldiers many times in Jerusalem but never so many in one place, warriors with their great horses and swords and armor.

And the market! It was many times larger than the one in Shiloh. Capernaum was on a caravan travel route, and its traders stopped there to sell foreign and exotic wares. What fun it would be to barter for her household needs here. That many traders meant more competition for her business. She felt a slight surge of confidence.

They traveled down the rough main road, everyone laughing as the carts jostled them to and fro, Marah clutching the side of the cart with white knuckles. The road was paved like the streets in Jerusalem, lined with black stones that shone in the sun.

The town was large, at least several thousand people. They passed street after street and several large lodging houses, much larger than the little family inn of Shiloh. But they did not stop, for Marah's family would stay at the house of Jarius. Jarius assured them there was ample room.

There was the synagogue. It was old and imposing. Jarius had not misspoken. Her husband would be an important man.

What did shock the noisy clan into silence was the home of Jarius, the home where Marah would soon be mistress. No wonder Jarius needed help. Marah cared for an old inn of ten tiny rooms, a small stable, a worn courtyard, just a shabby spot on the road through Shiloh.

It was no comparison to this.

The stately home was U-shaped, the two-stories on all three sides towering above them. Outside balconies faced the paved street and with balconies inside overlooking a vast courtyard covered with tile and inlaid mosaics. How many rooms were there? Where was the kitchen? Oh goodness, was that a second, private courtyard? Look at the size of the stable!

It will take me a month not to get lost, Marah thought. She stood for a moment with her father in the courtyard, Asa, her sisters and their husbands silently behind them. Her father's mouth was clamped shut, as though to keep some inappropriate quote of Moses from escaping. He squeezed her arm in amazement.

"Oh, Marah," he murmured. "Oh, oh, oh. Oh, Marah."

"It will be all right, Father."

It *will* be all right, Marah thought fiercely. I told Jarius I would be all he needs for a wife, and I will be. I will! He must never know that I am even the least bit scared about running this house. I have always been able to do anything. I can do this, and do this well. I must. She gritted her teeth. It was just a house, after all.

*"It is just a house, after all."* Marah ignored the mocking whisper.

Marah saw her future husband standing in an open door. He looked amused, watching Marah and her family in the fine courtyard, gawking in amazement with wide eyes and open mouths like yokels who never set foot out of Shiloh.

A fire blazed up in Marah, forging a fierce decision within her.

She might be a poor nobody from Shiloh. She might not deserve to be the wife of a rich ruler. Jarius might look down on her, for he knew what she really was.

But she would never, ever allow him to look down on her family or her father.

Marah saw the occasional wealthy Jewish woman at the inn, with the rare servant and her self-important airs and confidence. Marah could act like those women. She refused to be known as the daughter of a poor innkeeper any longer. Instead, beloved Naaman would be known as the father-in-law of the future ruler of the Jewish synagogue in beautiful Capernaum.

Marah pulled her thin face into a smile, a big one that showed her dimples. Her long, heavy hair lay loose on her shoulders under a carefully draped, beautifully embroidered veil. She wore her loveliest new tunic and the necklaces, bracelets and earrings Jarius delivered weeks ago as part of her dower. The freckles and calluses on her hands were still there, but her nails were even and shining. Her sisters had groomed her with care.

Marah pulled herself to her full and formidable height, her back straight as an arrow. As Jarius stood there, she looked him directly in the eye, staring at him from across the courtyard. She saw a flicker of surprise at her defiant stare, which Jarius at once masked with a polite smile.

See? Marah thought. She could pretend to be anything she set her mind to, even fool a future ruler into thinking she was confident and beautiful. Never mind that her knees were shaking like a leaf. She flashed her dimples again.

*"Not quite the rough country girl he left a few weeks ago, are you? You can wash dirt off a pig, can't you Marah? But it's still just a pig when you're done, even if it has a gold ring in its snout."*

Marah steeled herself. The whisper might know how she felt. Clean on the outside, unbelievably dirty on the inside. But no one else ever would. No one!

Jarius stepped into the courtyard to welcome her and her family. Marah held up a hand to halt her family. "Wait here."

"But, Daughter…"

"You too, Father."

She walked out to meet her future husband alone, nervous to the point of physical illness, her chin high. They stood facing each other.

"How were your travels, Marah?" She strained to hear his low voice.

"Fine." She deliberately pitched her voice even lower than his.

"Marah, I am glad to speak to you alone, just for a moment. I must hear you say this before we go one step further."

He took her hand, her knees shaking so hard she thought he surely could feel her trembling from head to toe.

"Do you remember your vows to me, the things you promised?' His soft voice was gentle, but the words were hard as iron. They pierced her like a dagger.

Marah's heart fell. Her fierce stare did not fool Jarius. He knew exactly what she was. He could shame her and her family if he wanted. That power would always be his.

Her eyes were wide with dread, the fear she tried to tamp down bubbling up within her. Did Jarius change his mind? Was he going to pronounce her shame and her guilt to all? Was she finally going to get the punishment she deserved?

"Have you told anyone about what has happened?"

Marah shook her head.

"You have told no one? Not even your sister Miriam?"

She shook her head again, this time with such vigor her ears rang. But it was not enough.

"Say it, Marah! Have you told anyone what we did, what happened between us?"

"No, Master Jarius."

"Do you promise to honor the vows you made that day? To keep your silence, to care for my father, to manage my household?

Marah nodded.

"Say the words, Marah."

"Yes. I promise, Master Jarius."

"Do you promise to help me? To not hurt me or my father, to never harm his reputation in any way? Do you promise?"

Marah looked down, unable to meet his eyes. "Yes," she whispered.

"Marah, say the words." His voice was intense.

"As I vowed in the house of my father... Yes, Master Jarius, I promise." She did not want to mention God.

Jarius's face relaxed into an expression she could not make out. Was it relief? Compassion? Forgiveness? No, surely not that. She could not tell what it was, and she did not dare to ask.

He rubbed the calluses on her palms, scars of hard work that would probably never go away, a brooding look on his face. He shook his head and his expression changed.

"Well, then, Marah, if I am to be your husband and you are to be my wife, then... you must not call me 'Master' any longer. If... if it pleases you." His voice was kind. "If you please, Marah... call me Jarius."

Marah flushed. She had been so afraid of this meeting. It was so different than she had expected.

Here stood Jarius holding her work-worn hand, smiling, polite and welcoming. He was going to marry her after all, not humiliate her in front of her father.

She nodded stiffly, as straight and tall as the man beside her. For of all the things she imagined Jarius might say when she arrived, "Call me Jarius," was not one of them.

He smiled at her. "You look very beautiful, Marah. Let us go greet your family."

*"Beautiful!"*

Beautiful? Never in all her memory could Marah recall being called anything but a skinny stick, a Goliath, a boney, bosom-less girl.

She jerked her mouth into a smile. Jarius called her beautiful.

Jarius squeezed her hand, pulling her along as he walked out to Naaman, his other hand outstretched. "Welcome, Naaman, welcome to Capernaum. I trust your journey was good."

Her father smiled widely at his future son-in-law. They shook hands, and then Naaman grabbed Jarius away from Marah to squash him in an impulsive hug.

"Asa, I am glad to see you!"

"And I to see you, Jarius! Congratulations!"

"How is Miriam? And the new baby?"

The two men continued, grinning, pounding each other's backs.

Marah watched as Jarius took the hands of her oldest sister. He whispered a greeting Marah couldn't hear. Tears came to her sister's eyes, and she nodded, smiling at her future brother-in-law.

Jarius continued her family circle, shaking hands, receiving hugs, slapping backs, smiling and laughing with each member of Marah's familial entourage.

*"What's wrong, Marah? He wasn't going to stone you in the courtyard after all. Even if you deserve it. And here he stands, welcoming your family like a good son-in-law should, saying the things a future husband should say. He even called you beautiful. And all he wants is for you to call him Jarius!"*

Her only true companion was relentless in its ridicule.

Marah's jaw was as rigid as stone in a fierce determination to keep her dimples in place. She would not stand for that whisper, not now, not here.

She was rescued by her father's lapse into a babble of

excitement, bobbing up and down with eagerness. "Jarius, it was a wonderful trip, riding in carts, a luxury! Thank you! We are so glad to be here, to celebrate this wedding of my daughter and her marriage to you!"

"I'm so glad you are here, Master Naaman. May I have the honor of showing you the home that your daughter Marah will share with me, or shall I take you to your rooms to rest after your journey?"

Naaman shook his head, suddenly quiet. "If it is all right, Master Jarius, perhaps someone else can show Asa and my other daughters to their rooms. Before I do anything else, I wish to pay my respects to your father, let him welcome me to his home for the first time, welcome me as I know he would if only he were well. I want to introduce him once again to my daughter Marah. He has not seen her for years."

*"What he means is he only remembers you as a servant girl, not as a bride for his only son."*

"That is, if my old friend is well enough to receive guests."

"You are kindness itself, Naaman. Father is feeling better today. He's waiting, anxious to visit with his old friend." Marah saw a glint of tears in his Jarius's eyes. "You are the friend my father thought he would never see again."

Jarius turned to Marah. "Are you ready to see my father, or do you need to freshen up from your journey first?"

She took the arm Jarius offered to her. Say something, Marah, her mind ordered. Don't be a stray dog with no bark. She had not said one word since Jarius uttered those quiet three words: "Call me Jarius."

She took his arm, nervous to meet his forbidding father. But never, ever would Marah let Jarius know of her fear and doubt. She had told him she would be the wife he needed and that was what she intended to do. Even if it killed her. Never would Jarius know that she was afraid, she thought fiercely. Never.

Marah tried to pull her lips over her teeth into a semblance of a smile. "I am anxious to see your father as well." The sound that croaked out was a scratchy rasp.

She cleared her throat and tried again. "My family is glad to be here. I mean, I am glad to be here, Master Jar— "

She stopped, flustered.

Smile, Marah, and smile big, she commanded herself. You're

only pretty when your dimples show.

She straightened up to her every inch of her imposing height and looked Jarius directly in the eye. Her smile was so wide, all her teeth were showing.

"I am glad to be here… Jarius."

Jarius threw back his head and laughed.

Is it possible he was as nervous as me? Marah thought. After all, this is no small thing they were doing.

*"This is no small thing you are making him do,"* the whisper corrected her.

To her great surprise, Jarius took her hand, raised it to his lips, and, in front of her father and family and Asa, kissed it. He wore a wide grin as he led her to the room where his father waited for his friend and the new bride of his only son.

Naaman followed only a few steps behind, muttering. "Oh, my beloved wife! See! Our daughter is marrying a synagogue ruler! This big house is her home! Your little baby Marah! As it says in the Book of Moses, 'Let us go over and see this strange sight…'"

"Who are you talking to, Father?"

"No one, my Marah. No one at all."

They walked from the sunny glare of the courtyard through a stone arch into the cool dimness of the house, Naaman right on Marah's heels.

Marah could have sworn she heard him mutter what only she would understand, his evening blessing to the woman he still loved: "God keep you, wife."

Marah glanced over her shoulder to see her father's wide grin.

"Just talking to myself, Marah. Just talking to myself."

# CHAPTER 10

From the moment Marah first stood in Jarius's courtyard, nothing was turning out the way she expected it. From small surprises – like Jarius kissing her hand – to outright shocks – like their wedding celebration – every preconceived notion regarding the future she had grabbed for herself was wrong from top to bottom.

"What have I done?" she whispered over and over again, as she ran into the handsome, laughing stranger that was her betrothed again and again. She roamed about the huge mansion that was now her home, knelt for the sincere blessing of the aged man that was her frail future father-in-law, and met servant after bowing servant, all curious about the oddity who would become Master Jarius's wife.

Her grinning father and giggling sisters were no consolation whatsoever.

Marah was overwhelmed, with no one to talk to and nowhere to turn. She would wring her hands, her plea for her ears alone: "What, oh, what have I done?"

*"What have you done? Oh, Marah, you only did what you had to do. Need I remind you?"*

There was an upside to the constant newness and hubbub. The whisper found itself hard pressed to be heard over the commotion.

But it was not until the celebration of her wedding that Marah at last understood the enormity of the path she had forged for herself, how different her life would now be.

Because of the frail health of his father, Jarius and Marah's wedding celebration lasted only two days. A private ceremony was held on the first day, a simple affair attended by her family, Asa, and Jarius's father and a lifelong servant named Deena.

"She's my family," Jarius smiled.

Jarius stood first to speak, eloquent and articulate, smiling at Marah as though she were a beautiful bride instead of the devious snake she knew she really was. He quoted a long passage from the Songs of King Solomon, some of which might have made Marah blush had she been listening.

But she did not, for her brow was wrinkled up with anxiety over the few words of Solomon that Miriam chose for her to recite, drummed into Marah night after night the last few weeks. When it was her turn to speak to her groom, Marah stumbled over word after word, red-faced and stammering. The collective sigh of relief at her final shaky "Selah" was almost audible.

Even as she listened with knees wobbling, Marah's heart broke for the pain Jarius's father endured for the sake of his beloved son. He stood only long enough to pronounce the blessing required of him as both the synagogue ruler and father of the groom. His words were stilted and halting, harsh stutters interspersed with grunts of agony.

Conversely, when Marah's father stood to bless this union, he cried so hard his blessing was not much better than that of the dying man. No one could understand much of what he said, his words punctuated by loud sniffles and a few outright sobs. All Marah gleaned was a garbled quotation from her father's constant companion: "They may marry anyone they please, so says my old, old friend… Moses."

Marah was certain Moses never said anything vaguely like that, but who was she to point out her father's misquote at a time like this?

Asa stared straight ahead, but finally glared a fierce warning as Marah's four sisters dissolved into giggles. Much to Marah's relief, when Naaman finally seemed at a loss for words, Asa jumped in with a solemn and eloquent prayer.

The disjointed, uncomfortable ceremony was over at last. They were married.

One day down, Marah thought to herself. Tomorrow I do

not even have to speak, just sit and smile and show off these stupid dimples. How hard can the celebration tomorrow be?

The next morning, Jarius himself would host an abbreviated version of the traditional week-long wedding feast, an affair for the Jewish citizens of Capernaum to be held in the grand courtyard of his home.

At least then Marah knew what to expect. She attended many such events in Shiloh, including the six celebrations for her older sisters. Of course, she had known the fifty or sixty people that attended those events, but how much different could her own wedding be even here in this big house and strange place called Capernaum? Brides didn't have to do anything but sit and smile, anyway.

She did not get a chance to ask her new husband, for Jarius's father took to his bed as soon as the final words of the wedding ceremony were uttered. He had a difficult afternoon and night, desperately ill, his body wracked with pain, strength sapped by the simple act of speaking at his son's wedding ceremony.

Jarius rushed from the wedding to his father's bedside. He returned to join them for the evening meal, a quiet, subdued affair, but excused himself almost at once with an agitated apology as he rushed the side of his father's bed.

"Jarius is afraid his father might at last go the way of the earth. Today may be the day he gives up his spirit to death," Marah's father whispered to her.

Marah was too unfamiliar with death and far too timid of her husband to join him at the bedside of his father, as another new bride might have done. She stood at the door and watched him weep at the side of his father's bed. Jarius shook his head at her presence.

"I am sorry, Marah. I am afraid to leave. I am sorry."

"Sorry... girl..." The old man's voice was a tortured gasp.

"Don't speak, Father." Marah heard the anguish in Jarius's voice. "Please, rest. Marah, just go. Forgive me. I will see you tomorrow, God willing. Thank you, Marah."

She knew he meant if his father made it through the night.

A better woman would have gone to comfort her husband, but Marah seemed to have left her courage behind in Shiloh. She ducked her head in acknowledgement and, not knowing what else to do, fled.

So, on her wedding night, Marah went to bed alone, sleeping

in the bedroom adjacent to her new husband's. It was a spacious chamber set aside for the mistress of the house, a room she was surprised to learn would be hers alone. She did not know any married couples with their own bedrooms, separated from each other by a closed door. She stared into the darkness long into the night.

"It doesn't matter," she muttered. She had no expectations whatsoever about her wedding night or any other nights with Jarius. But she could not shake the niggling memories of Miriam and Asa, heads pressed together in quiet murmurs of private conversations and gentle smiles, or the familiar camaraderie and boisterous laughter that punctuated the marriages of her five sisters and their equally jovial husbands.

She claimed to have no expectations, but if she were totally honest with herself, a marriage with a closed door between husband and wife at night never crossed her mind.

Oh, well. It didn't matter.

*"Of course it doesn't matter, Marah. You're not Deborah, after all."*

It doesn't matter, she thought again, fiercer this time, determined not to lose control of her emotions now. So she would not share a bedroom with her husband. It would not matter. That was not part of the bargain she struck with Jarius.

Her eyes hardly closed when her sisters trouped in. It was early even by Marah's standards. They helped her bathe, dressing her with the greatest of care in the beautiful bridal gown and jewelry. When her sisters made sly references to her wedding night, Marah shook her head and steeled herself for the certain teasing ridicule she knew would follow.

"Jarius did not come to me. He tended to his sick father all night long."

She was surprised by their babbled responses.

"Such a good man!"

"Rich, handsome *and* nice. Oh, Marah."

"A husband who loves his family will love his wife, too."

"You can be sure of it."

"You are so lucky, Marah!"

"Of course Jarius stayed with his father."

"It's a miracle the man made it through the night at all!"

"And to think he is so much better today. A miracle, an answer to prayer. Father is practically delirious, he is so happy Jarius's father is better."

A round of titters at the mention of Naaman.

"He was quoting Old Moses to anyone who would listen."

"Even to the servants!"

"Oh, our father!"

"Stop worrying about Father and help me get this robe on Marah."

"Good grief! How many layers of fabric are there? Who sewed this?"

"Marah, Jarius is truly a fine man. God has blessed you, Marah."

"God's hand is on you, that Jarius has chosen you."

*"God blessed you? Jarius chose you?"*

But it was impossible for the whisper to take hold with the noisy, buzzing chatter of Marah's four sisters. As busy as they were getting Marah ready, they were equally as secretive about what would soon transpire.

"Oh, sister," said one and then another.

"Oh, our sweet Marah!"

"You cannot imagine what is going on in that courtyard!"

"You can't imagine!"

"Don't tell her!"

"Just wait, Marah," one sister knowingly exclaimed after another. "Oh, just wait till you see!"

See what? She could not imagine and she did not ask. Marah let them fuss over her as though she were once again their four-year-old sister. She was silent as they combed and perfumed and oiled and powdered and rouged, never a break in their chatter.

"Don't forget to smile, Marah."

"You are so pretty when you smile."

"And smile big, like you mean it, Marah."

Her dimples were worn out before the day even began.

As befitted a bride, Marah did not have anything to do with the planning of this wedding. But she heard the noise long before she entered, escorted by sisters. A large, loud crowd was already gathered in the courtyard of Jarius's home. At the appearance of the bride, they burst into boisterous cheers.

Marah almost fainted when she saw the mass of smiling, laughing strangers in a festive courtyard she didn't even recognize from yesterday.

Her father rushed to her side and burst into tears. "Marah!

116

You are so beautiful! Oh my daughter, as Moses would say…"

She was swept away before she heard the pronouncement. Jarius came to meet her with a grin, leading her away from her sisters and father and steering her into a new life marked by the noisy applause of strangers.

Overnight, the courtyard had been transformed, festooned with flowers and a lavish bridal table under a heavy huppah for Marah and Jarius. There were tables and tables of food, and large vats of what Marah assumed were wine. And there were people. Lots and lots of people.

Much to Marah's shock, three hundred people came to pay their respects to Jarius and his new wife, jostling each other in the courtyard as they vied for a spot close to the future synagogue ruler.

Except for the crowds of strangers in Jerusalem, Marah had never seen so many people gathered together in one spot in her entire life. Two dozen families lived in tiny Shiloh.

Her husband, on the other hand, knew all the people milling about by name, calling out a greeting to one man after another.

Marah had never met so many strangers, never forced a smile for so long, and never, ever spoke so often in her life. Her husband talked with every single person, man and woman. He jovially introduced her to one person after another, smiling at her stilted 'thank you,' laughing as he acknowledged their good wishes. He enjoyed a sip of wine with everyone who came to congratulate him and ogle this awkward surprise of a wife. He appeared to be having a good time, jumping up from his seat beside his new bride to speak to friend after friend.

On the other hand, Marah's face hurt from smiling, her jaw ached from being clenched tightly so that her ridiculous dimples would show, and her head throbbed for all the other reasons. The day was interminable; Marah could not swallow a bite of food and took only the occasional sip of the fine wine. The roar of the people could not compete with the roar inside her head.

The day-long reception flowed into the evening. Although officially over, people lingered, talking and laughing, refilling wine cups by the dim yellow-gold lantern light. Her sisters were socializing and watching the dancers and musicians, while Naaman talked loudly with old friends and new. Asa and Jarius stood guffawing with a cluster of men who alternated between slapping Jarius on the back and slapping their knees in hilarity.

No one was watching the bride.

Marah fled. She slipped to her new room without a word to anyone, escaping the noise, the well-wishers, her family, the grinning Asa, her father who beamed at her all day long, and especially the jovial man who was now her husband. She undressed and took to her bed at once, mentally and physically exhausted, relieved and unexpectedly thankful for a bedroom all to herself.

"I would rather shovel out a stable all day than do that again," Marah muttered to herself. She lay in the dark, not even wondering about her groom, knowing he was probably chatting with the myriad of people she could still hear celebrating outside. Three hundred people!

She jumped at the brisk knock. The door that separated the adjoining bedrooms of Marah and Jarius swung open. Her husband stood at the door.

He grinned at her. Without a word, he walked to her bed, pulled off his tunic, lay down beside her and then took her in his arms.

There was no conversation between them, the intimacy strictly physical. Marah kept her head turned and her eyes closed, afraid to look at Jarius, trying to keep the image of what happened that other night far, far away. Before she even gathered her wits about what was happening between her and her new husband, it was over.

Marah was surprised when Jarius sat up at once, pulled his robe over his head and stood up from her bed. At the door, he turned to her with an apologetic look on his face.

"Marah, you will find I sleep very little. So as to not disturb you, I always sleep in my own room." He stopped, searching for words to ease the awkward moment. "It is my... habit, my custom for many years, to read, to study late into the night." His look was hesitant. For once, Jarius sounded unsure of himself.

Trying to soften his abrupt leave taking, his escape from his wife, she thought.

His face brightened. "I am right next door if you need anything, Marah," he said happily, consoling himself and his wife. He paused, as though searching his mind for anything else he might be required to say.

"Good night, Marah." His duty done and excuses made, Jarius nodded once and left with a broad smile on his face.

118

What a day and what a night.

What a wedding. What a marriage.

Oh, what had she done?

Marah lay awake for hours, her eyes wide in the dark room.

ଓ

It only took a few days of marriage for Marah to realize her life in Capernaum would be full, even busier than her days at the inn. She was relieved, for she liked it far better that way. Most of the time, she was alone. She did not like to be idle in any circumstances, but she especially needed to stay busy when she was alone.

She was married to man she knew as an acquaintance her entire life, one who was now more of a stranger than ever. Jarius left at first light, coming home to check on his father and to join her for a late dinner, if at all. The members of the synagogue council often met with Jarius at night, closed up in the upper room of their home where Jarius kept his many scrolls and parchments.

At Jarius's request, they had already hosted four dinners at their fine and beautiful home, inviting the council members and their wives and other influential people of Capernaum. Everyone wanted to meet the wife of the synagogue ruler's son. The food and setting of these meals so far were exceptional. Every detail was infinitely attended to by Marah and Cook, the rotund man who had overseen the kitchens in the house of Jarius since he was a young boy. He begrudgingly shared this duty with Marah.

"Better than we have ever had, Marah," Jarius told her after the last dinner. "Wonderful."

His praise did little for her confidence; these dinners left Marah nervous and exhausted, too worn out to even speak when they were finally over. But she was weary because of the dinners themselves, not the work to prepare them.

At these social gatherings, Marah was forced to do something far worse than prepare her home and cook a meal; she had to visit with the other women, the wives of the other men. And if she could not think of much to say to the elegant, handsome man that was her husband, she really did not have one word in her head to say to these worldly, wealthy women.

They were all older and former friends with Deborah. They were kind to Marah, never condescending or rude. After all, Jarius

119

would soon be the synagogue ruler. Marah just didn't know how to carry on a conversation with anyone other than her sisters.

Oh, if only Miriam were here! As soon as she married Jarius, Marah learned Asa was moving to Jerusalem as a bona-fide teacher of the law, rubbing elbows with the Temple leaders. Jarius told her about it one evening; he had written a few letters to acquaintances in the Holy City.

Even in faraway Capernaum, Jarius was a man of influence.

Miriam would live in Jerusalem, even farther away from Marah than she was now. If only they were moving to Capernaum instead! Graceful, beautiful Miriam would fit right in with Jarius's high society crowd. Miriam could have added the polish that Marah so desperately desired.

Instead, Marah the new bride sat at her own splendid dinners, dressed up in fine robes that felt alien to her, a stiff, tense smile on her face, a nod her typical conversational response. After a while, the women gave up in the face of Marah's aloof, tongue-tied silence, talking around rather than to her.

Yet, Marah soon realized it was much better to host the dinners than to attend them at the houses of the other women. In her own home, Marah could at least excuse herself as often as she needed, her hostess duties a ready alibi to escape the women and gather her wits for a few minutes. When dining elsewhere, Marah sat the entire night like a lump.

If Jarius noticed how inept his new wife was, he never pointed out her shortcomings to her. As a matter of fact, he was always thoughtful and considerate to Marah, as one might be to a welcome guest in one's home. His behavior confused her more each day, a nervous stutter her only response to his kind words and jovial greetings. Jarius appeared genuinely happy to return to his home each evening, even when it meant the company of his tongue-tied, awkward new wife. Though his late-night visits to her bed were conducted in an odd sort of silence, he came to her often. Marah could sense the simple pleasure he enjoyed when he was with her.

The longer she was married, the less she knew what to expect from this stranger that was her husband.

But then again, what had she expected? Raging anger and frenzied shouting from good-humored, easy-going Jarius? A displeased, stony silence from the man whose face spread into a happy smile whenever he spied someone he knew? Private and critical lectures where he reminded her that he was the son of a rich ruler forced to marry the ignorant, sinful daughter of a poor innkeeper from Shiloh? Harsh words from Jarius, who probably had never spoken an unkind or thoughtless word in his life?

Impossible.

*"A husband who might like you? Even a little? Impossible…"*

She clenched her jaw. Of all the things she left behind, why couldn't it have been the dreadful whisper always clawing its way into her heart?

*"Impossible."*

So, because Marah did not know what to expect, she expected nothing. She only waited, waited with the whisper to see what would happen next.

In the meantime, Marah did the only thing she knew how to do: She worked.

# CHAPTER 11

Once she was somewhat settled into her grand home, once the novelty of the strange, odd wife of Jarius wore itself out, Marah began to erase the quiet traces of the much-loved first wife of Jarius. Only if you paused and intently listened could you hear the echo of Deborah's spirit.

Well, only Marah could hear it. To everyone else, Deborah, the wife to Jarius for only one short year, was only a sad but infrequent memory.

*"Still, it's hard to get rid of someone like Deborah, isn't it, Marah?"*

Deborah was born to one of the best and most influential of Jewish families in Capernaum.

*"Not like Marah. She's just the youngest daughter of a penniless innkeeper in the middle of nowhere, wearing ragged hand-me-downs and smelling like onions, stables and sweat."*

Deborah was Jarius's confidante, his spiritual and intellectual equal.

*"Not like Marah. She's not an equal to Jarius. But she might be equal to the servants, for she can cook and clean and muck out manure! Just like a hired hand, except she's free! A real bargain!"*

Deborah was a faithful Jewish woman, respected for her piety and devotion to God.

*"Not like Marah. She couldn't recite a psalm if her life depended on it. She used to say her prayers, but... She never heard one single word back from*

*God. God never ever spoke to you, did he, Marah?"*

Deborah was the wife Jarius loved.

*"Not even remotely like Marah."*

It was apparent to Marah that Jarius did not hate her, or dislike her, or even mind that she lived in his house. On the contrary, Jarius was unfailingly kind and courteous, always deferential and polite. As the days went by, he seemed to be pleased with Marah's quiet personality and appreciate her efforts in his home.

In only a few weeks, he began to trust her capable judgment in most things pertaining to their household. It was obvious to Marah that Jarius cared nothing about the details of his home, and he and everyone else could see that Marah was a shrewd business woman and household manager.

*"Either that, or he is just too trusting and too dumb for his own good."*

It was a marriage of mannerly politeness and brief conversations about ordinary daily events, a detached, respectful marriage of strangers. Despite his kind and gentle demeanor, Marah was confident that Jarius could not love her.

For after all, Marah did a monstrous thing, something so evil she could never confess it to anyone. She committed a horrendous sin and so she would be punished. She knew Jarius would someday come to hate her, for she ruined his life. She enticed him to sin with her and then threatened to blackmail him. She forced him to marry her or risk losing everything dear to him.

Her sin pressed on her continually, a constant pressure in her heart and her mind. Oh, to have the burden lifted. But she could not discuss it with anyone. To do so was to risk certain divorce and shame. Jarius made that clear that morning in his courtyard.

Why had she done this terrible thing? To satisfy her own selfish, stubborn, sinful ambition.

Marah still had the same opinion of herself that she had that morning months ago, the morning after she slipped into Jarius's bedroom. She was a worm.

So Marah the worm waited every day, every night, every moment for the harsh judgment she knew was forthcoming. She waited for Jarius's anger, for his revulsion, for his revenge.

She waited for her punishment.

It never came.

Marah began to suspect something: Jarius had forgiven her. He forgave her and moved on with his life

It took Marah some time to fully realize this. But when she did, it was as though she had been struck by a frightening bright blue bolt from the raging black sky of her own fear and guilt.

Marah did not know what to do with his forgiveness. She never asked for it. She knew she did not deserve it. Thus, Jarius's quiet acceptance of her as his wife was confusing and unsettling. As each day passed, she became more troubled about this ominous, disturbing turn of events. Forgiveness! Jarius forgave the unforgivable. He had forgiven her.

She did not know what to do.

She hid behind a shy mask of detachment, on guard every moment, watching and waiting for accusations never spoken, punishment that never came, and for the anger she deserved.

Anger, accusations, punishment… they simply never came.

It changed her.

Marah was no longer the quiet, strong-willed girl who married Jarius, self-assured and confident of her ability in her own little world.

Now, she was a married woman, a wife alone in a foreign and alien home. She questioned her every decision, her stomach tense with nervous anxiety. She did not know or understand the man she married. She tiptoed around this stranger, waiting for him to finally give in to a rage that surely lurked somewhere behind his polite demeanor.

The longer she waited, the harder she worked, the more afraid she became of what would happen to her.

*"But why are you afraid, Marah? Didn't you get everything you wanted? Didn't your little scheme work exactly the way you planned? Don't be afraid. I'm here for you. You and I are in this together."*

"There is no 'you and I!' Marah gave up trying to drive out the scornful whisper that haunted her. "You are me, you awful, horrible…" She could not think of what the whisper was.

*"You're right. I am you and you are me. But you hate me, remember? I guess that means you hate yourself, too. Just like Jarius hates you."*

"You are not real! Leave me alone!"

*"I am not real? I am not real? I am the only real thing you have. I am the one who knows you, the sinful, shameful you. I am all you have. No one hears you but me. If I leave you, you will truly, forever and ever, be alone in this world and the next world and the world after that."*

Oh, if anyone ever knew about the conversations she carried

124

on with a dreadful imaginary whisper that tortured her so. Her husband would not only hate her, he would know she was only one short step away from the edge of the cliff. If she didn't fling herself over it, he probably would throw her over himself and be rid of her.

No. She was not crazy. She was not! She was only sinful. Not insane.

*"Only sinful. What a relief, to be only sinful! Sinful, sinful, sinful Marah. Your father would be so proud."*

Her father. Oh, her father. "Will you never be silent!"

*"Of course! I will be silent. Silent to everyone but you. Your shameful secrets are safe with me, Marah."*

"Leave me, please leave me." She could hear her own begging desperation.

*"Never,"* was the whisper's sneering reply.

Marah could feel the tears behind her eyes.

*"Oh, Marah, are you crying? Did I make you cry?"*

She lifted her chin and spoke her answer out loud, defiantly, her tears forgotten. "Never."

❧

Surprisingly, the servants took to their shy and silent Mistress almost at once. The oldest two worked for the family since Jarius was a boy, coming even before his mother died when he was only eight. Deena and Cook were intensely loyal to Master Jarius. As such, only their respect for him and his revered father would keep them from weighing judgment on this young, uncouth upstart of a wife.

The seventh daughter of a poor innkeeper! They would serve but not like this destitute, unsmiling girl from some tiny country village. As befitted their superior positions in the household, they never gave voice to the unspoken, collective thought:

"Why in the world did our Jarius marry *her*?"

However, despite their first opinions, they found themselves inexplicably and irresistibly drawn to Mistress Marah.

For one thing, they did not know what kind of wife she was, but they soon learned Marah was a master at all things in the household realm. Nothing in this big and grand house seemed to unnerve this stoic young woman.

For another, since Cook and Deena worked servants all their

lives, they could at once see their young mistress possessed something they treasured. Mistress Marah had a servant's heart.

And so, they liked her in spite of themselves.

Mistress Marah seemed uncomfortable giving orders to the servants, although that was what they expected from the mistress of such as fine household as this. Instead, Mistress Marah seemed much more comfortable, whether they liked it or not, *working* beside with the servants.

Unbelievable!

For one thing, the servants soon learned that no matter how early one arose, it was impossible to get up earlier than Mistress Marah. For another, they kept finding their new mistress doing their chores.

The evening before, Marah would shyly tell Cook, "I think we might need to grind wheat for flour tomorrow. Our supply bin seems a little low." As if she had to tell him that! Why was she even looking in the storage room, anyway? He already planned to have the kitchen girl do just that first thing tomorrow. He would nod respectfully, his lips set in a firm line.

Early the next morning, Cook would find her in the kitchen grinding the wheat herself.

Impossible!

"Mistress, stop!" he would cry when he found her, embarrassed and fearful that Jarius would think under his supervision the kitchen girl was shirking her duties. Surprised, Marah would stop and Cook's helper would nervously skitter over to take on the laborious task.

Both Cook and the girl would look in admiration at the flour Marah ground, sifted and fine and fit for use in the best of Cook's cakes.

They would no more than settle into their routine of daily chores than they would find Marah on her knees, scrubbing the pavers in the courtyard.

Unthinkable!

"Please, Mistress Marah, please!" They would run to find the household boy. Appalled, he would at once take over her brush and bucket, careful that his efforts were just as meticulous as the Mistress' work would be. Before Mistress Marah arrived, they only scrubbed the courtyard... well, they actually only swept the courtyard. No one could ever remember actually washing down the outdoor tiles.

When they pointed this out to Marah, she looked aghast. "Not mop these beautiful tiles? Look how they shine in the sun."

Deena would stride up the polished hall to the Master's chambers, keeping watching on her aged, frail employer of so many years.

But there would sit Marah, holding his hand, listening to his fevered ramble, a bowl of fresh water by his side, a cool cloth on his fevered head. Marah would jump to her feet at the sight of Deena in the doorway.

"Stay, Mistress Marah, stay. I was only checking..."

Marah would nod, unable to hide her fearful look at the sight of Deena. But at the gray-haired woman's approving nod, she would again kneel down beside the bed of her father-in-law.

At first light, Deena would walk up the long stairs to attend to her life-long task, to make up the two adjoining bedrooms shared by her Master and Mistress. But both beds would be empty, tidy and neatly made. The night clothing would be neatly folded, Master Jarius's tunic from the previous day gone, already set aside to be washed. The water bowls would be emptied, the soiled towels removed, even the night jars would be gone.

The night jars!

The first time it happened, Deena said nothing, thinking it an odd, newlywed, country girl sort of fluke. But this routine continued. Finally after a week, Deena went to find Marah.

"Mistress Marah," she scolded, put out. Her age and long tenure in this home gave her certain privileges. "Why are you doing this work every morning? The wife of a synagogue ruler does not get up earlier than the roosters! It is not fitting that she makes up her own bed. Or her husband's bed. Or tidies the bedrooms."

Deena's voice took on a certain outrage at the final shocking unsuitability. "And the wife of Master Jarius should not empty the night jars!" She stood with her hands on her hips, silently demanding an explanation for such inappropriate behavior.

Marah looked at her, startled. A long silence stretched out between them.

Then, for the first time since she arrived, Marah laughed.

Deena did not even smile, still put out with this shocking behavior. But the laughter surprised Deena. Since the wedding celebration, she did not think she had even seen Mistress Marah smile, and even then her smile was taut over wide, startled eyes.

Deena hadn't noticed a shred of happiness on the bride's face, and she watched for it day after day.

But lo and behold, when Mistress Marah laughed, the most beautiful dimples transformed that stark countenance into a face that was surprisingly pretty.

"Deena, from my first morning here, I have laid awake for nearly two hours waiting for this household to come to life. I cannot stay in bed any longer than I do. When the morning light comes, I must get up." She laughed again. "And the first thing I learned to do was to empty my own night jar."

"But Mistress…"

Marah looked away from Deena, not meeting her eyes. Her jaw was rigidly set. "I have tried to stay in bed longer, just as you suggest. But I cannot and so… And so, as mistress of this house…"

Marah took a deep breath, as if to gather up some vestige of courage. She stood stick straight, which in turn made her very tall. She threw back her shoulders and lifted her chin high, a defiant look on her face.

"And so, as mistress of this house, I will get up when I want. Even if it is before the roosters!"

Such a show of courage for such an incredibly innocuous proclamation caused both Marah and Deena to fall silent. Then, as one, they both started to laugh.

It felt good! Marah could not remember the last time she had laughed. Perhaps not since her father had shouted about frogs.

Deena was still laughing when Marah added, "Besides, Deena, what else am I to do?"

Deena saw the sad shadow that passed over Marah's face. Behind this silent façade was a frightened woman determined to do her best, even if she was afraid. After all, Mistress Marah was just a young girl and a new bride who was very much alone.

And certainly, a woman of Mistress Marah's status was free to get up whenever she felt like it.

Except, Deena had wondered to herself, typically the mistress of a house such as this began her day late in the morning, with breakfast served in bed and toiletry and dressing needs attended to by someone like a faithful Deena.

It did not mean getting up while the last gray of night was fading away. It did not mean dressing one's own self, and making up one's own bed. It did not include making up the bed of her husband.

It most certainly did not mean emptying one's own night jars! Mistresses had fine gowns and airs, not calloused hands and a willingness to work.

Deena looked at the plaintive, wistful face of Mistress Marah. Her bravado might fool Cook or Master Jarius, but it did not fool Deena. Something in this young woman's melancholy expression touched Deena's heart.

At that moment, Deena found her mission: to make certain that Master Jarius's new wife would be successful.

It was not to ensure her position with the family. Marah did not have a servant to bring with her to replace Deena. Jarius would never let Deena be sent from his household, anyway.

It was not to protect Master Jarius from Marah. Deena could sense there was some sort of odd bond between Master Jarius and Mistress Marah. After this many years, Deena knew the family secrets. All of them, except for the secret this girl carried. Whatever it was, Deena would protect it just as fiercely as she had protected Master Jarius for so many years.

It was not because she liked Marah. Indeed, she hardly knew this girl.

It was because Deena instinctively knew that this young woman was what Master Jarius needed in a wife.

Deborah was outgoing, friendly and well-liked. She was knowledgeable of the scriptures and enjoyed philosophical discussions with like-minded pious Jewish men and women of her own social stratum. She attended every dinner and social event in Capernaum, out somewhere nearly every evening. She loved to talk and laugh. She was breathtakingly, stunningly attractive. People still talked about her great beauty.

Deborah had been all those things and more, all things but one: Deborah had no idea how to be a good Jewish wife.

At least in Deena's opinion.

The only child of wealthy parents with an esteemed ancestral lineage, Deborah did not understand or even care about what needed to happen to make a house a home. Time after time, Master Jarius attended to household questions and issues. Those were Deborah's responsibilities!

At least that's what Deena thought.

Even with the long hours he worked at the synagogue, Jarius would come home to approve the market lists or menus from Cook, discuss repairs with the house boy, or even check the guest seating in the dining hall for a dinner that very night. While he did these things, beautiful Deborah would be dressing for the evening's splendid affair, her lifelong maid at her side. Her maid was as beautiful as her Mistress, and except for grooming her beautiful Mistress, brought no value to the household.

In Deena's opinion.

For years, first his father and now Master Jarius met with a business manager for hours each week. Jarius would stay for hours, listening to his reports, taking notes and asking questions, trying to understand his father's many holdings. At first, Deborah joined them every week, then every other, then not at all. Deena overhead Jarius asking her to stay, but Deborah laughed, declaring those matters to be far beyond her as she left to meet her friends.

In Deena's opinion, the shortcomings of a beautiful, laughing young wife might be fine for any other young man, but not for Master Jarius. He was soon to be one of the youngest rulers ever, and in a significant city like Capernaum. He was too important to be worried about menus and repairs and money for the market.

Deena felt a pang of guilt at her disapproving spirit, for her beloved Jarius loved his Deborah. But then again, who didn't Master Jarius love? She was proud of his kind and gentle manner to people both great and ordinary. Jarius loved Deborah, and Deena loved Jarius like the son she never had. She grieved for him when he wept for the loss of his wife and son.

But Deborah was gone. Mistress Marah stood in her place.

Mistress Marah was independent and hard-working and most of all, smart in the things that counted. She was not anything like Deborah at all. And that was a good thing. At least that was what Deena thought.

Mistress Marah would be the help Jarius needed. She would free him of the routines of daily life so he could wholeheartedly pursue the calling Almighty Jehovah placed before him. Deena felt it in her middle-aged bones. Marah would help Jarius.

Not like Deborah.

May God let her faithful soul and the baby rest in eternal peace, of course.

The thin, trembling woman still stood before her, the flash of courage and bravado ebbing away, her eyes flicking nervously between the intent Deena and the floor.

Deena's voice and smile were gentle. "Of course, Mistress Marah. Forgive me, I spoke out of turn. I am here to help you anyway I can. Together, we shall build the finest household possible for our Master Jarius."

Deena could feel the relief coursing through the young woman, who smiled widely and then ducked her head to return to her work at hand. Deena watched her for only a moment.

It was too bad that Master Jarius, whom Deena loved as a son, could not love this wife the way he once loved Deborah, but no matter. Marah's servant's heart would prevail.

Deena would make sure of it.

# CHAPTER 12

After Jarius so abruptly left her bedroom that first night, Marah soon learned that what he told her was not an excuse but actually true.

Under the door that separated their two rooms, Jarius's light burned late every night. Although he would frequently come to her bed, he would always leave and return to his own room, the dim light of his lantern a slit under the door. Marah assumed he was reading or writing or perhaps praying. There were as many scrolls and parchments in his large bedroom as there were scattered about on the table in the upper room. If he slept for more than four or five hours, Marah would be surprised.

She often remembered her father laying in his bed, his conversation with God and Moses audible through the thin wall, each night ending his commentary with a long sigh and the words that haunted her all her life:

"God keep you, wife."

How her father must have loved her mother. How Marah wished her mother hadn't died bearing her.

She would whisper the four words to herself, a small comfort in her nighttime homesickness for her inn, her father, for Miri, her life. The words her father spoke each night before he closed his eyes, as long as Marah could remember.

"God keep you, wife."

Surely those words signified love.

Marah, on the other hand, had not yet spoken one word to her husband when he came to her at night, instead laying there as silent as a stick. But what to say? She could not think of anything.

Finally, she thought of four words, and four words only. She knew she wanted to say something, but she could not think of anything else.

"God keep you, husband." Her voice was soft, but Jarius paused at the door to look at her for a long moment, startled. He nodded, ducked his head and left. Marah knew he was surprised and no wonder. She seldom spoke to Jarius in the daylight, and she was nothing but awkward and silent during these nighttime encounters.

The next time, as Jarius sat up to leave, Marah said it again. "God keep you, husband."

This time, he touched her cheek. "And you, too, Marah." As before, Jarius left for the privacy of his own room.

Marah never asked him to stay, and never followed him to his room. She never tapped on his door for conversation or interrupted him there. What would she talk about, anyway? She knew nothing of his world. She couldn't think of anything to say to her husband in the bright shine of the day.

*"What in the world could you say to him in the shadow of night?"*

ⓒ𝒮

One morning, while the house was still asleep and dark, Marah stole down to the silent kitchen and prepared a breakfast for two. She set it out in the warm comfort of the kitchen, not in the echoing formal room where she and Jarius took their evening meals. At night, the food she helped prepare was served to them by Cook and the kitchen girl as Jarius and Marah ate in silence.

Marah stood in the hallway, looking at the door to Jarius's room. After nearly six weeks, she knew his habits. He would leave soon for the synagogue. She stood there in the stillness of dawn, afraid. What would Jarius say?

She stared at the door, wishing for an answer.

It came before she could knock. The door opened and Jarius burst out, running into the lurking Marah.

"Marah!" He grabbed her arm, saving her from a sprawl on the floor. "I'm sorry! Are you all right?"

Marah nodded, frowning and rubbing her ribs where Jarius

133

inadvertently elbowed her. Jarius started to laugh. He was always in an agreeable mood, Marah noticed. So like her father. Marah smiled too, just a little.

"Were you looking for me, Marah?"

She nodded.

"Is something wrong?" His brow wrinkled as though he were truly concerned.

Marah mutely shook her head no. Say something, she thought. She took a deep breath, her words tentative. "I see you leave so early each morning. I am an early riser, too. I cannot stay in bed once… after the sun comes up."

Jarius looked puzzled, but he smiled at her.

She felt a surge of encouragement. "I wondered, if you have time, and if you don't, it's not a problem…"

He waited, silent. She supposed he was curious as to what this gawky, silent stick of a wife might want with him.

Her words came out in a rush. "I wondered if you would like to eat breakfast before you left every day. Eat breakfast with…. with me." The last two words were almost whispered.

Jarius looked at Marah for a moment, surprised. He seemed to choose his words with great care, rubbing his chin. He did not look at her. "Marah, my duties require me to be at the synagogue early, very early every day." But his voice was gentle.

Another rush of words popped out. "When you leave, I have usually been up for several hours. Really, Master Jarius, you can ask any of the servants. I drive them to distraction because I get up so early."

His eyes crinkled in a smile. "I would never think to question the servants about you, Marah."

Marah felt stupid. Of course he wouldn't ask the servants about his wife. He thought of the servants as, well, servants. She considered them friends. Her only friends. She was completely absurd. What was she thinking?

"Marah, do you have breakfast prepared for me this morning?"

Marah nodded stiffly, trying to swallow past the huge lump in her throat. All the words she had for Jarius were used up.

"Well, then…" he offered Marah his arm. "I would be honored to join you for breakfast."

Marah caught her breath and then smiled at him, a real smile.

They walked in complete silence. Jarius started to enter the dining hall, but Marah steered him into the kitchen.

"It is pleasant and comfortable in here. Just… for the two of us, just for breakfast." She cleared her throat to force out the last word. "Jarius."

He looked around the kitchen. Marah realized he had probably not eaten here since he was a boy, perhaps not since his mother was alive.

But this big kitchen is a wonderful place, thought Marah fiercely. Full of warmth and pleasing aromas and the morning sunlight. It's… friendly. The nicest place in this enormous old house, a good place to begin one's day.

As if in answer, Jarius knelt at the low table under the large window whose shutters she already opened. The earliest of the morning birds chirped a welcome to the golden gray light of dawn.

And so began their breakfasts together. It was where nearly all of their conversations took place. Jarius would talk, and Marah would listen intently and nod her agreement or understanding.

Jarius would tell her about some event they would attend, or inquire about the menu for an upcoming dinner. The household fund was always full, but he would often ask if she needed more. How were the servants? How did she find the Capernaum market? Good?

He would ask her to purchase things such as fabric or soap at the market, describing exactly what he wanted. No, their household did not make their own soap. Yes, he would prefer they use a tailor to sew new gowns for her, and a new cloak and an embroidered prayer shawl for him. Would she go to the tailor and make the arrangements?

Marah could not imagine such an extravagance. A girl who grew up in castoff tunics would never again spin thread or weave cloth or sew her own clothes.

Every morning, Jarius would compliment Marah about the delicious meals she and Cook prepared, on the well-kept beauty of their home, or of her watchful efficiency in managing the household funds.

He was genuinely and tearfully grateful for her compassionate, conscientious care of his father, who lay sick and suffering day after long day.

Without even having to ask, it was at breakfast that Marah at last learned about what she might expect of this new life.

Several times a year, Jarius told her, they would make the trip to Jerusalem. They would stay at the home of Asa and Miriam, who just moved there with their four children, into a spacious home that Jarius found for them. It was important Jarius attend the festivals and different meetings in Jerusalem. And, just as she could spend time with her sister, he enjoyed conversations with his friend Asa.

Would this be acceptable to Marah?

They would always break their journey at the little Shiloh inn, just as he had done so many times since he was a boy. On the return trip, they would stay for one or even two days so she could spend time with her father, see her sisters and their families. He would busy himself meeting with the ruler of the little Shiloh synagogue and its council members, or visit with her father, whom he always liked. Sometimes, she might prefer to stay with her family while he continued on to Jerusalem.

Would this be all right with Marah?

From time to time, Naaman might return with them, spend some time in Capernaum with his daughter and Jarius. There was plenty of room and Jarius's father loved to visit with the cheerful Naaman. He knew Marah missed her father, she worked by his side for so many years.

Would Marah like this?

Jarius worked with the family's business manager, a man responsible for the land and the farms and the flocks Jarius's father owned. They met several hours every single week. Marah was to make sure all was ready before the man came. Jarius would show her what to do. If Jarius was delayed, Marah would need to situate the gentleman until Jarius arrived. Jarius would like Marah to stay for these meetings. He wanted a second set of ears and did not want to share details of their family wealth with anyone but his wife.

Would this be agreeable to Marah?

Jarius had a good friend he wanted her to welcome in their home, an influential and important man, the Roman centurion of Capernaum. He was quite wealthy, the same age as Jarius, a patron of their synagogue and as devout a follower of Jehovah as Jarius. They were discussing the construction of a new synagogue, and this Roman, Augustus was his name, wanted to contribute money. Jarius and Augustus even dined together, much to the silent dismay of many of the influential Jews of Capernaum. But Augustus strictly observed the stringent Jewish laws about food, not in deference to

Jarius but because he followed the laws of Jehovah. Jarius had a true respect and affection for the man. It was important Augustus be treated as an honored guest and, more importantly, a friend.

Would Marah be willing to do this?

He would like it if Marah went to the synagogue more often than just the Sabbath services. She would come alone to the services, for Jarius always left early to prepare. Come sometimes to these meetings, he said, sit in the place set aside for you as my wife, just to listen. It's less formal, with much debate among the men.

Only here did Marah balk.

She attended the Sabbath worship in Capernaum every week. During the service, she would look around to see both stealthy glances quickly diverted and frank open stares. She could hear their collective thought: "Why in the world did the handsome wealthy important son of our synagogue ruler marry *her*?"

*"You know why he married you."* The whisper was not even remotely opposed to following her right inside the synagogue doors.

Jarius must not see how the other people looked at Marah, because he was gently firm in this request. It was important that his wife be in frequent attendance if he presided over these meetings. He wanted her there with him. He wanted the people of his synagogue to know Marah was his wife. It was important. Jarius did not explain why, and Marah was too shy to ask.

Would Marah please make time to support him on his path as the future ruler of the Capernaum synagogue?

It was at breakfast that Marah learned she would often travel to Jerusalem and stay with her beloved sister Miriam, and visit her father and sisters and nieces and nephews at her little inn in Shiloh.

Over warm wheat bread dipped in honey, she learned that Jarius was a wealthy man, with great holdings in lands and vineyards and flocks.

As they ate sliced melons and almonds, Marah learned about Jarius's friends, especially the man he considered his equal, the influential Roman centurion. Like a brother, Marah thought. Jarius felt about Augustus the way she felt about Miriam.

Over the rare boiled egg and fresh pomegranates, she learned what Jarius expected of a synagogue ruler's wife.

That's me, she would remind herself.

*"A synagogue ruler's wife! That's you?"*

It was at breakfast that Marah learned just how thoughtfully

Jarius intended to treat his wife. She was amazed by his compassion, indeed, his concern for Marah. Yet, the more kindly Jarius treated her, the more comfortable he became with her, the more afraid Marah grew.

Marah knew she didn't deserve the life she was living. She wasn't sure how to act around Jarius, for someday, surely someday soon, she would do something wrong, and he would remember what she really was. He would finally be angry… as was his right. Marah deserved punishment, not happiness.

She would whisper her anxieties only to herself in the darkness of night where no one might overhear what they must never know. If only there was someone, anyone Marah might talk to, a friend to listen to her fears, to hear her confession of the certain truth: After all she had done, she didn't deserve any of this.

*"You have someone to talk to, Marah. Here I am. And you finally got something right; you don't deserve this. Not a sinner like you. You don't deserve it. Not any of it. Not you."*

Marah had no answer for the whisper in her head.

# CHAPTER 13

Each day, Jarius's father grew more frail. Marah was certain he could not weigh more than a young boy, so wasted was his body, but she shared this with no one, least of all her husband.

Marah sat with her father-in-law for long hours in the afternoon, listening to his fevered rambling, sponging the sweat from his brow, placing the warm stones wrapped in cotton in his bed in a futile attempt to fight his chattering chills. Despite the culinary efforts of Cook and Marah and the pleading of Jarius, the old man had not eaten for nearly a week. His skin was wrinkled, paper thin, his eyes sunken in his head.

Always a light sleeper, Marah took to checking on him two or even three times at night. If he was awake, she would sit with him, holding his hand in the lonely hours of solitary pain and black night.

Having grown up in a house so full of people everyone knew what the others were doing, saying and even thinking, Marah felt that to be alone in the silent dark with only pain and death for company…

Well, that would be a very lonely thing indeed.

One afternoon, Marah, breathless, found Deena at her chores. "Send for Jarius. Quickly."

The old man's room was dark, the shutters closed. He could no longer stand the light. Jarius held the hand of the man he loved, his only family in the world. The old man motioned for Marah to come, a grunt accompanying this simple gesture. His hand crawled across the bed covers to grasp Marah's in a claw-like grip. He nodded at her, the smile on his face a terrible grimace of pain, too. His breath was a long, slow rattle.

Quietly, Jarius began to pray, words of comfort for his father, the faithful Jew and man of God. He did not have to pray for long.

In the fourth month of his son's marriage, after three long years of illness that ate away his body but never touched his mind, with his son and his daughter-in-law at his side, the ruler of the Capernaum synagogue drew his final breath.

The burial was huge, with many attending. Paid mourners led the way, old women clad in black from head to toe moaning and weeping, throwing dust in the air to show their terrible despair. Jarius and Marah stood at the head of the long procession, with Deena and Cook only steps behind them. The sounds of wailing and flutes pierced the dusty heat as they made their way to the hillside of graves. Caverns for the dead. The people formed a long trail of sorrow, weeping and crying.

The ruler of the Capernaum synagogue was dead.

When it was over, Jarius withdrew from everyone, refusing to eat or shave or leave his room. Anyone who walked nearby heard the rare sound of Jarius's raging grief. Only Marah dared to slip in and out with food and drink, calm and silent in the face of his heartbroken sorrow. Jarius did not tell her, but Marah knew that the death of his father marked the start of a new life for her husband, one he desperately wanted and yet feared.

She did not know how she knew this. She just knew.

Had she looked harder, she would have seen the same desires and fears in her own self.

After two weeks, Jarius quietly tapped on her door, visited her bed, and returned to his own room. "God keep you, wife," he whispered as he left. The next morning, wearing somber clothes of mourning, he joined Marah for the breakfast she faithfully prepared each day in readiness for the return she knew would most certainly come. He was silent, and so was she.

After breakfast, he stood, placed his hand on her shoulder and then, without a word, returned to the synagogue.

Fourteen days later, the mourning period was complete according to Jewish custom.

As expected, Jarius was named the synagogue ruler of Capernaum, taking over the role he unofficially held during his father's illness of nearly three years.

Only days after he was named ruler, in the warmth of their kitchen, Marah shyly told Jarius what she suspected for several weeks but whispered only to his dying father: without a doubt, she was with child.

Jarius was ecstatic.

Marah was certain Jarius did not love her. How could he? But contrary to what he told her in the office of the little inn only a few months ago, he did not act sorry that he married Marah. Indeed, he even seemed content with her, pleased that she so easily took on the responsibilities of his home, thankful that she was such a quiet, compliant wife who required so little attention.

She knew he was unspeakably grateful for her care of his dying father, for he understood she did not mind doing it, her quiet heart aching as death slowly claimed the old man for its own.

And now, he was delighted that she carried his baby. She would look up to find him gazing at her with an intent look in his eyes, a look she did not recognize. Perhaps Jarius was happy.

And so, for the first time in many months, Marah was happy, too. Just a little bit.

Jarius started returning home two or three times a day to check on his wife. Marah did not understand this. Because she had so few words to muster for Jarius, she did not know how to ask him why. She just kept doing the things she knew to do. What else was there?

One day, she was walking about in their large stables. She loved her little donkey, one Jarius said would be hers alone, a gentle creature with soft brown fur and bottomless brown eyes. The stable boy was working, but she picked up the rake to show him again how to muck the straw so the animals would stand only in fresh bedding.

"Marah!" She straightened up to see Jarius standing in the doorway. The sun behind him, she could not see his face.

"Marah! What are you doing?" Startled, Marah heard something she never heard from Jarius since she arrived here: anger.

Marah stood there, uncertain. "I'm… I'm just…"

Jarius strode over to her and snatched the rake from her hand. His face was white with rage. He turned his fury on the uncomprehending boy.

"You… you lazy, incompetent boy, this is your job! What sort of servant stands by while his mistress, the wife of a synagogue ruler, works in the stable? You should be turned out at once!" He threw the rake at the uncomprehending boy. The youngster ducked, and the rake clattered noisily against the stable wall. Marah's little brown donkey brayed at the commotion.

Jarius grabbed Marah's arm and started dragging her to the stable door. "And you, Marah, you! Have you no sense? That you would be doing this hard work! You are the mistress of my house!" The words burst out of him, clipped and angry. He glared at her and clamped his mouth shut, as though any other words that might escape were too terrible for a synagogue ruler to even utter. Marah was afraid to speak.

Jarius was angry.

He pulled her across the courtyard, his lips set in a firm line. He pulled the door to her room open, his other hand gripping her elbow like a vise, and then pushed her down on to the bed. "Lay down! Right now! Do not get up, do not even leave this bed until I return!"

He turned to face her at the door, a livid stranger staring at her. "I am… Marah, I am very angry with you!"

Marah stared his back as he strode away, at the door that swung shut behind him, alone in the sudden silence.

Jarius was angry with her.

Finally, the anger she thought had died away, the anger she anticipated for months, the anger she knew she deserved… the anger finally erupted within Jarius's heart. He was angry.

For the first time since that day she laid in her own stable, worrying about what would happen to her at the hand of Master Jarius, Marah started to cry.

*"That's right, cry, 'Mistress Marah.' He is finally angry with you, angry with the Marah that deceived him and tricked and forced him to marry her. Cry, cry, cry. You knew this would happen sooner or later. Jarius hates you. Finally! He hates you as you deserve to be hated."*

The relentless whisper wound itself around her, squeezing her heart. *"Ha! You thought this baby would make a difference. It will not! As if you were worthy to have the baby of a synagogue ruler. You are not! When Jarius returns, you will finally get the punishment you deserve. Ha!"*

She wept as though her heart was broken, loud sobs that tore at her throat. She knew Jarius did not love her, but she found herself hoping that perhaps, just perhaps, this baby would make a difference. Why was Jarius so angry with her now, after all these months, when she carried his baby? Marah did not understand.

She heard a light tap on the door.

"Mistress." It was Deena.

Marah forced herself to be silent. She did not want anyone, much less a servant, to see her in tears. Even if it was Deena, who was so kind to Marah. But she would not let anyone see her cry, not now, not later when Jarius made her shame public, not ever.

"Just a moment." Much to her disgust, her voice was shaky. Marah sat up in her bed, wiped her eyes and face and tried to smooth her tousled hair. She rubbed her face, hard. It was no use, she was a mess.

She started to stand up, but then remembered Jarius's harsh voice. He was angry with her.

She stayed seated on the bed. "Come in."

Deena carried a platter with a cup of wine and a plate of fresh bread, cheese, and Marah's favorite, olives. She silently set the platter down on the low table by the bed and began to do something she had not done in these past five months. She began to serve Mistress Marah. Marah was mortified to again feel tears in her eyes. Why was Jarius so angry with her?

Deena held out the cup. "Drink, please, Mistress." Marah obeyed, like a small child.

"Please, Mistress, eat." Marah took a piece of soft, fresh bread from the tray. Deena sat down on the beautifully woven couch across the room, watching her.

"Mistress Marah, I heard what happened today in the stables." Marah was ashamed that Deena, this woman who had known Jarius since he was young, heard him berating her so loudly and so publicly. Or perhaps the boy ran to tell her and the servants of her shame.

"I heard you in here crying."

Marah looked down, stoically chewing the bread, humiliated.

"Do you know why Master Jarius was so angry today?"

Much to her frustration, tears slid down Marah's cheeks. Yes, she knew why he hated her. But she had vowed to Jarius that she would never, ever speak of it.

"Mistress, you have lived here now for five months. Although he does not yet understand it, you are good for Master

143

Jarius. I have worked for this family all my life. You are quiet, but you are so hard-working, so fair and kind.

Fair and kind? That was how one described Master Jarius, not her.

"Jarius's father knew what kind of wife you would be, he saw what I also know. And you took such good care of the old Master. And now, you work so hard for the good of young Master Jarius. For those two things alone, I will always respect you."

Marah's tears would not be stopped. They rolled down her cheeks.

"Please forgive me if I speak too freely, Mistress. I know why Master Jarius is upset. Do you?"

How could Deena know of Marah's secret?

"Tell me," Marah whispered. It took all her courage to summon those two words.

*"She knows, Marah. Deena knows everything. She knows why Jarius is so angry, that you tricked him, you trapped into marriage, that you are a lying, deceitful, promiscuous wife!"* Marah closed her eyes to listen to Deena, willing the whisper to be silent.

"Master Jarius is unfamiliar with… a woman like you. You are not a woman like any of the other women he knows."

*"Because he doesn't keep with sinful, lying women. Deena knows you are not the woman he wanted for a wife or to be the mother of his child."*

Deena continued talking. "You most certainly are nothing like his first wife, may God have mercy on her soul."

Marah knew what Deena must think of her. She was the ugly daughter of a poor innkeeper. She was nothing like the beloved Deborah.

*"And you never will be."*

"You say very little. You work so hard to make this big empty house a home, a pleasant place for your husband and for those of us who work here, all of us. Forgive me, but you have the heart of a true servant, a heart that puts others' needs before your own."

Marah didn't understand what Deena was saying. What did this have to do with Marah's pitiful unworthiness? What did this have to do with the anger Jarius finally felt for her?

"Mistress, Master Jarius loved his first wife a great deal." Marah felt sad. She knew this, she reminded herself of it every day.

"But Mistress Deborah was nothing like you. She did not know how to run this house. She was an…" Deena smiled the smallest of smiles. "She was an 'intellectual,' a rich woman of great learning." The slight emphasis on 'intellectual' told Marah that this particular wifely trait was of little value to Deena.

"Mistress Deborah liked to read and write, dress in fine gowns, enjoy dinner with Jarius's important guests. In that sense, Jarius and she were quite well-suited. But that was before he was ruler, when he was but a young man. Now Mistress, for whatever reason, God gave him a holy calling and a new wife. And this time, the wife God chose was you."

*"God chose a new wife for Jarius? How absurd! She thinks GOD chose a new wife for Jarius! Aren't you relieved, Marah, that Deena doesn't know? God did not chose you for Jarius, you chose yourself."*

It was difficult for Marah to focus on Deena with the horrible whisper clattering about in her head.

"I do not know anything about you. But I see your hard work. You are a very capable young woman. Your work allows Master Jarius to do what he will do best, rule our synagogue here in Capernaum. Everywhere, Master Jarius is known as a kind, intelligent and most learned of young men. He is well-liked by the entire Jewish community." Marah could hear the pride in Deena's voice.

*"How she would hate you if she only knew your secret…"*

"When he was first elected to the synagogue council, many took their questions to Jarius first before presenting their case to the ruler, Jarius's father, for he was respected but also feared." Deena smiled at the memory of her formidable employer. "The people just wanted Jarius's opinion on which way his father might be leaning that day.

"Jarius rules far differently than his father. He is not only fair-minded and reasonable, but also compassionate. He does not just study the law, he tries to live the law, to live a life that is honorable to God. He is such a good man."

Marah knew this to be true, for she, the one who deserved it less than anyone, had experienced the kindness of Jarius first hand. After all, he forgave her appalling sin, without Marah asking for or even deserving it.

Marah looked at Deena. She still did not understand why Jarius was so angry with her.

Deena saw the questions in Marah's eyes. She knew her shy mistress would not ask. Her voice was gentle. "Mistress, Jarius may not yet love you like he did his first wife, but he will. Especially

145

now."

"Why?" Marah forced the word out. She needed to know.

"Why, Mistress, because you are going to have a baby! A baby!" Deena clapped her hands together.

Marah shook her head. She still did not understand.

"Mistress, surely you know how Jarius's wife died?"

Marah and Jarius never spoke of Deborah. But of course she knew how Deborah died. She died in childbirth.

*"She died having Jarius's baby, and you saw your chance, didn't you Marah?"*

It was the wild grief of Jarius that allowed Marah to prey on him, to subvert his sorrow to her own selfish intentions. She lowered her eyes, shamed. "Deborah died in childbirth. His son died soon after."

"Yes, Mistress. And the saddest day it was for us all, for Master Jarius could not be consoled. Mistress, Master Jarius not only wanted a wife, he wanted a family. He mourned the child as much as he mourned his wife."

"Yes."

"So you don't understand why Jarius was upset today?"

Marah shook her head.

"Because you were doing what you do best. Working! You were working and working hard! But Jarius only knows what women of his station do when they are pregnant, and that is to retire and rest and be waited on; that's how rich women prepare for the birth of their baby. That is what Deborah did. That is what the other wives of rich men do. And it is what Jarius expects from you, because he does not know anything different. Rich women who are with child do not go out and work in the stables or the kitchens or the courtyard. They rest."

"They rest? Rest until the baby comes? For the next six months, I must... rest?" Marah heard the shock in her own voice.

"Yes, Mistress, you must. It is only six months, after all. You must rest and not do the hard work you have been doing. The wealthy - not servants like me - think hard work might cause harm to your baby. So, even if you don't feel like the other rich women, you will do what they do and what your husband expects you to do. You will rest as you wait for the birth of your baby." Deena crossed the room and sat on the bed beside her.

"Mistress Marah, I speak to you as your own mother might

146

speak: Master Jarius does not want to lose another wife or child. He does not want to lose you."

"Me?" The word squeaked out before Marah could stop it. Deena nodded and smiled.

Marah sat in the silence that followed, thinking. This baby was so important. Perhaps with the birth of this child, Jarius would finally forgive her, forgive her for real. Perhaps this child would allow her to become Jarius's friend.

Perhaps they could someday have a marriage like her parents, a marriage of love. Perhaps Jarius would love her someday.

But right now, he was not angry with her for what she was. He was angry because he did not want to lose the baby.

Even though Deena said he did not want to lose her, she knew Jarius only cared about their baby. But still…

Relief flooded over Marah.

"Oh, Deena, I did not know. My mother had seven children, my six sisters all have many children, and all the women in my family have always worked, pregnant or not. Where I come from, a pregnant woman is not a frail woman; she is a woman with more work and even less rest!"

"That is how it is where I come from." Deena laughed. "Seven children! Seven daughters! Goodness! Just like the wife of Moses, Zipporah and her sisters! Except you are the youngest, not the oldest."

The wife of Moses came from a family of seven sisters? She laughed at this new-found knowledge of her father's Moses. "Yes, seven daughters. We were such a noisy crowd, my poor father did not know what to do with so many of us. We used to have so much fun. My father ran an inn…" Marah realized she was rambling. It was so nice to talk with someone! Still, she forced those words back into their hiding place. So far, she had managed to keep the real Marah secret.

*"And you did it once again, Marah. No one knows the real, sinful you…"*

"Deena, thank you. I did not know, but I understand now. I understand what Jarius expects. I will do it." Marah paused, wanting to say more but uncertain of the words. "So, thank you. This, I can do. For Master Jarius's sake."

Deena took her hand and smiled. "Mistress Marah, I believe you can do anything you set your mind to, especially when it is for

Master Jarius's sake."

☙

That evening, sitting up in her bed, Marah apologized to Jarius. Although he tried, she would not allow him to apologize to her.

"No." She ducked her head and held up her hand, interrupting him. "No." She would not hear a single word of apology from Jarius. He tried twice and then stopped to smile down at her.

His relief was visible. Marah realized that Jarius did not like conflict in his home. His home was his sanctuary from the demands, the stress, yes, even the cruelties of the synagogue.

Marah respectfully asked Jarius if she could still walk about the house and meet with Cook and Deena. She promised she would stay off her feet for most of the day. She would not do any cooking or cleaning, nor would she go to the market or lift or carry anything. If she went to the stables, it would only for a bit of fresh air and to offer a treat to her little donkey and the other animals there. Her only trips outside the home would be to the public baths and the synagogue.

Jarius is smiling at me, as though he really cares for me, Marah thought. Like maybe he… loves me. Her heart ached at the idea.

Jarius took her hand and kissed it. That night, very late, he came to her room. Before he left, he sat on the bed, picked up her hand and held it tight as he spoke.

"Marah, thank you for all you have done for me. I am sorry I lost my temper with you today. Thank you for taking care of yourself and this baby." He looked years younger, the cares of his father's death and his new role at the synagogue forgotten in the moment. He grinned at her. "Our baby, Marah. Our baby."

He looks happy, thought Marah.

As was his recent practice, Jarius laid his hand on her cheek. The gesture felt tender to Marah. He smiled and walked to the door of his room. He turned to face her, speaking before she could. "God keep you, wife."

Marah nodded, grateful Jarius could not see her sudden tears in the dimly-lit room.

"God keep you, husband, "Marah answered softly, her voice

148

husky.

He looked at her shyly. "Thank you, Marah." He left her alone in the silence.

A small curl of happiness fluttered in Marah's heart.

*"Thank you, Marah! Thank you!"* The whisper was laughing!

*"Jarius stands at the door to thank you, just as you did many months ago, the night you seduced and deceived him. 'Thank you Marah,' indeed. Do not fool yourself. He has not forgotten. He loves this baby, not you. He will never forget. He only thanks you to mock you."*

And the whisper began a singsong refrain, like a child taunting a playmate, *"Thank you Marah thank you Marah thankyouMarah thankyouMarahthankyouMarah…"*

She put her hands over her ears. Her happiness vanished with the whisper. He only loves this child, she thought, disconsolate. He couldn't love her, just the child.

She felt the lump in her throat and lay down. Today had been a gut-wrenching day for Marah.

"Well, I must do what I must do, and right now, that is to take care of me and this baby," she whispered. "I can do anything if I set my mind to it. Deena said so. I must take good care of my baby."

*"Your baby?"*

She thought for a moment and spoke out loud. "Our baby!"

The whisper was silent in the face of her defiance.

# CHAPTER 14

Marah was true to her word.

She missed the hustle and bustle and barter of the market, but Cook assured her the shopkeepers still asked after the Mistress of the House of Jarius. She hadn't cooked in months, but still the delicious smells prepared at the hands of others only caused waves of nausea to rise to the back of her throat. With the begrudging consent of her husband, Marah's only treks were to and from the stables to pet her little donkey's brown nose. She waddled down to the stables so often, Deena joked she wore a rut in the shining tile courtyard.

Marah had just left the little animal moments ago. She arched her back and rolled her head from side to side, stiff from the hours she spent in bed today. Mid-stretch, a wide dimpled smile covered her face.

She rested her hands on the considerable presence that was kicking her ribs with a belligerent strength.

"Soon enough, my baby," Marah whispered, cradling her belly. "I know you want out."

She bent to fluff up the pillows on a courtyard bench; the warm sun coaxed her to sit.

The long months were alien to Marah, whose entire life was a routine of work and chores and hard labor. But the lethargic days of pregnancy took over, creating a new and comfortable rhythm to her life.

Marah closed her eyes and sunned herself, glad for the rare solitude and peace of her lovely courtyard.

Most of the time, she was surrounded by people. Deena and Cook checked on her all day long. For several glorious weeks, Miriam and Asa came to stay with their four boisterous children in tow. Her father and two sisters made the trek in carts rented by Jarius.

And Jarius… Jarius spent every moment he could with his wife.

Sometimes when he looked at her, Marah would tremble, her knees wobbly, hands shaking. He was so intense, so caring, so kind, so… tender. More than once, she thought perhaps, just perhaps, he might love her.

He never said it, so she didn't really know. But still, people loved each other.

Maybe Jarius loved her.

They enjoyed their quiet breakfasts alone in the morning, Jarius's one concession to Marah's forbidden workload. They would eat a light meal, Jarius talking about his upcoming day, his outing the night before, matters of the house, her pregnancy or… their baby.

Jarius would talk about their future.

And his prayers! He prayed for her continually. His prayers were intense, full of love, beseeching God's hand on his wife and his baby. Marah felt safe, sustained by the faith of her husband. She could not feel God, she could not hear God, she knew that God wanted nothing to do with her. But her husband knew and feared God, and he was praying for her. That was enough for Marah.

She would never give voice to the thought that secretly nagged in a corner of her mind. For the first time in all the years she could remember, Marah was not tormented by the doubts and fears and anger that resided in her head. The dreadful hiss that pointed out all her faults and flaws, mocked her, chided her, hated her, was silent. She was afraid to ask herself why, fearful that the hint of an inquiry would rouse the whisper from the dark recess where it slept.

She only knew the more she was in the presence of Jarius's prayers, the fainter the memory of the whisper became. His prayers for her became her armor, a fortress again the feared evil whisper that once sought to hurt her.

She was also afraid to question her unshakable confidence in a matter others would not discuss, a fear they would not voice, frightened by an all-too-often reality of Jewish life.

Marah knew her baby was going to live, and so was she.

She knew about the pain and rigor of childbirth, witness to the multiple births of six fruitful sisters. She knew what happened to her own mother. She knew what happened to Deborah. But she did not care.

Nothing was going to happen to her or the precious child she carried.

For although she did not know God, she knew that he could not be so merciless that he would punish a man as good and faithful as Jarius a second time.

God would not condemn the second wife and second child of his faithful servant Jarius to death.

Marah's days were a far change from her lifelong habits. But she did not mind her idle days, filled with dreams of her baby boy or girl. There was a peaceful silence in her head. She was married to someone who was attentive and caring. She felt protected from harm by her husband's faith and the tragic fates he had already endured.

She heard the light step of Deena.

"Enjoying the sun, Mistress?"

"Sit with me, Deena."

They sat in a companionable silence, the warmth of the sun soothing and tranquil.

"Soon your baby will be here."

Marah smiled. "Very soon."

"I cannot wait much longer, Mistress!"

"Nor I, Deena, nor I…"

An unfamiliar stab in Marah's belly bent her in two from pain and from surprise. "Ow."

"Ow?"

Marah felt the slow warmth spreading beneath her. Familiar with the pregnancies of her six sisters, she knew at once that the water that held the baby had given way.

"Deena, I believe I might have ruined this cushion."

"What? Oh!"

Deena jumped to her feet and ran, hollering for the house boy. "Run to the synagogue, get Master Jarius! Hurry! Hurry!" She stuck her gray head in the kitchen. "Cook! Boil the water! Lots of water! It is time!"

She whirled around and bustled back to Marah. "Oh, Mistress, I am sorry! I ran off and left you!"

Marah's smile flinched into a grimace of pain, but she shook her head. "I'm fine, Deena. Just get me to the room we have prepared."

Deena pulled Marah to her feet. Every servant in their household was scurrying.

"It's time, Deena. My baby is coming." She clenched her teeth against a wrenching cramp.

"Don't be afraid, Mistress! It will be over soon! You can stand the pain, and soon will hold your son or daughter. Soon, Mistress!"

"I'm not afraid, Deena." Marah lumbered across the courtyard, leaning on Deena's arm, to the room on the first floor prepared for the birth of her first child. "I'm not afraid."

ༀ

Marah gazed at the bundle in her arms, little eyes squinted shut, a rosebud lower lip sucking in and out as she breathed, a mass of black fuzz on the little round head.

Jarius rushed in. "Marah, are you all right?" His eyes were bloodshot. He stood outside the door pacing for the entire four hours of her labor.

She nodded and then smiled. "I am fine. It's a girl, Jarius." A surge of fierce emotion ran through her. This tiny bundle was not a much favored son, as Jewish men wanted. It was a girl, a tiny, beautiful, perfect girl. She held the tightly wrapped baby up for Jarius to see. "Our baby."

Jarius lifted her from Marah's hands, his finger tracing the child's nose, her lips, her tiny chin. "Oh, Marah. She is perfect."

Gazing at her husband, she saw his tears fall freely on his daughter. She felt her fear ebb away. Jarius loved this tiny girl.

"Marah, I would like to name our daughter Abigail."

No one in Marah's family was named Abigail.

"Abigail means the joy of the father, Marah. I have always wanted to name my first daughter Abigail."

Jarius hadn't been thinking about continuing his lineage through the birth of a son, he was thinking of names for his future daughters.

She wondered how her father felt naming girl after girl after girl. No little Naamans for him. But Naaman loved all of his daughters. Everyone knew it, Marah most of all.

"Do you like the name Abigail, Marah?"

She nodded and stretched out her arms. Jarius laid the tiny girl on Marah's breast and wrapped his arms around the both of them.

He kissed Marah on the cheek and brushed a light finger on Abigail's tiny nose, which wrinkled up in response. Marah and Jarius both chuckled at her expression.

"Hello, Abigail," Marah whispered. Jarius touched a tiny hand with his finger. Abigail grabbed hold with a tight fist.

Strong, like her mother, Marah thought. Strong like me.

With one arm around his wife, and his finger in the grasp of his new daughter, Jarius began to whisper his prayers, prayers of thanksgiving for his wife and his daughter and their new life.

Marah knew she was safe, safe in the prayers of her husband.

೮೩

Lovely Abigail, the daughter of Jarius and Marah.

Not a son like his first wife gave him, some whispered.

Marah and Jarius did not care one bit. It was as though God poured everything perfect, everything wonderful into this tiny, beautiful girl.

Jarius spent every possible moment with his daughter. As the weeks went by, Marah knew Jarius loved Abigail. Perhaps he didn't love me like I had hoped, she thought. Only our child.

But she did not dwell on the thought, busy with her child, husband and new life. She was happy that Jarius loved his daughter – their daughter – so much. For Marah too loved Abigail, more than her own life.

With the birth of this baby girl, a new chapter in their odd, cobbled marriage began, a new chapter with one main character. Abigail.

She was the light of their lives. So many Jewish men thought daughters were a curse, a misfortune from God. Jarius treated Abigail as though she were something precious, a treasure to protect and to love. He always had time for his bright, happy daughter.

He would sit for hours with her tiny hands clutching his, a laughing baby wobbling on her toes and standing tall for her father.

"Pah!" It was her first word.

154

"She said Papa! Papa was her first word!" Jarius shouted.

Marah marveled with him that tiny Abigail already gurgled her first word.

Jarius came home earlier and earlier every day to seek out the blossoming Abigail. Marah wanted to be jealous but how could she? Abigail was perfect, and she, of course, was not.

Jarius would walk in, pick up Abigail awake or asleep, smother her in kisses and begin a quiet litany of prayers for his daughter. He was grateful.

Marah would listen and remembered Jarius praying for her when she was pregnant, fervent and intense. He prayed for their daughter now.

Abigail was a new breakfast topic, gurgling through their morning meal.

Marah would feel Abigail's gum. "A tooth is coming."

"Her first tooth!"

"Mah!" Abigail would holler, smiling a dimpled, toothless smile at her mother.

Marah and Jarius would peer into the drooly pink gums with the greatest anxiety. Abigail would grab their fingers and chomp down greedily, gnawing with contentment. A tooth!

"I think today may be the day Abigail may try to crawl," Jarius would murmur with excitement.

"You might be right, she is so close."

"Oh, I wish I could be here when she does!"

"Oh, you will be, Jarius. She always reaches for her Papa first!"

"Bah!" Abigail would clamor in agreement.

"Please stay close to her. When I was small and learning to crawl, I fell and hit my head on a stone. See? I still have the scar." Jarius pushed back his hair to show Marah a scar that she would have never ever known about, if not for Abigail.

"I remember when Miriam's first child fell learning to walk. He got a lump the size of an egg on his little head! We were so worried, but he was fine. I thought Miriam would never stop crying."

Jarius laughed. "I can see Asa standing there wringing his hands."

"Gah!" Abigail would add, sitting right between them.

There was no longer just quiet conversation at their breakfast table. There was laughter.

The little family sat in the warm kitchen, the shutters open, a morning bird piercing the morning air.

Even though she could not truly talk, Jarius asked Abigail the same question he asked every day, always supplying the answer himself.

"What does Abigail mean?"

"Pah!"

"That's right! The joy of your Papa. Joy!"

"Oy!"

"The joy of your Papa! She said it, Marah!"

"Pah!"

"Oh, you are my joy, Abigail, you are my joy." He took the girl in his arms, tears in his gentle eyes, his lips moving with a silent prayer soft against her round cheek.

Jarius loves our daughter, Marah thought. His prayers will always keep her safe. He loves her more than anything.

*"He loves her more than you, Marah…"*

So clear, so close was the whisper that had lain dormant for these long months, so near was the hated enemy Marah thought finally abandoned her, so loud was its torment, its mocking jeer…

The clay platter she was holding shattered into a dozen pieces on the cold tile floor, the crash as loud as thunder in the still morning.

"Marah!" Jarius's voice was loud in the quiet kitchen. Abigail let out a shriek, frightened as much by her father's shout as the crash of the platter. Jarius patted her back. "There, there, Mother didn't mean to scare you…" His voice was loud over the wailing of his daughter. Marah reached out to touch her daughter.

"No!" Abigail recoiled at Marah's touch, burst into new wails and hid her eyes in the crook of Jarius's neck.

Marah drew her hand back as though bitten by a snake. Abigail didn't want her.

"There, there, Abigail, it's all right. It's all right." Jarius's voice was loud over Abigail's cries.

Marah stared at them. Her daughter did not want her. She wanted her father.

*"Of course she wants her father, Marah. He's the good parent. You are one whose sin has never been confessed or forgiven. But I haven't forgotten your sins, your many, many sins. Our Abigail wants her father, a good and holy man. Not you."*

156

Our Abigail.

Marah sank to her knees on the cold floor, sick to her stomach, unable to breathe.

"Marah! What is wrong?"

She bent to hide her face, afraid, unable to tell Jarius about the evil that just invaded the sanctuary of their kitchen, driving beloved Abigail away from her sinful mother into the safety of her father's arms and prayers.

*"She wants her father, not you, Marah."*

"Marah! Are you sick, Marah?" Jarius plopped the crying Abigail down on the floor and rushed to his wife's side, his hand on her shoulder. "What is wrong?"

*"Everything is wrong. Jarius is a holy man married to a sinful woman, a liar, a fornicator, a murderer... If only your mother could see this child, but she is dead, murdered...."*

"What is wrong?"

She shook her head, unable to speak, not sure who she was answering.

Jarius grabbed her arm, trying to pull the limp Marah up, when they heard Abigail's shriek of pain. For the first time ever, she crawled.

She crawled straight to the kitchen fire

A bright red coal from the fire lay on the floor, a red welt already growing on the soft fair skin.

"Marah! Abigail burnt her hand!"

She heard the fear in Jarius's voice even as it turned to anger.

"Oh, she was so quick! It only took a moment for her to get hurt! What if something worse happened!"

Jarius picked up the screaming child even as he looked down at his wife slumped on the floor. "Marah, Marah, what is wrong with you?"

*"Everything is wrong with you. There is not one thing about you that is right..."*

Abigail's wails bounced off the stucco walls of the kitchen.

"Cook! Deena! Help, please help!" He bent to grab Marah's hand, slinging the screaming Abigail over his shoulder like a sack of ground flour.

Marah realized she did not have the strength to stand about the same time Jarius figured out he couldn't pull her up. He plopped down on the floor beside her. "Wife, what is wrong?"

*"Yes, Marah, what is wrong?"*

Perhaps Marah could tell him. She had felt so safe in his care the last months. He had prayed for her, worried about her. Perhaps he loved her. Perhaps he could love their daughter and her, too. Her father loved her mother and seven daughters.

*"But you killed your father's wife, didn't you?"*

Perhaps she could once again be safe in the prayers of Jarius. Perhaps she could tell him of her fears, of her torment.

"Jarius, I…"

*"Tell him about me, Marah. Tell him you live with me in your head. Tell him you have something evil in you, a sinful woman, living in the house of a holy man who believes in God. Go ahead. Share your insanity with Jarius…"*

Abigail was still crying.

"Marah?"

Jarius prayed once for her and kept her safe. She would tell her husband, surely he would pray for her again.

"Jarius…"

"What happened?" Deena ran over to pick up Abigail as Cook lumbered behind. Jarius scrambled to his feet. Cook's giant hands lifted Marah up as if she weighed no more than Abigail.

The moment to confide in Jarius was lost.

"Are you all right, Mistress?" The big man had a tight grip on her arm to keep the swaying Marah from falling.

Jarius was wringing his hands. "She dropped a plate, Abigail started crying, Marah just sank to the floor, like she fainted, then Abigail crawled – she crawled! She burned her hand in the fire… What is wrong, Deena? I don't know what's wrong with Marah? Marah, what's wrong?"

"She will be fine, Master!" Deena looked at Abigail's hand and to Marah's surprise, kissed it. "Hush, little one, now hush." Deena rocked the child for only a few moments, and then handed the baby to back to Jarius. Although fat tears stood in her eyes, her sobs were reduced to an occasional hiccup over a thumb stuck in her mouth.

Deena turned to Marah. "Come to me, Mistress." She pulled Marah over to the low bench. "Cook, get some wine with water, just a splash in a cup."

He dashed to the counter, amazingly spry for such a rotund man, and handed the clay goblet to Deena.

"Drink." Marah's stomach wrenched, but she took a sip at

158

Deena's stern tone.

"Get one for Jarius, too, Cook."

"No, Deena, I don't want one. What is wrong with Marah?"
Marah heard the fear in his voice.

"Mistress, what is wrong?"

*"Tell them, Marah. Confess to everyone what is wrong."*

She shook her head.

Deena leaned in, her voice low. "Are you with child,
Mistress?"

Marah shook her head again, trying desperately to find her
voice. "No," she whispered, so softly only Deena could hear. "No,
I'm not." She heard the sadness in her own voice.

Deena nodded, stood, and turned to face Jarius. "Master,
Mistress Marah is fine."

I am not fine, Marah wanted to shout. I am afraid!

*"Tell them, Marah! Confess!"*

"Mistress just had a baby. After something so great as that, a
woman must heal, find her old strength. Sometimes it takes months.
Our Mistress Marah is not yet as strong as she thinks she is."

I am not strong. Help me, Marah thought. Someone please
help me...

*"There is no one to help you. No one but me."*

"It is no easy thing to care for this big house and a baby and
a husband." Deena smiled at Marah. "Marah, you work too hard!
You always have, taking care of everything and everyone, and now a
baby, too."

"And Abigail? Is she hurt?"

"Master!" Deena was laughing. "She is fine, can you not
see?"

Jarius looked down at his daughter as though he forgot she
was in his arms. Abigail gurgled at him, grabbed his sleeve and stuck
it in her mouth, the red welt on her hand forgotten.

"Thank goodness." Abigail grunted as Jarius squeezed her
tight.

Marah heard Jarius's voice, a quiet prayer of thanksgiving for
his daughter. Marah looked around the room, at Deena and Cook
intently listening to their Master, Abigail reaching out for her father's
beard.

She had nearly told Jarius her secret. She almost confessed
her fears, her guilt and her sin. The words were so close. If only she

had told him. If only he would pray for her the way he now prayed for Abigail.

*"Tell him, Marah, tell him! He is a man of God. Ask him to pray for sinful Marah instead of our perfect Abigail."*

Our perfect Abigail. Marah found her hidden rage, her only defense against the whisper that had ravaged her peace of mind for years. Not ours. Never. The evil whisper could not have her daughter. Abigail belonged to her.

*"She belongs to Jarius."*

Marah stared at her husband and daughter. The whisper never lied. She saw the truth at once.

Jarius loved God. Jarius loved Abigail. Abigail belonged to her father. Marah was the one who did not belong. She was sinful from the moment she drew her first breath and her mother breathed her last. God didn't want her, a sinful unworthy woman who clawed her way into the world and stole the life she now lived so many months ago.

*"Sinful, sinful, sinful…"*

The evil whisper that lived in her would never die until Marah too drew her last breath. If it were to ever leave her, surely it would merely find another soul to haunt, another heart to torment.

What if that tender heart was Abigail?

*"Murderer, murderer, murderer…"* Marah closed her eyes, the echo of the childhood taunt loud in her head.

She looked at her daughter, safe in her father's arms. Abigail smiled back at her with dimpled cheeks. "Mah."

*"She seems safe with her father…"*

Abigail was safe with her father. Better for Abigail to love her father, to have the protection of his prayers and his God than for her to love her mother. Marah would give up anything for this child to protect her, even the child's love. Marah would sacrifice her own worthless life if need be. For her life was nothing compared to the precious life of her daughter.

*"Is your worthless life really a sacrifice, Marah? I might demand something more precious than you. What's most precious to you, Marah? That's what I want…"*

"No!" her voice was a shout in the quiet kitchen. Four sets of eyes fixed on her.

"Marah?" She heard the anxiety in her husband's voice.

He must never know. Never.

She jumped to her feet and forced a dimpled smile. "Sorry for the commotion, everyone. I don't know what in the world was wrong with me. I'm better now. Everything is fine. I am fine."

"Marah, what's wrong? Please tell me."

"Mah!" Abigail reached for her mother.

Marah's resolve wavered before her husband's concern and her daughter's outstretched arms.

If only Jarius still prayed for her. She was safe when he prayed for her.

But Jarius prayed for Abigail now. His prayers would keep her daughter safe. Marah would fend for herself.

She lifted her chin and pulled her thin frame into a tall, determined stance, as tall as her husband and towering over the others seen and unseen in the room. She smiled brightly.

"I… am fine."

Jarius and Abigail must never know.

The normal cheer of the bright kitchen returned, ahs of sympathy over the hand of the now-cooing Abigail, Cook and Deena helping themselves to food, Jarius giving his wife a tight hug and returning to his food.

She watched them with sadness. She was a woman apart from the love in the room, a woman alone.

*"Not alone, Marah. I will always be with you. Always."*

# CHAPTER 15

## *Eleven Years Later*

In the dark hours of the night, when her husband was away and she was left to manage things on her own, or on those late midnights when the light under his door at last died away and she knew for certain he would not come to her bed, at the blackest hour when her daughter was asleep and her house was silent...

Marah walked the halls of her great home alone.

Her obsessive steps were quiet and practiced, and no one, not her husband or daughter or servants or even faithful Deena were ever disturbed. Indeed, none of them even knew of her lonely prowling in the darkest hours of night. No one did. Marah walked with no one but the relentless whisper in her head.

Never did she feel more lost than when she walked alone in the darkness. As her eyes scoured the familiar shadows, her heart would long for someone to find her, to hear her unspoken cries, to pray for her to that unknown God of Jarius and Naaman, to end her desperate solitude. Perhaps one night someone would find her awake and alone and afraid. She wished someone might rescue her as passionately as she hid her secret nighttime wanderings from all who knew her.

She would move from one room to another, examining her latest purchase, mulling over its price and quality and the bargain she had made. She would check the kitchen, the faint outlines familiar in the darkness. Was it clean? Was the storeroom full? Was everything laid out and ready for morning?

The dining hall where they entertained was set with fresh linens, three long tables awaiting the guests that would most certainly come. The often-used guestrooms were immaculate and inviting, ready for the next traveler from afar.

She would glance into the stables at the sleeping animals in their fresh straw, or walk to the balcony to look down the street one direction and then the other. She never saw anyone. She would check and check again the locks on every door and gate, protecting her household and husband and daughter from things she could not name.

The upper room would stare back at her with its echoing emptiness, parchments in their place, comfortable cushions lined up in a precise row on the low benches. Her husband spent hours in this room, in prayer and study and conversation with friends and other holy men. The meticulous, methodical order of the room she herself arranged would mock her with its tidiness.

The only place she would linger was at the door of her daughter's room. Sometimes she would steal to the side of Abigail's bed, but she never reached out to touch her, to smooth the long tangle of black hair, stroke her soft cheek or kiss her gentle smile. From an early age, the girl was as light a sleeper as her mother. Marah was afraid to wake this precious gift.

So she would stand in Abigail's room, gazing at her in wonder, this creature with the perfect countenance and peaceful dreams, marveling that only eleven short years ago such a beautiful child had come to be hers, a miracle she knew she did not deserve, a blessing she knew she was not worthy to call her own.

*"Oh, Marah, are you really worthy of anything? Is there anything you have that you truly deserve? I don't think so. For you know what you are. You deserve none of this. None of it. You know I speak the truth."*

At the first hiss of the hated whisper, Marah at once would leave Abigail's side to resume her well-worn lonely path, ever fearful the dreaded demon of her imagination would escape the mind of Marah to haunt her daughter instead.

She often wondered why she just could not stay in her bed, stay where it was safe and warm and protected. When she could not sleep – which was almost always – then why couldn't she stay in her room, next door to her resting husband, near her sleeping daughter, close to faithful Deena, far away from the bitter and frightening world that waited just outside her own bedroom door?

But she could not stay in her bed any more than she could banish the dreaded whisper that haunted her by day and tormented her by night. To stay in her bed was to do nothing but listen to its incessant, malicious venom.

*"Oh, Marah, you think that now, in the dark of the night. But if I didn't talk to you, who would? But for me… you are alone. I am your only friend, the only one that knows the real you."*

To walk was to keep her hated companion at bay, not gone, but at least shoved back to an insolent, seemingly indifferent stroll a few steps behind her, waiting and watching.

To walk was to see her sleeping daughter, the closed door of her husband's bedroom, her gracious home, all the things that surrounded her, the signs of her life, the familiar objects and routines that defined her and made her real.

To walk was to run, run away from her fear and her guilt and her shame.

To walk was to hide from the wicked whisper that squeezed her heart so painfully in the blackest hours of night.

And so, alone and in the dark, Marah walked. She walked through the long halls, up one set of steps and down another, across the courtyard, from the dining hall into the kitchen, over to the stables, to one wing of bedrooms and then to the other, by her husband's upper room and through the courtyard again, around and around, upstairs and down, to the front, to the back, in and out, around and around and around… a silent, furtive, frightened stranger in the place that was her home.

Marah walked alone, save for the whisper in her head.

# CHAPTER 16

Marah watched her husband's aimless stroll through the empty synagogue. The beautiful willow of a girl that was her eleven-year-old daughter chattered non-stop at his side, her father smiling and nodding at her words.

She could not share in their joy any more than Jarius and Abigail could temper their excitement, even in the face of Marah's paralyzing grief.

"Marah, his time had come." Her husband's gentle voice did not console her.

The messenger arrived earlier that day, sent by her brother-in-law from Shiloh. Her father was buried the day before. Jarius came from the old synagogue at once to tell her the sad news.

"You were born to your father late in his life. He lived for many years, a long and full life. And you were his greatest joy, my wife. Take comfort in this, Marah. Almighty Jehovah will certainly reward such a good and faithful Jewish man."

Jarius suggested she stay home and rest, but Marah went to the new synagogue with Jarius and Abigail as planned. She did not want to be alone with her thoughts.

For even if she were to be left by herself, she was never alone.

Today, however, the whisper had not found her. Instead, her father stood before her, laughing, waving his arms, quoting the book of Moses to anyone within earshot. She tried to clear her head of the image; it was too painful. Naaman was dead.

"I have become an alien in a strange land! So says the Book of Moses," her father exclaimed as he backed out of a room where his seven tittering daughters braided ribbons into long plaits of black hair.

"As it is written in the Book of Moses, give us meat to eat, Marah!" Naaman was calling for her, asking her to help him with their many guests at the inn.

With shrieking grandchildren clinging to his back, Naaman was shouting, "I shall be like Moses and hide my face from you! You are a perverse generation!" Naaman would indeed hide but, to the delight of his giggling herd of descendants, he could be found in the most obvious of places like behind the skinniest stick of a tree.

"You will find them if you seek them with all your heart and your soul, so said mighty Moses," he would exclaim, his eyes closed and arms outstretched as he took his turn to try to find one grandchild or another. "I am seeking you!"

Naaman reached up to hug his tall, skinny daughter. "Does it not say in the Book of Moses, do not be hard-hearted towards your daughter?"

Her heart ached. Her father never denied her anything. He taught things no other man ever taught a daughter. He praised her intelligence and accomplishments to anyone who would listen and often to those who did not.

"Ahhhh!" Naaman's hands were thrown in the air. "It is just as Moses said! How long will you refuse to humble yourself before me, my stiff-necked daughter!" Marah could hear the exasperation in his voice as though he stood right beside her. His stubborn daughter was the only child who dared to stand beside him as an equal, even when she should not have done so. But Naaman loved that daughter as no one else did.

Even though she was the daughter who cost him a life with his beloved wife.

Look how she repaid her father's love, by forcing herself on a godly man outside of the marriage bed, forcing him to marry her. If Naaman had learned of his daughter's sin, he would have died of heartbreak years ago.

"As foretold in the book of Moses, the Sovereign Lord has shown his greatness to his servant Naaman." As far as Naaman was concerned, it was beyond greatness that a synagogue ruler was his son-in-law. That this synagogue ruler was as nice and as wealthy as Jarius was just …added greatness. His smart, beloved, stiff-necked daughter was the wife of a synagogue ruler! Marah could almost see his barrel chest in its ragged tunic expanding with pride.

She remembered their parting a few days after her marriage, as he and her sisters and Asa were leaving to return to Shiloh. Only her father was crying, crying so hard it was difficult to understand his final words to his youngest daughter.

"Be strong and courageous. Do not be afraid, my daughter, or terrified, for the Lord God goes with you; he will never leave you nor forsake you. That's what God told… Moses." He had choked on the last word. Marah knew the words of Moses were more for his benefit than for her own. He was despondent to at last be parted from his Marah.

Oh, and how often her father used the ancient Patriarch to poke fun at himself. "Ah, just like the great Moses, I too am slow of speech and tongue." Or, "As for this fellow Naaman, we do not know what has happened to him, so says the Book of Moses."

But now, Marah wanted to know. Yes, Moses, she thought. Now that he is dead, tell me what I must know. What has happened to this fellow called Naaman, my beloved father?

Neither Moses nor God spoke in the echoing silence of the synagogue.

On her last visit to Shiloh, she watched as Naaman caught a particularly naughty grandson in his iron grip, scolding him, "The Lord does not leave the guilty unpunished, young one. So says the Book of Moses."

Yet her father never learned of Marah's great sin, and she had never been punished according to the firm laws of her father's champion. Surely her father would not learn of her great sin now that he had entered the realm of a thousand years, the place of all knowledge and understanding.

Marah remembered shouting at her father, exasperated by his continued ramblings while she tried to finish her work at the inn. "Enough of Moses, already! I have listened to his words more than the poor Israelites! Enough!"

Once, her father had responded by placing his arm around the tall bony shoulders of his youngest daughter. "Moses told me this, my daughter: 'Take to heart all the words I solemnly declare.

They are not just idle words for you, they are your life.' The words of Moses are my life, Marah."

Marah bowed her head at the memory. For over seventy years, wrinkled, smiling Naaman hid himself in the words of his beloved Moses. Perhaps now, he would meet the Ancient Moses in the place Marah knew she would never see.

Moses would be lucky to get to meet my father, she thought belligerently. Naaman was not to be blamed that his daughter Marah failed to live a life according to the precepts of Moses. Her sin was not his fault, for he was the best of fathers. Jehovah better not dare to punish her father for the sins of his worthless daughter.

*"Hmmm, what does Moses say about a worthless, sinful daughter, I wonder? Oh, I remember! For I, the Lord your God, punish the children for the sins of the parents, the third and fourth generation of those who hate me!"*

Marah could hear the malevolent whisper as clearly as she had heard her father's happy voice only a moment ago.

*"Don't worry, Marah. God will not punish your father for your sin. No, no. God punishes the children for the sin of their parents."*

It took Marah a moment to grasp the meaning of the words.

*"Just as Moses said, just as Naaman said, God will punish your children for your terrible sin. Your children, not your father. Why Marah, that's Abigail, isn't it?"*

"No! No, no, no!" Marah's voice was a scream in the echoing hall of the synagogue. The idle conversation between Jarius and Abigail broke off as they rushed to her.

Abigail was the first at her side. "It's all right, Mother, it is all right." Abigail's strong arms clasped her neck. "I am here, it is all right!"

Marah was shaking.

"I know you mourn for Grandfather, I know you do. Papa and I will miss him, too." Abigail held her mother in a tight embrace.

Marah clung to her daughter as though Satan himself were about to snatch her away.

*"Tell her why you really mourn,"* came the snide whisper. *"Naaman, a good and faithful Jew has gone to a place you can never go, you with your unconfessed sin. Your father will go to the Gates of Heaven to join your mother and someday, Jarius, too. But not sinful Marah and not poor Abigail, for after all, the daughter must pay for the sins of her mother. Isn't that what Moses said?"*

Marah began to cry, great sobs wrenched from her gut. Her

husband and daughter stared. Their quiet, stoic wife and mother never cried.

"Marah." Jarius did not know what else to say, for this grief-stricken Marah was alien to him, this Marah who sat there naked in her sorrow, her torn heart set out for anyone to see. "Oh, Marah."

"Hello, my favorite family!" Marah, Jarius and Abigail jumped at the sound of the loud voice.

At once, Augustus saw he'd interrupted something private. Jarius rushed across the wide room to whisper in his ear. Augustus shook his head at the sadness of the message and then crossed the room in a few great strides to take Marah's hand.

Romans were, after all, much more casual in their exchanges with women than Jewish men. But Augustus was at the home of Jarius at least three nights a week. Even Marah loved Augustus, although not as much as Jarius and Abigail. She was mostly just grateful for the one man who was a true friend to her husband. She saw how the other men who called Jarius friend too often carried secret motives and furtive plans. But never the Roman centurion Augustus.

"Marah, I am so sorry to hear about the loss of your father. It's hard to be far away from the ones we love, is it not?"

Augustus's mother died two years ago in Rome, with Augustus stationed here in this remote outpost. A life of great responsibility and a journey of many weeks separated Augustus from those he loved. His only loved one here was his life-long servant Quintius, who fought and commanded beside Augustus for twenty years. "He means more to me than my own father," Augustus often said. "A true friend."

He is so far from his family, too, she thought. But not even Augustus could know her guilty pain.

Encouraged by her imperceptible nod Augustus smiled at Marah. "Your father was a good man. I am honored he counted me among his friends."

On his visits to his youngest daughter and her important husband, Naaman broke bread and freely shared the wisdom of Moses with this Roman friend of Jarius's on many, many occasions.

Naaman did not care one shekel that Augustus was a centurion who commanded many men, that he was the only son of an influential senator in Rome, or that he was heir to a vast Roman estate. He did not care that Augustus chose this life in Capernaum to escape the politics and debauchery of Rome, to be free to seek and worship Jehovah. The law of Moses was for anyone with ears, as far as Naaman was concerned, and Augustus the Roman was no exception.

Marah often heard the laughter of her father and the two men in the upper room. She tried to smile at the memory, but could not. She looked down.

"Your father was faithful to Jehovah, and the Lord's reward to him will be great." Augustus took Marah's chin and turned her face up to him. "For does it not say in the Book of Moses, 'The Lord will bless Naaman and keep him, the Lord will make his face to shine upon him, the Lord will turn his face towards him and give him peace.' Those are the words of Moses that describe the unshakeable faith of Naaman, Marah."

Marah nodded. She was always amazed that Augustus, this Roman, loved the God of Jarius and her father as intensely as they did. He spoke the truth. Naaman deserved the peace of God. He earned it, she was certain.

"Thank you, Augustus." But her voice wavered, for now fear pierced her heart, not sorrow. A fear she could share with no one.

"I will miss your father, Marah. For he was a rare man, in that he was truly happy." Marah nodded again. Her father was happy, the happiest person she had ever known.

"I shall always treasure my conversations with Naaman, for no one else has ever used the words of Moses to call down such terrible plagues on the people of Rome – and especially on me – except for your father. Remember?" He pitched his voice higher, a spot-on imitation of Naaman's self-assured and often agitated voice. "'If you do not let my people go, the Lord will send swarms of flies on you and your officials, on your people and into your houses. But on that day the Lord will deal differently between *MY* people and your people.' So says the law of Moses! *MY* people, Augustus!"

Marah laughed a little; she could not help herself. She was joined by Abigail and Jarius. Many evenings their friendly debates would end with Naaman reminding Augustus that God once sent many plagues to torment the non-Jews. As a non-Jew, Augustus most certainly could be tortured by God, too, if he did not stop hounding poor Naaman once and for all.

Oh, how she would miss her father.

"Thank you, Augustus. You always know what to say." Her

voice was stronger. The whisper fell silent, but Marah felt its presence lurking nearby.

"Don't feel as though he only picked on you, Augustus. When we first announced our betrothal, Naaman's first prayer for me was that my house would be free of frogs!" Abigail and Augustus both joined in Jarius's laughter, remembering beloved Naaman.

But Marah froze, for she remembered that day, too. It was the day her forced marriage to Jarius was arranged, the day of her great deception to her father. The morning after her great sin and shame, the dishonor she never confessed to her father or to her God.

*"Does it not also say in the Book of Moses, 'If your very own daughter sins, show her no pity. Do not spare her or shield her. Your hand must be the first in putting her to death! Stone her to death, because she tried to turn you away from the Lord your God.'"*

Her father never knew of her sin. It would have broken his heart forever, for he would have not been able to reconcile the perfect Law of Moses, the foundation of his faith, with the dreadful sin of his own daughter, the girl that he loved.

Augustus and Jarius began a familiar circle of the completed synagogue, looking at it in admiration as though they had not walked these same steps almost every day but the Sabbath for the last three years.

Abigail stayed with Marah, sitting beside her, holding her hand, using the corner of her lovely veil to wipe away tears she had never before seen her mother shed.

"Don't cry, Mother. As King David tells us in the holy psalms, 'Blessed are those who dwell in your house; they are ever praising you. Better is one day in your courts than a thousand elsewhere. Selah.' Today Grandfather is praising Jehovah in his courts."

It was always unsettling to Marah that her daughter could quote from the Holy Scrolls with so little effort, as though the words meant something significant to her. Abigail possessed the same confident understanding of those alien words that Jarius did and Marah did not. Marah nodded her head, even as feelings of panic continued to attack her.

She tried to focus on the voices of Jarius and Augustus, echoing off the walls of the large empty room.

"A house of instruction, where the philosophy of the Father and all virtue may be taught."

"A place where we can gather to hear the law and the prophets."

"A house of prayer."

"A house of worship."

Three long years of work was complete. The first Sabbath worship would take place in this new building in only three days, followed by a week of celebrations and feasts. The synagogue was a testimony to the growing importance of Capernaum, a symbol of the years of devotion Jarius and his father dedicated to the Capernaum Jews, and a witness to Jarius's firm belief that although the Jews were God's Chosen, the grace of God was for Jew and Gentile alike. Especially for his friend Augustus, no matter what some members of his own synagogue might think.

For anyone who truly listened to Augustus could never doubt his firm belief in the One True God of the Heavens, the King of Glory, the Almighty Lord, Yahweh.

"For all classes of people, rich and poor."

"For Jew and Gentile, my brother."

"For all people."

"For all who believe."

Funded largely by the wealth of Jarius and Augustus, the synagogue was imposing and spacious, over eighty feet in length, and two-thirds as wide. Built from the black basalt stone found near Galilee, the walls were as thick as one of Marah's long arms stretched out. The ebony stone created a dark and shadowy interior, yet light streamed in through narrow, evenly-spaced windows. It would be cool and inviting here during the hot months of Galilee.

Stone benches for the elders and council sat in front of the twelve gray marble columns positioned on both sides of the sanctuary; spacious hallways ran behind them.

At the front of the room on a raised podium sat the ruler's throne, or Chief Seat, as Jarius always referred to it. He refused to let the word "throne" be used in his presence and corrected anyone who said otherwise. "The throne is reserved for the chosen one from the line of David. For God says, 'I will establish his line forever and make his throne firm through all generations.' This is only the Chief Seat, a seat of great responsibility and honor. Never is it a throne and never is its position to be abused or taken for granted."

No matter what his son-in-law said, however, Naaman called it the Throne of Moses, refusing to hear any of Jarius's gentle arguments to the contrary.

And though he always corrected everyone else, Jarius made an exception only for his father-in-law. Naaman was as proud of his son-in-law as Jarius's own father would have been, a fact that moved Jarius.

"A sanctuary for those who fear God."

"Yes, a sanctuary for those who fear Jehovah."

"A sanctuary of praise."

"A sanctuary of worship."

The floors were lined with stone pavers, smooth to the touch. Two doors led to the other synagogue rooms, including the sacred mikveh, the bath for the ceremonial cleansing rituals. Augustus built water-channels to this room from the Galilee, an innovation unheard of to Marah. If only that luxury had been around in my little inn, where it was really needed, Marah had thought. She remembered lugging the many bowls of water to the inn's sixteen rooms three times each day. She never forgot the hard work of her youth.

Several meeting rooms were also located here, and the treasury where the offerings for the Holy Temple were kept until Jarius and an envoy of elders could transport their synagogue's gift to the priests in Jerusalem.

The worshippers would sit on mats on the floor at the feet of the elders and the synagogue ruler, facing southwest towards Jerusalem as the law required.

This synagogue did not have a separate women's gallery like the one of Marah's youth. Jarius and Augustus were both in firm agreement on this point.

She remembered their excitement as they discussed the new synagogue over dinner, how it would be beautiful, and magnificent, and most of all, different.

"Even in the time of the great prophets, the law was given to men and to women. 'Ezra the priest brought the Law before the assembly, which was made up of men and women and all who were able to understand.' All who could understand, Augustus, everyone!"

How Jarius could quote the writings of the prophets with such ease still amazed Marah.

"Yes, Jarius! 'Ezra read the Law aloud from daybreak till noon in the presence of the men and women, and all the people listened attentively to the Book of the Law.'"

That Augustus, a Gentile and a Roman, could so readily respond with the rest of the passage flabbergasted her.

To the side of the Chief Seat would sit the precious rolls of the Law and the Prophets. The sacred scrolls would be moved here in two days, carried by a reverent procession of Jarius and all the elders and followed by the faithful worshippers of Jehovah.

On the other side of the Chief Seat was a raised platform where elders, teachers and other Jewish men could stand to read or speak about the Law.

"A place of new thoughts and of honored traditions."

"A place of teaching and of learning."

"A place we have built, Augustus."

"A place we have built with humble hearts to honor Jehovah, Jarius."

"Yes, to honor Jehovah Almighty."

Marah watched the two men as they wandered through the synagogue. Jarius was proud and Marah was proud for him. This was as fine a synagogue as any she had seen in Jerusalem.

"Let Jehovah's teaching fall like rain and his words descend like dew, like showers on new grass, like abundant rain on tender plants."

"I will proclaim the name of the Lord. Oh, praise the greatness of our God!" Jarius's voice was joyful.

"He is the Rock, his works are perfect, and all his ways are just. A faithful God who does no wrong, upright and just is he."

"Remember the days of old; consider the generations long past. Ask your father and he will tell you, your elders, and they will explain to you." Jarius turned to smile at Marah, his voice echoing across the wide chamber. "So says Naaman's Book of Moses, Marah."

Ask your father and he will tell you, thought Marah dully. *"Too late to ask him now, isn't it Marah? He would have told you. But you never listened to your father anyway."*

She looked at the beauty around her. This synagogue was nothing like the dusty gathering place she knew as a girl in Shiloh. Her father was been amazed to see this place being built for faithful Jews like himself. He was so proud of the husband of his youngest daughter, his Marah. His son-in-law, the synagogue ruler.

"My father," Marah said aloud. The pain of regret carefully hidden away for so many years burst forth in her anew.

"Oh, Mother, don't cry, Remember how much our Father Jehovah cares for you. 'His love endures forever.' That's what the Psalmist says. 'His faithfulness continues through all generations.' From grandfather to you to me, God is faithful to us, Mother. His love endures forever."

*"From generation to generation, God is faithful. Faithful to punish generation after generation, from mother to daughter…"*

With a gentle hand, Abigail again wiped away her mother's fresh tears. "His love endures forever, Mother…"

# CHAPTER 17

Marah and Miriam stood in the courtyard, first laughing, then hugging, and then jumping up and down.

Jarius and Asa stood watching, smiling and embarrassed, their hands hidden under their prayer shawls, nodding at the sheer delight their wives shared at their reunion.

Marah was so happy to see Miriam standing in her courtyard. Asa and Miriam traveled all the way from Jerusalem to surprise them and attend the first worship service in the new synagogue tomorrow.

"Marah." Her older sister cried as she held her sister tight.

"Miri," whispered the younger, lapsing into the pet name of her childhood, left behind in dusty Shiloh so many years ago.

"Our father…"

"Yes, Father…"

And the two clung to each other even tighter, Marah's face a mask of sorrow and Miriam sobbing, both women grieving the death of their father Naaman.

"Did you see him before…"

"Yes, Asa and I were there just hours before…"

"Was he… Could he… talk? Did he know you?"

"Oh, my goodness, yes! Father knew everything that was going on. When he found out we were coming here, he knew why at once. The new synagogue! He was so proud of Jarius."

Marah nodded and looked down, her heart breaking. Her

father was indeed proud of Jarius, and of Asa, too.

"Father's last words were of you, my sister."

"No…"

As if she could read her mind, Miriam put her hand on her chin, and forced Marah to look in Miriam's eyes. "Marah, he told me to be certain to tell you this, that he loved you above all, the daughter of his heart. He said he loved his stiff-necked, smart, stubborn, beautiful baby daughter best."

"He couldn't have said that."

Miriam laughed. "That is exactly what he said! And those are the words he used to describe you!" She shook her head. "My feelings should be hurt that he loved you best, but we all knew it, Marah. After all, Father had to be both father and mother for you. We knew how much he loved you. No one cared, for we all loved you the best, too."

Marah's eyes filled with tears again. Why would anyone love her best? She was the worst of the lot. Certainly her father should have hated her.

*"Ah, yes, for you murdered your father's wife. At least he never found out about your great sin, did he? Lucky for you Naaman died and never had to know that his favorite child, his beloved Marah, was nothing more than a great deceiver who lied her way into this life. Not a good Jewish girl married to a fine Jewish ruler, but a sinful, evil, conniving…"*

A fierce tremor ran between Marah's shoulder blades.

Miriam mistook the passionate shake of Marah's body. "It's true, Marah, you were always special. Especially to Father. Isn't Marah special, Jarius? Didn't Father love her best? Asa? Jarius?"

Jarius smiled and nodded. Asa stepped in to save him from the forthcoming flood of female emotion from his wife. "Yes, wife, it is true. Jarius! Come show me the new synagogue. I am anxious to see what you have accomplished here in Capernaum."

Jarius nodded again, happy. Marah knew Jarius was touched that Asa had come for the first worship service in the new synagogue. She answered her husband's unspoken question.

"Yes, Jarius, please take Asa to the synagogue. And if you do not mind, and if Miriam doesn't care, we will stay here and catch up before Abigail returns from her friend's house. Is that all right with you?"

The two men scrambled to get out of the house so fast that once they were safely out of sight, Marah and Miriam had a good laugh at their expense. "Like two foxes with their tails tied together!" crowed Miriam.

Marah slid her arm through her sister's. She was so glad to see her.

"Come," she said shyly to Miriam. "We have made many changes to the house since you were here. May I show you what we have done?"

"Yes!" exclaimed Miriam. "What little I have seen is beautiful, Marah!"

While Jarius busied himself with the new synagogue, Marah used some of the same craftsmen to remodel his old family home, the place where he lived all of his life. The work she started several years ago was finished. Marah felt self-conscious about the many changes. She thought her work was beautiful. Everyone said so. But what else would they say to the wife of the synagogue ruler?

How good it was to have Miriam here, someone who truly loved her. Miriam would speak the truth about the work of her hands. She longed for Miriam's approval.

*"I speak the truth, Marah…"*

The two women stood alone in the deserted street, looking at the house's new façade. Every stone on the entire house was whitewashed a pale yellow-white, the color of ripened wheat. Six new columns stretched from the foundation up to the second story roof, graceful, huge and very imposing. Painted a deep gold color, they rose from their rounded bases to form graceful tapers up to the second floor balcony, ending with scrolled ornamentation at the roofline.

The wooden balcony railing between the columns was carved with an intricate winding pattern of flowers and vines. The windows of the upper room opened to this new balcony, their wooden shutters stained a deep mahogany color to match those of the dining hall below. The effect was impressive. There were few homes in Capernaum like this. But then, there were few houses like the home of Jarius even before Marah had made her changes.

"Beautiful!"

Despite herself, Marah grinned at her sister. "It took more than a little pestering to get my husband to agree to these columns, that's for certain."

"How did you get the idea to do this?"

"Well, it started as much needed repairs to the old balcony; it was unsafe to even walk on. It just kind of… grew to a full-blown redo inside and out. Everywhere I looked, something in this old house needed repair. These columns were the last thing that Jarius agreed to, for they, um… kind of cost a lot."

"Kind of cost a lot?" her sister laughed. "You paid for something that cost a lot? I don't believe it, Marah!"

"Well, they did cost too much, and they might be too presumptuous, that was the other thing that Jarius said. But once they were complete, he was pleased, I know." At least she thought she knew.

Not for the first time, Marah silently repeated her excuse to herself. Her husband was an important and wealthy man. He deserves a home fitting of his stature.

But was his stature as great as these big, imposing columns? Jarius was many things, but she knew the people did not think of him as imposing. He was the kindest, most accessible and agreeable man one could hope to meet. Everyone loved the ruler of the Capernaum synagogue.

Who could know what a friendly ruler might like? Marah tired of constantly second-guessing the answer.

"Please tell me the truth, Miriam," Marah said, wringing her hands. "What do you think? Is it… good?" If only her sister would approve.

"Magnificent. Wonderful. Really!" her sister exclaimed.

"You don't think it's too…" Marah searched for the right word and in the end could only think of her husband's description. "Too presumptuous?"

"Of course not. Your husband is an important man. It's certainly appropriate, fitting for someone of his stature." That Miriam's words were almost the same as Marah's own thoughts encouraged her a bit. If only she could be certain.

"I'm not sure he thinks that."

"Men never do until other men approve what they just did. As soon as our cart stopped, Asa already said he would love to have columns like this in our home in Jerusalem. He and Jarius were already talking about it in the courtyard, and your husband is acting like it was his idea. He likes it, Marah. It's beautiful, it's perfect. You did a marvelous job."

"Thank you, Miriam," Marah said gratefully.

Marah saw her sister only a few times a year and then almost always when Marah and Jarius traveled to Jerusalem. This visit was a rare treat. For one thing, Marah was so glad to see her sister just days after her father's death. That Miriam left her four children with their aunts and many cousins in Shiloh was an added pleasure. Marah would have Miriam to herself, except when Abigail stole her away.

If only she had a friend, a confidante here in Capernaum to guide her and give her advice! But Marah had no one. In twelve years, she knew most of the women, as befitted the wife of the synagogue ruler. But she had no friends. She did not know why. She never questioned this fact. It was what it was.

The lone person Marah ever dared to confide in was Deena. But she never asked Deena for advice. Never. Marah could not bring herself to show this weakness to Deena.

She looked up again at the house before her. It looked imposing, as though important people lived inside. For the briefest moment, Marah took pleasure in the sight of her home. How did this happen to her, a poor girl from Shiloh?

There was a ready answer, of course. *"You know how it happened. Don't play dumb, you know how you came to be here, by your own hand and evil intentions. Remember? 'I must do what I must do.' So says the Book of Marah."* The whisper mocked her in a hissing tone. *"You know how you got here."*

Standing in the street next to her older sister, Marah flushed with shame. That was twelve years ago! One horrible mistake! Must her terrible sin haunt her every moment? Couldn't she just for once have some peace?

"Enough!" Marah was startled to hear her voice.

Miriam looked at her and laughed. "Fine! Let's go in and see what else you have done. You are a funny girl, my sweet Marah."

Marah ducked her head, careful not to meet Miriam's smiling eyes.

They walked together through the massive iron gate into the courtyard, Marah showing her sister the other changes made during the long months of remodeling. Miriam noted with approval the spotless courtyard tile gleaming in the hot sunshine. She exclaimed over the benches decked with the bright cushions Marah picked up from the tailor last week.

The water in the stone fountain made a soothing, bubbling sound as it splashed to the pebbles below. Replacing the old leaking fountain was another extravagance Jarius at last conceded to, Marah confided to Miriam, but only after much wheedling on her part.

The old, carved doors facing the courtyard were stained a dark rich color and were oiled to a high sheen, as was a fitted corner table that held a large, beautiful ceramic bowl. "To fill with flowers, when we have special guests," Marah shyly told Miriam.

"Flowers! Such an extravagance! Such a good idea!"

The two women inspected the long, narrow reception hall, where two massive benches now sat on either side of the dining hall's double doors. Each was large enough to seat six people. Ornate carving covered each bench, the wood was stained the same rich, dark color of the impressive entry doors. Water bowls of a rich bronzed hue sat at each bench, along with clean towels for drying hands and feet. A woven covered basket of deep jewel tones stood ready for the used linens. Eight lanterns of a burnished brown metal were set in individual alcoves.

"Look at these lamps! I suppose when they are lit, the lighting is wonderful."

"Yes, they make this long narrow room feel warm and inviting."

Miriam was silent when she entered the dining hall. She gave Marah's arm a squeeze of approval. "Oh, Marah, this is so very lovely." Marah flushed with pleasure.

Four large windows were the focal point of the room. They looked out to the porch under the new balcony. Unshuttered, dinner guests would have an unobstructed view of Marah's gold-colored columns and the street outside.

Low benches faced each other on the two side walls, each covered in cushions of rich jewel tones. But what caught Miriam's immediate attention were the murals of floral and geometric designs painted above the benches.

"Look at these walls! Paintings!"

"Yes, it was hard to get Jarius to agree to these murals. He thought that might be a bit too 'Gentile,' to use his words. I had to promise not to paint any people or places, for other Jews might think they were 'idols.' As if there would be idols in the home of the synagogue ruler! What nonsense."

"How did you get him to give in? I want to do this in our home!"

"My tactics probably won't work on Asa," Marah smiled. "Remember Augustus, the Roman centurion?"

Miriam never shared with Marah what Asa thought about Jarius's friendship with the Gentile Augustus. But Marah, always silent and listening, knew. When he was the center of attention with his cronies in Jerusalem, Asa conveniently forgot that Augustus was the most generous patron of the Capernaum synagogue. Marah knew that Miriam found Augustus charming, courteous and quite sophisticated. And to the Roman's face, Asa was respectful and congenial to Jarius's closest friend.

After all, much of Asa's good fortune the last ten years was due to the fervent support of the wealthy synagogue ruler from Capernaum.

Asa's becoming as pompous as some of the oldest Sadducees in the Temple, Marah thought. But she would never say it aloud, any more than she would give voice to what both women knew: Asa did not think as highly of Augustus as Jarius thought he did.

"Ah, Jarius's good friend Augustus," Miriam smiled. "Of course, I remember Augustus."

"Well, I reminded Jarius that he just admired the same thing at the residence of Augustus. Once he remembered that, he not only agreed but used the same artist Augustus used for the work in our dining hall."

"Smart thinking, sister. Men can always talk other men into things far more easily than we women can. We just need to get them talking to each other!"

Marah felt the warm flush of happiness color her cheeks.

She pointed at the beautifully carved tables anchoring either side of the door. "This is where the servers place platters and wine during the meal. It is quicker than making trips back and forth to the kitchen."

"I have seen this done before in the finest of Jerusalem houses. How smart of you."

The head table where Jarius and other honored guests reclined sat in front of the wall of windows. The table was covered in a cloth of a deep red and gold, woven from a fine and expensive linen. Marah had purchased a large bolt of the fabric from one of the shopkeepers a few weeks ago, who finally threw up his hands in disgust at her hard-nosed negotiations and told her to take the price or leave. Bold words for a merchant to the ruler's wife.

The two guest tables on each side were covered with linen

cloths of a gold fabric, each trimmed with a wide border of the same red-gold shimmering cloth of the head table.

"It's beautiful, Marah! Where in the world did you find this linen cloth?"

"One of the shopkeepers here. He trades for it from somewhere up north, Caesarea Philippi, perhaps? Some woman weaver there, he said. He sells her work almost as soon as it arrives and always at full price. Isn't it amazing?"

"I see why you paid full price for it. It's the colors of a sunset. Amazing. This is the most beautiful room in your home, Marah."

"Thank you, Miriam." Marah's rare dimples flashed a grin of relief. "I am so glad you are here. It will be good to have you here tomorrow, both for the worship service at the new synagogue and for the dinner we are hosting tomorrow evening. We are hosting the entire council, their wives and many other guests, too. Jarius will be so proud Asa is here!"

Miriam hugged her youngest sister. Miriam never forgot what Marah once confided, that to sit through those dinners was nothing short of pure misery for Marah. "I cannot think of anything to say to them, Miri." She had sounded so sad when she said it.

Miriam, on the other hand, could talk to anyone, and she would most certainly talk at great length to these women, for the sake of her sister. She would be certain to express her admiration for the beautiful home of Jarius and Marah to the other women. She would mention how amazed she was at the work Marah had accomplished. Repeatedly, if she needed to.

Her sister was an important woman, and Miriam would make sure the other women knew it. After all, she herself was the wife of an honored teacher of the law in Jerusalem.

"Everyone will be in awe of you and your home, Marah."

"Oh, I don't know about that, Miriam!" Marah rolled her eyes, but she was pleased. "Thank you, though."

"Aunt Miri!" The shriek that accompanied Abigail's shout made them both laugh. Abigail threw herself on her favorite aunt.

"Ah, so beautiful," Miriam murmured to Marah.

"Say Aunt Miriam, Abigail, not 'Miri.'" Marah flinched at the sound of her own voice. She sounded as though she were angry. She wasn't! Marah only wanted to teach her daughter to be properly respectful.

Marah never shared with Abigail that Miri had been her own pet name for her sister when she was a little girl.

Abigail smiled at her mother. "Sorry, Mother. Hello, Aunt Miriam." Abigail laughed again. She was excited, surprised to see her aunt. "Why are you here? When did you arrive? How long will you stay? Did my cousins come, too? Why doesn't anyone tell me about these things?"

Miriam and Marah both laughed at this onslaught, delivered without Abigail even once taking a breath.

"Oh, my beautiful girl, who could answer so many questions? As your grandfather would say, compared to you I am 'slow of speech and tongue,' just like Moses. "

At the mention of Naaman, all three fell silent, but only for a moment.

"Mother, may I please show Aunt Miri my new gown? Please?"

"Aunt Miriam, Abigail."

"Yes, Mother. May I PLEASE show Aunt MI-RI-AM my gowns?"

Marah nodded. After all, the first thing she had wanted to do was to show her things to Miriam, too. Everyone needed Miriam's approval, so it seemed.

Abigail yanked on Miriam's hand; Marah had to laugh at her impatient daughter. "Give us just a few more moments alone, Abigail. Then you may have your aunt's full attention."

Abigail dropped her aunt's hand. "No problem, Mother. I will give you two moments." She wiggled two fingers at her mother.

"Thank you, Abigail," replied Marah. Miriam was laughing now, too. They watched her walk away, a skip in her step.

"She is beautiful, Marah," Miriam said again.

"Yes, she is, isn't she? She looks like her father. And she is quite smart, too." Marah tried to hide her pride, but the words burst from her.

"Oh, Miriam! I am so proud of her! Abigail can read and write and recite any passage of the scriptures as well as her father. She surprises me every day. And Miriam, she is so perceptive. Do not discuss anything in front of Abigail you do not want to hear repeated, even days later. She doesn't miss a trick. That girl understands conversations as though she were a wise old woman, not an eleven-year-old girl. Sometimes, it is just unnerving." Marah shook her head.

184

"Such a mature head on her shoulders. She is too smart for me.

"And Miriam, she has such a kind heart. She is so compassionate, always worrying about me or her father or a friend or someone in the synagogue. Just the most gentle heart you could ever imagine!" Marah was suddenly self-conscious. "Forgive me, Miriam. I am sorry to brag. I am just so proud of her. My Abigail is like her father in every way."

Miriam turned and looked at her sister for a long moment and then shook her head with a chuckle. "Abigail is not like her father. She is like her mother. She is like you, Marah."

*"Like her sinful mother?"*

Marah's laugh was one of ridicule, not humor. "Me? Oh, Miriam, that is absurd."

"Abigail is her mother's daughter in every way, Marah. She is just like you."

"She is not like me, Miriam. Jarius is the handsome one, the smart and wise one, the one who reads and prays and writes, the one everyone loves. I am only a housekeeper, a shopper, a cook. Just like a servant. Not that there is anything wrong with that. But Abigail! She is nothing like me."

Miriam looked again at her sister, then walked over to one of the long benches and sat down.

"Remember that family that stayed in our stable, Marah?"

"What?"

"Remember that family that used to stay in our stable, many years ago? Remember them, Marah?"

Marah had no idea why Miriam brought them up now, but she never forgot that poor family. She nodded. "Of course I remember them. They reminded me of us, so many children traveling with their mother and father."

"They were like us, yes, except much poorer. When they arrived for the first time, there were no empty rooms. Which was good, for when the man inquired about the cost, they would have left anyway. But before they could leave, who came up to them and suggested they stay in the stable?"

Marah shrugged her shoulders. She knew, but she didn't want to say.

"It was you, Marah. You, and you were only what? Five years old? 'Father,' you said, with your hands on your hips, as wise and knowing as though you were forty years old, 'Father, we cannot turn this family away, they must stay somewhere. I will make them a place.' And that is what happened.

"And then you said, 'Father, this family must eat, but I think they do not have much money.' You were so careful to whisper this! 'Father, we have extra bread and cheese, we will not miss it. I will bring this family some food, Father.' And you did. You were so determined, no one dared to question you.

"And then, after you brought them some food, there was this: 'Father, this family should join us in the courtyard, they do not need to hide from the other guests, out of sight in the stable with the donkeys. I will get them and make them sit with the rest of us. They are our guests, too.' And that is what happened.

"Looking at Father, with your little chin in the air: 'Father, this family will need a place to stay when they return from Jerusalem. But they will not want our charity." Charity! That is the word that popped out of your little mouth! I will never forget the look on Father's face! 'Father, go ask them to stop here again when they return. Tell them it is a great help that they stay in our stable, stay for free in exchange for keeping watch over Donkey and our guests' animals while we sleep. We will be grateful for their help at such a busy time. That is what you must tell them, Father.' And that is what happened.

"Now Marah, we never had anyone stay in the stable to watch the animals at night in little Shiloh. But the family did not know that and they so readily agreed to this in exchange for a safe place to stay. I will never forget the mother crying in the kitchen, thanking Father for his kindness. And there you sat, listening, silent, nodding wisely at Father, making sure he would not give away the secret.

"You did not say a word, yet you were the one, the only one, who noticed and understood this poor family's problems. You have always had a good head and a better heart."

For the second time that day, Marah's eyes filled with tears.

"You say your daughter can read and write as though this were something special. And Marah, truly it is. But... Abigail has had many teachers and many hours with her learned father. Her days are not filled with long hours of work as yours were when you were a little girl.

"And yet you, a poor girl from Shiloh, learned to read and write just by watching our father, scratching letters and numbers in the dirt with a stick! You learned how to add, and keep numbers and count money! No one, no one could believe how smart you were. Except for Father, of course.

"If something needed fixing, you could fix it. How did you know how to do those things? If people came when we did not expect them, you jumped up and at once made a big dinner, enough to feed everyone! Who taught you to cook like that, for so many people? If something needed to be purchased, you bought it for less money than anyone else in the market could. How did you learn to add up numbers in your head, to outsmart even the savviest merchant?

"There is a reason we all loved you the best! You were our little wonder child, smart and hard-working, your little forehead wrinkled up with a frown as you solved this problem or that. And with only me to fill in as a mother..."

*"Whose fault was that?"*

Miriam stood up and put her hands on her sister's shoulders, looking up into her tall sister's eyes.

"Oh, Marah, when you say Abigail is smart, or perceptive, or wise... When you say she is kind, and has such a good heart... Those are the same words we all used to describe our baby sister so many years ago. You were, just as you say about Abigail, unnerving! Surprising! Amazing. Our amazing baby sister.

"When you say she is beautiful, can't you see your own tall stature, your long beautiful hair, that same flash of dimples that lights up your face? Abigail looks like you and you look like our mother.

"And so, you were always the one Father loved best. The one everyone loved the best. And no one cared, no one was jealous. How could we be? You were perfect."

Marah pulled away from her sister and stood there crying. She heard her sister but could not speak. For if she had the voice to speak, she would have to then find the words to contradict, to correct, yes, even to chastise her beloved older sister. That Miriam thought these things of her touched her deeply. That Miriam was so wrong broke Marah's heart. She was none of the things Miriam had just spoken about. How could she be?

*"You murdered your mother..."*

It was too much to bear. "Miri, it is my fault our mother died! Mine!"

"Marah, Marah! You know that is ridiculous. That is simply

not true!"

"That not what my other sisters thought."

"What?"

"You remember that day... That day. Murderer, that's what she called me. And it's true. I..." Marah spoke the unspeakable, her voice a whisper. "I killed our mother. Murderer. That's what I am."

Miriam stared at Marah. "Marah, that day so long ago... I can't believe you still remember. Children say mean things to each other, things they do not mean or even understand. Your sisters love you and they always have. I love you."

Marah turned away from Miriam. She wanted to believe, but she knew it was not the truth.

*"After all, what else can Miriam say? That you really are a murderer?"*

Marah could not contain her sobs.

"Oh, Mother, are you crying again? Please don't cry." Marah heard the footsteps of her daughter approaching before she felt Abigail's gentle arms around her waist. "Please, Mother."

"Marah, stop crying." Miriam reached out to wipe away the tears with a gentle hand. "We all love you. We were so proud of you, just as Father was so proud, bragging about you to anyone who would listen after all these years."

Abigail chimed in. "I am proud of you, too, Mother. You are the strongest, most beautiful woman I know. Every day I pray that our Lord will bless you and give you peace. Please, don't cry."

Marah looked down at her daughter. Her daughter prayed for her! Peace. The one thing that eluded her for twelve long years was the very thing her own daughter asked God to give her. Was she really that transparent, that even a young girl could see Marah's inner turmoil?

*"Hmmm. Maybe you're not as good at keeping secrets as you think, Marah."*

Marah shook her head and squared her shoulders, trying to compose herself. "I have much to do yet today and tomorrow." Her voice was much louder than she intended.

She cleared her throat and tried again. "Goodness, a week of temple dedication ceremonies, plus the banquet we are hosting tomorrow evening." She mustered a weak smile for her daughter. "I have used up far more of Miriam's time than the two moments I promised, haven't I, Abigail?"

Abigail and Miriam exchanged glances. Marah had changed the subject. All three of them knew it.

"Why do you think I came looking for you two? But it's all right, Mother. We all want to spend time with lovely Aunt Miri, don't we?" Her voice was gentle. Abigail was letting her off the hook.

"Yes, we do." Marah turned to her sister. "Miriam, Abigail is about to have a fit, she so wants to show you her new things, just like I couldn't wait to show you what I have done to the house."

"Then she must show me! Are you coming, too?"

"In a few minutes."

Miriam took her sister's hand. Her voice was gentle. "Are you sure you are all right?"

"Of course. I will be with you in just a few minutes. I am fine."

Those who loved her knew she was intensely private; whatever she was thinking, she would not speak of it now no matter how they might encourage her. All they could do was try to tell her how much they loved her.

"Remember what I told you, Marah. All of us, Father and ever sisters, we all loved you best."

"I love you, too, Mother. Please come when you are done. Please?"

Marah nodded and watched her sister and daughter walk away. She stood alone at the door of her beautiful dining room, looking at the courtyard with its tiled floor and its bubbling fountain of stone.

If one didn't know better, they would think a prominent person, someone of significance, lived here. One only had to look to see the evidence of a woman's touch. A woman of grace and elegance and substance must live in this beautiful house.

"Not just plain old me," thought Marah.

*Don't worry!* Marah cringed. *Unless Jarius tells them, no one will ever know it's really plain old you living here! Look how you fooled your own sister for these many years. Marah, Marah, the innkeeper's daughter, with a worn-out tunic that smells! Jarius won't tell, he's as ashamed of it as you are!*

No wonder I never have a moment's peace, Marah thought crossly, with a wicked, irritating whisper clanging around in my head night and day, year after year. Go away. She was still shaken about the things her sister had said to her, things she knew were not true.

"Go away," she hissed. She had much to do today with no

time for the whisper and its blathering.

Marah swore she heard the whisper laugh.

*"Oh, Marah, don't be angry with me! Why do you quarrel with me, daughter?' That's what old Naaman and his older friend Moses would say."*

"Don't speak to me of my father!" Marah was startled by the loud echo of her voice in the empty courtyard.

If Miriam ever knew Marah had carried on these ridiculous arguments with an imaginary whisper in her head day after day after day, she would without a doubt change her mind about her. For Miriam would absolutely, undeniably think her youngest sister was out of her mind.

Jarius and Asa would soon return. Much excitement lay ahead for her husband's big day tomorrow. Marah was the wife of a synagogue ruler. She was a woman of significance that lived in this beautiful home. She was someone who mattered, at least to Jarius, Miriam and Abigail.

*"Someone who matters?"*

"Yes."

Marah lifted her chin high and straightened her back, every inch of her formidable height rigid with determination. Then, as though she were indeed a woman of great worth, she swept through the courtyard of her magnificent home with an imperious stride, leaving the whisper behind.

# CHAPTER 18

Marah heard Jarius enter his room late that night, just as she heard him every night, returning from council meetings, from dinner with Augustus, or even from a late gathering in the upper room of their own home.

She was always alert to the coming and going of her husband, in case he came to her bed, which he often did, or he needed her for some reason, which he never did. Jarius did not come in to discuss his evening activities with Marah, saving that for their breakfast conversations.

This was fine with Marah. She took part of his evenings far too often for her anyway. They entertained once or twice each week in their beautiful home, and these preparations consumed much of Marah's time. Every few days, someone wanted to entertain the synagogue ruler and his wife, dinners which still consumed her with worry, the fear of making polite conversation gnawing at her stomach. Jarius had his frequent meetings in his upper room, presiding over loud conversations between the influential Jewish men of Capernaum. Marah would slip in and out, bringing full wine flasks and replenishing the platters of food.

Much more enjoyable were the frequent nights Jarius, Marah and Abigail spent with Augustus. Augustus enjoyed these evenings, she knew, for Jarius was his closest friend and she and Abigail were like family to him. They were comfortable in each other's homes, simple dinners filled with laughter and conversation. Abigail and Marah loved to hear the colorful stories about Augustus growing up in the cosmopolitan city of Rome. Faithful Quintius attended the four of them at his own insistence, although Marah long ago realized he was not just Augustus's beloved servant, but also a man of great influence among the company of soldiers Augustus commanded.

Except for faithful Deena, loyal Cook, her husband Jarius and beautiful Abigail, Augustus was the only other person Marah counted as a friend in Capernaum.

All day long and the other evenings, too, Jarius was gone, even on the Sabbath where his many duties required his presence. Abigail and Marah would entertain each other with games or reading or shopping at the market or walking in their city. At night, after she tucked in Abigail, Marah would remain awake in her room, alert should her husband's gentle knock announce his intentions. Jarius was always quiet when he came home, careful not to disturb the sleeping household, the lamplight under his door noticed only by his watchful, silent wife. As she promised many years ago, Marah did everything in her power to be a good wife for Jarius. Save the dreadful whisper in her head, theirs was an orderly marriage without disruption or turmoil.

Tonight, however, something was different.

Marah sat up in her bed, listening, uncertain as to what to do. For tonight, make no mistake, Jarius was making a racket.

His bedroom door slammed shut. It did not latch, for he pushed it shut again, once, twice, then a third time with a bang. She heard him throw something heavy down on the small table by the door.

But whatever he threw down tipped over the table as well, and sent it and a jar crashing to the floor. The water jar, she was certain. She heard his uttered oath.

In twelve years of marriage, Marah never heard Jarius curse. An oath! That was it.

Marah stood and did something she had never done in all these years of marriage: she knocked on the door between their bedrooms.

There was no answer. Yet so loud was his breathing, Marah could hear Jarius panting through the door that divided them, great noisy gulps of air. Something was wrong with her husband.

"Jarius?" Her voice was soft. Should she bother him?

Silence was the only response. What if he had fallen over in a seizure or fit? It happened to others! She knocked again, this time with a sharp rap loud in the quiet of night.

"Jarius?"

Still no answer. What was wrong with her husband? Panic gripped her.

"Jarius!"

She pushed open the door. Her gentle, dignified husband sat on the floor, his legs stuck out in front of him like a child. A widening pool of water was spreading around him. His robe was torn; Marah had never seen her husband this. His head was bare, his normally neat hair messy, loose and wild, as though he had been running his hands through it.

He looked up at her as though he had never seen her before, confused, his mouth open but mute.

"Jarius! What is wrong?"

At the note of panic in his wife's voice, Jarius shook his head. "Nothing," he whispered. "Nothing is wrong."

Shaken, Marah took a quick step to the chest and picked up the towels she set out that morning. She threw several down to stop the spreading water, then knelt to pick up the shards of broken pottery strewn across the room.

"What kind of man makes a cripple walk, Marah?" Marah was startled by the strange fervor in Jarius's low whisper. She froze, holding the sharp pieces of broken clay in her hands.

"The man is a nobody. Yet he teaches and hundreds come to listen." Jarius's voice was louder. "I have heard him myself, in my own synagogue. He speaks and four fishermen - men of my own synagogue - leave everything to follow him. He lays his hands on the leper and the leper is clean. He touches a woman and her fever leaves her at once! What kind of man is this?"

Marah didn't know this Jarius in such fervent, intense turmoil. A finger of fear skittered between her shoulder blades.

"It is one thing to hear of a leper or a fevered woman. But Marah! It is another thing altogether to see it yourself, to see someone healed right in front of you! Someone healed by a man who blasphemes, healed by someone who calls himself the Son of Man, one who claims to forgive sin! One who claims to do what only God can do! Yet in the face of this great sacrilege, this, this, this… blasphemy, the man heals, and heals as though he had the power of

God."

His voice was soft. "What kind of man is this, Marah?"

He stared ahead with unseeing eyes, his words an odd litany. "The noise, the heat, the roof tiles crashing down. The man's bed lowered through the roof. Right in front of me and those infernal Pharisees. The man's friends could not get him through the crowd. But they knew. They knew their friend had to see this man. How did they know, Marah? How?"

"I... I don't know, Jarius." Her voice was uncertain.

He jerked his head to stare at her, a look in his eyes Marah could not fathom. "Of course you don't know, Marah! How could you know, you who are so down to earth, so, so... simple, so uncomplicated?" For some reason, Marah felt shamed by his statement.

"I, on the other hand, I, the synagogue ruler, with all my learning and authority, I, who am so important," Jarius spat this last word out, "I cannot understand any of it! I cannot!" Jarius slapped at Marah's outstretched hand, sending the pottery she still held skittering across the room. The clay shattered both the silence and the unfocused trance that held Jarius.

They both looked down at Marah's hand that had held the clay shard. Blood welled up from a small cut.

"Marah." His remorse was immediate. He grabbed a wet towel and wrapped it around her hand. "Marah, I am so sorry. Let me take care of this for you, I am so sorry."

Marah snatched her hand away. "No, Jarius, do not touch me! I'm not hurt. I don't want you to be made unclean by my blood. Look, it is just a nick. Please, do not touch me, you have far too many important things to do this week to be made unclean by me!"

He looked at her and laughed, a hollow, odd sound. "Important? Unclean? Oh, yes, ceremonially unclean. Yes, of course, I am not a man who can touch a leper or the unclean or even my own wife if she bleeds. God commands it. But then again, I can't help any of those people, either, can I, Marah?" He crawled up from the floor, shaking his head, uncomprehending of his own words. "I can't."

He looked at Marah kneeling on the floor. "Come sit with me."

"Jarius, please be careful not to touch the blood!"

He shook his head, calmer. "I am not worried about that."

Marah looked at him, shocked.

"Please. Come sit with me." He pulled her to her feet and led her to the long couch by the upended table. They sat for some time, unspeaking.

Just ask him, Marah thought. "He wants to talk, and he asked me to stay. He wants to talk and to talk to me, of all people. *"To you, of all people!"*

She took a deep breath. "Jarius, what happened tonight?"

He did not answer for some time, and Marah was too shy to repeat her question. But when he spoke at last, his voice had its usual calm, reasonable tenor. "This evening, I went to the home of the fisherman Simon. He attends our synagogue, but I do not think you have ever met him. Perhaps you know his wife or mother-in-law."

Marah did, but they had never spoken. She found it hard enough to speak to the people she knew without trying to talk to mere acquaintances.

"There are Pharisees here in Capernaum, Pharisees from Jerusalem and some of the other cities. Men I know well. They went to meet the man who now lives here, the man from Nazareth who stays at the home of Simon the fisherman. So I went there, too. This man," Jarius's voice held an odd note of amusement, "this man is a teacher. A teacher with many followers, and more every day. I am told several hundred people gathered at the Sea of Galilee to hear him preach yesterday. And of course, everyone is talking about him, for he is a great healer, after all."

"A great healer?" Marah wanted to make sure she understood what Jarius was saying. "You mean, like a doctor?" She remembered the many physicians who tended to Jarius's father in his last days, arrogant and self-important men of medicine. As far as Marah could tell, they hadn't done her father-in-law one bit of good. *But then again, what would an uncomplicated, down to earth, simple girl from Shiloh know? What would you know about a teacher and a healer, Marah?"*

"No, not a physician, nothing like that. He is a healer." He tilted his head to look at her. "A worker of miracles."

"A worker of miracles?" Marah felt stupid repeating everything Jarius said, but she did not understand.

"Yes, Marah, miracles." Jarius leapt to his feet. "And a forgiver of sin, Marah! How about that?" He pointed a shaking finger at her. "A forgiver of sin! No man can forgive sin, no matter how amazing his acts of healing might be. Forgiveness is of God and God alone!"

Marah reached up and took Jarius's hand, pulling him back to a sitting position. "Tell me what happened tonight, Jarius." This time her voice was firm. "What happened?"

"What happened, what happened," It seemed as though he could not remember exactly what had happened. Still, the strength of her voice calmed him.

"Well, there were many people at the home of Simon the fisherman. Inside were the elders of my own council, the Pharisees from Jerusalem, some of the Teacher's disciples and followers, the Galilean himself, me, and also some women. Outside, you could not even walk through the crowd. People waiting and shouting and begging for this man to come out. I thought I would not be able to get inside."

Jarius rubbed his forehead and closed his eyes. "But I am a synagogue ruler, after all, so the people must make way for someone important like me." There was no mistaking his sarcasm.

"That's not how you are at all, Jarius."

"Once I got inside, I listened. You know that is my way, Marah, to listen first and to reserve judgment. But the Pharisees who have been following this man were angry, asking him questions about the law, the traditions and rules for our daily life, the laws and practices that have set the Jew apart from the sin of this world since the time of Moses. And his answers, Marah, his answers…

"He said he has not come to uphold the law, but to fulfill it. To spread the good news of the Kingdom of God. Marah, the Pharisees say the man claims to be the Messiah. The Messiah, Marah! He all but said so tonight. The Son of Man, he called himself, just as the prophets foretold. And he lives right here in Capernaum, in my city, under my jurisdiction."

Although this was important, Marah could tell it was not what had upset Jarius tonight.

"We were sitting in this hot, crowded room, listening to this man, when all of a sudden I heard a great commotion above me. Roof tiles were being pulled off, one at a time, dirt and dust sifting down right on the man from Galilee. But he didn't care! He just watched what was happening, almost amused at what was going on above him."

"What was going on above him?"

"I wondered the same thing, Marah." Jarius laughed a little. "All of sudden, there were four faces looking down on the entire room, young men I know, looking through this big hole they had made in the roof. Two of them were waving at me. At me! Then, those four men lowered something carefully with ropes through the hole, very slowly, very carefully."

"What were they doing?"

"They were lowering a bed."

"A what?"

"A bed! Down it came through the hole in the roof, until it rested on the floor in front of the Nazarene." Jarius laughed again, an odd bark in the midst of this confusing story. "Several of the Pharisees were not only covered in dirt but also in danger of getting a bed dropped on their heads." Marah, trying hard to understand, did not laugh.

"The whole room got quiet. For Marah, you cannot guess what was on the bed, who was in it."

Because she could not, she was silent.

"Eri, the son of Mattius. You know his wife, Rebecca."

"Eri?"

"Eri."

"Eri, the young man who fell while he was working on his father's boat years ago? The one who still comes to the synagogue so often? His friends carry him in? That Eri?"

"The very one."

Marah did not understand. "Was there no other way that he could hear this teacher except to come through the roof? After all, doesn't this man teach in our synagogue from time to time?"

"Eri did not come for the teaching. He came to be healed."

"I see." Marah did not see at all. She had no idea what Jarius was talking about.

Jarius stood again, his back to her. "So, the Teacher just watches as the bed comes down to the ground. Eri is lying there, right in front of him. His friends are still up above, all four looking down at him through the hole they had made, looking at the Teacher and Eri laying on his dusty bed. The Galilean never said a word. He just sat there looking up at the four men and then down at Eri. Up. Down. Up. Down." Jarius was looking up and down, too, as though he expected the four men to peer through a hole in his own roof.

"At last, after what seemed to be an eternity, he spoke. And

197

do you know what he said, Marah?" Marah shook her head at Jarius's back.

Jarius turned around and looked at Marah. "He spoke to Eri. 'Friend, your sins are forgiven.' That was all he said. Your sins are forgiven."

Marah scrunched her eyes up, closed against her confusion. "Jarius, why did this young man work so hard to get to this teacher, just for... forgiveness? Isn't that what the Temple sacrifices are for? Forgiveness?"

"Marah, I know it seems confusing to you, but oh! The outrage in that room over those four words, 'Your sins are forgiven.' It was unbelievable! I knew the Pharisees were not there to learn about the Teacher, but to trap him. And the Galilean knew it, too.

"The Pharisees started muttering to each other and to me. 'Blasphemy! Sacrilege! Who but God can forgive sins? Blasphemy!' "

"Blasphemy?"

"Yes, Marah, it is a terrible blasphemy, after all, to claim you can do the things that God alone can do. It is the same as cursing the name of Jehovah, and it is punishable by death, Marah, by death."

"Will the man be put to death?" Marah shivered. She above all others feared the fierce Jewish penalties for sin. After all, had she been found out, had Jarius chosen to cast her aside, the penalty for her sin was death, too.

"No, he will not be put to death. At least not right now. For although the Pharisees whispered among themselves, the Teacher knew what they were saying." Jarius wore that same strange look. What happened to her husband at the fisherman's house with this itinerant teacher? "He knew what they were saying and he answered his accusers as though he was just teaching in the synagogue, calmly and without fear. 'Which is easier to say,' he asked them, 'that your sins are forgiven, or to say, get up and walk?' "

"Get up and walk? What?"

Jarius did not seem to hear her. "The room got so quiet, Marah, it was as though everyone was holding their breath. Then the teacher said in a loud voice, so all could hear: 'That you may know that the Son of Man has authority on earth to forgive sins....' and he turned to Eri, laying there in front of him, and said to him, 'I tell you, get up, take your mat and go home.' "

"What happened?" It was hard for Marah to get the two words out. She was afraid of the answer.

"Eri got up, Marah! He stood up in front of the entire room, picked up the bed he was laying on and took a few steps. Then he starting laughing, and suddenly he was running and jumping and hugging everyone he knew. He hugged me first! This young man whose legs I saw with my own eyes, withered and useless and wasted… Eri was running and jumping!"

Jarius stretched out his arm, as though he were addressing a synagogue full of worshippers. "As the prophets would say, 'He was leaping and dancing before the Lord.' " An odd, desperate sound escaped him. " 'And they despised him in their hearts.' The Pharisees despised him, Marah…"

At that, Jarius sat back down, as though the strength of his own legs left him in the telling of this story.

Marah had to ask the obvious. She could not help it. "Eri, the son of Rebecca, is healed?"

Jarius nodded.

"He walks? Eri walks?"

Marah was silent. She did not really know how to say what she was thinking. Handsome Eri, the son of kind, friendly Rebecca, healed? She decided just to say it.

"Jarius, isn't this wonderful news, that this young man is healed?"

Jarius looked at her. She was shocked to see his eyes fill with tears. "Jarius! What is wrong?"

At her question, he was overcome, sobbing before her, great wrenching cries as though he were in physical pain. She put her hand on his shoulder and felt him shaking. Her gentle husband, whose eyes would fill with sympathetic tears at the least thing, had not cried like this since his father died, or since that night at the inn so many years ago.

Marah pulled him close as she did when her daughter cried, murmuring soft, meaningless words, stroking his hair. She could not remember ever touching her husband so intimately without him touching her first. They sat like that for many minutes. Finally his sobs quieted. He lifted his head, sighed and looked at her with eyes as sad as Marah had ever seen.

"Marah, I believe I made many enemies tonight." Marah looked at him, startled. "But what else was I to do?"

"When Eri was first healed, there was complete silence in the room. Everyone was gripped with awe. With awe! Everyone in that room knows old Mattius and Rebecca. Everyone knows of their great love for their son, both when he was strong and even more so now, for all these years he has laid lame in his bed. But soon, I could hear it, the quiet angry buzz of the Pharisees. 'Blasphemy, blasphemy!' How could they say this, Marah, after witnessing what we had just seen?"

He took a deep breath, and for a moment, Marah thought he would break down again. But he continued, a curious note to his voice. "So I stood and asked what you just did! 'The Teacher has healed this young man who was lame,' I said. 'Is this not good news? He walks! His father and his mother and his friends are rejoicing! How can this act be blasphemy?' For my first reaction was the same as yours: How wonderful that Eri, the son of beloved Mattius and Rebecca, is healed!"

He exhaled loudly. "Alas, my question was not well-received."

"What do you mean?"

He shrugged. "Even here, far away in Capernaum, it is not a good idea to make enemies of the leaders and teachers of Jerusalem."

Marah looked at him, suddenly suspicious of his torn robe and disheveled hair. "What happened?"

"They started arguing, shouting at the Teacher and at me. After a few minutes, I stood to leave. I wanted to speak to old Mattius if he was outside. But several of the Pharisees followed me out, and we exchanged… hmmm… words."

"Words?" A finger of fear stabbed her in the back. "Jarius, did they try to hurt you?"

Jarius laughed. "No, Marah, just shove me around a bit. And this," he looked down at his torn robe, "this is how my robe is supposed to look. As the synagogue ruler in a city where such horrific blasphemy exists, I am to rip my robe to show my great sorrow and distress. I am not supposed to rejoice with one of my families over this miracle. Oh, no!" He touched his robe. "One of the Pharisees ripped my robe on my behalf, since I did not fall to the ground in my great dishonor to do so myself."

Marah was outraged. That anyone would dare to touch her husband, who was so beloved and respected, angered her. There was no other word for it. Marah was angry.

"We must do something!"

"No, Marah. There is nothing to do and yet there will be

much to do. There will be many arguments tomorrow at the synagogue, in my upper room, with the council, with these strange men, and the next time I go to Jerusalem." Jarius shook his head, defeated. "And soon, Asa comes here with Zedekiah, remember? They finally are coming, after all this time, to thank Augustus for his help in building our new synagogue."

His laugh was a short, bitter bark. "I have been duped, thinking Jerusalem sends the brother of the High Priest to thank my friend Augustus. And to think this Zedekiah comes with my good friend and brother, Asa." She heard the pain in his voice.

"The real reason Zedekiah comes is to spy on this man from Nazareth, this Teacher of the law, this man who heals the sick and…" he looked at her, his eyes unblinking, "…forgives the sinner."

"What can I do?" Marah did not know what to do. Jarius would have to tell her.

Jarius sat down beside her again. He took her hand and felt the calluses on her palm. After all these years, her hands were still rough with work and labor. She had never mastered the art of being the refined and sophisticated wife of a wealthy, important synagogue ruler.

"Oh, Marah what can you do?" He kept rubbing her rough hands. "Tomorrow, I will awaken early for my private prayers with my God." He was silent for a moment, thinking about his God.

"Then, I will eat breakfast with you and Abigail, enjoy the food you so lovingly prepare for me each day. I will sit where I always sit, where the light comes through the window and warms the morning chill. Before I leave, I will listen to my daughter laugh and talk, and I will hear about your quiet plans for your busy day. A world of chaos is right outside my courtyard gate. I will enjoy my home and my family at breakfast before I go to meet it."

He looked at her. "That is what you can do for me, Marah, the same thing you have done for me nearly every morning for twelve years."

Marah flushed at his words. She felt as though he were making fun of her. "I would do that anyway, Jarius. That is nothing." She heard the stiffness in her voice. "I only wished to help."

Jarius looked at her, surprised. "Marah, what you would 'do anyway' is your greatest gift, what I treasure the most. You told me years ago that you were the wife I needed. I did not believe you at the time."

Marah remembered that night too well. It haunted her every day. Why did he mention this now?

"But you were right, Marah. You are what I need. You have created a place of refuge, a place I love, a home. My mind is always racing, thinking, worrying; it never rests, until I am here with you and Abigail. You are calm and deliberate. You are…"

What am I, Jarius? What am I? She dared not speak the question her mind was shouting.

"Peace. You are peace, Marah, the peace I so desperately need."

Peace, her mind echoed. She heard her father's faint voice, "'I will grant peace in the land. You will lie down and no one will make you afraid. So says the Book of Moses.'" Peace.

He still traced her calluses, preoccupied. "Just as Abigail brings me joy, you give me peace, Marah. My home is my sanctuary, and I have you to thank for that. Do I never tell you this? The things you do are so important to me, Marah, more important that I can say. I am sorry I have not told you that."

The truth was, he told Marah all the time. Marah just never felt the simple work she did was worthy of his gratitude. There was a lump in her throat.

"Well… I will be glad to do that for you, Jarius. It's an honor to sit with you and Abigail each morning." Her words sounded stilted. But in her heart, she knew they were true.

*"An honor you don't deserve, do you?"*

For once, she lashed back at the whisper. Be gone! To her husband, she was peace.

It slithered away.

She heard Jarius continue, his voice much calmer. Marah had brought him peace.

"Let us begin our day tomorrow in the same manner as always, Marah, in the ways that are familiar and comforting and precious to me, before this inevitable turmoil is so ruthlessly thrust upon me."

He sighed. "Because tomorrow, Marah, my life will be different. I have already set it on a different path. Tomorrow, I must meet this man from Nazareth alone, find out more about the teacher from Galilee. I go to meet the man they call Jesus."

# CHAPTER 19

Marah saw her husband standing in their courtyard, talking with a man she did not know. Only Marah would know that behind the stoic expression he wore, Jarius was upset. Her controlled husband seldom allowed anything to agitate him, at least not that anyone else would know. To the world, he was always smiling and approachable. But the slight cock of his head, his arched eyebrows and his pleasant but unsmiling countenance at once told Marah something was out of sorts with her husband.

Who was that man, and what was wrong with Jarius?

The man was still speaking, nodding as if agreeing with his own words, punctuating the air with emphatic gestures. He looked pompous and pretentious to Marah. His rich robes told her he was a person of some importance.

It was very hot, the mid-day sun beating down on Marah's gleaming tile floors. Why didn't her husband invite him in out of this heat?

The man pointed at a parchment in Jarius's hands, jabbing the paper with his finger, and then pointed at Jarius, talking non-stop. Jarius did not seem to be paying any attention to him, all his attention now focused on that parchment. Marah could see his jaw clenched tight, a small tic twitching in his cheek.

Marah walked across the courtyard. Jarius glanced at her with an imperceptible shake of his head. "Don't speak," was his silent request. She stood listening, watching her husband's face.

"Yes, they know you have many duties here at the synagogue, especially this close to the Passover. However, your presence is needed at once in Jerusalem." The man was short and fat, his silk robes richly embroidered. Marah's practiced eye recognized their expense at once. He shifted his considerable bulk from one foot to the other, but Jarius made no move to offer him a seat. Circles of sweat were forming under the man's arms, ruining the brilliant purple fabric.

"I come as a representative of the High Priest himself, to summon you to Jerusalem. There are many problems here in Capernaum. You are the synagogue ruler. Thus, you are the man who must account for them." With a grating high pitch that tended towards a squeak, the man's voice undermined the authority he was trying so hard to convey.

"No one is saying you have done anything wrong, of course. Not yet, anyway. But the man teaches in your synagogue. Many of his disciples are men you have known for years." He removed his heavy linen kippah to reveal a bald head perspiring profusely, shining in the brutal sunshine. Rivulets ran down his face into the fat creases on his neck.

Let him sweat, Marah thought, a pleasant expression carefully masking her anger. No wonder Jarius did not invite him in. If it were her, she would have left him standing in the street.

"As the ruler of your synagogue, you must have some knowledge of what this man plans to do. We must know! The people think he is a Messiah, come to rule all of Israel. We know he is nothing more than a charlatan! What does he plan to do?" He poked the parchment once more for emphasis, the large gold ring on his chubby finger flashing in the sun. Marah noted the fingernails on his fleshy white hands were chewed down to nothing.

There was a nervous sneer on the man's face, as though he wanted to be haughtily superior. But because he did not quite have the confidence to pull it off before the aloof calm of the synagogue ruler, he came off as whining and petulant.

"When this man was in Jerusalem, he cleared the Holy Temple with a whip, driving out the money changers and those who sell the holy sacrifices! He is a rebellious revolutionary, an insubordinate pretender trampling all over our sacred laws and venerated holy rituals! He makes Capernaum and your synagogue his home."

Each time he spat the words "your synagogue," the shrill voice rose a notch. Marah decided he was jealous that Jarius was the synagogue ruler and he was just a menial, trivial messenger from Jerusalem.

"And so, you see by the sacred seal before you, you have been summoned to Jerusalem to appear before the Sadducees and tell them everything you know about this renegade, this Galilean they call Jesus of Nazareth. You... have... been... summoned." He punctuated the final word with a loud wheeze through his nose.

Summoned! Jarius was summoned to Jerusalem!

Her husband smiled, bobbed his head in a pleasant nod and then spoke three words. "I will go."

Jarius turned his back on the man and walked away at such a quick pace, his deep blue robe billowed behind him like a storm cloud. The man stared, unsure as to whether he should follow him or leave after such an abrupt and unexpected dismissal.

He looked at Marah with bulging eyes. "Where did he go?"

Marah looked down at the annoying, ostentatious little man. She did not know him, but she hated him with a sudden fierce passion. He had summoned her husband to Jerusalem!

As strong as she was, she could pick the little man up with the greatest of ease and then throw him out the gate into the street, where perhaps he might crack his head open on its gleaming black stones. While he lay there, she could add a swift kick or two to his posterior for good measure.

"I ask again, where did he go?"

Perhaps she could roll him out into the dirt of their stable, sit on him and pummel him until he screamed, as she had often done to every one of her much bigger sisters, except for Miriam, of course.

"Woman, did you hear me?"

As short as he was, she could undoubtedly grab his neck in the crook of her arm and squeeze him until his face was bright red. His eyes might burst from his head like two pits popping out of ripe green olives.

"Woman?"

Marah pulled herself up to every inch of her full and very imposing height and moved closer to the man, looking down on his sweating, shining head. He had the good sense to cower before her, just a little.

"I would say my husband has gone to speak to someone he trusts about your… summons."

"Wha--- Who is that? Who is that? Who would he go see about this summons?" Panting with excitement, he bounced on his toes in his excitement to find out who the synagogue ruler might trust more than a messenger from Jerusalem bearing a parchment with a seal. He craned his neck up at this Goliath of a woman towering over him. "Who!"

"When my husband seeks counsel, he goes to be alone with his God, to listen for his guidance. I am certain he has retired to his prayers." The man looked surprised and then crestfallen.

Marah stared down at him as though he were a worm, but when she spoke, it was in the most refined, Miriam-type voice she could muster. "Since you are leaving, please close the courtyard gate behind you."

She looked at him with the most condescending look she could muster, her chin high. Tossing her head, she turned and walked across the courtyard just as her husband had, leaving the man to splutter alone in the glaring sunshine of Marah's immaculate courtyard.

☙

Marah went at once to find her husband. He was already packing his things. No matter what Marah said, Jarius would not be swayed. He was going to Jerusalem.

"I must, Marah, I have no choice." He was imperturbable in his cheerful humor. "I think I will need more tunics, Marah. Where is that gray and green one?"

She stared at him. Just this once she would not be silent. "Jarius, why must you go?"

"Why, Marah, I cannot ignore a summons from Jerusalem."

"But why do they ask you about this Jesus? You must not go!"

"Marah, I don't want to go. But to stay here after I have been summoned by the Sadducees, by those closest to the High Priest, is unthinkable. I have no choice. I must go and answer their questions.

"The Sadducees! There are plenty of Sadducees and Pharisees from Jerusalem here right now, here in Capernaum, slinking around to hear the man preach! Let Jerusalem question their own about this Teacher, not you! Do not go, Jarius!"

Jarius stopped his careful preparations to stare at Marah with a grin on his face.

Which completely unnerved her. "Why are you smiling?"

"Because you are arguing with me. You never argue with me. Can it be, Marah, after twelve years of marriage, we are having our first fight?" He was laughing as he said it, and she knew he was teasing her, trying to chase her worries away.

But Jarius's laughter was no match for the whisper, snaking its way around her heart. *"Yes, Marah, pick a fight with Jarius. People are angry when they fight and we all know Jarius should be angry with you…"*

"Jarius, I am afraid for you to go." Her voice shook just a little. She would not listen to that hateful whisper right now, she would not.

He laid a hand on her shoulder. "Marah, the man from Galilee is just a teacher, and that is what I will tell the men in Jerusalem. A very good teacher, and one who does possess some great power from God. One who does indeed have the ability to heal people. But he is nothing more than that, just a teacher and a healer. He is not a Messiah, not a God, not the future king of Israel. That is the truth, and that is what I will tell them."

He resumed his packing. "I am not worried about the trip any more than I will worry about anything here while I am away. I trust you to take care of my daughter, my house, my affairs, everything else. Don't worry, Marah. He's just a simple Jewish teacher from the little town of Bethlehem."

Marah stared at her husband and then nodded, looking away.

Just a simple teacher, Jarius said. Marah might not know everything about her husband, but she did know that for the first time, Jarius was not being honest with her. The man from Nazareth was many things, but of all people, her husband did not think this Jesus was just a simple teacher from Bethlehem.

❦

That night, Jarius held a rushed meeting with the members of his council. Later, he sat beside the bed of his daughter until her chatter fell into the easy breathing of an untroubled sleep. Augustus came later, well after the council had left, and stayed long into the night talking with his friend. Late, very late, Jarius came to Marah's bed, and for once, he stayed with her for a long time before leaving for the solitude of his own room.

He whispered to Marah, as though even in the safety of her room, the Jewish ruling class might hear him speak. "Today, they demanded he show them a sign, a miracle," he said, a shocked tone in his voice. "They wanted a miracle performed at their command, like he is an entertainer in a traveling caravan! And do you know what Jesus said? 'Only a wicked and adulterous generation would ask for such a thing.' He called the Pharisees wicked!" Marah could hear his awed apprehension.

When he finally rose to leave her, she could hardly hear his whispered words before he closed the door between them. "God keep you, wife."

"God keep you, husband."

He did not answer.

Marah did not leave her room that night, both fearful and hopeful that Jarius might knock a second time on her door. When she finally fell asleep, his light was still burning.

The next morning, he took his time over breakfast with his wife and daughter, smiling and laughing, teasing Abigail and nodding reassurances to his wife.

Breakfast behind them, he at once prepared to leave for Jerusalem.

His words were soft in her ear as he hugged her goodbye outside their home. "Marah, do not speak to anyone about the Teacher while I am gone." Abigail's arms were tight around him, her thin body wedged between them. "I know you would not, but just in case. And if you must, only speak to Augustus, no one else. And do not worry. It will be all right." He smiled at her and mounted his donkey.

Marah and Abigail watched him ride away until he was lost in the crowd in the street.

Jarius's calm demeanor hand not soothed Marah's worries. If anything, each day she was away from him with no word of what was happening, her fear grew, cultivated by the fertile soil of concern for her husband.

How dare they challenge Jarius as though any of this were his fault? It's not as though he were here in Capernaum ruling over this mess alone. For months, different teachers of the law had shown up to question the Galilean. Sadducees and Pharisees came to stay, even some men from the house of Herod! Jarius said they spent hours discussing the law and how they might ensnare him in his own words.

"No matter what those 'learned' men ask, they never trap this Jesus." Marah heard the admiration in his voice.

How could it possibly be Jarius's fault that some men in his synagogue decided to follow the man? Bah. Mere fishermen, the brothers Simon and Andrew and the Zebedee boys, James and John. They dropped everything, their boats, their nets, their fathers and their families, everything, in order to be the Teacher's disciples. How could Jarius possibly stop them? Those crazy fishermen had nothing to do with Jarius!

"Not fishermen," Jarius said to her, shaking his head, mystified. "They told me they are fishers of men, now. They are not fishermen anymore."

And then, how could anyone blame the thing with Old Beker on her husband? Old Beker, the widower with the misshapen and deformed hand, sat in the synagogue with everyone else that Sabbath, listening to the Galilean. Old Beker did not ask for healing, and the Teacher did not ask if he wanted to be healed. The Galilean only asked what Marah thought was a simple question: "Is it lawful on the Sabbath to do good or to do evil, to save life or to destroy?" Even Marah thought she knew the answer to that.

But then he told Old Beker to stretch out his hand and just like that, after years of deformity, Old Beker's hand was healed! The tiny, clenched claw with its red misshapen stubs stretched out into a flat palm with long, strong fingers! No one could believe it, least of all faithful Old Beker, who cried and cried as he clutched that new hand to his chest. The Teacher did not say, "You are healed!" He just told Old Beker to stretch out his hand, speaking to him as if he alone understood the deepest scars of the old man's heart.

Marah almost fainted. Abigail screamed in happy amazement. The old man thanked the Teacher again and again, his words almost incomprehensible, and then ran to hug Jarius before the crowd of friends pushed them apart.

But there was no joy in the synagogue. No, there was only the shouting and accusations and anger of the visiting Pharisees.

"Not one was happy for poor Old Beker. Not even one," Jarius said to her with real sadness. Her kind husband could not understand such bitter hatred standing beside such kind compassion, especially to someone as faithful and unassuming as Old Beker.

How could it possibly be Jarius's fault that Levi, the most well known and most desperately hated Jew in Capernaum, quit his job as tax collector so he could follow the Galilean? Or that this Galilean would eat dinner not only with his new disciple Levi and his tax collectors friends, but also invite the Pharisees to eat with them, too? And they went! Jarius did not even go to that dinner. Why was anything to do with Levi the tax collector remotely Jarius's fault?

"Pharisees eating with tax collectors! A year ago, they wouldn't even speak to Levi or any tax collector, much less eat with them!" Jarius said this with his jaw and fists clenched.

And why did the Pharisees have to argue over and over in Jarius's synagogue about whether or not this Teacher and his disciples broke a Jewish law? Harvesting wheat on the Sabbath? Oh, for goodness sake! All they did was eat a few grains of wheat. They were hungry! And the Pharisees were right there when they did it, skulking after this little vagabond band, prowling behind as silent as sly foxes in the field, waiting to pounce on their unsuspecting prey.

"There's always a loophole in the law, Marah, a way for the righteous holy men to condemn miserable sinners like the rest of us," Jarius said with a tone of true contempt.

Marah hoped Jarius would hide his growing scorn for the Pharisees better when he was in Jerusalem than he did while eating dinner with her, Augustus and Abigail.

So, Jarius had been summoned to Jerusalem. Questions needed answering, and Jarius dutifully went. He was due home any day now, with Asa and the brother-in-law of the High Priest due to arrive soon after.

Jarius was especially disappointed that Asa was accompanying Zedekiah to Capernaum now of all times. "I know that Asa must be unaware of this ruse, he must… As if the brother-in-law of the High Priest is here to thank Augustus for his gift! What a farce! Surely Asa does not know his real intent. Zedekiah does not come to thank Augustus but to find a way to disgrace the Galilean, whose crimes are indeed monstrous: teaching God's law and healing those who cannot be healed."

Marah hoped Jarius would be able to hide his bitter sarcasm from Zedekiah, the honored brother-in-law of the High Priest. She doubted he would hide it from his brother-in-law and friend Asa.

# CHAPTER 20

For the tenth time that day, Marah walked out into the street,
wringing her hands, looking for her husband. When would Jarius
return from Jerusalem?

A worker stood outside her home, touching up some nick on
the ornate golden columns at Marah's watchful direction, the last of
the work to be done before the important dinner that would take
place here in a few days.

Jarius was due to return home from Jerusalem today. Marah
was certain he would arrive no later than the mid-day meal. Where
was he?

Throughout their marriage, Jarius traveled often. In his
absence Marah managed their home, their finances, their business
transactions, their servants and their daughter. Nothing changed
except for his presence. It was a point of honor for Marah that when
Jarius was away, he could be certain everything he held dear was
tended to by his dutiful, capable wife.

But it was different this time.

For one thing, his visit in Jerusalem was certain to have been
difficult. The Sadducees demanded he come to them, and the
Pharisees, too. The Sadducees! The ruling party of the Temple had
summoned her husband! Jarius made the long trip to Jerusalem to tell
them what little he knew about someone he had no control over, this
itinerant teacher from the dusty town of Bethlehem. He had been

gone for ten days with no word. Marah was beside herself with worry.

Two days ago, Marah and Abigail walked aimlessly in Capernaum. They fell in with a growing crowd, wondering what was happening. The crowd halted at the shores of the Sea of Galilee. She kept a tight hold on Abigail's hand, for there were hundreds of people pushing for the best spot to see and hear. It was hard to get through the crowd. They saw the man from Nazareth standing in a boat. They did not get close, although Abigail wanted to stay and listen.

"Mother, we have heard him in the synagogue! The words he speaks are wonderful. Please, let us stay and listen to the Teacher some more."

Marah had heard him speak at the synagogue, too. But everyone knew the synagogue ruler's wife and daughter. To stay here and listen to this man was to be unfaithful to her husband, so beleaguered these last few weeks. She would not stay to hear the man who was causing so many problems for Jarius.

"We cannot stay to hear the Galilean," she said to Abigail. "Not with your father away. Not today."

Wise beyond her years, Abigail nodded. "You are right, of course."

Those two days were now an eternity ago, Marah watching diligently for Jarius's return. She was frightened, for her husband, for their life together, even for her daughter. But most of all, she was frightened about what she did yesterday.

Where was Jarius? Marah needed Jarius to come home. She could not wait any longer for his certain anger with her. She felt faint with fear.

She looked down the street from her second floor balcony. She did not even remember walking up there. Marah had not heard from Augustus today, but she was too anxious to see her husband to worry about Augustus. He would let her know if something had changed with Quintius.

For ten days, Marah worried non-stop about Jarius and his troubles.

Now, she was worried about herself. For in his absence, she feared she might have done something terrible, perhaps unforgivable. Yesterday, Marah did something for Augustus, something she perhaps should not have done.

212

Did she do something right or something terribly, dreadfully wrong? Which was it, good or bad? She did not know. She was sick with worry, afraid that at last Jarius would be angry with her, that he would be done with her. Jarius would finally see her for what she was and give her what she really deserved.

*"This IS it, Marah, you don't have to wait any longer. Your punishment is coming. You've finally going to get what you deserve."*

"Go away!" Marah shouted the words out loud, startling the poor man working on her beautiful columns of gold. He scrambled to pick up his tools, careful not to meet her crazy, wild-eyed glare.

Only then did she realize she was back downstairs again, standing outside the courtyard gate by her new columns, wringing her hands, looking up the street and down for her husband.

When, oh when, would Jarius come home?

∞

Yesterday began like any other. Marah was busy with her chores. She was in the upper room putting away some of Jarius's parchments, when she heard the urgent shouting in the courtyard below. Her first reaction was fear. Jarius! She threw down the parchments and rushed to the gate. Cook's corpulent presence already stood there, talking to the deep voice of the friend she knew so well.

"Marah!"

"Augustus! What is wrong? Tell me!"

She was shocked by his appearance. His eyes were swollen and red, his face puffy.

"Marah, when does Jarius return?" He took her shoulders and gave them a small shake.

"Tomorrow, Augustus, why? What is wrong? What can I do?"

He walked past her into the courtyard and plopped down on one of the benches, squishing one of the cushions she so carefully fluffed up each day.

"Close and latch the gate," Marah hissed to Cook. "Stay here with me and Augustus." Even in this moment of distress, she would give no person any opportunity to question why the synagogue ruler's wife was seated alone with a Roman man in their courtyard. Even one as respected by the Jews as Augustus. She sat down beside the soldier who held his head in his hands.

"Augustus, what is it?"

He did not lift his head. "It is Quintius."

"What? What is wrong with Quintius?" Marah could think of no one stronger or more energetic than Quintius. She could picture his flashing blue eyes, steel-gray hair and muscular build, hear his booming voice and laughter. He was fifteen years older than Augustus, but his long years of soldiering made him as fit as the commander he so faithfully served.

Quintius was the father Augustus always longed for, the only one he considered family except for his dead mother and Jarius. Augustus loved the servant Quintius as much as Marah loved Naaman. Quintius!

She asked him again. "Augustus, what is wrong with Quintius?"

"He is dying."

Marah closed her eyes. Oh, death and its immortal pain! Even after several months, the death of her beloved father was still raw, a sudden piercing pain at unexpected moments.

"Oh, Augustus, what? What has happened?"

"I found him this morning in his room, struck down by a terrible curse. He fell from his bed to the floor, and he cannot move his arms or his legs. His eyes follow me, I know he understands me, but he cannot speak. He can only make these sounds, these... grunts, as though he is begging me for help. He cannot move. He cannot..." His voice broke. "I know he is dying. I have seen this before. If he is not helped, and soon, he will die."

Marah placed her hand on his shoulder. "Did you want me to send for Jarius's physicians?"

Augustus leapt to his feet and spun around to look at her. She was a little frightened by the wild look in his eyes. "Physicians! No! Marah, he cannot die, he cannot. He is all I have! I have already sent for the best of physicians! They have come and gone to no avail. I have seen this before and no physician can help him!" He dropped to one knee and buried his face in his hands. "Oh, if only Jarius were here."

Marah did not understand. If Augustus did not want physicians, then what could he possibly want?

"Marah, you are the only one who can help me."

At once she knew. She knew. Oh, no, Augustus, no...

214

"Augustus, you ask too much."

Oh, the heated discussions these last few weeks between Jarius and Augustus, the only man her husband trusted. The stories were as wild as their conversations. The man from Nazareth had cleared the Temple in Jerusalem, Jarius knew this for a fact. The man was preaching all over Galilee, but he always came back to stay right here in Capernaum. Hundreds of people came to hear him wherever he preached, Jew and Gentile alike.

He even read the law in their synagogue, as did every other Jewish man in Capernaum. He taught there too, in the beautiful new synagogue built by Augustus and Jarius.

"Well, my brother," Augustus mocked his friend over dinner last week, "we said we wanted a place for honored traditions AND new thoughts, didn't we?"

Jarius had not answered.

Most gripping were the healings. Stories about the deaf, the mute, the blind, shriveled hands, withered feet, fevers and leprosy and who knew what else, all cured by this Galilean.

Young Eri, lame for five long years, walking and jumping for Jarius, the Pharisees and the whole world to see.

Old Beker, who never, ever knew the power of two firm hands, standing with his shriveled hand straight and strong, lifted up in a fierce, alien joy.

The mother-in-law of Simon the fisherman, cured of her fever by just a touch a touch of the Galilean's hand.

Marah caught her breath.

Augustus still knelt before her. "Please, Marah. Your husband would do this for me. I ask you, please. Please help me."

Would Jarius do this? Marah didn't know. To ask the Galilean to heal someone was to act as though one believed he could do it.

"As it says in the Book of Moses, the Lord will have compassion on his servants when he sees their strength is gone." She jumped. Her father's amused voice was as clear as though the small, smiling man was standing right beside his beloved youngest daughter.

If only someone could have saved her father, struck down just like Quintius! Old or not, she missed him. She didn't want him to die. Her father loved Augustus, a Roman, and he loved him only because his beloved daughter's husband Jarius loved Augustus first.

Augustus was her husband's closest friend, as dear to him as a brother, as loved by Jarius as Miriam was by Marah.

There was only one answer. "Of course. I will go to Nathaniel; he is the elder that Jarius trusts the most. We will send him to get the Galilean. Jarius trusts him." She saw the relief on Augustus's face.

"Yes, that is who Jarius trusts the most."

"No, Augustus. The person Jarius trusts the most is you."

He nodded, overcome for just a moment. "I will go to the elders with you, Marah. Yes, we will ask them to go to the Teacher on my behalf. "

Now that they had a plan, his voice sounded stronger. To be alone with one's grief is to be weak, Marah thought. Grief is made to be shared, or it can overtake even the strongest man.

Still, she hesitated. Should Augustus come with her? Even with Deena in tow, should she be seen walking with Augustus when Jarius was so prominently and conspicuously away? Jewish women were not supposed to even speak to Jewish men, much less to Romans when their Jewish husbands were away.

She shook off her doubts. There was no time to waste.

Marah turned to Cook. "You will leave the kitchen and come with us." She would just chase away the innuendo by bringing an entire entourage with her.

Marah and Deena returned moments later, Abigail trailing behind.

"But, Mother, why can't I go with you?"

"Abigail, you may not. Please do not ask me again." Marah winced at the abrupt tone in her voice.

Augustus looked at her daughter and dropped to his knee. "Abigail, Quintius is very sick. I need your mother to help me. Please, Abigail. You can come another day, when Quintius is better."

Abigail nodded. "I will wait, Augustus, and I will pray for my friend Quintius. That is what Papa would do, he would pray. As it is written: 'Hear my prayer, O Lord, listen to my cry for help. Do not be deaf to my weeping.' " She laid her hand on his shoulder, loving him.

Augustus looked at her, moved. He cleared his voice and finished her psalm. "'For I dwell with you as an alien, a stranger, as all my fathers were.' Yes, Abigail, I am an alien among you, and your father would call on the Lord for me." He coughed, in part to cover his tears. "That is what your father would do. Thank you, for praying

216

to Jehovah for Quintius and for me. Oh, Abigail."

She sat down on the bench. "I will pray, Augustus, and the Lord will hear my prayers. Augustus, remember. 'His love endures forever.' Mother, I'm not moving until you come back."

"Thank you, Abigail." Marah was touched at the sight of her daughter's dark head already bowed in prayer, her lips silently speaking the words of King David, words etched in her young heart like the commandments chiseled in stone for Moses.

Miriam was wrong. Abigail was absolutely, without a doubt, exactly like her father.

Augustus, Marah, Deena and Cook fled through the gate into the crowded and busy street. They paused only for Cook to lock the gate behind them.

Marah turned to Deena and Cook. "Keep up," was all she said.

ဆ

Cook was panting behind her. Never had he walked so fast for so long. His many years in the kitchen standing, stirring and tasting made this pace hard for him. Marah glanced back at him, proud that he had not once complained. She remembered how Cook spent many long evenings in the kitchen with Quintius, laughing, playing that game with the smooth stones, enjoying some of the Mistress's wine, waiting for their Masters to retire.

If Cook or Deena were sick, she would want what Augustus wanted.

All four ran to the synagogue, for the morning services should just now be ending. It was time for the noon meal. Marah saw him at once.

"Nathaniel!"

The aged man jumped at the sound of his name called out by a woman. He was the oldest elder on the council, a man faithful in his dedicated service to Jarius and his father before him. He looked startled at the odd and urgent group standing before him: Augustus the centurion, Marah the synagogue ruler's wife, her aging maidservant and Jarius's fat cook. All four were sweaty and wild-eyed, the cook gasping for air.

"Nathaniel." Before Marah could speak, Augustus greeted the man he knew well.

"Augustus, Marah, what is it? Has something happened to Jarius?" Marah was touched that the man's first concern was for her husband. They recognized that these were trying times in Capernaum, most of all for Jarius.

Marah spoke. "Jarius is traveling. I am sure all is well with him. I expect him tomorrow or the next day. Because he is away, we come to you for another urgent manner."

The man looked at the ruler's wife, surprised to hear her speak. They'd dined together many, many times. His wife often commented it was like conversing with a rock, the poor thing.

"What is it?"

"Quintius, the servant of Augustus, is ill. He is dying. He is dear to Augustus, like a father." Marah tried not to think of Naaman. "Quintius has been seen by physicians but to no avail. I need you, the most senior elder of our council, to go to the house of Simon the fisherman and ask the Galilean to go to Quintius, the servant of Augustus."

"What?" Nathaniel stared at her as though she just suggested he step outside and part the Sea of Galilee, just as Moses once separated the waters of the renowned Sea of Red.

"In the absence of my husband, I need you to go to the house of Simon the fisherman and ask the Galilean to go and see Quintius. The Teacher must go to the house of Augustus, for Quintius stands at the edge of death." Her voice broke a little. "Quintius cannot go to the Teacher."

Although she repeated her request twice, Nathaniel stood dumbfounded. At last he spoke, shaking his head with his answer before the words left his lips. "Mistress Marah, I cannot go to the Galilean to ask for this, for, for… healing! Think of our problems with Jerusalem already! What would Jarius say?"

What would Jarius say? What would her husband, kind, gentle, compassionate Jarius say?

At once, Marah realized she was not asking. She remembered a Marah of old, strong and tenacious, the girl she had lost so many years ago in her guilt and her shame. Marah drew herself up to her full and imposing height. Her voice was commanding.

"As the synagogue ruler, my husband Jarius would do this for Augustus, and not just because Augustus is his friend, one dearer to him than any brother. Jarius would do this to repay a debt of gratitude to Master Augustus, a debt that you also owe to him.

"Need I remind you that due to the good will and patronage of Master Augustus, this beautiful new synagogue stands in our city? The synagogue where you sit as the most respected elder would not have been built without this Roman commander who stands before you.

"And you should do it for yet another reason, without my having to asking you yet again, for you know as well as my husband that Master Augustus is a kind man, who keeps our laws and loves our people. He is a man who loves your God as you do. You will do as I ask."

Five pairs of eyes stared at Marah and her imperious speech. There was no mistaking the authority in her voice, the fire in her eyes. All were shocked except for Deena, who smiled knowingly. Here was the woman she knew was hidden inside her Mistress' heart!

*"Who are you to talk of loving God, Marah?"*

Marah dropped her eyes, waiting for Nathaniel's answer. Only Deena saw Marah's confidence shrivel away.

"Nathaniel, please. I beg you." His voice was so soft, Marah only just heard Augustus.

Nathaniel stared at them for a long moment and then nodded his head. "Of course, Augustus, of course."

He looked at Marah. "You are right, Mistress Marah, of course. Jarius would most certainly honor this request for Master Augustus."

He bowed his head to Augustus. "I would be honored to seek out the Galilean on your behalf, to request this favor for one who has done so much for the Jews here in Capernaum, to even have built this synagogue where we stand. Out of respect for your position and gratitude for all you have done for the Jews, we will go at once. I shall find several of the other elders to accompany me."

What a crafty fox, Marah thought. Of course! Nathaniel's first action was to position this as a favor to an honored Roman who built their synagogue, not as Jewish elders asking the man they were growing to despise for an incredible miracle. Nathaniel was smart. He was already turning the situation around to protect Jarius from the criticism that was sure to follow. Relief flooded her, that that Nathaniel would try to protect Jarius, too.

They parted ways at the synagogue, each one with their own worries.

"I will send word to you," Nathaniel said to Augustus.

"Thank you, Marah, thank you." Augustus covered her hands with both of his, fear etched in his face. He rushed away, back to the bedside of Quintius.

Cook was weary from the walking and the upsetting worry for his friend. What would happen to poor Quintius?

Deena wondered about the woman she loved walking beside her. She was so proud to see Marah stand up to old Nathaniel; Deena always disliked the pompous windbag anyway. Poor Mistress, she thought. She is always frightened. What haunts her so?

Marah had only one thought. She was already feeling sick, claws of anxiety tearing at her stomach.

What would Jarius say?

∞

Quintius lived.

Cook brought her the news late that day, breaking down with sobs mid-sentence. She stared at his heaving shoulders. "Healed," he whispered. "Quintius is healed."

The Galilean healed the servant of Augustus the Roman Centurion.

She wanted to ask Cook more, but Jarius's whisper was etched on the stone that was her heart: "Do not speak to anyone about the Teacher while I am gone."

"Good," she nodded to her faithful servant. She went to share the news with Abigail.

Marah wiped away her daughter's tears and listened to her fervent prayers of thanksgiving. They ate a late dinner alone. Abigail dropped off to her own dreams almost the moment she lay down in her bed.

Marah however, did not sleep at all, prowling throughout the house until gray light broke the night sky, the hiss of her hated companion tormenting her all night long.

*"I always knew you weren't fit to be a ruler's wife."*

Today, she accomplished nothing, spending all her time looking down the street, first from the balcony, then through the gate, then through the window in the upper room, hoping to catch sight of Jarius returning home.

Finally, she heard the sound of his voice approaching the

courtyard gate, greeting someone in the street. Jarius! Marah rushed to meet her husband. She ran across the courtyard to him.

"Marah."

She stopped before him. Oh, he sounded so tired. How she wished she did not have to tell him what happened last night, what Augustus asked her to do. Oh please, that he would not be angry with her.

She stood, not knowing what to say.

"You did the right thing, Marah. It was right to help our friend."

He knew! He was not angry with her! How did he know?

Marah's knees gave way. She sank to the courtyard floor, faint in her relief.

"Oh, Marah…"

"Papa! Mother?"

Jarius smiled at the sound of Abigail's voice. He took Marah's hand, pulled her to her feet and held her hand tight against his chest, his arm around her waist. "Are you all right, my wife?"

She nodded, speechless, and pulled away just as Abigail threw herself on her father.

Marah looked at the two of them clinging to each other. Abigail suffered when her Papa was away. This time, Marah understood how it felt.

Everything had taken its toll: the weeks of anxiety about the man from Nazareth; the stress of Jarius's absence and what might be happening with him in Jerusalem; the terrible illness of Quintius and piercing grief of Augustus; tossing and turning and prowling about her house, sleeping so little the prior night… worrying that Jarius would be angry with her. Marah did not realize how exhausted, how mentally worn she was.

"Jarius, I am so glad you are home." She rubbed her face, weary to her core.

"I am glad to be home, Marah. I am glad to be home."

How did… ?"

"We will talk in a few minutes, Marah." He looked at her with a gentle smile. "Don't worry any more, Marah. Don't worry." He smiled at his willowy daughter whose arms were still wrapped around him.

"Abigail, my greatest joy!" His voice was heartier than Marah knew he felt. "Tell me what you have done these last days."

Abigail was chatting animatedly, starting with the excitement of last night. Marah watched them walk away. Even her bones felt weak with relief.

Jarius was not angry with her.

CB

Later, Jarius told her the whole story. This morning, Augustus sent out two soldiers to watch for Jarius. The moment they spotted him approaching Capernaum, one rode back at a full gallop to tell Augustus, the other rode with Jarius. "An escort, I guess," Jarius said flatly.

Augustus then raced his own great white horse out to meet his friend miles before the city gate. Augustus told Jarius everything, especially how grateful he was for Marah. Jarius told her how proud he was for what she said to Nathaniel. She was pink with embarrassment.

As Jarius neared Capernaum, Augustus talking non-stop, he spied Nathaniel and two other elders waiting just outside the city gate, so *they* could tell him everything. Capped off with Abigail's animated version of just a few minutes ago, Jarius had already heard more versions of this story than he wanted.

Marah's relief was evident to Jarius. She could not hide it. He touched her hand. "Marah, thank you for doing what you did for Augustus. I know you did not know what to do, but you made the right decision. And it was the hardest of decisions to make. I'm sorry I was away when this happened."

Marah could only nod. She was still weak over her actions, her fear of Jarius's disapproval.

"The Teacher went to see Augustus, then?"

Jarius looked at her with an amazed look on his face. "You... you do not know?"

Marah shook her head. She was suddenly shamed that she had not gone to Augustus's house, to see his beloved servant who had been so sick, to sit with Augustus.

"No. I'm sorry, Jarius. I... I just assumed the Galilean went to Quintius. Cook told us the good news that Quintius lived, and then he returned to his friend. I did not go to Augustus. I always worry what people might say... And I was worried about Nathaniel.... I... I wanted to talk with you first," she whispered.

222

"You told me… you said not to talk to anyone about the Teacher… And I… I…"

Jarius looked at her, kindness in his eyes. "That's right, Marah. Of course. I did tell you not to talk to anyone about the Galilean. And you should never visit our dear friend's house when I am away. Of course. Once again you are right about everything."

*"You are right about everything?"*

She shooed the whisper away, afraid to ask what she knew she must.

"What happened with Quintius… and the Galilean, Jarius? Quintius… he is all right?"

Jarius shook his head. The look on his face was unfathomable. "Oh, yes, Marah. He is not only all right, he is up and feeling better than he has in years. I saw him with my own two eyes, talked with him, walked with him in the street."

A wave of relief for Quintius washed over her. "So the healer, this Jesus, he went to Augustus's house, like with Eri or the fisherman's mother-in-law? He went to the house of Augustus, even though he is a …centurion?"

"The Galilean never went to Augustus's home."

"What?" She could not hide her shock. "What? He would not go? But then, how…"

Jarius stood up, pacing. "Oh, the man from Nazareth agreed to go, Nathaniel said. He left the house of Simon to go with Nathaniel and the elders at once. Much to Nathaniel's dismay, however, all his disciples and a big crowd of followers went too, even though Nathaniel protested. Off they went, Nathaniel, the other elders, the Galilean, his disciples and all these people, everyone on their way to the home of Augustus.

"But before they got there, they were met by two of Augustus's soldiers. According to Nathaniel, this is what the soldiers said to the Teacher. 'Our Master Augustus says to tell you this: "Lord, don't trouble yourself, for I do not deserve to have you come under my roof. That is why I did not even consider myself worthy to come to you. But say the word, and my servant will be healed."'

"Augustus sent the healer away?"

"Not exactly. Instead he asked the Galilean to perform an even greater miracle, to say the word and heal Quintius. He asked Jesus to heal Quintius from afar, without even seeing or touching him."

Marah remembered that day in the synagogue. The Galilean never even touched Old Beker. "Stretch out your hand," he said.

Jarius continued his story. "Nathaniel said this was Augustus's message to the Teacher: 'For I also am a man set under authority, with soldiers under me. I say to one, "Go," and he goes, and to another, "Come," and he comes and to my slave, "Do this," and the slave does it.'" That was the message Augustus commanded two of his soldiers to tell Jesus."

Marah nodded, confident Augustus's message would be delivered word-for-word. Men always obeyed the commands of Augustus. If she had not spent long hours listening to him speak, or seen his tenderness toward Abigail, laughter with Naaman, brotherly affection toward Jarius... If they did not know and love him so much, Augustus would be an imposing and fearsome man.

"When the Teacher heard this message from Augustus, Nathaniel said he was amazed. Jesus spoke to the entire crowd: 'I tell you, I haven't seen faith like this in all the land of Israel.' Jesus of Nazareth, the so-called Messiah of the Jews, was amazed at the faith of my friend, the Roman centurion Augustus.

"Of course, Nathaniel and the elders were quite angry, for everyone was talking about the amazing faith of the centurion. After all, Jesus made this pronouncement to the entire crowd of people. 'The faith of the centurion Augustus, the faith of the Roman,' the people said over and over. Nathaniel said it did not sit well with the council elders, that this Galilean would praise the faith of Augustus more highly than the faith of the Capernaum Jews." Jarius shook his head and laughed, the odd, disbelieving snort Marah had heard so often as of late. "You know how Nathaniel and the elders are."

She didn't care about Nathaniel. "So, what happened to Quintius?"

Jarius did not answer her for a moment. When he spoke, his voice was soft. "Marah, it happened as Augustus knew it would happen. Jesus of Nazareth healed Quintius without ever seeing him or touching him."

"What?"

"The very moment that Jesus met the soldiers, the very moment they told Jesus of Augustus's faith... Augustus told me at that moment, Quintius sat up in his bed, healed. Jesus did not even enter Augustus's home, yet Quintius was healed of his seizure."

Marah sat still, trying to understand. She did not even dare to take a breath.

"Augustus told me he thought Quintius would die at any moment, die before the Galilean could heal him. So his message to Jesus was one of faith, a desperate, believing faith, that Jesus alone could heal Quintius before it was too late."

Marah took a deep gulp of air. "And Quintius is healed." It was a statement.

"He is healed."

Jarius hesitated. "I am not being completely truthful, Marah. What Augustus also told me is this: 'If a man can heal a leper with a touch, rebuke a fever with a word, tell a young lame man to get up and walk, stretch out the hand of an old man… why would that man need to see Quintius to heal him?'

"This is what my friend, my brother said to me: 'Why would a man as great as Jesus, the son of our God Jehovah, come to see an unworthy sinner like me? I am not even a Jew. Why would he come to me, Jarius?'"

Marah could feel Augustus's pain in those words. She knew what it was like to be unworthy before God.

"Marah, Augustus knew that Jesus could heal Quintius if only he, Augustus, believed. He believes Jesus is what he says, the son of God."

Marah looked at her fatigued husband. She laid a hand on his arm, but he jumped at her touch as though she stabbed him. His turmoil over the man from Nazareth had returned. His eyes were wild and unseeing.

"What kind of man commands a disease, an illness, by only speaking a word?" His eyes burned with an intense gaze, the torment in his eyes evident. "What kind of man can banish death when he is nowhere near the dying?" He turned away from her.

"What kind of man can do that, Marah?"

Marah did not know.

She could barely hear his whispered plea, begging her for an answer. "What kind of man is this Jesus, Marah?"

Marah had no words for her weary husband. She simply did not know.

# CHAPTER 21

Marah stopped so abruptly that Deena, following a few steps behind, ran right into her. Had Deena not juggled her packages to grab her elbow, Marah would have found herself sprawled in the street.

"Ow! Be careful!" Deena bowed her head, waiting to see if Marah would enter their home, continue standing in the street, or just scold her some more.

Marah looked at the top of the graying head. "Sorry! I am just so nervous." She heard the insincerity in her apology.

Deena smiled and nodded, but remained silent. Marah felt as twitchy as a trapped sparrow, ready to jump out of her own skin. She laid a hand on the small woman's shoulder. "Deena, I am so sorry."

"Marah! How graceful you looked!" Miriam laughed at Marah's near tumble to the bumpy black stone street. She and Asa arrived yesterday for tonight's dinner, traveling with Zedekiah, his wife, and their entourage of servants and Temple guards. "I thought you were going to go head over heels into the street."

Miriam was not afraid to poke fun at her sister's skittishness, but changed the subject at the look on Marah's face. Her tone was conciliatory. "Anyway, what do you have to be nervous about? Honestly, you worry more but do everything better than anyone I know."

"Well, this is important," Marah replied, feeling defensive. "When is the last time you entertained a group like this? A Roman centurion meeting the brother-in-law of the High Priest… If this were your dinner, you'd be nervous, too."

"If this were my dinner, I would just get my sister to take care of it. Everything she does is always perfect."

They stopped talking at the giggling from the balcony above their heads. Marah could see one bright eye peeking at her from behind one of the new columns above.

"Abigail, what are you doing?" Marah tried to ignore the sharp sound of her voice. She did not mean to sound so terse, it was just how her words came out. Everything was upside-down and inside-out, an ever-widening circle of turmoil.

Their simple, ordered lives had been disrupted by some impoverished Jewish teacher from Nazareth who decided to make Capernaum his home.

Capernaum, where easy-going, affable Jarius was the synagogue ruler. If he knew his only son would be ruling over such mess, Jarius's father would have packed him off to live in the dust of little Shiloh, thought Marah crossly. She was ready to move there herself.

"Hello, Mother, hello, Miri." Abigail leaned over the edge of the balcony rail and pushed back her long black hair, transformed from playful girl to graceful young woman by that one simple motion.

"What did you bring me from the market, Aunt Miri?"

"Aunt Miriam, Abigail, not Miri. We did not buy you one thing," Marah answered for her sister. "We only went to market so I could get fresh fruit for the dinner tonight. You know this."

Behind her, Deena winked at Abigail. She knew there were a few extra fresh figs for this girl with the dazzling smile. Her mother purchased the girl's favorite food herself.

"What are you doing up there, Abigail?" Marah wanted to get on a different track, one where she was not scolding her daughter.

"You told me to sit down somewhere and stay put, so I wouldn't get dirty before I got dressed for the evening. Remember, Mother? You TOLD me to sit down somewhere. So here I sit!"

"Oh, that's right, I did. Thank you, Abigail. Why don't you come down with me to the kitchen? I would like to hear your recitation one last time."

"Mother! I have done it a thousand times already."

"Abigail." Marah's voice was disapproving. "We have

227

important guests coming. It is important that you not embarrass your father and me tonight."

The sight of her daughter's stricken face plunged Marah into remorse. Why did she say that? Abigail never embarrassed the father who unabashedly adored her. Angry with herself, Marah felt the wrinkle between her brows forming.

Miriam stepped in to rescue both niece and sister, the latter growing more flustered by the moment. "Marah, she has done it twice for us already, perfect both times. You don't have to worry about Abigail, you have taught her well. Let her come with me instead. I would like that very much."

Marah hesitated. What her sister said was true. But anxiety reared its fretful head. Did Abigail do enough? Worked hard enough? Given her best? Marah was as hard on her daughter as she was on herself.

She hated herself for it.

*"But still, you don't want Abigail to embarrass you, do you Marah? You're her mother! You know what it's like to not be good enough. Make her do it again and again and again."*

That did it. If the whisper thought Abigail should stay, Marah would absolutely send her off with Miriam.

She shrugged, and then regretted the uncaring attitude the casual gesture seemed to suggest. What was wrong with her! But she knew what was wrong. If only this dinner, this day, this week, this year of problems was over.

Marah chose her words with care. "I am sorry, Abigail. Miriam is right. You will be wonderful tonight. Your Papa will be so proud of you, as will I. For now, yes, please go with your Aunt Miriam. After you are dressed for the evening, would you please come to my room and help me?" Marah hated the formal, stilted tone to her voice.

"I will, Mother, and thank you." Abigail's voice was cheerful, as though she had not just been wrongly scolded in front of her favorite aunt. She disappeared from sight; Marah heard her clattering footsteps on the stairs. She popped into view through the open doors and walked straight to her mother, hugging her in a tight embrace.

She loves me so much, thought Marah. Why did it always seem she didn't love Abigail when in truth she was everything to Marah?

*Well, someone has to be the strict parent. Too bad that has to be you,*

*Marah. For Abigail's father certainly spoils her shamelessly! No one ever doubts how much Jarius loves his Abigail."*

Marah shook away the whisper but in her mind's eye could see her husband and daughter standing together in laughter or conversation or prayer. Abigail, the joy of her father.

*"At least his daughter brings him joy. Not like poor Naaman, whose youngest daughter…"*

"Let's go to my room, Abigail," Miriam's voice startled the whisper into silence. "Come! I will tell you stories of how naughty your mother was when she was a little girl." She winked at Marah, who tried to smile.

"Yes, Aunt Miri." Abigail clapped a hand to her mouth. "Oops! I mean, Aunt Mi-ri-AM. Sorry, Mother!"

Marah watched the two walk across the courtyard and turned to Deena. "Why don't you bring them a few of the figs we bought, Deena? And maybe some cheese? It will be a long time for Abigail to wait for dinner."

"Yes, Mistress." Deena hesitated. "Don't worry, Mistress Marah. Everything is perfect. Please, don't worry anymore." She hurried off to her many tasks, determined to do her part to make sure no detail was overlooked for her Mistress.

Marah was alone in the silent courtyard.

The quiet echo of Jarius's voice came to her, the soft conversation they shared last night in her bed, before he left her for his room.

"This dinner tomorrow is important, Marah."

"I know, Jarius."

"I feel so foolish. I thought Zedekiah was coming to pay his respects to Augustus, to honor him for what he has done for the Jews here."

"I know."

"Instead, Zedekiah is really here to meet the Galilean, to make a report to Caiaphas about him."

"Yes."

"And he will certainly report how the man from Nazareth called Capernaum home, and how he teaches in our synagogue, the one Augustus helped us build."

"I know, Jarius."

"And without a doubt he will tell Caiaphas all the things the Capernaum synagogue ruler is and is not doing, along with all the things he should and should not be doing, to say nothing about what he has and hasn't done about this Jesus."

Marah had trouble following that statement, so she settled for a safe answer. "I see."

"And Augustus, oh Augustus! I feel so terrible for Augustus."

"Augustus understands, Jarius." Jarius could no more keep the truth about this visit from Augustus than he could keep from smiling at the sight of Abigail.

"If only he will not speak of Jesus and Quintius to Zedekiah. I know it is a lot to ask of him. I know what happened is a miracle! I know it! I love Quintius, too! But with the arguments and unrest going on outside these walls, I just need for this to be a quiet, civil dinner."

"I know, Jarius." Marah thought a moment and then added, "Augustus knows, also. You are his closest friend. He will not let you down, Jarius. He will not."

He touched her cheek and smiled the sad smile he wore so often as of late. "God keep you, wife."

"God keep you, husband."

His light had burned dimly for hours, Jarius as sleepless as his wife on the other side of the door.

Marah sighed at the thought of her husband's sleepless night and sat down in the courtyard. This Jesus situation was going to drive her husband to insanity.

There were whispered reports, Deena told her, that the man might be moving on to Jerusalem for good. It could not happen a moment too soon for Marah.

*"But what about Quintius? And Eri? And Simon's mother-in-law and Old Beker and the blind man and leper and all those people this Jesus healed? Isn't it wrong of you, Marah, to want to get rid of someone like that?"*

On the contrary, there was no question that Marah would be happy to get rid of anyone who caused such worry for her husband Jarius, who ruined the peace of Marah's calm and ordered world.

Especially one who caused as many problems as this Galilean.

Worry gripped her over the ominous significance of tonight's dinner. If only things would go well and Jarius would be pleased. Perhaps that would help. She jumped to her feet. Surely there were still things for her to do.

If only this dinner would go well.

If only she could please her husband Jarius.

&#9752;

Marah walked to the kitchen. Cook was supervising a dinner that promised perfection. Long ago, Cook and Marah recognized each other's superior cooking skills. Together, their dinners were unmatched in all of Capernaum. Even the cosmopolitan Augustus exclaimed over their work.

She took a deep breath in the doorway, unaware of the dimples she flashed at Cook. At last, a place of comfort for Marah. Her sanctuary.

Cook smiled back, as nervous as she. They labored over this special menu for days. He motioned to her. "Come, Mistress, let me show you what is done thus far."

They walked over to one of the large counters, laden with many items. "The wine is set aside over here; we will fill the cups on the tables for the guests, refill the pitchers and leave them on the side counter in the dining hall. That way, the servers can refill wine without having to return to the kitchen. We will be certain to keep the wine cups full, Mistress."

They nodded a silent agreement. Perhaps the wine would make the guests expansive and relaxed, not tense and testy and itching for a fight.

"The platters of cheese and olives are prepared." He pointed to the three large platters, a twitch in his cheek betraying his anxiety. "What do you think? Do you like how I arranged the food on these trays?"

"Wonderful, Cook. They look wonderful. Now, when do the servers arrive?"

"In an hour, Mistress." He answered before she could ask. "Three, as we discussed. I know the three men well, as you do. We have used them before. They are very good."

Marah frowned, but Cook knew this was a sign she was thinking rather than one of disapproval.

"Next we will serve your famous stew, which we prepared this morning. It has been simmering all day, Mistress Marah. It is wonderful, the best you have ever made! We have not left it unwatched for a moment."

Marah bent over the large pot to inspect the broth. The wonderful aroma of meat, onions and lentils wafted up to her. Oh, if Cook allowed the stew to scorch for even one second, she would be furious. She took a taste. "Mmmm. Perfect. Delicious."

The stew was every bit as good as if she tended it herself. Yet, she felt a small wave of nausea wash over her. Nerves, she thought, not the stew. After all, who could eat at a time like this? Her stomach gurgled in agreement.

"Here is the bread, Mistress, ready for the ovens at just the right moment." The loaves of risen dough, made from wheat flour ground so fine it was practically a powder, would be baked under Cook's careful supervision. The guests would dip fresh, hot bread into the stew as a prelude to the main course.

They walked to the private courtyard, where the lamb roasted over the fire pit. Seasoned with the best spices and herbs, the lamb had been cooking since early morning, brushed with olive oil as the house boy turned the spit with a slow, steady motion. This would be the highlight of the meal, worthy of a king. Her stomach groaned again at the aroma.

What was wrong with her?

"Very nice, Cook." They walked back into the kitchen. "But make certain you bank the fire once the meat is ready," Marah added.

Cook nodded his acknowledgement even as he silently forgave his jumpy Mistress for such an unnecessary reminder. When it came to roasting lamb, Cook was the acknowledged expert.

On the back counter sat several white cakes, drizzled with a liberal dose of honey and sprinkled with silvers of roasted almonds. Even Marah would readily admit no one could bake cakes like Cook. Dates and the expensive, rare oranges would accompany these rich cakes, a fitting end to their feast.

"Well done, Cook, truly well done." Marah's face was serious. "This will be our best dinner yet."

Cook stood a little taller and smiled. Because she was such a perfectionist - to say nothing of being such a good cook herself - any praise from Mistress Marah was appreciated. Truly well done! That was high praise indeed.

Tonight, Marah and Cook would serve their most unforgettable meal to their most important guest ever, the brother-in-law of Caiaphas the High Priest. Caiaphas, son-in-law of the powerful ex-High Priest Annas and one of the most powerful men in

Jerusalem, was sending a family member to distant Capernaum. King Herod might hold the scepter of the Jewish throne, but the true Jewish royalty held the Temple scrolls and the title of High Priest.

"Cook, help me think. What have we overlooked? Have I forgotten anything?"

Before he could answer, they heard voices in the courtyard through the open door.

"This is the room where we will be serving the meal." There was an undeniable note of authority to Abigail's voice. The evening's entertainment had arrived. Marah looked at Cook, who was trying to look stern and not to laugh out loud. She smiled for both of them and then stepped into the courtyard.

"Thank you, Abigail," Marah said, "I will help the musicians get situated."

"As you wish, Mother." Abigail nodded at the men. "Thank you," she said in her best, most polite, "I-am-almost-a-grown-woman, Mother" voice. Marah knew she wanted to stay and watch the musicians. She loved music, and had the same melodious voice as her father. But Marah would not let her daughter stay without a chaperon with two grown men, and everyone was too busy at the moment for something so frivolous. Her daughter could hear the musicians tonight.

"Abigail, come here." Marah put her arm around her daughter's waist and walked into the courtyard with her. Abigail could almost look her mother in the eye. "Thank you for helping with the musicians. And Abi…" Abigail smiled at the use of Jarius's pet name for her. Her mother never called her that.

But Marah corrected herself at once. "Abigail, I am sorry I scolded you earlier. I am worried and took it out on you. You will do a wonderful job, I know. I am proud of you, so very proud. Now, go back to your Aunt Miriam. And thank you."

Abigail sighed. "No, thank you, Mother. I know you are worried about the dinner tonight, and about Papa's troubles with that awful Zedekiah from Jerusalem. If that man would only meet the teacher called Jesus, perhaps he will understand the position Papa is in. The people love Jesus. It is a troublesome thing.

"I will do my best tonight, Mother, I promise. Don't worry any more about this evening. Everything will be wonderful. Papa will be proud of you and you will be proud of me." She gave her mother a hug, and whispered in her ear. "Don't worry, Mother. I will make you proud."

She left in search of Miriam.

I am always proud of her, Marah thought to herself.

She was taken aback at her daughter's quick perception of all that went on around her. Awful Zedekiah? That was exactly what Marah thought of him. Jarius and Marah did not speak of their recent troubles in front of their daughter, but her clever mind missed nothing.

*"She is as clever as her mother, isn't she? We all know how clever you are, Marah."*

Before it could whisper anything else, Marah turned her attention back to the musicians. Productive work always soothed her and banished the whisper from her presence. As they tuned their instruments, Marah made one last inspection of the place where the dinner would take place. She hoped no one could spill any of the wine on her beautiful new tablecloths, especially the red brocade. Marah could get any stain out except wine.

Jarius, Augustus, Asa and the so-called honorable Zedekiah would sit at the head table. Zedekiah, who Jarius assumed was here to thank Augustus, the generous benefactor of the Capernaum synagogue.

It was a bitter disappointment to realize the visit was only a ruse. Zedekiah would provide Caiaphas and Annas a firsthand report about the man Jesus, and, most likely, a report about what the Jewish ruler Jarius was and was not doing about the situation.

Oh, this man, this Jesus, Marah thought to herself.

Marah met Zedekiah for a few moments yesterday. He and his wife rented rooms for their stay that would accommodate them, their considerable entourage of servants and several of the Temple guard that accompanied them from Jerusalem. Marah found Zedekiah to be dour and impatient. If only her dinner would please Zedekiah, and prove her husband's worth to him!

Marah sighed. The wife of Zedekiah would sit at the table on Jarius's right, closest to the head table. Also at the table would be Miriam, Marah and Abigail. Marah deliberately placed Miriam beside Zedekiah's wife. They were both from Jerusalem, and Miriam could carry on a conversation with anyone.

At the opposite table would be six others, Nathaniel and the two elders who asked Jesus to heal Quintius, and their three wives. The men were the oldest and most respected leaders on the synagogue council. And they know as much about this Jesus as Jarius does, thought Marah.

Her home was immaculate, the food would be excellent, the musicians were ready. Deena was probably dressing her daughter in her new tunic, smiling at the girl's idle chatter as her aging hands arranged the beautiful black hair. Her sister Miriam was clothing herself in a rich gown befitting the wife of an esteemed teacher of the law, ready to lend moral support to the sister she loved. Everything was perfect.

All that was left for Marah to do was dress herself too, and wait with her husband to receive their guests. If only Jarius would be pleased. She had never wanted something to be perfect so much in her life.

*"Your home, the food, the music… Perfect. Your daughter, your sister, your husband… Perfect. Everything is perfect except for… you! The only flaw in this perfect picture is you, Marah!"*

Marah shook her head. All right, everything was perfect but her.

Tonight, almost perfect was good enough for her.

# CHAPTER 22

Jarius caught Marah's eye and gave her an imperceptible nod. She flushed at his silent acknowledgement of her hard work. The meal *had* been superb. How wonderful to have Jarius think so too.

Conversation was quiet and polite, interspersed with occasional laughter. Talk centered on the wonderful food, Jarius's beautiful home and the construction of the synagogue. Miriam outdid herself entertaining Zedekiah's standoffish wife, making sure silent Marah was as much a part of the conversation as though she actually said something. Abigail spoke only when spoken to first. Her answers were articulate and gracious, her manners impeccable. Marah's heart expanded with pride just to look at her accomplished daughter.

Servers stood at the ready, refilling glasses and replenishing plates, silent and efficient as they cleared each course. The musicians continued to play their lyre and flute softly, not more than the briefest pause between songs.

So far, so good, Marah thought cautiously.

The meal was finished, the cakes were gone, and the guests had enjoyed their fill of wine. Everyone exclaimed over the food, although Marah was unable to take a single bite. She was too worried, her stomach jumping at the smell of food.

It seemed as though an eternity passed before it was time for Abigail's presentation. Marah's stomach was in a knot. "Please, please, please," she whispered. Let Abigail bring honor to her father

236

Jarius before this sour old man from Jerusalem. She clenched her hands in her lap, the only way she could keep from wringing them.

Jarius stood and clapped once, silencing the musicians. At a nod from her father, Abigail stood, poised and self-assured. The tall, lissome girl made her way to the center of the room, standing to face the four men at the head table.

Her embroidered gown was a pale pink linen, set off by heavy embroidery and a belt and veil of deep burgundy. Bracelets hung at her wrists and heavy earrings grazed her neck. Her dark eyes were wide and serious above her sharp cheekbones. Abigail's skin glowed like sunshine on golden desert sand. Her long black hair gleamed in the light of the lanterns. She carried herself with the comportment of a princess.

Marah caught her breath to see what she already knew: her daughter was stunning.

Both Asa and Zedekiah watched the young woman with sharp eyes. Abigail was, after all, not only a young woman of incredible beauty and the only child of a wealthy and influential man, but also a girl approaching the age of betrothal.

Marah shot a glance at Jarius. Surely there would not be a match for their daughter with some unknown Hebrew from far away Jerusalem.

Abigail waited a few moments, making sure all eyes were on her. Miriam leaned toward Marah with a soft whisper. "Where did your daughter get this flair for the dramatic?"

Marah smiled and breathed back the answer that made Miriam grin. "Her grandfather Naaman, of course."

Just as Abigail's long silence began to make Marah nervous - had she forgotten the first words? - Abigail tossed her head and held her chin high, her back as straight as an arrow.

The way she tossed her head! Such courage, such… grit, thought Marah with admiration. She had no idea that Abigail's resolute stance was a mirror image of her own.

Abigail's gaze was unwavering and direct as she looked at the four men seated before her, the most important one to her being the one she called Papa. She gave him a confident smile and began to speak.

"Give thanks to the Lord, for he is good; his love endures forever." She paused.

"Let the redeemed of the Lord say this, those he redeemed

from the hand of the foe, those he gathered from the lands, from east and west, from north and south." Abigail swept her arms into the air, as though to emphasize the vast distance Jehovah had traveled to gather those he had redeemed.

"Some wandered in desert wastelands. They found no city to dwell in. They were hungry and thirsty," Abigail's voice dropped to a mere whisper, "…and their lives ebbed away."

She continued in a louder voice, as if to emphasize the anguish of the Israelites. "Then they cried out to the Lord in their trouble, and he delivered them from their distress. He led them by a straight way to a city where they could settle."

Abigail pressed both hands to her heart. "Let them give thanks to the Lord for his unfailing love and his wonderful deeds for men!"

She went on, for many woes befell the Chosen People. The Israelites sat in the deepest gloom, suffered as prisoners in iron chains, were subjected to bitter labor. Some became fools because of their rebellious ways, suffering afflictions caused by their sin, drawing near to the gates of death. Others went out in ships on the sea, where the Lord spoke and stirred up a tempest, waves lifting high to the heavens and down again to the deepest depths, peril the fate of those on the sea. The anguish in her voice made it clear that these wretched souls were her people, the ancestors of Abigail.

"Then they cried to the Lord in their trouble." Abigail uttered these somber words again and again, each time sounding as though she herself were beseeching Almighty God.

But in the answering refrain, her exultation was unmistakable, each chorus joyous, wonder in her expressive voice. "And he saved them from their distress! Let them give thanks to the Lord for his unfailing love and his wonderful deeds for men!"

She told how the Lord undid the people's chains and broke down the gates of bronze. She spoke of God healing his people and rescuing them from the grave. He stilled the storm to a whisper and guided his people to a safe haven. As Abigail spoke, the dry words came alive for Marah, a living, fluid story. She was entranced and bewildered.

In the stillness of the room, Marah heard God's voice in the words she'd heard her daughter recite countless times.

"He turned rivers into a desert, flowing springs into thirsty ground, and fruitful land into a salt waste, because of the wickedness of those who lived there." Marah shivered at God's wrath for wickedness.

*"Has God ever punished you for your wickedness, Marah?"* Marah's heart fell. She had hoped to be free this evening, at least while her daughter spoke. But Abigail's words strengthened her. "His love endures forever." She turned her back on the whisper. It would not judge her with the words of my daughter.

Her heart was pierced by her daughter's passionate testimony to God. Had she not heard these words a hundred times before? And yet, Marah never before understood them.

"He who pours contempt on nobles made them wander in a trackless waste." The judgment was made harsher by the severity of Abigail's tone.

*"If God pours contempt on the nobles, he will certainly poor contempt you. You, pretending to be noble in your fine house, seated at your fine table in your fine gown. You can dress like a noble, Marah, but God isn't fooled. He will make you wander in a trackless waste, just as Abigail says."*

Marah closed her eyes, suddenly drained. The whisper that never left her would not even allow her to glory in her daughter's accomplishments, much less to ever celebrate her own insignificant, trivial triumphs.

Marah lost the thread of Abigail's recitation, unable to listen to both voices at once. She opened her eyes to see Abigail gazing at her, the silence a dramatic pause giving weight to her final words: "Whoever is wise, let him heed these things. And let him consider the great love… of my Lord."

With a last look at her mother, Abigail turned to the head table. She sank to her knees before her father and his honored guests. Her back was straight, her head bowed in respect, her eyes closed. She sat unmoving, quiet and waiting. The room was mesmerized, spellbound by Abigail, "The great love of my Lord," a soft echo in the room.

Marah felt a sob in her throat. "Oh, Abigail," she whispered. God made her daughter perfect in every way. She couldn't understand how this perfect young woman came to be her daughter. Abigail didn't deserve to have a mother like Marah. She deserved a mother that God spoke to, listened to… loved. A mother who heeded God. Not like unwise Marah. The little she had known, she certainly had not heeded

*"You certainly didn't, sinful Marah, mother of perfect Abigail."*

No one spoke or even moved, all eyes riveted on the beautiful young woman kneeling on the floor.

Loud clapping shattered the silence, the sound ringing in the room.

Augustus was standing, his face covered with a broad smile, nodding with satisfaction at the girl he loved. After a moment, Zedekiah and Asa stood to also applaud, albeit in an unsure manner, as though clapping were an unfamiliar, alien ritual. The other guests jumped up and followed suit. Marah stood, but did not clap for her own daughter. She was too moved to do anything but gaze at this girl she loved so much.

"Brilliant, beautiful Abigail, incredible! Wonderful!" The first to speak, Augustus was unabashedly glowing with his praise.

Only then did Abigail lose her composure, covering her cheeks with her hands in embarrassment. She stood to make a quick, embarrassed bow to her father, and then raced back to her seat by her mother. She had won over everyone in the room, but no one more so than Jarius and Marah.

"Abigail," Jarius said, "Come. Stand before me." Suddenly shy, Abigail went to stand once again before her father as the guests took their seats.

"My enchanting daughter." Jarius shook his head in astonishment. "You honor me when you speak the words of our forefathers, and speak them with such love and passion. Not even King David could surpass your rendition this evening." Jarius's words were met with a murmur of agreement.

"Every single word of one of King David's longest psalms. Amazing, Abigail! Simply amazing!" Augustus clapped his hands a few more times for emphasis.

Zedekiah looked surprised that a Roman centurion even knew what a psalm was.

Jarius smiled and held up a hand to silence his friend. "Although God has not given me a son, no child could be more favored or beloved than you, my beautiful daughter. You are truly God's gift to your mother and me. And tonight, I have a special gift for you."

Jarius pulled out a wooden box from under his couch. He handed it to Abigail.

"Thank you, Papa." Abigail's voice wavered, the confident young woman of a few moments ago gone. She was uncertain what to do with a gift from her father in front of these strangers. She stood looking down at the box.

"Open it, look what is inside." Jarius was anxious to see his daughter's reaction. Abigail looked at her mother. Marah nodded her encouragement even as she wondered what special gift her husband might have found.

Abigail opened it and slowly lifted out an intricate gold chain as heavy as Marah's little finger. At the end of the chain dangled a beautiful medallion, shaped like a flower and set with a large center stone that sparkled red.

A ruby, thought Marah. The sight of the stone and her years of experience in the market at once marked the exceptional value of the necklace.

Expensive stones in all the different shades of red were set around it, row after row. Small diamonds glittered.

Pearls, too, thought Marah. Where did Jarius find this?

The medallion was large, almost three inches across. It looked old and precious.

It was the most beautiful thing she had ever seen.

There was a collective intake of breath. Even with the all costly things Jarius gave to Marah during their marriage, even with all the dinners she'd attended where the women trotted out their finest jewelry, Marah had never seen anything like it.

Abigail was speechless.

"Put it on, Abigail." She clasped the necklace behind her heavy hair under the veil. It was even more stunning hanging around her neck, the pale pink linen of her gown setting off the red rubies, translucent pearls and sparkling diamonds to perfection.

Abigail picked up the medallion on its long chain. "Oh," she said, more of a sigh than a statement.

Jarius smiled at the sight of his daughter. "It is beautiful, isn't it, Abigail? And with a lovely story, too." All eyes turned to Jarius. He looked happy at Abigail's quiet wonder. He had not been happy about much these last months, Marah thought.

"This medallion was once worn by a family of Jewish women at their weddings, given by each generation of the oldest son to his new wife, handed down year after year from father to son. Now, it will be worn by you too, when the day comes for you to take a husband. But not anytime soon," Jarius said with a laugh, looking around the room. The others laughed with him. Not Marah, however. Not a husband for Abigail, not yet!

"Someday, my beautiful daughter, you shall take a groom, and your mother and I will do all we can to make sure you are happy. This bridal medallion will be part of your dowry when the time comes – as it surely will – for you to marry. Someday."

Marah saw tears in Jarius's eyes. Just the thought of his daughter leaving touched his heart.

He smiled, self-conscious about his emotion before these stoic men. "But I repeat, not any time soon." Polite laughter masked the obvious: Abigail was certainly of an age for betrothal.

Not yet, Marah thought. Not yet.

"Well done, Jarius! What a magnificent piece," said Augustus. "Your daughter is so lovely she doesn't need any jewels. But surely no one can wear them with more grace or beauty than beautiful Abigail."

Abigail turned pink. She tried not to grin at him. She clamped her lips together, but her dimples gave her away. She made a deep curtsey to Augustus and then to the other honored guest, who sat there silent and, Marah thought, disapproving.

Her daughter stood before her father, unsure of what to do next. At the sight of ever-confident Abigail's uncertainty, at the memory of what her daughter just did before a man who could only bring ill will to Jarius, Marah found a sudden surge of courage.

She stood and walked out to the center of the room to take her daughter's hand. Her knees shook as she stood before the surprised assembly, her husband the most astonished of all. The squeeze of Abigail's hand reassured her.

Marah cleared her throat. "My husband, you honor me by honoring our daughter." Her voice quavered; as she never imagined she might speak, she had no words prepared. But who could prepare for a night like this?

She cleared her throat again. "You are the best of fathers and the kindest and most honorable of men. You always honor God in all you do. May God bless you, and honor you, as I honor you…" She lost count of how many times she used the word honor, but knew it was a lot, "… and, um, may his peace be with you… all your days. Thank you, Master Jarius."

It was all she could think of to say. Unlike Abigail, her words were stilted and nervous. But she was touched at Jarius's public generosity to their only child and wanted everyone in that room to

242

know what a truly wonderful man he was.

Marah bent to whisper in Abigail's ear. "Go to your father."

Abigail ran around the table and did what her manners kept her from doing only a moment ago. She threw her arms around her father's neck. "Thank you, Papa, thank you!"

She looked so happy, relieved even. Perhaps her confident daughter was the tiniest bit nervous, too. "Papa, may I take my leave?"

"Yes, Abigail, it is time for you to retire, beloved girl."

As if from nowhere, Deena stood at the door. Marah knew she was listening in the reception hall, ready to whisk Abigail away the moment her father commanded it, to steal away with her and exclaim about her wonderful performance and beautiful necklace for the rest of the evening. Marah wished Deena could whisk her away, too.

Abigail bowed formally one last time to the important group, walked to the door and took Deena's arm. "Good night, Papa! Good night, Mother!"

Everyone smiled at the cheerful farewell of the beautiful girl. Marah thought her heart would explode with pride and love. "Oh, Abigail," she murmured.

Even the face of sour Zedekiah wore a twisted grimace of yellowed teeth.

"Is that a smile?" Miriam whispered. "Who would have thought that old codger could even pull his frozen lips apart?"

Marah's lips twitched but she didn't smile. She looked at Zedekiah with a raised eyebrow. It probably was the first time he smiled since he first found his mother's breast two hundred years ago, she thought. She tried to hide a surreptitious giggle.

She turned from Miriam and was startled to see Abigail still at the door. Their eyes met for a long moment, and then Abigail gave her an exaggerated wink.

"We did it, didn't we, Mother?"

A ripple of laughter rounded the room. Abigail grinned, and with a wobbly curtsey to the assembly of important dignitaries, she skipped from the room with an airy wave to her father and mother.

# CHAPTER 23

"Wherever did you get such a beautiful necklace, Jarius?" asked Asa. Everyone turned to hear the answer.

"I bought it this week from a man, a visitor to the synagogue. It is a beautiful necklace with a wonderful history and a tragic ending. Serving as the synagogue ruler, I hear things that grieve me, make me sad for the things in our world caused by sin."

"What's the story?"

"One of the locals sent a message to me, asking I meet a Jewish man outside the synagogue. When I walked out, there stood a stranger, distraught and agitated. He needed to sell this medallion, for he spent all he possessed on doctors for his dying wife. He needed money to complete his journey. He was a sad man, a man whose wife was sick and unclean for twelve years."

"Twelve years?" said Zedekiah. "She died, then?" At the mention of synagogue business, he was all ears.

"No," replied Jarius. "But, according to her husband, she will soon. She was deathly ill, he said."

"What is wrong with her?"

"I am not sure, but it sounded like a tragic thing. She has a bleeding disorder of some sort, a bloody discharge for twelve years. Ever since they were first married."

"Twelve years!" exclaimed Miriam. "And these many doctors, they could not help her?"

"The husband said no, though they tried everything. They used to live in Caesarea Philippi, but moved years ago to Caesarea on the Sea, where they could seek better physicians. Now, the husband is intent on returning his wife to Caesarea Philippi to live out her last days, to die there, he said. The wife wished to go to her mother for her last days. The man must return to Caesarea on the Sea where he works as a trader. He said he had many, many financial obligations there. I also finalized a divorce for the man, since he now had money to pay the fees." He shook his head. "Heartbreaking. A tragic story."

Oh, to be ill for twelve years, thought Marah. And with a bleeding disease, unclean and untouchable under Jewish law for so many years. Such a curse on that poor woman. Thank goodness she didn't have to face such a terrible fate.

*"Yes, for if anyone deserves a terrible fate, it's you, isn't it Marah?"*
She forced herself back to the conversation in the room.

"How can the poor woman manage the trip to Caesarea Philippi if she is so ill?" asked Miriam.

"I do not know how she will manage the trip, I did not ask." Marah alone sensed a bit of irritation in the polite tone of her husband. "While it may not make sense to us, the husband was unwavering in one thing, Miriam. His wife begged to be taken to her childhood home, at any cost and by any means, so that she might be with her mother when she died."

At that, the group nodded their understanding of the stranger's reasons. Of course, the woman would want to die with her mother holding her hand.

"So, if she is about to die, why did the man divorce her, Jarius?"

Marah turned to glare at Miriam. Why was her sister questioning Jarius? Marah gave serious thought about kicking Miriam under the table. She knew that Miriam was only doing what she did best, making conversation.

But talk about something else, Miriam!

"The man was very upset to have to divorce his dying wife, Miriam. But there are two reasons he would seek a divorce now. First, if he divorces her, the dowry is indisputably hers. If they remain married and she dies, it is his. That is the law. It is easier this way, it ensures what little she has remains hers legally. And who knows what family assets she may still have in Caesarea Philippi? He divorced her so her dowry would stay with her in her final days. And, when she

245

dies, what's left will go to her family, not his. It is in the best interest of his wife."

The men nodded in approval. Women, of course, could not be expected to know the law. Marah's eye twitched; how easy it was for a man to divorce his wife.

*"Jarius could easily get rid of you yet, Marah."*

"There was a second reason for the divorce, one quite urgent. The man hired many doctors for twelve years to attend to his wife, for all the years they were married. He will take the woman to her mother, say his last goodbye to his wife, and then return to Caesarea on the Sea to try to repay his many debts. He said he has difficult financial obligations. He divorced her so in his absence, all decisions will belong to his wife and to her family. He seemed to be a good man in terrible circumstances trying to do the best thing."

"It would be difficult to say goodbye to someone you loved knowing you would never see them again," Augustus said.

*He is so far away from those he loved as a boy,* Marah thought.

"Yes." Jarius nodded his agreement. There was a moment of collective silence in the room over the tragedy of the dying woman.

"Anyway, the man had one thing left to sell - the medallion. The medallion had been in his family for many generations, but his parents are dead and he is an only child. He has no heir to wear the medallion at their own wedding, for his wife could never give him any children. The woman he loves is dying, and he said he could never remarry.

"He acted as though his heart was broken, telling me how beautiful she was twelve years ago as a bride wearing this beautiful heirloom. I asked if he was certain he wanted to sell it, but the man said the medallion only reminded him that the Lord did not see fit to give him any of what he hoped for in his life."

Jarius shook his head. "The poor man needed money to repay the debts he incurred trying to keep his wife alive, and to continue their travels, so he might honor his dying wife's wish… to be with her mother."

Marah thought of her own mother.

Augustus could see this story was getting the best of Jarius and stepped in to help. "You did a good thing, Jarius. You are a ruler with a heart for your people. Now… did you pay a king's ransom for this incredible piece, or make the shrewdest deal like our clever

246

Marah in the marketplace?" He smiled at Marah, so all would know he meant this only in the kindest way.

He is always good to Jarius, Marah thought. And to her.

Jarius laughed. "I paid what was probably a king's ransom, Augustus, more than he would have gotten in Jerusalem or even great Caesarea on the Sea." Zedekiah's eyes glittered, as though he wished he'd had the opportunity to purchase the medallion. He would not have been as fair to the man as Jarius, she thought.

"It is indeed a fine piece, Augustus, and probably worth more than the great amount I paid for it. But I wanted it for Abigail, and the stranger was satisfied with the price I offered, saying it was plenty to pay for his wife's travel, her future care, and of course, for the divorce he was seeking."

"I'm sure he hated to part with it, Jarius." Miriam was still employing her greatest skill, making conversation.

"I don't think he cared about the medallion any more, Miriam. All in all, it was a heartbreaking day for the man."

Marah's heart was touched at her husband's endless compassion for all people, those he knew and those he did not.

"There is of course a third reason for you to grant a divorce to the man, Jarius. The most obvious and important reason." For some reason, Zedekiah stood. He had spoken little during the dinner, allowing people instead to cater their words to him. His contemptuous voice took center stage.

Jarius's smile was deferential, but Marah sensed his immediate nerves at Zedekiah's statement. "Of course, Zedekiah. What reason did I overlook?"

Marah wanted to shout, "He didn't overlook anything, you jackal!" But her face was as still as marble, her eyes unblinking.

The man exhaled loudly and looked around the room. "A woman who bleeds is unclean in the eyes of our Most Holy Lord, unclean according to the sacred laws of Moses." He looked as though just speaking of a woman who bled was as vile as walking by a dead jackal rotted by the road.

"Thus, this man, this stranger, has most likely been unclean before the Lord for years." Zedekiah gazed at his audience. Marah shuddered. She wanted to hide from his malevolent stare.

"No faithful Jewish man should be forced to remain separate from God due to the sin of his wife. You say he is an honorable man, Jarius, and you probably meant well. But he should have divorced his unclean, bleeding wife years ago. A true follower of God understands and obeys the laws of Moses. The woman was unclean and sinful. His need to divorce the woman is incontestable.

"Now, he can make the sacrifices to atone for his sin, be forgiven by the priests and be fully accepted back into the good grace of the Jewish faith. The man was sinful to live in such a state for so long. He has sinned in ways we cannot know in this room. For why else would God punish this man with a sinful, bleeding wife?

"But his greatest sin was that he did not divorce his unholy wife years ago."

At this, Zedekiah sat back down.

*"God punished the man because he did not divorce his sinful, unholy wife years ago. Surely God will punish Jarius, too."*

A smile was pasted on Jarius's face. His burning eyes told Marah he was seething inside.

How dare Zedekiah pronounce judgment on a woman he never met, Marah thought. How dare this arrogant, self-important ass correct her husband in this public setting, criticize Jarius who was always good and kind, so loved by his people? After all, Zedekiah is only the brother-in-law of the High Priest. But for his own wife, he would be nothing! How dare he! Marah was outraged.

"You are right, of course, Zedekiah. We must honor the laws of Moses." Marah could not believe that calm, pacifying voice was her husband's.

The short, barking laugh belonged to Augustus. He leaned forward to address Zedekiah. "You refer, of course, to our strict laws about being ceremonially clean, is that right, Zedekiah?" No matter what Jarius wanted, Augustus would not allow Zedekiah's comment to pass without response.

Augustus continued in a quiet, reasonable tone. "According to the law, forgiveness cannot be given to the unclean until they have ceremonially cleansed themselves before God, correct? And forgiveness can only come to the unclean through the holy sacrifices offered by the priests on their behalf, yes?"

Zedekiah's nod was wooden. He was appalled that this Roman would so freely question him and even more that he so clearly understood Jewish Law. "That is correct. Forgiveness of the unclean, forgiveness of all sin comes through sacrifices offered by the priests."

"Yes, that's right, Zedekiah. I know this well. As a Gentile, I am very familiar with 'clean and unclean.' Although I have often wondered about forgiveness procured only through the blood of a perfect animal, that perfect animal, of course, only being perfect if it is purchased from the priests themselves! Seems strange, does it not? But it does buy forgiveness from the priests, who, interestingly, are flawed and sinful men themselves. We poor sinners cannot seek forgiveness from Jehovah directly. It seems the sacrifice of a broken heart and a spirit of repentance is not nearly as powerful as the sacrifice of a perfect animal available only by purchase from a priest."

There was nothing untrue in Augustus's statement. Yet the anger was visible on Zedekiah's reddening face. "The laws of Moses clearly state that the sacrifices are required." His voice was rough.

Jarius opened his mouth, but Augustus cut him off before he could speak. "I see. But Zedekiah, I am confused. Didn't King David say, 'O Lord, you do not delight in sacrifice, or I would bring it? You do not take pleasure in burnt offerings, Lord.' King David claimed that 'the sacrifices of God are a broken spirit, a broken and contrite heart.' " His laugh was congenial. "I'm sure Moses is turning over in his grave at those words from the greatest king Israel has ever known."

Zedekiah stared at Augustus. "How dare you, a Gentile, challenge the laws God gave to the Israelites, to his Chosen people?" He practically spit out the words "chosen people."

"Oh, you misunderstand me, Zedekiah. I do not challenge the law. I only seek to gain perspective from a wise and learned man such as you." His tone was civil, as though they discussed the weather.

Jarius cut off the vicious words of Zedekiah that were sitting on his curled lips, harsh words that would cause nothing but grave harm. "Gentlemen, you are both correct, of course. I cannot judge this man or this woman. I cannot say whether the man should have divorced her years ago or only this week, whether they are clean or unclean, whether he should stay with her until she dies or leave her with her mother to face death without him."

In the practiced and skillful manner that served him so well as synagogue ruler, Jarius was reclaiming control of the conversation and the room.

"I only met the man a few days ago and I have never met his wife. Their lives are heartbreaking for so many reasons, her illness, their many debts, her desire to see her mother, their inability to

249

worship as our laws state." He looked around the room. "On that we must all agree."

The elders nodded their heads in accord for Jarius.

"After I heard his terrible story, Augustus, the first thing I did was offer to just give him the money for his trip and for his wife's care, so that he would not have to sell something that, to me, seems so precious. But he refused my charity. He refused the charity of the synagogue. So, I did what I thought would best help him. I honored his wishes. I paid him generously for the medallion and I granted him the divorce. And, Augustus, I did this standing out in the street. For of his own volition, the man told me he would not even come near the doors of the synagogue, for he was unclean. The man said himself that he was unclean and unworthy before our God."

Jarius smiled at each man in the room, trying to pacify both his beloved friend and this offensive man disguised as a religious dignitary. Augustus nodded, at once regretful about the precarious situation he created for his friend Jarius by his amused toying with Zedekiah.

Jarius continued in a confident voice. "We all agree the purpose of the law is to benefit the people. That is why God gave the law to Moses, to govern us, to guide us, to teach us his holy ways. As sinful men, we do not always understand God's omnipotent will. But as God's follower, I only try, as a flawed and humble sinner myself, to abide by and uphold the laws."

"You are an astute and wise ruler, Jarius." Augustus voice was respectful. He and Jarius might argue long into the night in Jarius's upper room, reading the word, discussing each point for hours. But Augustus would never argue with his friend in public; he would be a pillar of staunch support in front of the odious Zedekiah.

At this, Zedekiah stood and held up his hands. The room fell silent. "Jarius, your actions are commendable. As the Centurion says, you have served as a fine ruler for these many years, following in the footsteps of your honored father, enforcing the laws of Moses handed down by Jehovah God for the benefit of his Chosen People, the Jews."

He turned to Augustus. "Without any sacrifice, we forgive you, Master Augustus." Jarius stared at the man, stunned. "Your inquiry is to be expected from one raised by pagans in an idolatrous home. It is difficult for someone like you to truly… appreciate the laws of the Chosen People."

There was a shocked hush at those insulting words.

Soldier that he was, Augustus betrayed no emotion to the Jewish man parading as a dignitary.

Jarius started to stand, but Zedekiah held up his hand. He had tired of this conversation and these people. The law was the law. Zedekiah wished to end this dinner with this Roman as soon as possible. "Like Jarius, I too have a special gift to present this evening. For you, Master Augustus."

Marah felt his comments were both offensive and ostentatious, coming on the heels of his cruel disrespect to the godly and righteous Augustus.

Augustus rose to his feet, his soldier's stalwart posture a stark contrast to the small, slump-shouldered man in his rich robes.

"I come bearing a gift of gratitude from the High Priest of the Jewish people, the High Priest of our Holy Temple in Jerusalem," Zedekiah continued in his reedy, grating voice. "We understand from our friend Jarius how you have helped the Jewish people of Capernaum. Without your financial support, the new synagogue would not exist. Without your aid, it would have been many years before the synagogue would have been complete."

He held out a large wooden box. "I speak for my brother-in-law the High Priest when I thank you. I offer you this token of our gratitude."

Marah knew what was in it, for Jarius purchased it himself. Asa told Jarius when he was in Jerusalem that Zedekiah would arrive bearing a gift, a gift of gold and silver from the Temple treasury.

Jarius confided this to Marah over breakfast. "Augustus is a wealthy man, far wealthier than you and I. To offer gold and silver to a man who already has both! Why don't they just give him bags of copper coins, instead?" He shook his head at their crass, mindless gift. His friend Augustus could not be bought.

So while in Jerusalem, Jarius took the gold and silver, added his own money to theirs and purchased this gift for his friend.

Augustus opened the box and lifted out the long scrolls of parchments with their intricately engraved silver caps. "It is our Law, all of our Law," Jarius said. "That you may continue to pursue the righteous ways of Jehovah."

Augustus held the scrolls in his hands. A muscle in his cheek twitched. Marah knew that Augustus saw the hand of Jarius behind this costly and meaningful gift.

"You are like King Solomon, my friend, who asked God only for wisdom and knowledge, not for wealth or riches, not for honor or a long life. Therefore, just as God gave these gifts to Solomon, may God give wisdom and knowledge to you, his faithful follower." Jarius's voice was quiet. "Thank you, my friend, for all you have done for me and for my people here in Capernaum. In all you do, you honor Almighty God."

Zedekiah frowned, looking at the two men in suspicion. He cleared his throat, intent that the last word to this heathen Roman would come from him. "Yes, Master Augustus, on behalf of the High Priest of the Temple, we thank you." His smile at Augustus was nothing more than a sneer. "You have shown yourself to be a man of honorable ways, attempting to follow the Laws of the One True God, unlike the ruthless, unwanted Romans in Jerusalem and the savage Gentiles of Rome."

The only sound in the room was a roar of silence, inaudible gasps as each guest took in the atrocity of Zedekiah's scathing words to Augustus, smugly disguised as a tribute of thanks.

With an arrogant sneer on his face, Zedekiah's nod was triumphant as he sat down, satisfied with his final words.

Jarius looked as though he had been struck by lightning, so great was his rage that Augustus, his friend and his brother, suffered such vicious insult in his home.

Augustus stood unmoving for what seemed like an eternity to Marah. When he spoke at last, his voice was that of a gentleman. "I am honored with this gift, Zedekiah. But, as my friend Jarius knows, your God has already rewarded me. This generous gift is appreciated. But I am even more thankful for the greater gift given to me through our mutual faith in Yahweh, Jehovah God."

There were soft murmurs of assent from the elders, surprised and thankful at Augustus's conciliatory tone in response to Zedekiah's appalling insolence. What was this imbecile from Jerusalem thinking?

But Marah saw her husband; he stood frozen, staring at his friend, willing Augustus not to speak. Jarius knew what the greater gift was.

Augustus shook his head sadly in response to his friend's unspoken plea. He would not be silent in the face of such evil. He was, after all, a soldier, a man unafraid of the enemy or battle.

He turned to Zedekiah. "Yes, God has already rewarded me

with a far greater gift than anything you or all of Jerusalem could give me." Zedekiah looked at the Roman quizzically.

"And what is that greater gift, Master Zedekiah? Why, it is the gift of life itself. Life, given to my beloved servant Quintius as he lay dying. Life, given to him by the Son of Man himself. The Jewish teacher. The Galilean." Augustus's voice grew louder, each syllable clipped and distinct. "Yes, I received the gift of life from the man called Jesus… Christ…."

If Marah had jumped up and stripped naked before them, there could not have been a more flabbergasted hush in the room. The elders sat with their mouths agape, pillars of salt as the fire rained down. Zedekiah was turning purple. Perhaps he will just have a stroke and die right here in my dining hall, Marah thought desperately.

Augustus smiled at the vile man before him. "Honored Zedekiah, please send my most heartfelt gratitude to your ruling council and to… your wife's brother…" No one missed the ridicule in Augustus's voice. "My appreciation to the High Priest, Caiaphas. Your travel of such a great distance, all the way to Capernaum to meet with me, is in itself a great honor."

The biting sarcasm was clear. If they wanted to honor Augustus for his gift, they would have done so when the synagogue was completed.

"Zedekiah, without your God, who happens to also be my God, without the man from Galilee, whom you choose to persecute but I choose to follow, without Jesus Christ… my servant Quintius would surely be dead."

Zedekiah wanted to speak, but there was no interrupting this man, a soldier and centurion who commanded armies and defeated enemies.

"Anything I have done for this synagogue was repaid to me a thousand times, when Jesus healed this man I have loved since I was a young man." Augustus sounded as though he was speaking to hundreds of soldiers armed for a certain conquest. "What little debt owed me by you was paid a thousand times over… when Jesus saved Quintius from his certain death."

Zedekiah was making a gurgling sound. Augustus smiled, in control of the conflict, exultant and confident in the certain outcome. "And Jesus, the Son of Man and Son of God, healed Quintius without seeing him or touching him. He healed from afar, without speaking a word to him."

Augustus drew closer, certain of his opponent's impending demise. "Jesus Christ healed him because of *my* faith in Jehovah. My faith, Zedekiah, the faith of an unworthy, unclean *Gentile.*"

He made the final assault, his victory assured. "And Zedekiah, know this. 'I have not found such great faith, even in Israel.' That, Zedekiah, is what Jesus Christ said about my faith. That is what Jesus said about me… He had found no greater faith in Israel than mine."

The battle was over.

Zedekiah's mouth was opening and closing like a fish, eyes bulging in his purple face, a wounded man gasping for air on the front line of war.

The cheerful voice was jarring and loud. "Augustus!" Jarius strode over to his friend. "We are grateful that your servant was healed, for I know he is like a father to you. Our own servants Cook and Deena have been with us many years and are like our family, aren't they, Marah?" He looked at her and grinned, a weird caricature of a smile.

Startled at the sound of her name, Marah jumped to her feet. "Yes!" she blurted out. "They are!"

Jarius voice was smooth and allowed no interruption as he took over this dangerous conversation. "Augustus, it is an honor to have you worship with us at the synagogue you built." He looked to the council members sitting there, stunned. "We cannot say enough about the many good things you have done for the Jews of Capernaum. Can we, my friends?"

Nathaniel and the two elders came to life at once. All three stood as one and began speaking at the same time. They did not want Augustus to say another word either.

For after all, they were the elders who went to find Jesus. In the absence of Jarius, they spoke to the Galilean on behalf of the centurion. They were standing right there when Jesus exclaimed over the great faith of the Roman, greater than any he had found in all of Israel. No, there would be no further conversations about Jesus and Quintius.

As the elders began talking, Asa also stood and joined in. The explosive moment was lost in a babble of voices, all vying to divert the attention of Zedekiah elsewhere.

Only Marah stood close enough to hear Jarius and Augustus.

"The time is not now, my friend." Jarius had pulled Augustus to the center of the room, away from Zedekiah, his arm around his friend's shoulder. "Please. For our friendship. Forgive me for asking you. But please, the time is not now."

Augustus looked away, the set of his jaw visible to Marah. His voice was intense. "You know what Jesus said. 'A time has now come, when the true worshipers will worship the Father in spirit and truth.' The true worshipers, Jarius! You know this Jesus speaks the truth, you know it! I say this to you in his truth! He is a man of authority, the authority of Jehovah God. I cannot deny the Son of Man."

"I understand what I ask of you!" Marah heard the pleading in Jarius's voice. "But please, Augustus, not now, not with Zedekiah in my home here with my family. Please."

Augustus looked at him. "Jesus is speaking tomorrow at the Sea. Bring Zedekiah to hear Jesus. If he hears Jesus, he will know."

"I am taking Zedekiah to meet him." Jarius spoke as though the thought pained him. "But Zedekiah will not listen. He will not hear or understand."

The other men were still talking loudly to Zedekiah. Miriam stood with the silent prune that was Zedekiah's wife, listening to a shrill conversation between the three elders' wives talking together. All spoke of everything but Jesus. The cavernous room echoed with the commotion.

Augustus took Jarius's arm and pulled it off his shoulder, his words passionate. "This is what Jesus said, that he had never seen a faith like mine. Jesus said that about me, Jarius, me." His voice broke. Marah was shocked to see tears in his eyes. "I cannot deny the man from Galilee."

He shook his head. "But neither can I deny you. I will never do anything to harm you, my friend and my brother, or hurt the family I love as my own."

Zedekiah was watching the two men, but could hear nothing but the babble of Asa and the three elders.

"Most gracious Zedekiah," Augustus's voice boomed across the room, silencing everyone, a vivid demonstration that hundreds of men obeyed his commands. "With great regret, I must take my leave. Please express my gratitude to the High Priest for this generous and holy gift. Asa, I am pleased to see you once again; you have come so many miles to visit my beautiful city. Jarius and Marah, you have entertained us tonight as though we were kings. It has been an exceedingly interesting evening, but I must return to my command."

He came to Marah, still standing alone in the middle of the room, and took her hand, bowing low over it. She flushed a deep red that he would recognize her first, before these important men. Then, one by one, Augustus bowed first to the council members, then to Asa, and last to Zedekiah. Zedekiah nodded in return, his face ugly with hatred.

Augustus turned to Jarius and gripped his hand. "The time is now, my friend. The time is now." A joyous look crossed his face. He laughed, and releasing Jarius's hand, strode towards the door.

But before he could leave, a small, graying figure blocked his way.

"Mistress Marah, Master Jarius, come, come right now!" There was no mistaking the frightened urgency in Deena's voice.

"Abigail is ill!"

# CHAPTER 24

Marah rinsed out the cloth in the cool water and smoothed back
Abigail's damp hair. She laid the cloth on her daughter's forehead.

"I am so cold, Mother." Abigail was shaking, her body
covered in goose bumps. The cold her daughter felt was from
somewhere deep within, for the outside of her body was burning hot
to the touch.

Why had she worried so about something as foolish as
musicians or a perfect stew or where her guests would sit? If she had
known how sick her beloved daughter would be that same night, she
would have let those people sit in the street and beg. Why had she
worried about something as insignificant as that terrible dinner, when
that same night her daughter would fall so desperately ill?

When Marah first arrived in the room with Deena, she was
shocked at how swiftly Abigail went from a laughing, curtseying
young woman at an elegant dinner to the thin, pitiful girl curled up in
her bed. Deena showed her the night jar with a sober look on her
face. Abigail vomited up all of her dinner and the dates from that
afternoon, even her lunch and breakfast.

Her beautiful face was flushed, mottled red spots that stood
out in stark contract to her clammy skin.

Marah sat beside her, holding her head, trying to help Abigail
as she vomited again and again and again, now producing only a
dribble of water. Or worse, nothing at all. The spasms racked her

entire body, but there was nothing left inside her thin frame to throw up. After each bout of gut-wrenching, shuddering spasms, Marah would pull Abigail close, stroking her hair, trying to calm the sobs.

Each time the wracking heaves would subside, Marah's heart would constrict at the small tearful voice.

"I'm sorry I ruined your dinner, Mother."

Nothing Marah said could convince her fevered daughter that she did not care one whit about that dreadful, horrible dinner. If only she had not scolded Abigail about her recitation. If only she had not been so hard on her, making her repeat it over and over and over. If only Abigail knew how wonderful she had been. If only.

Now, Abigail did not cry because she was sick. No, Marah's daughter cried for fear that she ruined her mother's atrocious, vile, awful… stupid dinner! If only she knew that her mother did not care about that stupid, stupid dinner! Marah cared only for Abigail, only for her beautiful, precious daughter. If only Abigail knew.

*"You made sure Abigail knew what was really important, didn't you Marah?"*

If only, if only, if only.

Chill bumps covered Abigail's skin, and despite the fever, she moaned about the cold. Marah tried rubbing her hands and feet, piling more blankets on the bed and holding her in a tight hug, but nothing she did would melt the icy cold raging inside the girl.

"Water, Mother, water. So thirsty." Marah held the cup to Abigail's lips. She drank greedily, as though dying of a great thirst. But after a few moments, the terrible heaving would come upon her again. She would throw up every drop of water. Then she would cry out, begging Marah for water, more water, only to repeat the cycle over and over again.

And the heat from her body! Marah saw the fear in Deena's face and the shock of her sister Miriam. Marah was frightened. With her army of nieces and nephews, she had seen many, many childhood fevers. But never had Marah felt anyone so hot. Never had she seen anyone struck down so quickly by a fever.

Abigail's back was on fire, her cheeks flaming, her forehead blistering. Yet she shivered and begged for more blankets, crying loudly when Marah tried to cool her daughter's hot, hot body with the cool cloths, great sobs begging for mercy from her Papa, her Mother, her God.

"Please, Jehovah, please…" Abigail's voice was a frightened

whisper.

They pulled her bed away from the wall, Marah scurrying about on one side, Jarius seated in terrified dread on the other. Between the bouts of vomiting, he clutched her hand. Uncertainty lined his face, his panic betrayed by wild eyes and shaking hands.

"Papa." At the sound of his name, Jarius's eyes would fill with tears.

"What should we do, Marah? What should we do?"

*"Yes, Marah, you are the mother. What should a sinful mother and holy man like Jarius do?"*

Deena and Miriam scurried in and out with water and clean bowls and fresh cloths and more blankets.

Asa and Augustus sat outside the door in the courtyard, waiting and praying.

Cook did not sleep, sitting in the kitchen waiting to see what, please dear God what, he might prepare for sweet Abigail when she got better.

Jarius sat at the side of her bed, murmuring fervent prayers, his eyes asking Marah an unspoken question: When would Abigail get better?

Marah tended to her daughter and spoke to no one.

For as each hour of the dark night crept by, the thin fevered girl did not get better. With every sip of water, every cry of pain, every desperate glance at her mother, beloved Abigail got worse.

# CHAPTER 25

The morning dawned hot. Warmer than usual, Marah thought. Her daughter was resting in that fitful sleep of one who is very ill.

Marah and Jarius had not left Abigail's side all night. Marah, who had nursed various childhood ailments of nieces and nephews for years, tried to hide her fear from her husband. She had never seen a fever of such sudden intensity in anyone.

Jarius, whose only experience with a sick child was the death of his infant son so many years ago, was beside himself with worry.

From time to time, Abigail would jerk up to a sitting position in her bed and shout. "Mother!"

Marah would almost jump out of her skin. Abigail would lie back down, roll over and throw the blankets to the floor. Marah would scramble to tuck them around her fretful daughter.

"Papa!" Abigail would yell, bolting up in her bed. "Papa!" Jarius would leap to answer, the terror in his voice unmistakable. Abigail would lie down and pull the blankets tight around her, Jarius fumbling to tuck her in.

So soft was the soft cry, Marah almost did not hear her daughter's words. "Mother? Mother?"

"Yes?" Marah could hardly get the word out.

"My back hurts." She was crying, tears coursing down the fevered face.

"Shall I rub it for you, Abigail?"

Her nod was almost imperceptible. Marah rolled her over and began to rub her back with a gentle touch. "How is that?"

Abigail did not answer her. *Her back is as hot as a smoldering fire*, thought Marah.

Abigail's lips were chapped and cracking, both from the fever and the bouts of vomiting. Marah tried to rub ointment on them. "It stings, Mother. No, it stings." Abigail's tears began anew.

"Oh, if only this was happening to me and not you, not my sweet Abigail."

*"For I the Lord your God am a jealous God, punishing the children for the sin of the parents…"*

Marah started in terror at the familiar words, words of Moses, words of her father Naaman, words of the God of Jarius and Abigail.

*"Why would Abigail's God punish her, Marah? She is perfect. No, God is punishing you, her sinful mother…"*

"Mother?"

"I'm sorry, Mother, that I ruined your important dinner."

*"After all, that dinner was so important, wasn't it, Marah? More important than anything. Abigail ruined your perfect, perfect dinner."*

*No she did not ruin anything! Who cares about that dinner! That stupid, awful, terrible dinner!*

"Oh, Abigail," Marah tried to smile, wiping the tears from Abigail's eyes. "You did not ruin that dinner! We don't care about that anyway. All we care about is you. Everyone said how wonderful you were when you spoke. You looked so beautiful, like a princess. You alone made that dinner wonderful. I was so proud of you."

"And Papa, too?" The little voice sounded as though she might finally fall asleep.

"And me, too, Abigail. No one could have been prouder."

"Thank you, Papa, for my necklace." Her eyes closed. Jarius stared at her with eyes full of tears.

Marah looked at her daughter. Even with this raging fever, even as she suffered, Abigail only thought of her mother and her father.

*"God punishes the children for the sin of the parent… for the sin of the mother…"*

*No! That was so long ago!*

Soon the fever would break, Marah thought. A new day was beginning, this horrible night was ending, and soon the terrible illness tormenting Abigail would be over, too. It had to.

03

Jarius sat across from Marah, one hand holding the hand of
the sleeping Abigail, the other holding his bowed head, waiting.
Hunched over on his stool, Marah could not tell if he was praying or
if her weary husband finally slept, too.

"Jarius." She heard the voice outside the door, but did not
turn around. All she cared about was the thin girl twitching in a
restless sleep before her. "Sleep, Abigail, sleep!" she muttered
fiercely. Years of experience with her sisters' children taught her that
sleep was often a prelude to a break in a fever.

"Jarius!" More urgent this time. Jarius raised his head at the
sound of Asa's voice. Marah turned to look; he stood not quite in the
doorway, as though fear of the unknown illness barred him from
entering the sick bed of his niece.

"Jarius!" His voice was loud.

Jarius sighed, put down his daughter's hand and walked to
the door.

Marah could hear the voices but not the words exchanged.
She did not care. Until she heard her husband shouting. Jarius
shouting?

"I will not leave, Asa. I will not!"

"But Jarius, Zedekiah comes as the representative of the
High Priest to meet this Galilean. The man has worshipped in your
synagogue many times. You promised to introduce this imposter of a
rabbi to Zedekiah, so he could speak with him and report what he
finds to the Sadducees. The ruling party of the Holy Temple, Jarius!"

"I cannot leave Abigail or Marah, Asa."

"Jarius! If you do not accompany Zedekiah to meet this
Teacher, it will be a great insult to Zedekiah!"

"Asa, please, I cannot leave my daughter. Find Nathaniel! He
has served as elder of our synagogue for many years. He will help you
in my place. I will not leave Abigail."

"This man from Nazareth is preaching today. You need not
be gone for long, just long enough to introduce Zedekiah to Jesus.
He claims to be a Messiah and you are the synagogue ruler here
where he lives! Zedekiah must meet him and you must introduce
him. Then you may leave. That is all I ask, Jarius. Abigail will be fine,

262

these children's fevers never last long."

"No, Asa, I cannot. I will not leave Marah and Abigail!"

"Jarius, you have a responsibility! A responsibility to the Jews and to the Temple! And to me! You must come with me, I demand it!"

"Asa!" The voice was sharp. "Asa, come away at once." Marah could hear the fury in Miriam's voice.

"This is not your business, Miriam."

"Asa!" There was no mistaking Miriam's rage. "This is my sister and my niece! Abigail is sick, very sick. More the power to Jarius that he cares enough for his own daughter to sit at her bedside. Let him be!"

"Leave us, Miriam. This does not concern you."

There was silence in the room.

"'The pride of your heart has deceived you.'" Marah had never heard the tone she heard in her sister's voice now. "Is that not the law you so often teach?"

Her voice dripped with sarcasm. "'The terror you inspire and the pride of your heart have deceived you, you who occupy the heights of the hill.' Isn't that how your scripture goes, Asa?" Her laugh was grating, a bitter sound. "And, oh my husband, what do you yourself teach that the Lord promises to the proud? 'The Lord will bring them down.' I have heard you say it many times. Your pride will bring you down, Asa, from the heights of that Temple hill you so wish to climb.

"And to think what you have achieved in Jerusalem was only possible through the goodness, the patronage of this man you now berate! Jarius, who is like the brother you never had!

"Jarius has chosen the right course, to stay with his sick daughter. But you! You are concerned with the opinion of a man who does not matter, a man who only comes to serve his own purposes, a man you hope can someday help you on your supposed journey to greatness! How can you ask Jarius to place someone like Zedekiah above the needs of his daughter?"

Asa looked as his wife as though he had never seen her before in his entire life.

"I am ashamed for you, Asa. Today, and yes, many other days, too. Any compassion you might have once had has been replaced by arrogance and yes, by the pride you once railed against. You have succumbed to the sin you condemned, the sin of arrogance and pride." Miriam sounded sad at these last words. She went to stand next to her sister sitting by Abigail's side.

"Leave this room at once. You bring only ill will here. Leave, and tend to your important business, the business of the Holy Hill. Make certain," her voice was like iron, "that you speak to Zedekiah on behalf of your brother-in-law and the reason for his absence."

Asa stared at his wife. He looked cornered, as though he were left with only one disagreeable option.

Jarius's voice was soft but firm. "I will not leave Abigail. My brother, I cannot leave my wife or my daughter."

Asa looked only at Jarius, his posture and his voice stiff. "My apologies, Jarius. I did not understand. I will tell Zedekiah of your terrible circumstances. I am confident he would not want you to leave your sick child. Nor do I, of course. I will pray for Abigail. Of course."

As Asa left, he bowed his head towards Marah, but he would not meet the eyes of his beautiful, angry wife standing resolutely at her sister's side.

◖◗

Deena crept to Marah's side. "One of the doctors Jarius summoned has arrived," she murmured. Marah nodded. Finally! They certainly took their sweet time. It was easily mid-morning. Jarius sent for them at the first light of dawn.

The stranger came in and examined Abigail. She woke to his strange touch, and clutched her father's hand in fear. "It's all right, Abigail, it will be all right." The tremor in his voice did not make things sound all right at all.

What this doctor prescribed was just what Marah feared: to bleed Abigail. Whatever evil things had taken root in Abigail's body would wash away as her blood trickled out. It was a common remedy of city physicians, and worthless in Marah's unsophisticated country experience.

As synagogue ruler, Jarius could not touch his daughter while the remedy of bleeding was taking place. He could not be defiled by the unclean blood. He stood at her side in anguish, wringing his hands, reaching out to touch her and pulling his hand back again and again.

Marah never once let go of her daughter's hand, however.

She did not care about the blood and the laws of Moses. Unclean or not, she did not care. She would not let go of her daughter's hand.

*"No one cares if you are soiled and defiled, after all... Dirty, sinful, shameful Marah..."*

Marah clenched her jaw.

"I'm fine, Papa." Abigail spoke to her father in a tiny, thin voice. She gave Marah's hand a weak squeeze. "Tell Papa I will be fine."

Marah watched doctors undertake bleeding before, but not since the last weeks of life for Jarius's father. Still, to see her daughter's strong dark arm laying limp and white across the bowl, to watch her daughter's own blood drain from her in a slow, throbbing drip, was a different thing altogether. She watched with a fierce anger, never taking her eyes off her daughter's face.

Breathe, Abigail, breathe, Marah thought. She herself could not draw a breath past the bitter taste in her mouth. Her stomach was balled up in a painful knot. After an eternity, the doctor set the bowl aside and wrapped a tight bandage around Abigail's arm. He busied himself with a few other things and then carried the bowl of blood from the room to be buried. Abigail's blood. Would this help? Did the bleeding rid Abigail of the horrible scourge that was racking her body?

"Water, Mother, please. I am so thirsty."

Marah held the cup to Abigail's lips, now cracked and parched. Abigail drank greedily.

"Not so much, Abigail. Not so fast." She heard the pleading in her own voice.

Moments later, Marah held Abigail's head over the large bowl, helpless as she watched her daughter roughly vomit up the water over and over. The retching went on forever, Abigail reduced to dry, racking spasms. So much pain for so little water.

What was happening to her beautiful Abigail?

Soon, a second doctor arrived. He carried a large clay jar and a small packet. The doctor poured the packet into a cup he produced, added water from the clay jar and stirred the concoction with vigorous strokes.

"Holy water from the ancient springs of the Valley of Baka," he said, nodding to Jarius in approval. Jarius nodded, too, but he did not look convinced.

"She must drink this," he said to Jarius. Jarius nodded again, even less certain.

"She will not be able to keep it down," said Marah. A few minutes later, her sad prediction proved true.

The doctor watched as Abigail vomited again, terrible heaving interspersed with her pleas for mercy. Marah felt as though she would scream. At last, the terrible bout passed and Abigail lay as though dead on her bed. The doctor nodded with approval. "Good!" he said. "Just what she needed."

Marah wanted to slap him.

He then removed a cork stopper from the jar. The dark, rich, overpowering aroma filled the room.

Marah leapt to her feet. "What is that?"

*"You know what it is... It is costly. It is rare. You have seen it many times at the market. It is myrrh, the ointment of death..."*

"It is myrrh and rue, mixed with oil. We need to rub it all over her body, it will help her breathe, help the air get into her. To vomit is to rid the body of evil, of sickness. To breathe is to restore her spirit."

As if Abigail didn't vomit all night before you ever showed up, thought Marah angrily. There's nothing left in her at all. But she held out her hands, her jaw set to the odious task. She would be the only one to administer this next useless treatment to her daughter.

*"Yes, Marah, you rub the balm of the dead on your daughter's body..."*

For an eternity, Marah rubbed the oil into Abigail's hot body, the smell nearly overpowering both of them. It did not help. If anything, it seemed to make her hotter.

"Mother, stop, please stop," Abigail moaned.

"Marah shook her head. "Abigail, I cannot, the doctor... the doctor thinks this will make you better."

"It hurts, Mother. Please stop. It hurts."

"I know, my sweet girl, I know. I am so sorry, Abigail."

"Patience." the doctor said. "We must have patience."

Marah felt a huge ball in her stomach, a bitter, seething knot of hatred. It moved up to her chest, where it sat like an anchor, squeezing and piercing her heart as though it were clasped in a band of iron. Abigail moaned in pain.

"I know it hurts, my brave girl. Just a little longer. You will be better soon. I am so sorry."

"All right. If you say so, Mother."

266

Finally, the doctor nodded his approval. At once Marah stopped the agony she was inflicting on her poor daughter.

"Water, Mother, please, water."

Marah hesitated, but then held the cup to Abigail's bleeding lips. Only a few moments later, she again threw up the little she drank, sobbing and vomiting at the same time.

"Oh my sweet girl," Marah could feel her own tears so close. "It's all right, Abigail."

"Thank you, Mother." Abigail's voice was a sigh.

*"Thank you, Marah, for torturing your own daughter…"*

A burning pressure grew behind her eyes. No. The whisper would not provoke her not now. She would not cry in front of her daughter and husband. Marah did not want Abigail to see her cry.

She again rubbed oil on Abigail's cracked and bleeding lips, ravaged and swollen from the fever and the vomiting. Abigail moaned at her painful touch.

Sometime later, a third doctor came in. He carried with him a large cloth. Even over the lingering odor of the pungent of myrrh, she could smell a scent she knew well but could not recognize, like a sweet aroma from her kitchen. Surely he would not try to feed Abigail anything?

"It is hot," he said. "Lay it on her chest. It will help her breath, and draw some of the heat out of her body."

"What is it?"

"A poultice of figs."

Marah laughed for the first time in eighteen hours. How ironic that a poultice of Abigail's favorite food would be the suggested cure for this terrible travesty that ravished her body.

"What is that, Mother?"

She thought Abigail was asleep. "A poultice, sweetheart. A medicine for your fever." Marah stroked her hair.

She could barely hear the tiny voice that answered her. "It smells like figs, Mother."

"Yes, Abigail."

*"Figs! Her favorite food! What a good mother you are!"*

"I'm not hungry right now. Is that all right, Mother?"

Marah nodded, a lump in her throat. Abigail drifted into sleep even as Marah laid the smelly concoction on her daughter's chest. The whispers were so soft, she almost missed them.

"You always take care of me, Mother…"

267

*"You always take care of things, Marah. But you take care of things your own way..."*

Almighty Jehovah, foreign God of her father and husband and daughter: What, oh what was happening to beautiful Abigail?

# CHAPTER 26

The red gold rays that crept across the floor of Abigail's bedroom were soon replaced by the shadows of night that Marah knew so well.

How many nights had she stood in this doorway, watching her daughter, silent, cautious, afraid any sound might awaken Abigail from her fragile sleep? She had not sat on Abigail's bed to smooth her hair or to caress her soft cheek. She had been more worried about her daughter's rest than loving reassurances for a slumbering little girl.

Since Deena called them the night before, neither Marah nor Jarius left Abigail's side. Each avoided the other's glance, knowing that to look into each other's eyes was to acknowledge a truth they both knew:

Abigail was very sick.

Marah knew it from the moment she entered Abigail's room last night. Despite the calculated ministrations of the physicians and the frantic efforts of Marah, her sister and Deena, her daughter only seemed to get worse.

Marah was terrified.

What frightened Marah the most was Abigail slipping in and out of consciousness. When she was awake, her voice was soft, breathy, almost gasping. It was as though she could not draw deep enough to catch her breath. She would look at her mother with a silent cry for help until her eyelids fluttered shut, her body limp, her breath imperceptible. The fall of her chest, as gentle as a butterfly's wing, was all that told Marah her daughter still lived. That and a body that was fire hot to the touch.

Marah felt the darkness growing, threatening and surrounding her, so dark she could not see, smothering her, a blackness she could not fight. Marah had never been afraid of the night, but she was frightened by this. She sat gripping her daughter's hand, the darkness covering her and Abigail. Who could fight such a dark night as this?

*"You, Marah. No one knows the darkness like you…"*

"Mistress Marah?" Marah nearly jumped out of her skin at the sound of Deena's voice. "Shall I light the lamps?"

"Yes! Yes, please. Light all the lamps." Her voice was shaking.

Her back straight, her chin high, Marah turned back to her daughter, the dim lamps no match for this darkness.

൙

"Mother?"

If Marah was not been inches from her daughter, she would not have heard the faint words.

"Yes, Abigail, here I am."

"Water, please Mother, water."

"Of course, Abigail, but just a little.

She held the clay cup to her daughter's mouth. Abigail drank in great slurps, as though she were gasping for water.

"Only sips, Abigail, only sips," Marah knew what lay ahead, she knew.

"I am so thirsty, Mother."

"I know. But just a few sips, Abigail."

Only a moment later, Abigail sat up, the violent spasms gripping her, the terrible retching sound mingled with her heartbreaking sobs.

This time however, Marah was silent, staring at the bowl, struck dumb at the terrible sight. Abigail was not vomiting up water. She was vomiting up blood, dark and red.

Marah showed the bowl to Jarius, whose eyes widened in fear.

"Abigail," he whispered. "Abigail."

ભ

Faithful Miriam and Deena slipped in and out with fresh water, emptying the bowls of bloody vomit, bringing in fresh, clean cloths and water. Despite the midnight hour, all three of the doctors returned to check the welfare of the synagogue's daughter.

The first doctor declined to bleed Abigail again. "She is too weak," he said.

How profound, Marah thought. Even an ignorant woman from Shiloh can see that.

Abigail tossed on her bed from side to side in a fitful sleep, twitching at the covers. She wouldn't answer Deena or Jarius or even her mother. She no longer opened her eyes.

After the doctors left, Jarius knelt by Abigail's bed. He spoke in a low voice.

"I am the man who has seen affliction by the rod of his wrath. He has driven me away and made me walk in darkness rather than light; indeed, he has turned his hand against me again and again, all day long."

Marah's hair stood on end. Darkness instead of light?

"He has made my skin and my flesh grow old and has broken my bones. He has besieged me and surrounded me with bitterness and hardship. He has made me dwell in darkness like those long dead."

Those long dead!

"Jarius." Marah's voice was soft.

"He has walled me in so I cannot escape; he has weighed me down with chains. Even when I call out or cry for help, he shuts out my prayer."

*"Not even Jarius can pray to God with the unforgiven sin that lurks in this room…"*

"Jarius!" Jarius opened his eyes and looked at her, surprised. No one had ever interrupted his prayers before. Ever.

"Jarius, do not speak of darkness and those long dead and no escape before my daughter!"

He sat frozen. "I am sorry, Marah, these are the words of Job, a true man of God. I am only… God found favor in Job… His words… I was just…" His voice trailed off.

Marah's impatience was immediate. He would not pray the

prayers of the dead over her daughter. Never!

Unbidden, the words came to her. "Jarius. These are the prayers of Abigail." She knelt beside Abigail's bed, her fevered daughter's hand clasped in her own.

"'Give thanks to the Lord, for he is good; his love endures forever.'" Marah was surprised that the words came to her. She could never remember the words of David or Solomon or Job, and indeed, only a few of the words of her father's Moses. But her daughter's clear voice rang in her heart.

"'They cried to the Lord in their trouble, and he saved them from their distress. He sent forth his word and healed them; he rescued them from the grave.' He rescued them from the grave, Jarius! 'Let them give thanks to the Lord for his unfailing love and his wonderful deeds for men.' This is the prayer of our Abigail, one of healing and rescue and unfailing love."

"He rescued them from the grave." Jarius whispered the words, tears in his eyes. He looked at Abigail and started crying in earnest, the agonized sobs of a man without hope.

Marah gazed at her husband; his heart was breaking. She got up, walked around the bed and helped Jarius to his feet, half-supporting him as they walked to the door.

"Jarius." He looked at her as though she were a ghost, some alien creature calling out his name. She shook his arm, trying to snap his unfocused trance.

"Jarius. Go eat something. Rest for a moment, and come back to us." She motioned to Deena, who stood at her side at once. "Find Augustus. Master Jarius needs to eat something, to be away from this room for a moment. Augustus is who my husband needs. He can help him the most…"

Before she finished the sentence, Augustus stepped around the corner and stood at his friend's side. He must have been waiting at the door, Marah thought. Waiting all this time.

"I'm here, Marah." Augustus's voice was gentle. "Come, Jarius. Come with me, brother." He supported Jarius as he led him away.

Deena stood at the door, staring first at her adored Abigail, then at her much-loved Master, broken and weeping, and longest at the straight back and stone-faced countenance of her Mistress.

"May I bring you something to eat, Marah?" Deena's voice was gentle.

Marah shook her head and turned back into the bedroom. She looked out the window, the darkness forced back by the lanterns' dim light. They were well into the night. Abigail had been sick for more than twenty-four hours with no improvement.

Jarius was out of his mind with worry.

On the other hand, Marah's mind seethed in a silent, calculating rage. She could not rid herself of the bitter ball of hatred planted squarely in her chest.

With each hour, with each shallow breath her daughter drew, the hatred grew, clenching her heart, robbing it of its pulse and feeling and emotion, until she knew that soon her rage would rob her of her life, too.

*"'For I the Lord your God am a jealous God, punishing the children for the sin of the parents...'"*

The ball of hatred in Marah's heart pushed its way to a throbbing pain behind her eyes at the mention of a jealous God of vengeance.

03

A short time later, Jarius returned with Augustus at his side. Augustus did not let go of Jarius's arm until he sat down in the chair at Abigail's bedside. Jarius did not once take his eyes off his daughter.

Augustus stood at the foot of the bed, looking at the girl he loved as if she were his daughter.

Marah thought of the times this commander of men teased her daughter, brought her gifts from afar, been startled by her impulsive hugs. One night, at Abigail's insistence, Augustus let her try on some of his armor, her knees buckling under the weight as she staggered around the room, her exuberant delight contagious. She could not even lift the heavy iron shield and instead drug it clattering behind her, calling her imaginary troops into battle. How they laughed that night.

Augustus would grant any wish to Abigail, this girl that he loved.

Now, the face of this commander of men was an unreadable mask. He had seen death many times. Marah wondered what this soldier, this commander, this follower of Yahweh was thinking, watching a young innocent fight such a fierce battle with such an unforgiving opponent. As if reading her mind, he spoke.

"Tell me what to do, Marah."

She stood, took his arm and walked him to the door. "Just stay close, Augustus, please stay close. For Jarius."

He nodded, understanding. Jarius needed him now. "There is nothing else?"

She shook her head. "No one else can do what I need for you to do, Augustus, and that is to help Jarius. No one but you."

He covered her hands with both of his, both sets calloused and rough from the effort of their daily work. He shook his head sadly and left Abigail's dark room.

ɔ

Sitting in the deep silence of the night, Marah heard the wind and rain begin. It was unexpected and violent, a fierce storm seizing the city by the Sea.

How fitting, thought Marah. Even God's creation is angry that someone so precious lays here so sick.

*"Not your God. The God of Naaman and Jarius and Abigail. Not yours."*

As if in answer to her thoughts, lightening flashed through the window. The profile of her daughter was thrown into sharp relief. Marah cried out, for in the brilliant light, her daughter looked as white as marble statute, the stone effigy of a beautiful young woman, peaceful, unmoving, lifeless.

Marah's scream was drowned out by the crash of thunder, thunder like none she had ever heard.

Jarius jumped to his feet at his wife's scream of terror, running to her side. "Marah, Marah, it is all right, it is only a storm."

Marah still stared at Abigail as though she were a ghost. But then Abigail opened her eyes and smiled at Marah.

Abigail was smiling!

Marah thought she might faint. She could no longer sort out reality from the terror growing inside her own mind.

"Mother, don't be frightened. 'The God of glory thunders, the Lord thunders over the mighty waters. Worship the Lord in the splendor of his holiness.' It is only the voice of God."

As quickly as Abigail opened her eyes, they closed again in her fitful, feverish sleep. Jarius and Marah stared in shocked silence at their daughter, her words echoing like the noise of the storm.

The ominous thunder rolled again, threatening her. "The voice of God," Marah whispered. She didn't know.

Her dying daughter heard in the thunder what Marah could not: the terrifying, fierce, unbending voice of God.

# CHAPTER 27

It had been a terrible, terrible day.

Marah sat by Abigail's bed, exhausted. Night was falling. This day could not end a moment too soon.

But what would the night bring? Perhaps it would be even worse than this day from hell.

After the thunderous storm last night, Abigail slept for several hours without waking. She slept! Marah was so encouraged. Indeed, Marah even dozed off, sitting up on a stool beside the dreadful illness of her daughter.

Any flicker of hope, however, was banished with the rising of the sun that morning. Morning. It seemed so long ago.

Marah was rousted from her fitful sleep by a loud gasping sound. She froze at the sight of Abigail.

Abigail lay in her bed, eyes open and staring, unseeing. Her arms and legs were straight, her body as stiff and rigid as petrified wood. Marah squinted. Abigail seemed to be turning blue! She was not breathing, but she was definitely not dead, either. Marah sat for just a moment, puzzled, unsure of what was happening.

Like a slow wind moving over grass, Abigail's arms and legs started shaking, first her fingers and toes, then her arms and legs and finally her entire body, an odd twitching with its own silent, relentless rhythm. Marah could not understand what was happening.

Suddenly, Abigail's limbs jerked at once in wild, awful,

uncontrollable spasms. Her eyes rolled back in her head, and a loud ragged gasping sound came from her lips.

"Jarius!" Marah's cry was a scream.

They both jumped up and looked at their daughter, but neither knew what to do.

"What is it, Marah?" Jarius shouted. "What is happening?"

Abigail was making horrible grunting sounds, drooling, choking, twitching, her body flailing in violent, frenzied jerks.

Marah could not breathe. "I don't know, Jarius." She choked on the words. Her voice sounded strange and far away to her.

The commotion summoned Deena, sitting on her chair just outside the bedroom door. She stopped at the door for a shocked moment, and then ran to shove Jarius out of the way.

"Hold her shoulders, Mistress, so she does not fall from the bed!" In all their years together, Marah never before heard Deena shout. As though slapped from her stupor, Marah gripped Abigail. The terrible jerking nearly wrested the thin frame from her hands.

Deena snatched a damp cloth from the corner of the bed, and used both hands to pry Abigail's mouth open. She forced the towel in Abigail's mouth and with an iron grip both held her jaw open and the towel in place. Abigail was making terrible, inhuman sounds Marah had never heard before in her life.

"Don't let go!" she commanded Marah. Jarius stood behind Deena, frozen with shock.

Her daughter's ragged gasps for air were punctuated by dreadful grunts, as though she were possessed by some demon. The terrible spasms shaking Abigail's thin body were so violent, it was as though a terrible storm raged out of control in her. It went on forever.

And then… it was over.

Abigail's eyes returned to normal. She looked at the three people in the room and said only one word.

"Mother." Abigail dissolved into an uncontrolled weeping.

But only for a few moments, for she stopped, looked up at her paralyzed mother, and fell asleep in Marah's arms. She could not be wakened. If she had not been breathing, Marah would have thought she was dead. The sleep of the dead.

Marah perched on the edge of Abigail's bed in a state of shock, rocking her daughter. Jarius still had not moved. Deena stood, holding the towel she had forced into Abigail's mouth, looking down at the charge she loved so much.

"Deena, what was that?" Marah's voice was a whisper. Deena knew what had happened. Marah could sense it. But Deena would not tell unless she was asked. "Deena. What is it?"

Deena raised her eyes and stared at Marah. "Mistress, it was a… a seizure. It happens sometime when the fevers are high. I have seen it before, when I was young."

Marah was still rocking Abigail back and forth, just as she did when this precious girl was just a tiny baby.

"A seizure." It was a statement, not a question. Marah kept rocking. Deena would tell her more.

"Yes, like a fit. When fevers do not give in, the body is often tormented by such seizures." Deena sounded perilously close to hysterics; Marah could hear it in the quiet gray-headed woman's voice. Oh, beloved, faithful Deena!

"What do we do?"

"Mistress, all I know to do is what we did. You must hold her tight, keep her from thrashing around. And, you must put something in the mouth, force Abigail's jaw open when a seizure takes hold, or they might… she might…" Deena did not seem to know how to finish her sentence.

"Tell me, Deena. Why did you force the towel in Abigail's mouth?"

"For two reasons. To help her breathe, and to… to keep her from biting her tongue. The seizures are so fierce, Abigail could bite her tongue…" Deena's voice trailed off.

Marah knew what Deena would not say. In the face of violent spasms that threatened to throw Abigail's body off the bed, Abigail could easily bite her tongue off.

Marah closed her eyes, wishing she could escape this nightmare

*"It's as if demons are in control of your perfect daughter…"*

She promptly opened them, seeking to take control of the situation and the ghastly whisper.

"Deena, would you please get us some clean cloths and fresh water?" Deena nodded. Marah knew the aging woman needed a task to do, anything to distract her from what just happened. She was met at the door by Miriam, never far from Abigail's room, either.

"Jarius, would you sit down with us?" Marah's question to her husband was gentle. He nodded and sat down, still staring at

Abigail. He's in shock, Marah thought absently. With good reason. The seizure was traumatic for all of them, but perhaps worst for Jarius, who only stood by as Marah and Deena fought the demon in Abigail.

But the seizure that so frightened them was just the first of many. Marah could not imagine a more horrifying day.

The seizure would come upon Abigail, taking over her body, torturing her every muscle and her mind, teasing her with suffocation. Her body would flail about in a helpless spasm, her face a frozen, unseeing mask of terror and pain, the horrible grunting and gasping loud in the silent room. Deena and Marah took turns forcing open the clenched jaw, holding the towel in place over the insensible girl's tongue. Marah never experienced anything so horrible in her life.

When it was over, Abigail would say only one word, in a voice so soft and sad it was unimaginable. "Mother." Her daughter would dissolve into inconsolable sobbing and then sink into the inexplicable, death-like sleep... until the next seizure gripped them all.

And still, her fever raged.

Marah lost count of the seizures. The doctors returned, Deena and Miriam and Augustus and even Cook and Asa came in and out, in and out, worried, praying, seeking to do anything. But there was nothing to do.

Nothing to do but wait.

ଔ

"Cold, Mother, cold." Marah jumped, startled from her reverie by Abigail's small voice. Other than the single word "Mother," it was the first thing Abigail had said all day.

"Oh, Abigail, I know." She nodded at Deena, who scurried off to fetch the warm, wool-wrapped stones they used to try to warm up Abigail on several occasions. There were so many blankets on her daughter's bed already. Jarius was not in the room, forced to leave by Augustus for some food, some water. No one even tried to make Marah leave.

"Cold, I am so cold, Mother."

At her wit's end, Marah did not know what else to do but to crawl into the bed with her daughter. The heat from Abigail's thin

279

body frightened her. That someone could endure such a harsh fever of two days, that anyone could survive seizure after vicious seizure was beyond comprehension.

Abigail was clinging to her last bit of life.

"I am so cold." Abigail's teeth were chattering so hard, Marah thought they might break. She placed her hand on Abigail's jaw, holding the thin, hot face close to her own, willing her warmth to steal into the shaking body of Abigail.

Only a few moments later, Abigail again threw off all the bed clothes. This time she was shrieking. "Hot, hot, Mother, hot!"

"Water, water, Mother, water."

Then the familiar retching into the bowl, each time laced with more and more blood.

Over and over Abigail repeated this cycle.

At least," Marah thought to herself, no seizures. She wanted to pray to God, the God of Abigail... please, have mercy, please no more seizures! But she did not know what to say to a God who spoke in the frightening voice of violent, roaring thunder.

Sometimes in the silence, Abigail's breathing was so faint, Marah would not breathe either, fearing Abigail breathed no more.

Then would come a loud gasp, a deep gulp of air. "It hurts, Mother, it hurts. I hurt."

And the terrible ritual would begin again.

Cold, hot, thirsty, vomit, blood. Hurt.

*"For I, the Lord your God, punish the children for the sins of the parents."*

Marah no longer had the strength to drive the whisper from her head.

*"For I, the Lord your God, punish daughters for the sins of the mothers."*

Please, no.

*"For I, the Lord your God, punish Marah, a murderer, a whore, a liar, one who has never called on my name..."*

I wanted to call on you, God, Marah thought. I wanted to hear your voice... Like Jarius. Like my father. Like my daughter, like my Abigail....

*"For I, the Lord your God, punish Abigail for the sins of her mother, Marah."*

As though she too heard the whisper, Abigail sat straight up in bed. Marah was horrified. Blood stood in the corners of Abigail's

280

eyes.

"The Father is near." Abigail spoke in a normal tone, her voice clear and lucid. Were her body not scalding to the touch, her lips and eyes not bleeding, her vomit not laced with blood, Marah's daughter might have just arisen from an afternoon nap,

Marah looked at her as though she were a ghost.

Abigail smiled, but the effect was so frightening, Marah thought she would scream. She spoke again, her voice even softer. "Don't worry, Mother, the Father is near."

Marah stood and dropped her daughter's hand. She walked to the door, never talking her eyes off Abigail. Deena sat sleeping on a low stool outside the door, her gray head leaning in the corner. "Deena," Marah whispered. At once, Deena jumped to her feet. Marah did not look at her, afraid to take her eyes off Abigail. "Deena, find Jarius."

Within moments, Jarius was at the bedside, but in that brief time, Abigail went back to her fitful sleep.

Marah forced her lips to move. "She sat up and… talked about you, asked for you, I think. She sounded as though she had never been sick. She just sat up and said 'Mother, the Father is near.'"

"I should not have left her." Jarius sat down and laid his head on her bed.

Marah sat back down. She felt rattled, as though her head was not connected to her body. She closed her eyes for just a moment. She was so tired.

*"For I, the Lord your God, punish the children for the sins of the parents."*

Her eyes snapped open.

*"For I, the Lord your God, punish the daughters for the sins of the mothers."*

She stood up and looked around, searching for the voice she knew was only in her head.

*"For I, the Lord your God, punish Abigail for the sins of Marah."*

"Mother, the Father is near."

Both Marah and Jarius jumped at the sound of Abigail's voice.

"Abigail, I am right here."

"Mother, don't worry. The Father is near."

"Abigail!" Marah thought Jarius would shake her. "I am right here!" He sounded hysterical.

281

Marah gripped Abigail's hand. "Your Papa is right here. Abigail, don't you see him, don't you hear him?"

Abigail smiled again, the same frightening smile. "Mother, the Father is near. I see the Father."

Jarius began to cry, great racking sobs that shook his whole body, his words almost unintelligible. "It is me, Abigail, me. Remember what Abigail means? The joy of my Papa? Here I am, and you are my joy! I am right here, Abigail, here."

"No, Papa, no. Mother, the Father is near. Don't be afraid, Mother. I see the Father."

*"For I, the Lord your God, punish the children for the sins of the parents. God is punishing Abigail for the sins of her mother...."*

"I hate you! If you are God, then take me! Take me, God!" Marah heard the words before she realized they came from her own mouth. "I am the one with the sin! Can you even hear me? I hate you, God! I hate you!"

Jarius jumped to his feet, staring at her. "Marah?" It was a sob more than her name.

*"Take you? God only wants a perfect sacrifice to atone for a murderous, adulterous woman who has never heard the voice of God, Marah!"*

The whisper was laughing.

Marah was shouting, screaming, anything to drown this evil out. "If you are God, take me! Leave my daughter, God! Leave her! I hate you, I hate you. I hate you!" She was out of control, hysterical. Everything was out of control. "I hate you, God! I hate you!"

She could not hear an answer, not from the weak voice of Abigail, not from her husband crying out her name, and certainly not from the roaring, thunderous voice of an unknown God.

The only one to answer Marah was the one she hated most, the whispered mockery of her own voice, the whisper that spoke the terrible truths she could not utter. *"I hate you, God, I hate you, God, I hate you, God!"* It was a singsong taunt. *"Like God cares that you hate him, Marah..."*

She looked at her sobbing husband and her feverish, incoherent daughter. Her friend Deena and sister Miriam stared at her, open-mouthed in the bedroom doorway.

*"I hate you God IhateyouGod Ihate hatehatehate..."*

Marah ran from the room.

ଔ

282

She found herself in the deserted street, the balcony with its columns of gold visible in the darkness. Only days ago, her daughter hid on that balcony, laughing at her mother and aunt, begging for treats from the market. Marah had seen her bright eyes and sweet smile, heard that soft giggle, felt that tight hug.

"Why are you doing this, God?" Marah was shouting and she did not care. "Why are you doing this? If you must punish someone, punish me! I am one who murdered my mother, who seduced my husband, who lied to my father, my husband even my daughter! I am the one who never heard your voice! I am the sinner! Take me, and spare Abigail, Lord! She is innocent! Take me!" Marah heard her own scream echo down the silent dark street.

"I know you can hear me! Speak to me, God! If you are God, speak! Speak to me!"

Nothing.

"I hate you, I hate you, I hate you! If you are God, speak!"

She felt rather than saw the strong presence of Augustus beside her. "Marah."

She whirled to face him. "Why won't God speak to me?" The sound of her voice echoed in the dark, empty street.

Augustus reached out to take her arm. She snatched it away.

"It is said that his voice is in the thunder! Abigail heard the thunder and told me it was the voice of God! And yet, I heard nothing, nothing! Where is this God that you and Jarius and Abigail worship? Where? Where? He is not here!" She fell to the ground, her voice angry.

She looked up at Augustus, her voice a terrified whisper. "He is not here, Augustus."

"Oh, Marah…"

Augustus pulled her to her feet.

It should be her dying, not Abigail.

He led her through the courtyard into her kitchen. She did not speak, and neither did Augustus. He led her to a couch and supported her as she sat down, the silence loud between them.

*"He heard what you said, Marah, about how sinful you are."*

God should punish me for my own sins, Marah thought dully, too weary to argue. He should punish me.

*"But he IS punishing you, Marah, in the most terrible way possible. He punishes by taking the very thing you love the most in this world."*

She watched Augustus pour a cup of wine and hold it out to

her. "Drink. You need to strengthen yourself."

*"Yes, Marah, strengthen yourself, for much worse is to come."*

"Please, Marah." Augustus raised the wine to her lips.

The smell was too much. Marah ran to the corner, vomiting in the scrap bowl with its old food leavings from who knew when.

She put one arm on the wall to steady herself. Augustus again came to her and steered her to the sturdy stool where Cook so often perched. "Sit." He poured some water in a bowl from the jar, dipped a cloth in it and brought the cloth to her. When she did not take it, he wiped her face with a gentle touch.

He returned with the cup of water. "Drink. You must drink." This time, he held the glass to her mouth and forced the water down. He handed her the smallest piece of bread. "The bread will give you strength. Please, Marah, please eat something."

As though she were an obedient child, Marah chewed, the bread a slimy, tasteless mass in her mouth.

"You will need your strength, Marah, for your daughter to get better and for your husband to survive. Abigail needs you to be strong."

Marah did not understand. She was not even listening. For at the words, 'your daughter needs you,' sudden surge of adrenaline roused Marah to her feet. What was she doing here in the kitchen, idly eating bread with Augustus? Abigail needed her!

Marah saw the gray rays of approaching morning pouring through the kitchen window where she, Jarius and Abigail sat for so many happy mornings. She threw down the bread and ran from the light. Abigail needed her.

Not knowing what else to do, Augustus followed as his friend, fierce and angry, ran to her dying daughter.

# CHAPTER 28

It was the third morning. Abigail still clung desperately to life. The sun was already hot, a bright white light through the narrow window, mocking the misery in the room. The confused babble of noisy voices disturbed her, but what was there to do?

"People from the synagogue, outside the gates," Miriam whispered.

"Why?" Why would people be gathered outside her gates?

"They have heard of Abigail's terrible sickness, and come to wait and to pray. She is, after all, the synagogue ruler's daughter."

Marah stared at her sister. She heard the laughter and conversations. They did not sound like they were worried or praying to her. She heard the babble of conversation and a woman's laughter.

"Vultures." She spat the word out.

"Marah, they mean well."

Marah pressed her lips together and turned from her sister.

Jarius, lost in his heartache and worry, was oblivious to the clamor in his courtyard.

For this, Marah was thankful.

ભ

"Mother," Abigail looked at her and smiled, as though she had not laid here in this bed at death's edge for two days. Tears seeped through the blood dried in the corners of her eyes, leaving ghastly red trails down her cheeks. Her face was as white as chalk, hollow as a skull. Her voice was a whisper, as she repeated the litany of the past hour. "Mother, the Father is near."

Jarius stared at his beloved daughter, uncomprehending. He sat at Abigail's bedside, still holding her hand. "Abigail? I'm here. Don't you know me?" But his was a stranger's voice that Marah did not recognize either.

Augustus stood at the door at the sound of Jarius's voice. Marah spoke to him. "She, she keeps talking about her father being near when Jarius sits right there beside her. Abigail does not seem to know... to know Jarius."

*"For I, the Lord your God, punish the children for the sins of the parents."*

No! But the shout of rage was only in Marah's head.

"Mother, the Father is near." Her voice was frail and breathless and yet... Abigail sounded happy.

Augustus looked at Abigail as in amazement. He shook his head in disbelief. "Of course," he said aloud. "Of course. Jarius, come with me."

"No, Augustus. I cannot leave her. I will not leave her." Jarius looked like a madman, unshaven and uncombed, his wrinkled robe of fine linen stained with vomit and blood. Jarius and Marah were still dressed in the finery of Marah's great and important dinner. Marah felt hysterical at the thought.

Augustus looked at Jarius for a long moment, as though pondering some unknown question. "My friend, do as I say. Come with me at once. Please."

"No."

"Jarius. Trust me as I have trusted you and our God these many years. Come with me. I beg of you." He did not sound like he was begging. No one could argue with the decisive note in his voice, eyes bright with a steely determination.

"Please, Jarius." Augustus's voice was softer, filled with pain for this family he loved as his own. "Come with me, brother."

Jarius stood as though he were a hundred years old. He bent and kissed Abigail's forehead. "I love you, Abigail." He kissed her again. "Please do not leave me."

They froze at her soft whisper. "I love you, too, Papa. Go with Augustus. And Papa, do not be afraid."

No one breathed. But Abigail closed her eyes and said no

more.

"Jarius. Come with me now." Augustus looked every bit the commander he was.

Jarius shuffled away from his daughter's bed, an aged, beaten man. He stopped to look at Marah. His eyes beseeched her for an answer she did not have.

Jarius nodded. There was no answer. He turned, leaving his wife to face his daughter's death alone.

&

The sun was hotter; morning was slipping away. For the first time in many hours, Marah was sleeping, sitting straight up on the low stool next to the bed.

"Mother, where is my necklace?"

Marah woke with a start and looked at the girl beside her. Was it all a bad dream? Here was her daughter talking as though she had not laid at death's door for two days and two nights! In her shock, she blurted out the first thing that crossed her mind.

"What necklace?"

"My necklace, where is my necklace from Papa?"

The harsh truth dawned. Abigail's beautiful face was gray and pinched. Her lips were swollen and cracked, her bed dirty and stained, the smells of sweat and vomit and blood overwhelming. Pools of fresh blood gathered at the corners of her lips and eyes. Her body was as violently hot to the touch as it was since she first fell ill. Marah could hear the noisy crowd as though they were right outside Abigail's window, a macabre rabble outside her beautiful courtyard, waiting for news, waiting for the death of the synagogue ruler's daughter.

Marah shook her head in disbelief. Of all things, after all Abigail had been through these two long days and nights, she thought of her necklace, the gift from her father.

"May I see my necklace from Papa?"

"Oh, my sweet girl." Marah jumped to her feet. The box sat on top of Abigail's chest where she first set it two long nights ago. She opened the box and lifted out the ruby medallion. It felt heavy, even ominous, to Marah.

*"For I, the Lord your God, punish the children for the sins of the parents. Perhaps that's why God caused that man's wife to die, for him to remain*

*childless, for him to die as the last of his line, with no one to ever wear his beautiful necklace. Perhaps he was punished for his father's sin as Abigail must be punished for yours."*

Marah carried the necklace to the bed. "Is this what you want, dear?"

Abigail sat up as though she had never been ill. Marah stared at her.

She smiled, but it was a ghastly, frightening grimace. "Yes, Mother!" She took the necklace from Marah and placed it around her neck herself. Then she lay back down and closed her eyes.

That Abigail had the strength to even speak shocked Marah. And yet, the girl too frail to lift her head just sat up, took the necklace and put it around her neck!

"Abigail?"

Her daughter did not answer.

Marah was afraid of what was happening in this room.

She picked up a fresh cloth and dipped it in the water. She would not give up. Perhaps this fever could still leave Abigail's blistered body.

*"For I, the Lord your God, punish the children for the sins of the parents."*

Marah continued to wring out the cloth. She would not acknowledge the whisper, that harbinger of evil.

*Isn't that why Abigail must die? For the sins of the mother?"*

Marah's lips were set; she would not answer. She wiped Abigail's burning face and neck burning with heat, softly smoothing away the traces of blood.

*"Aren't those the very words of Moses, the words of Naaman?"*

Weary, Marah slumped on the stool and lay her head down on the bed, the damp cloth clenched in her hand. She could feel the heat radiating from the feverish body of her daughter. She would not listen, she would not acknowledge the evil of the whisper. Not while her daughter lay sick in this room.

*"The sin of the mother, the mother, the mother...."*

"Yes." She heard the defeat in her voice. "The sin of Abi's mother..."

She heard another voice in the quiet room, the whisper of a real person. It came from the thin girl beside her, her daughter's faint voice.

"God is not punishing you, Mother. God loves you, he loves

Papa and he loves me, too." Abigail's voice was so soft, so gentle. How could this poor, sick, dying girl be speaking?

Marah crawled into the narrow bed, as close to her daughter as she could get, and pulled the blanket up over them.

"Do not mourn for me, Mother. And don't hate God. God loves you. He hears you. He has always heard you."

"But…" Marah found her voice. She had to answer this soft voice of her daughter. She could not help herself. "But if God hears me, he will not take you away from me. For that is all I ask God, that if he must take someone, he take me and not you! You are the gift God gave me. Why would he take you away? God is punishing me for my sin. And in punishing me, he punishes you! Forgive me, Abigail!"

For the first time, Marah was crying.

Abigail's hot hand stroked her face. "Don't cry, Mother. God is not punishing you. He loves you. He has always loved you, and so have I." She turned her head, her gaze direct, her eyes clear and happy. "I love you, Mother. Please tell Papa I love him too, more than anything. Tell him not to be afraid. The Father is waiting for me, Mother. I must go."

"No, Abigail, please don't go. Don't leave us. Don't leave me," Marah whispered. Tears streamed down her face. "Don't leave."

Abigail stroked her cheek. "Oh, Mother, don't cry. I have always loved you so much. Be strong for Papa, for he will need you. I go now to the Father. But I must go, Mother. It is my time. The Father calls me." Marah could hardly hear the last words. "I love you. I will always love you and Papa."

Abigail closed her eyes, the smallest smile on her face. Marah did not dare to move.

The wispy flutter of breath passed by Marah once, twice, three times, and then was still.

Abigail was dead.

Marah lay beside her daughter, uncomprehending. Her daughter, her beloved, beautiful Abigail, was dead. She told her she loved her and Jarius. Then, in the span of three short breaths, Abigail left her forever.

Only two days ago, Abigail stood before an audience of important men, pronouncing the goodness of her God. She laughed with her aunt, marveled over a necklace, told her Papa she loved him and left her mother with a wink and a wave.

And now she was gone.

Abigail looked so peaceful. Marah felt the thin body already growing cold.

Cold! Abigail would be cold! Her daughter would be cold. She did not want her daughter to be cold.

Marah pulled the blankets up around them both. She lay at Abigail's side, holding her close. She would keep her daughter warm. Marah would the cold of death away.

&#x6167;

She felt Miriam's hand on her shoulder. She saw Miriam touch Abigail's cold forehead and shake her head, her eyes filling with tears. She could hear Deena sobbing. Miriam pulled at her shoulder.

Marah did not know the voice, but it was not the whisper. It was a voice she did not recognize and yet, she knew it to be her own.

"For the Lord our God will punish the children for the sins of the parents. God has punished Abigail for my sins." The voice was cold and bitter. "After all this time, God has finally condemned me for my sin, for the death of my mother, for cheating Jarius of the life he deserved, for my lies, for my life. He gave me the greatest punishment possible, the punishment I have always known was mine. God has punished me by taking Abigail away. The sins of the mother are the sins of the daughter. God said so. Moses said so. Our father Naaman said so. God has taken my daughter away to punish me."

"Marah…" She heard the suffering in Miriam's voice. She shook her head and turned away from the two women standing beside the bed, back to the cold body of her daughter.

"Send for Jarius." She could sense the two women behind her, hesitating. Both of you, leave, and send for Jarius."

"Mistress…"

"Send for Jarius and get out of this room." Her voice was angry and biting. "Get out."

*"Get out! Leave sinful Marah with her perfect sacrifice, Abigail."*

"Get out!"

She heard the hurried footsteps fade away.

At last, Marah and her precious daughter were alone. Alone, just as that alien God intended.

# CHAPTER 29

Marah heard the noise outside, the murmur of many voices, the shrieking wails of mourners, and the piercing, trilling flutes. What was that racket, anyway? She could not imagine why people might be making so much noise right outside her courtyard. Next thing you knew, they'd come inside and want to be fed. People always wanted something from the synagogue ruler and his wife.

But these were only idle thoughts, and Marah did not lift her head to look. For in truth, she did not care about anything except the tranquil girl beside her.

She still lay beside her daughter, peaceful, beautiful Abigail. Marah raised herself to one elbow to look again at her exquisite baby girl.

She reached for a damp cloth that lay on the corner of the bed, and began to wash Abigail's face. Carefully, so carefully, she wiped the traces of dried blood from the corners of Abigail's eyes. Oh, her poor lips, cracked and blistered. She dabbed at the shreds of vomit clinging to those poor damaged lips.

She tried to smooth the tangle of Abigail's hair, hair that Marah had doused with water the night before, anything to rid her daughter of the fever. Abigail's hair was a mess. Marah tried to run her fingers through it, one long strand at a time. She wanted Abigail to look pretty when Jarius returned. The joy of her Papa, that's what Abigail would always be.

She could see the little girl just learning to walk, tottering to her laughing father.

"Joy of Papa!" She could hear the laughter in the happy voice.

There was that tiny five-year-old girl, her black head bent a studious concentration and tongue stuck out in determination as she sounded out the words of her father's scrolls.

A laughing girl teased Deena, begging for the fresh figs she knew the woman had for her favorite girl.

"Aunt Miri!" Marah could hear the joy in her daughter's voice. "Aunt Miri, you are here!"

"Aunt Miriam, Abigail." Marah cringed at the spitefulness in the mean voice.

She could hear the laughter. "Of course, Mother. Aunt Miri-AM!"

"It's important you not embarrass your father and me, Abigail." Was that awful voice really her own?

"Papa will be proud of you and you will be proud of me, Mother. I love you."

Marah whispered in the silence. "I am proud of you. I love you, Abigail. Oh, please, please know how much I love you."

She heard Miriam's soft voice at the door. "Marah."

She would not speak with Miriam. This time was for her and Abigail alone.

"Get out." She still sensed her sister's presence there. "Get out, get out, get out!" It was an incomprehensible shriek. Miriam fled.

Marah reached down and picked up the heavy necklace still draped around Abigail's neck. Her wedding necklace. Marah would never take it off her daughter, never. It would lay with Abigail forever, now.

If only she could lie beside Abigail forever, too, and join her daughter wherever she had gone.

*"You could go where she has gone, you know. Your daughter needs you. Your daughter is dead. If you don't join her, she will suffer alone for eternity, suffering your punishment for your sin alone."*

Yes, she should go wherever Abigail was.

But where did Abigail go? Marah pondered this as she held the medallion up. The light shone through the brilliant red rubies. Red like Abigail's blood, Marah thought. Beautiful.

*"If you join Abigail, you will know where she went. If you were a good*

*mother, you would go right now, and not leave your daughter alone."*

"But I don't know how," Marah answered. "How do I go to my daughter?" Her voice did not sound hateful anymore. This voice was sad and defeated. "Tell me, please. Tell me how to find Abigail. You have always told me truth."

*"Yes, I speak the truths you have always needed to hear. I will tell you how to go to Abigail, Marah. I will tell you what to do and you must listen."*

The noise outside grew louder. It sounded like a lot of people were standing in the street, outside her house, even inside the courtyard. Who were they? She did not want them to disturb her beautiful, tranquil, perfect Abigail.

She traced a gentle finger down Abigail's cold cheek. Abigail loved her. She did not want Abigail to be alone in death.

*"Yes, Abigail loved you! If you loved her, you would go to her now. She is calling for you, Marah. Don't you hear her?"*

Marah listened, but all she heard was the unfamiliar noisy din outside her home.

*You're not listening hard enough, Marah! I will help you."*

"Tell me."

*"Marah, for you to join your daughter, you must join her in death. You must die, too, Marah. Don't let Abigail suffer your punishment alone. Do what a good mother would do, Marah. It's not too late to be a good mother…"*

Of course. Abigail was dead. Marah could only see her daughter again if she died, too. It was so simple.

The noise outside her home was so loud as to be unbearable. Or was the roar only in her head?

She studied Abigail's wedding necklace and remembered her own wedding. Three hundred people, Naaman had said in awe. Many more people would come to mourn the beautiful daughter of the synagogue ruler, far more than those who came to meet the heathen woman who tricked her way into the noble, God-fearing home of Jarius.

Jarius would want her to take care of all these people. After all, she was the synagogue ruler's wife. She sensed a prick of sadness at the thought of her husband. Poor Jarius would again lose a child and a wife.

But she could not be concerned with that now. She had to listen to the whisper, to find out how to join her daughter, to at last be the good mother she always wanted but never managed to be.

*"Yes, you must join your daughter, Marah. For Jarius will truly hate*

293

*you now, anyway. When he finds out Abigail was taken for your sin, he will hate you as he has hated no other."*

After all this time, Jarius would finally hate her. She knew she deserved his hatred, but her heart was breaking. Because, like Abigail, she loved Jarius. She knew he did not love her. Hadn't she always known it, as she waited and waited for the anger and punishment of Jarius? He couldn't have loved her. And now, with Abigail dead, he would hate her.

*"Yes he will hate you. You will be dead to him, just like Abigail."*

A terrible loneliness welled up inside her. There was no one to comfort her in the loss of what she treasured the most, her daughter Abigail and yes, her husband, Jarius. If only someone could help her with the pain.

*"I can help you. I can make the pain go away. I can help you find your daughter. There is nothing else for you but death. Join your daughter."*

"But how can I?" A sudden rage flared. Always, always the whisper tormented her. Never, never did it tell her what it was she needed to do.

*"Oh, Marah, this time I will tell you what to do. But you know, don't you? You know. There are so many ways, and you have thought of them before..."*

No. On those dark nights when she walked her house alone, with only the whisper for company, those had been the evil mutterings of the whisper, not her.

Hadn't it?

*"You know the ways, Marah. You have thought of them before. Throw yourself from the roof above your beautiful presumptuous balcony to the black stones of the street below. Hang yourself from one of the strong rafters in your lovely dining hall with its heathen painted walls. Take the sharpest knife, the one that slices the lamb from the bone, and press it to your wrist in your friendly, inviting kitchen. There are many, many ways, and you know them all. But you must act quickly Marah, quickly. Before your husband returns. You must act now."*

Even as she wondered at the agitation of the whisper, she heard her husband's voice in the courtyard. He sounded so sad.

*"He is coming, Marah! You must act now! Hurry to join your daughter forever in death. If you do not act now, it will be too late. You must escape before your husband returns, the husband that will despise and hate you. Hurry!"*

Abigail was dead. The moment Abigail took her last breath,

the beating of Marah's heart stopped. She just needed to end the life of the empty shell that was her body.

She pushed herself up in the bed. "I am ready." Her voice sounded odd in the empty room. "I'm coming to you, Abigail."

At once she saw it, glittering on the chest. The physician's knife, the very blade he used to pierce Abigail's thin arm, lay atop the bandages. She remembered how the blood welled up at once. It would be so simple, so easy. Her life here would ebb away, and she would stand beside Abigail."

*"Yes, you will stand with your daughter. But hurry, Marah, hurry. Hurry to Abigail"*

She heard a different voice, one echoing in her courtyard. "Why all this commotion and wailing?"

It was a stranger, yet it seemed like a voice she knew well.

*"Hurry, Marah. Go to Abigail. You must hurry."*

The voice in the courtyard was speaking. "The child is not dead but asleep."

Marah heard laughing in the crowd, the babble of voices. There was more talking, and the noise continued, but it ebbed away, a softer, more distant hum, as though the crowd stood in the street.

She heard a man in the courtyard, telling the mourners to leave, forcing them out. The voice was steadfast and unassailable. Strong, like a fortress. Unfathomable.

"She is not dead." The man spoke with authority.

*"Marah, quickly, before Jarius comes, you must do this. Go to your death. Go to join your daughter. Pick up the knife. Do it now!"*

She stood, as obedient as a child, the knife heavy in her hand. Go to her death, the whisper told her. Death was the only answer, the whisper said. The whisper always spoke truth, didn't it?

And yet, the idea of her own death at her own hand pierced her heart. Oh, how heartbroken her father would be to see Marah now, grieving the bright light that was Abigail, committing murder to kill the dark demon that possessed Marah. Oh, how he would have wept. And Jarius. Wouldn't Jarius mourn for her? He was so kind and gentle and good. Surely he would grieve his wife a little.

*"He will not mourn for you! He will grieve for Abigail! Go to her! Do it, Marah."* The whisper would not relent, willing her to do the unthinkable.

She pressed the knife to her wrist.

"Help me." Marah heard the words in the room, weak and

beaten. "Help me, God of Abigail. Help me, God of my husband, God of my father. Help me, God. Forgive me. Only you can forgive me. Save me, Abba Father."

A sudden fear in the room loomed, a terror she did not recognize. Was it her own? She did not know. But the fear was real, like the presence of a living, breathing being. It stood with Marah's grief, the agony of her daughter, the hatred of her husband, the shame of her father. It gripped her, choking her, smothering her.

But her daughter looked so peaceful. Her husband did not hate her. Her father had loved her. All that was real was Marah's grief for her Abigail.

"The girl is not dead." Laughter answered the statement, but the man's voice was unshakeable. "The girl is not dead, but sleeping."

*"She is not sleeping, Marah! Go to her now! Steal away and hide. Go to your death in a secret place. The time is now, if you ever want to see Abigail again. Run, Marah, run from that voice. I am all that is real to you!"*

"For she cries out to the Lord in her trouble, and I will deliver her from her distress."

The words of Abigail resonated in Marah's heart, the psalm she used to proclaim the strength of her God. The strong words of her daughter echoed in the room.

*"Run, Marah!"* The words were shrill and panicked.

"Help me, God. Save me." The words welled up from somewhere deep within Marah.

"She cries to me and I will deliver her. My love endures forever." She could hear the strength of her daughter in the power of the words.

*"Don't listen, Marah! Don't listen! It isn't Abigail who speaks to you. Abigail is dead! Only if you end your life now will you ever hear Abigail's voice again!"*

"Why do you mourn? The girl is not dead." The voice in her courtyard was strong, overwhelming in its power.

"Be gone." Marah had never heard a voice like this. Quiet and calm and yet frightening in its might, a voice that resonated with the overlapping tones of Abigail and Jarius and Naaman... yet the voice was her own. "My love endures forever. She cries out to me in her trouble and I will deliver her from her distress."

*"Marah, to join your daughter you must die! Run away, Marah!"* It was a frantic hiss, hysterical in her ear. *"Come with me! Run! Now!"*

"'I will bring her out of the darkness and deepest gloom. I

will break away her chains. I will heal her and rescue her from the grave.' These are the words of my daughter Abigail, the words of Jehovah. I say, be gone."

*"Marah! Listen to me, Marah, to me!"*

"BE GONE! I WILL DELIVER HER! MY LOVE ENDURES FOREVER!"

The words roared in Marah's heart.

A terrible shriek, a keening, piercing howl of misery twisted around her, tighter and tighter. Marah closed her eyes, unable to raging frenzied shriek. "Save me, God," she whispered.

And then…

Silence.

How long did she stand in the silence, listening? Moments? Hours? Her entire life? She did not know; she only waited. She knew the voice would speak to her again. She knew the voice had not left her. There was calm in the room and peace in Marah's heart. She waited.

"Consider the great love of the Lord. My love endures forever." The voice was undeniable. Marah knew the words to be true. They were Abigail's words of praise, her daughter's exultant cry: "His love endures forever!"

A warmth grew within her, the ball of hatred lodged in her throat melting away.

The voice was as gentle as a soft rain, "My love endures forever, Marah, forever..."

Truly it was the voice of God.

The chains that twisted so tightly around Marah's heart loosened one by one, their iron grip broken. Her agitation and fear were gone, replaced by something she did not at first recognize.

Here in this room, this room where her beloved daughter lay dead, Marah felt her grief for Abigail take hold, a sad bitter heartache. And yet, she felt peace. "The Father is near," Abigail said.

She remembered once, in another lifetime, Jarius had taken her hand and told her that she, Marah, gave him peace. She had never forgotten, but she had never known peace herself. And yet, now, she held that peace safe in her heart.

Her daughter was safe with God. Someday she would see her daughter again. The God of Abigail and Jarius and Naaman had been the God of Marah all these years, keeping her in his protection. Abigail suffered no more. She was safe with Abba God.

"The Father," Marah whispered. "Abigail is with the Father."

"Marah." She heard the voice of the man she knew she had loved for years.

Jarius stood gazing at Marah and Abigail, tears running down his face. He had not heard Abigail's last, gentle breath, her soft words of love before she joined her Father Jehovah in Heaven. "The Father is near," Abigail said. He had not heard the war that raged in Marah's head, he had not heard the voice of God that saved her. He had not heard the voice of God, speaking to Marah, claiming her as his own.

No, Jarius only saw his daughter, dead and lost to him.

Marah had never seen such suffering on anyone's face. Jarius gazed at Abigail, stricken, unable to move.

"She is dead, Marah. Our Abigail is gone. Oh, Marah…" He was weeping.

"Yes, Jarius. Abigail is gone." She wondered at the gentle strength of her voice. "Abigail stands with her Father Jehovah, now."

Belatedly, Marah realized Jarius was not alone. Behind him were three men from the synagogue, Simon the fisherman and the sons of Zebedee, James and his younger brother John. They had never before been in her home. Why, she wondered abstractedly.

The Zebedee men were just boys really, not that much older than her own beloved Abigail. In some other life, young John might have been a bridegroom for lovely Abigail. Marah could picture him standing handsome and bronze from the sea and the sun, gazing in awe at his bride, the enchanting Abigail in her bridal veil and beautiful medallion. She would never see sweet Abigail standing beside her bridegroom.

The fishermen came into the bedroom, stricken at the sight of the still, tranquil girl.

The other man came in last. It was the teacher, the man from Nazareth, the healer of Simon's mother-in-law and Eri and Quintius and so many others. She knew it was his voice in the courtyard, telling all those noisy people that her child, her Abigail was not dead, but asleep.

It was his voice she heard in her heart only moments ago.

But how could that be? That voice echoed with the overtones of Abigail and Jarius and Naaman and Augustus and Miriam, all those that loved Jehovah and loved her, too. It was a voice of love and strength that fought back against the whisper, fought for her, and then cast the whisper of evil from her heart, stopping her from taking her own life. She prayed to the God of Jarius and Abigail and Naaman, and he saved her, her daughter's words of faith beating in her heart. How could that be the voice of Jesus, too?

Jesus gazed at her. Marah remembered what Jarius told her, the words of Jesus to Eri. "Friend, your sins are forgiven."

Jesus banished evil and forgave sins. She asked for salvation and God rescued her. All that remained was for her to ask Jesus to forgive her of the sin she had carried for so many tortured years.

All she had to do was ask.

She could hear the voice of her beloved father, faithful and happy Naaman. "Marah, my Marah! 'Although you are a stiff-necked daughter, I will forgive your wickedness and your sin.' So says the Book of Moses."

My father loved me and he would have forgiven me for anything. Why had it taken her so many years to understand this? And Jarius forgave her years ago. Why did she not see? And forgiveness from God stood right here before her, the man called Jesus, the Son of God.

The Son of Man had the authority to forgive sins, Jarius said. She only needed to ask, and forgiveness would be hers. Then she would stand with Abigail forever, but at God's appointed time. Not a time of her own choosing.

She heard Abigail's soft words echoing in her heart. "His love endures forever, Mother."

All her life, she had been tortured by a whisper of guilt and condemnation, waiting with apprehension for the punishment she deserved, condemnation and punishment that never came.

If I confess my sin, I will be free from my past forever, she thought. This is truth.

Marah gazed at the face of her daughter, so serene on her bed. She walked to the Teacher and knelt at his feet. She knew what she had to do. She could feel Jarius watching her. She looked up at Jesus, unafraid. She knew what she needed to do.

"Forgive me, Jesus, for I am a sinner. Many years ago, my birth caused my mother to die, leaving my father and sisters without her. I grew up with pride and anger. I committed a great sin against the Law of Moses, against my father, against…" she hesitated, but only for a moment. "Against my husband Jarius, a good and

righteous man. I sinned against… God. According to the law of
Moses, my daughter Abigail has been punished for the sins of her
mother. My punishment is her punishment, for God's punishment of
his children is just. God's law to Moses is clear: 'For I, the Lord your
God, punish the children for the sins of the parents.' My daughter
was taken for my sin. Forgive me, Jesus, forgive me of my sin. For
the sake of Abigail, who knows God and believes in you, forgive
me."

Jesus stood for a long time, looking down at her. When she
acknowledged her just punishment, that God punished Abigail for
her own sins, tears came to his eyes. He looked so very sad.

Marah bowed her head, waiting for the forgiveness she knew
would come.

Jesus bent and placed his hands on her head.

His hands were so heavy! Marah was strong, but she never
felt a weight like this. Never! Oh, such a weight pressing down on
her!

She heard his voice, but did not understand his words. He
was praying, and he was praying for her. She did not know how she
knew this, but she did. Jesus, the long-awaited Messiah, the Son of
Man and the Son of God, was praying for Marah.

The sound of his voice was so soft and yet it filled the room.
Oh, the miracle of that voice.

Jesus fell silent. After a moment, he reached down and
pulled Marah to her feet. As he did, the guilt and shame Marah
carried for so long fell away. Jesus placed her hand in Jarius's, and
held both their hands in his for a moment. Jarius stood unmoving,
crying, silent and uncomprehending.

Marah saw her husband's torn robe, his red eyes, his wild
face. She saw his broken heart. "Jesus forgave me, but it is too late
for our daughter Abigail. Oh, Jarius," she thought. "Oh, my
husband."

God be with you, Jarius, she thought softly. Please let Jesus
heal my husband Jarius. He will be forever broken unless Jesus heals
him.

She watched as Jesus walked to the bed and gazed down at
Abigail. There was no sound in the room. Marah closed her eyes. If
only Abigail had lived just a little longer, perhaps Jesus could have
healed her. But it was not the will of God.

"Talitha koum!" Marah's eyes flew open. "Little girl, I say to you, get up!"

She felt, rather than saw, Abigail sit up. It was as though something connected the two of them, something alive and breathing. When Abigail sat up, something strong, something powerful pulled on Marah's heart, pulled so hard she thought it would fly out of her chest. Abigail was alive, and so was she. She felt the first beat of Abigail's heart as though it were a fist beating down on her own chest, so strong was the pulse.

There was a rushing sound in the room, like a strong wind. Abigail, cold, dead Abigail, sat up and left her bed. She walked over to Jarius and Marah.

"Papa. Mother." Abigail smiled at them.

There was a shocked silence in the room.

"Abigail!" Jarius cried aloud. The spell was broken. He grabbed her in a tight hug, pushed her back to look at her again, and hugged her even more tightly. Abigail reached out to take Marah's hand. "Mother." She was smiling.

Marah stood, unable to move, her daughter's cold hand an iron grip on her own. She forced the words out. "Abigail. You're… alive."

"Yes, Mother. I'm right here with you."

The mesmerized spell was broken. The noise from the street came rushing in, voices and mournful wailing. Marah heard the shocked murmurs of the three fishermen. She heard her husband weeping with joy.

Marah thought she and Jarius might smother Abigail with their kisses and their tears. They were laughing and crying at once.

Abigail laughed with them. She looked at the man behind them. "Jesus! Father!"

Abigail knew Jesus; she called him Father. Why did Abigail call Jesus her Father? Marah's head wondered but her heart would not let her keep the thought.

Marah saw Jesus grin at Abigail. This man, this great teacher, this… Messiah was grinning at twelve-year-old Abigail, the girl he rescued from the dead. He had saved her from the grave, just as God most certainly saved Marah from death.

Abigail laughed aloud, and he laughed with her. Jesus was laughing.

Jesus turned to Jarius. "Give her something to eat!" He was grinning. Jarius nodded. Jesus smiled at Abigail again. He looked …

joyous. Abigail smiled back at him, her face a mirror of the happiness on his. They nodded at each other, as though they shared a secret.

Jesus turned and picked up Marah's hands. He looked at her for a long time. He knows, she thought. Jesus knows about Naaman and his faithfulness to Moses. He knew about the faith of Jarius and of Abigail. He knew about the sin she committed and the guilt she carried. He knew that Marah had never, ever heard the voice of God. But God heard her, God answered her, God… saved her. He saved her from the evil that has haunted her these many years.

"You forgave me, she whispered. "You saved me and my daughter. Thank you, Jesus."

She felt the tears running down her face.

Jesus smiled at Marah. He was still holding her hands. His voice was gentle. "Tell no one what has happened." She nodded. Never again would she wonder where the voice of God was. Today, she heard the voice of God. It would never leave her.

Jesus laid his hand on Jarius's shoulder one last time. Jarius nodded, but he had no words. Jesus looked at him for a long moment and then smiled.

"Give her something to eat," Jesus said to Jarius, his voice gentle. Then he laughed out loud, joyous. "Give her something to eat, friend!"

With his disciples following and shaking their heads in disbelief, Jesus left the house of Jarius.

"Mother! Papa! I'm hungry!"

No matter how they tried, Marah and Jarius could not hold Abigail tight enough.

# CHAPTER 30

Jarius and Marah sat beside each other at the low table, holding hands. The shadows of late afternoon crept up the wall of the warm, sunlit kitchen, alive with people and activities and laughter.

Cook burdened the table with more of the great quantities of food he was preparing. For once, Marah had no comment or even interest in his culinary efforts. Augustus and Asa stood in the corner, talking, laughing, snatching some bit of particularly inviting food from the groaning table covered with dishes and plates. Miriam and Deena flitted in and out of the room, stopping every single time to hug the thin girl sitting at the table.

Abigail was eating for the second time that day with the same gusto as the first, wolfing down as much of the great quantities of food Cook kept piling on the table as a girl her size could possibly stand.

"This is so good, Cook!"

Jarius and Marah looked at each other and smiled.

The thing most precious to them was restored. To look at Abigail, one would never know such a vicious illness had ravaged her body for two days and three nights.

They could not stop smiling at their daughter.

Just this morning, Jarius was wild with grief, his spirit broken, his faith in God robbed from him. "Your daughter is dead," Asa told Jarius, pulling him away from the Master.

"Don't be afraid," Jesus said to Jarius. "Only believe."
Jarius had believed.

Only a few short hours ago, Marah finally lost the battle waging inside her for so many years. The vicious, sinful whisper within her finally won. *"Marah, to join your daughter you must die!"*

Marah had accepted its harsh judgment and the punishment she felt she deserved. She resigned herself to the sentence of death standing before her, the death of her daughter and her own death, death to be brought about by her own hand.

"My love endures forever, Marah." She heard the voice of God. And at that moment, God rescued her, as no one, nothing else could. "My love endures forever."

As certain as she was that her daughter lived and ate breakfast at this very table, she knew that God had conquered death in more than one way in Abigail's bedroom. God restored Abigail to life, but he also claimed Marah as his own, forgave her, restored her, and banished the guilt that haunted her.

"My love endures forever."

The voice of Jesus would never leave her. God had defeated Satan, the evil one that so wanted to claim Marah as his own. She had been so close! She felt as though life was returned to her, just as it was given anew to her daughter. She was reborn.

And then, the laughter of Jesus with Abigail! His words as he left them: "Give her something to eat!" He seemed so joyous, as though Abigail were his own daughter, his own precious child.

Abigail practically leapt through the house the entire day, dancing from room to room with an energy that denied her three days of illness. As soon as Jesus left, she started her incessant talking and laughing, jumping up and down in the courtyard, looking out the balcony windows, hugging all she saw and eating, eating and eating.

As soon as she finished breakfast that morning, Abigail stood up and announced she was leaving for the synagogue.

Marah shook her head no. Abigail had been so sick! But before she could speak, Jarius put his rare paternal foot down.

"Not yet, Abigail. You were too ill. Not yet."

"But I must! I am better!"

"I understand, Abigail. Not yet."

"But---"

"Abigail, we can give thanks anywhere, even right here in the kitchen together. You were so sick and it is too soon. Please."

Abigail cocked her head with a complacent smile for her father. She looked as though she knew something he did not. But she did not argue. "Yes, Papa. But soon."

"Soon."

Marah watched the exchange with tears in her eyes. It was hard not to cry whenever she looked at her daughter. It was as though years of unshed tears were leaking from her at every turn.

She did not care.

Marah turned to see every person in the room looking at her with knowing looks.

"Sister," Miriam's voice was gentle.

"Marah." As always, Augustus's tone held a certain note of undeniable authority.

"Mistress?" In unison, Deena and Cook turned to their beloved friend.

"Mother!" Abigail's voice was certain.

"Wife," Jarius laid a gentle hand on his wife's shoulder.

"What!" exclaimed Marah, startled to hear so many voices directed at her all at once.

There was laughter in the room, that everyone spoke to Marah at the same time.

"Marah, you must go to bed, and you must go to bed now. You have not slept for three days." Her husband squeezed her shoulder. "You haven't taken a single bite of food, anyway. You need to rest, you're swaying where you sit."

Marah gave her head a stubborn shake. "When Abigail goes to bed, then I will, too. I want to be near her when she sleeps. I want…"

"Mother, I am well. Jesus did not heal me only to have me snatched away the moment you close your eyes. You look so weary. Please, go rest."

"I will not leave her side for one moment, Marah. I promise." Her sister's voice was firm.

"Nor I, Mistress, nor I." Deena shook her gray head for emphasis.

"This warm wine will help you sleep, my Mistress. Please, you must rest." Cook held out a cup to her. Marah waved it away.

"Come, Marah," her husband's voice was soft. "We will rest together. No one in this house will leave Abigail even for a moment, probably for weeks to come, perhaps for the rest of her life. Please,

Marah, please. Come rest. I will go with you."

"I will be fine, Mother. Please rest."

Marah looked around the room and the smiling faces, her heart full. She was surrounded by people who loved her.

People who were growing fuzzy around the edges. Three days of desperate worry, two nights of heartbreak, and a day of joyous celebration were catching up with her.

She smiled back at the people who loved her.

"You're right," Marah nodded. "All of you! Jarius, could you please come with me? I would like that very much. Abigail, come give me one more hug."

Nothing could describe the feel of her daughter's arms around her neck.

෫

It was dusk outside, and yet, sleep did not find the weary Marah or Jarius. The noise of their household faded away into the quiet of evening.

Marah and Jarius lay awake, talking. They had much to say to each other, hushed whispers as their family now lay sleeping. It was the most wonderful evening of Marah's life.

"Marah," Jarius turned to her shyly when they first entered her room. "Might we pray together, alone, to give thanks to God?"

She nodded. Not since she was pregnant with Abigail had Jarius and Marah prayed alone as a couple. Their prayers were reserved for meals, evening prayer times with Abigail, prayers for the Festivals, or Marah and Abigail listening to Jarius pray in the synagogue. But never did they pray together, just the two of them.

Her heart overflowed to hear Jarius speak words of fervent thanks for his daughter, for Jesus Christ, for how God blessed them. Marah cried at the final words of his prayer.

"Thank you, Lord, for sending me this woman I love for my wife."

Jarius thanked God for her, for Marah. Jarius loved her.

As they prayed together, Marah only spoke a few words, but Jarius gave voice to the emotion he knew she could not speak. And for each word spoken, Marah felt as though God nodded at her in encouragement.

"Jarius, there is something I must tell you."

Haltingly, Marah whispered how for all her marriage she had feared Jarius's anger and punishment, ever since that day so long ago when she had tricked him into sin and marriage. How something evil had whispered to her, torturing her, tormenting her all of her life, ever since that terrible day when she heard her sister's childish shout: "Murderer."

"The only time I really felt safe, that I was free from this evil whisper of self-doubt and guilt, was when I was pregnant. Remember how you prayed for me? For the first time in my life, I felt close to God, safe with you, free from fear in my life."

"Oh, my wife. I didn't know. You seemed so strong, always in control."

Marah shook her head. "My life has always felt as though something else controlled me. I have never felt the reality of God, never experienced the faith you and Abigail have, until today."

"Marah, I didn't know. Forgive me, forgive me for not knowing how you have suffered."

"I was determined to keep my fears from you! And now I understand that as long as I stand with God, I can face my fear alone." She smiled at Jarius. "I love to hear you pray for me, Jarius. Please, Jarius, always pray for me."

"I always prayed for you and I always will. And Marah, from this day forward, we will pray together." Jarius embraced her with strong arms.

Marah could not stop smiling.

They spent hours recounting what happened to each other.

Jarius told her how, once he realized the intention of his friend Augustus, they ran to the house of Simon Peter, pushing people out of their way, frantic to find the man from Galilee.

Marah told him of her shock when Abigail sat up, asked for the necklace and then lay back down. Of her repeated conviction that her Father - God the Father - was near to her. Of Abigail's courage. Of the quiet, peaceful moment before she breathed her last.

Jarius told her of the crowds that fell in behind him, pushing, shoving, as he and Augustus hurried, searching for Jesus, hoping they could find him before it was... too late.

It was hard, but Marah told Jarius how she had decided to take her own life. "So I might go... where Abigail went..." She cried at the words. "I am ashamed, and so sorry, Jarius. But I heard this voice speaking the words of Abigail's psalm: 'His love endures forever." I felt as though God were speaking to me! If I had not heard him, I know I would have done it. I was crazy, for I believed this terrible whisper telling me that by dying, I would again be with Abigail."

Jarius held her in his arms and cried with her.

"Oh, Marah, if only I knew. I have loved you almost from the very beginning. You have suffered for no reason. I forgave you the first time I saw you walking across my courtyard, your back straight and courage blazing out of your eyes! I knew I loved you when I saw you sitting alone at night beside my dying father. You've been my partner, my rock all these years. Tell me, promise me that you understand how much you mean to me. For I could not bear to lose you. I thought you knew how much I loved you."

Now that he knew he had nearly lost her, Jarius held her as though to never let her get away from him.

Jarius told her how Jesus stood at the door of Simon Peter's house before Jarius could even call out for him. He told her of the bleeding woman, how she reached out in the crowd to touch the robe of Jesus even as Jarius tried to pull him away, how the hushed crowds fell back to hear her words.

"She was healed by touching his robe?"

"Yes, she did not even ask for healing! She just believed in his power. She touched his robe and after twelve years of bleeding... She was healed. But Jesus knew something happened. He kept asking, 'Who touched me?' Peter and John and James were trying to get him to hurry, to come with me, but Jesus would not go. 'Who touched me?' he said.

"And the woman, oh, she stepped forward and told Jesus it was her. She told him everything, Marah! About her bleeding and her shame, how she touched the robe of Jesus in secret because she was afraid and alone, abandoned by her husband! Divorced and abandoned by her husband.

"Marah, her husband was the same man I gave a divorce to only three days before. She was sick and dying and alone and he abandoned her. And I helped him, Marah! I gave that man who abandoned his sick and dying wife a divorce! I am so ashamed of what I did."

"You did not know. Jarius, you thought you were helping. How could you know the man told you such lies?"

Jarius shook his head. "I wanted his medallion for my

daughter. I let him convince me of a story that I knew was probably false, telling myself how I helped him by giving him such a 'good price' for the necklace. I paid a great sum to ease my own conscience! I lied to myself, Marah."

"You did not know the whole story, Jarius."

"We must find her, Marah, and give the medallion back to her."

"Yes, we will do that. We will find her. Someone will know her."

He told her of the quiet murmur of the crowd when he heard the bitter news of Abigail's death. "Marah, when Asa and Cook ran up to say Abigail was … dead… Oh Marah, to hear she died! I felt as though someone struck me, as though my life was over, too," he said. "My daughter, my little girl!

"And, Marah, this is what Jesus said to me: 'Jarius, listen! Don't be afraid; just believe, and she will be healed.' He left with me at once, his disciples, Augustus and the entire crowd following along. I don't know what happened to the woman he healed…"

Marah could only shake her head in amazement.

"Oh, Jarius, I am so sorry. When Abigail… died," Marah still could hardly say the words, "Her last words were for you and I. 'Be strong for Papa,' that is what she said. 'He will need you.' And 'I will always love you and Papa.' That was the very last thing she said."

Jarius let out a shaky breath. "I do need you, Marah. I am so sad you were alone with Abigail when she died, alone with that terrible, terrible burden, tortured by something evil even as you were suffering. Oh, Marah."

"And I need you, too, Jarius. Please, please always pray for me. Your prayers bring me peace.'

"I always have, Marah, and I always will. From now on, I will spend everyday in gratitude to God for you and Abigail."

"Oh, my husband…"

"You are free, Marah. We have each other, and Abigail is alive. She was dead, and now she is alive!"

"Jesus gave her life, as he gave me life. She was… gone from us, but now she lives. Jesus did this for us."

"We must tell her," Jarius whispered to Marah. "For everyone knows. Jesus said to tell no one what happened in that room. But we must tell her what happened to her, or someone else will. For all the people knew she died. Even the mourners were here!

Such a crowd in our courtyard, outside our home, in the streets! And now, everyone knows she lives. Abigail must hear what happened to her from us."

Marah nodded.

"What shall we tell Abigail, Marah?"

"I don't know. When the time is right, you will know what to say. You will."

Jarius took her hand and kissed it. "I love you, Marah."

Marah's heart was full. She cleared her throat and whispered very softly. "I love you, too, Jarius."

They smiled at each other. They had never before said those words to each other.

Jarius loved her.

"God keep you, my beloved wife."

"God keep you, Jarius, my husband."

A drowsy tranquility covered her, gentle and peaceful. She heard the sound of her husband's breathing at last, quiet and even. He was asleep. It was the first time Jarius ever slept in her bed. He felt strong and reassuring beside her. He felt wonderful.

Abigail lived. Jarius loved her. Jesus forgave her.

Marah closed her eyes and slept.

# CHAPTER 31

The morning sun shone in the kitchen window where the small family sat at the table talking, alone and uninterrupted, just as they had for twelve years. Yet it was different this morning. Jarius's morning prayer was more fervent, more heartfelt than ever before. Marah wiped away a tear as she whispered her soft amen. Abigail looked thoughtful. "Amen," she said with conviction.

Their conversation was quiet and happy, full of the daily sundries that make up life. Yet, restless, unspoken words pressed them, insisting their presence be acknowledged.

What to say to Abigail? Marah thought to herself. Lord, please help me, for I do not know what to say to my daughter. Please, Lord, give Jarius the right words to tell her what has happened.

"Mother, Papa, we have sat right here at this table for many years, talking and laughing, haven't we? For as long as I can remember."

"Since before you were born, Abigail. As soon as we married, your mother made sure we would always spend some family time together every morning before we began our day. It is what has made our family strong."

Marah flushed with pride. It seemed like such an insignificant thing to her.

"Yes, Mother, you have made our family strong. And you are

strong. When I am a woman, I hope I am just like you."

Marah looked at her daughter and shook her head. "I do not want you to be like me, Abigail, for…"

Abigail reached over and put a finger to Marah's lips. "Shhhh. I want to be like the best of you and the best of Papa. Don't worry about what you think are your mistakes. Papa has made them, I have made them, none of us is perfect. Every day is a new day in the Lord!"

She picked up her bread and took another bite, chewing and talking. "We have talked about many things at this table. That too has made us strong. Isn't this true?"

Jarius and Marah looked at each other. What should they say?

Abigail knew she had been very, very sick. Indeed she remembered much of it, casually sharing details of the terrible ordeal, a sickbed perspective that shocked and hurt them. Some of her casual comments almost made Marah physically ill, to hear her daughter describe the pain she suffered, to know her daughter remembered the longs bouts of vomiting and the doctors with their medical treatments, the seizures and the fever, and the pain, the terrible searing pain.

Yes, Abigail knew she had been sick. But to tell Abigail she had died! The words were too terrible to speak. Their great joy could not be contained, yet neither one knew how to speak those words: "Abigail, my precious daughter, you were dead."

Neither one could say it.

So, here they sat, with Abigail sitting at the table, nibbling at bread with honey, looking at them with an expectant face. At their silence, she cocked her head and continued, her voice deliberate. "After all that has happened, we should not be afraid to tell each other everything that is in our hearts, should we?"

Jarius looked at Marah.

"Mother, Papa, now is not the time for secrets."

"Abigail… you are right. There is something we must tell you, something that happened when you were so sick. Something that happened to you."

Abigail stood and held up both her hands to silence her father. Without thinking, they both smiled at her standing with such authority before her parents.

"Mother, Papa." She smiled at them fondly, as though they

were the children and she was the adult. "I know what you are afraid to tell me."

Jarius and Marah looked at each other and then back at their beautiful daughter.

"I was very sick. I know this. But I was more than sick. I was dead."

Marah and Jarius stared at each other.

"My beautiful daughter." Jarius's voice was gentle. "Who told you this?" Marah heard the heartbreak in his voice at those terrible words. The worst fear of a parent, the greatest nightmare, the unspeakable had happened. Abigail had died, and she knew it.

Marah closed her eyes, trying to still her pounding heart just at the thought of those words. Abigail died.

But Jesus had banished death, and brought her daughter to life! Abigail was alive.

Marah opened her eyes.

Abigail smiled. "No one told me, Papa. I know I was dead, and what happened to me… This is the great secret I must share with you. We must tell no one what happened to us, but I must tell you my story. I cannot keep it inside. I was dead."

She turned to Marah. "I remember leaving you, Mother. I will never forget the terrible pain you suffered, lying beside me in my bed." Marah stared at her, shocked.

Abigail turned and stared out the open window. A bird was nearby, a morning song in its throat. "I heard your heart breaking, Mother. It was a terrible thing to see your pain." Her voice was husky.

"After I died, at once I found myself in a wondrous place. I cannot describe it." Abigail's voice was shy, as though she thought Marah and Jarius might not believe her. "I stood before a great throne covered in light, so bright I could not look at it and yet I could not look away. I know it was the throne of Jehovah. It was so beautiful! So beautiful…

"I did not speak to anyone, but I saw faces of … joyous people with faces that glowed like the sun." She reached out and touched Marah's face. "I saw Grandfather standing near me, Mother. He was so happy."

Marah felt as though she could not move. Her father?

"He stood beside a beautiful woman with long dark hair, just like yours, Mother. And she was so tall, like you and me! When she saw me, she smiled a smile I have seen every day of my life, the smile of you, my mother. The same dimples! You never met your mother, but I know that is who stood by Grandfather. I know."

Abigail turned to Jarius. "And a man, I had never seen him before, but I knew at once he was your father, Papa. How would I know this? He died before I was born! Yet I knew it to be true.

"I have been waiting to tell you this, for there is a very difficult thing I must say to you." Her look was hesitant. "This is my great secret, but I cannot keep it from you.

"I did not want to leave that beautiful place. I did not want to leave the people there. I did not want to leave." Abigail's voice shook. "And yet, I could feel your heartache, Mother. I could hear your pain, Papa. It was so strange. There was no sadness in this place. So I did not grieve for you, yet I knew your pain as though it were my own. I cannot explain it. But it was then that I knew it was not yet my time. It was not yet time for me to be in that place."

She looked at both of them and took a deep breath. "Talitha Koum!"

The words of Jesus. No one knew what Jesus said except for Marah, Jarius and the fishermen. As Jesus commanded, they told no one. Yet, Abigail spoke those words to them now.

"I heard the voice of Jesus calling to me. 'Talitha Koum. Little girl, get up!' That is what called me back to you. I knew I had to leave the Father, I knew I had to return, I knew you needed me. When Jesus called me, I could hear the anguish, the sorrow of your breaking hearts. You needed me and it was not yet my time."

Abigail knelt before her father, looking up at him. "Papa, Jesus told you to believe, even when those around you did not. And you did. You believed the Master when he told you I was only asleep. Because of your faith in Jesus Christ, he brought me to life. Because of your faith, Papa."

Tears were running down Jarius's face.

"But there is more, Father. Something evil was fighting for Mother, Papa, and it would have won. Her love for me is so great, her pain at my death brought her to the edge of death, too. The moment I died, the evil one saw Mother at her weakest. It tried to claim her for its own. There is evil here on earth that we cannot fight without God.

"But we are not alone. The Lord is with us."

She stood to place an arm on her mother's shoulder, her

314

voice a whisper. "And now you are free, aren't you, Mother?"

Marah nodded her head, mute with amazement. Abigail knew of the great struggle she endured. How could she? Yet, she did.

"Mother?"

"God has always heard you. You know this now, don't you?"

Marah nodded. She knew God had heard her; he saved her as surely as he returned her daughter to life.

"And so, in the middle of this great struggle, God heard your cries. Because of Papa's faith in God, his belief in Christ, your cry to God to save you... Jesus called me back."

Marah and Jarius sat there in silence. No one told Abigail anything, and yet she knew everything.

Finally, Abigail broke the silence. "I wanted you to know that I know what happened to me. But more than that, I wanted to tell you what happened to me after I left you. You alone. For Jesus said I should not tell anyone what happened to me. The same is true for you.

"However, we cannot hide what Jesus did. People know I was dead. People will soon see me alive." Abigail's smile was sudden and brilliant. "We cannot hide that from them!"

She jumped to her feet as if to prove her point. "For look what has happened to me! Jesus brought me back from death, returned me to life... this is a truth that will live forever! For years and years, for generations and generations, people will know of the great and mighty hand of Jesus! They will know how he taught the truth to all who would listen, how he healed people, how he even conquered death! My death!

"My life, my story will be, must be a testimony to the Son of Man. Papa, you believed because someone you love and trust believed first. And so we must do the same for others. The people that love us and trust us... we must tell them the good news! Jesus, the Teacher from Nazareth, the Son of Man... Jesus is the Messiah, the Son of God."

Her eyes blazed with a fire Marah had never seen. "The Messiah has come, and I must follow him." She threw back her shoulders, her chin high, her back as straight as an arrow, every inch of her tall frame rigid with resolve. "I will follow Jesus."

Jarius looked at her and then at Marah. He let out a long, deep sigh. "Abigail, when you stand like that, well... you look just like your mother. You are your mother's daughter."

"Which is, of course, the best thing ever," Abigail crowed. Jarius and Abigail laughed.

Like me, thought Marah. That's what Miriam said, too. My daughter is like me. And that is not a bad thing. It is a great and wonderful thing, something to be proud of. My daughter is like me.

"Yes, Papa, I am like Mother in that I have made up my mind and you will not be able to change it. For I know what I must do, and I also know what you and Mother must do." She put her hands on her hips.

"We must follow Jesus."

The moment Abigail spoke the words, Marah knew. She stood up and took Abigail's hand. "Yes. We must follow Jesus."

Jarius got up to gather both Marah and Abigail into his arms. His voice was strong and happy.

"As a very wise man said to me just the other day, 'The time is now!'" He winked at Marah. "Yes, we must follow Jesus, for truly he is the Son of God."

They stood like that for a moment, or perhaps a year. Marah had never been so happy.

Abigail pulled away to break the silence. She looked at her father.

"Now," she said in a serious tone, "There is another thing we must discuss. Tell me about the bleeding woman."

Jarius and Marah looked at her, shocked.

What happened to my daughter, thought Marah, that she knows these things? She spoke haltingly. "Abigail... you know about this, too? When you were ...gone from us... you saw these things happening? Or did... did God tell you... about this?" It was hard for Marah to utter something so amazing.

Much to Marah's shock, Abigail threw back her head and laughed out loud. "No, Mother. God did not tell me about the bleeding woman." There was an impish look on her face. "Aunt Miri did."

At the look on her mother's face, Abigail tilted her head and grinned. "Oh, yes. I mean Aunt Miri-AM, Mother!"

There was laughter in their kitchen again.

316

# CHAPTER 32

Marah rubbed the sleep from her eyes, gazing around her room with the befuddled stupor of a mid-day nap. She stretched her long frame, trying to shake her fog away.

Her house was still. What time was it? Marah listened and then bowed her head in the silence. "Jehovah," she whispered, "You are almighty and good, guardian of my soul and keeper of my family. Thank you for your rich blessings and for the goodness you have rained on me these many years. Thank you for Jarius and Abigail and Deena, and for all those I love. Help me to do your will. Thank you for sending us Jesus. Amen."

The terrible whisper, the demon of self-doubt and hatred that had haunted her for years, was gone. In its place stood a gentle peace, a calm understanding that she was a precious child held in the close care of Almighty Jehovah.

It was no problem for Marah to keep her promise to thank God at every moment. Gratitude welled up in her from the moment she opened her eyes until they closed in sleep at night.

Or, as had been the case of late, when she awoke from a mid-day nap.

Her lifelong limited patience was wearing thin at this new lethargy that dogged her footsteps and interfered with her work. She alternated between short bursts of frenzied energy to a bone-jarring weariness… ever since the long sleepless nights and days of Abigail's illness, the start of Abi's new life. Marah could not bring herself to call it anything else.

The well-meaning platitudes of her family did not help.

"Mother. You did not sleep at all for three nights! It's only been a few days. It will just take you a while to catch up."

"Relief and joy can wear you out as much as worry and sorrow, sister. It will soon pass."

"We will take care of things, Mistress! Do not worry, just rest."

"You work too hard anyway, wife! Come with me today instead…"

Marah accompanied Jarius somewhere daily, content to sit nearby and watch as he spoke at the synagogue. She nibbled while he dined with Augustus, or listened as he met with others in his upper room. But on more than one occasion, she found herself nodding off, dreaming of crawling into her own bed as soon as possible.

She made a few trips to the market, and once there paid asking prices with no more than a smile and an absent nod, much to the surprise of the familiar shopkeepers.

"Whatever you think," she murmured in response to the query about the week's menus, as Cook scratched his head in speechless amazement.

"No need to fret, Mistress. It's what you have been through these last months," nodded Deena when finding Marah in a mid-day nap. "Rest, Mistress Marah! Rest your body, your mind and your heart, my dear girl…"

Marah stretched again. Enough of this. She had never been this idle in her entire life, except for the months of Jarius-enforced confinement during pregnancy with Abigail. It was time to get with it. Life was passing her by as she lolled around in bed like one of King Solomon's sluggards.

She clambered up and crossed the room to the water bowl, splashing its cool contents on her face. She was reaching for her veil when the wave of nausea swept over her. She barely made the single step to the night jar before she lost the entire contents of her meager lunch.

It was the second time that day, one of multiple episodes that week.

"What is wrong with me?" she muttered, wiping her lips. She bent to pick up the night jar with its revolting contents when the wave of dizziness hit her. She leaned against the wall for support and took several deep breaths, waiting for her knees to regain their familiar strength.

"Mother!" Marah straightened, energized by the joyous shriek of her daughter, her weakness dispelled by the sound of Abigail's voice. "Mother! Where are you? I need you!"

"In here," Marah shouted. She shoved the clay night jar beside her chest, its lid tightly in place. "In my room, Abi."

Abigail's sandals clattered on the courtyard tiles. She stood at the door, hands on her hips. "Oh, Mother, I'm sorry. Did I wake you?"

"No." Marah felt guilty, like a child caught stealing a forbidden fig. "I was awake. I just can't seem to get back to my old self."

"It will come. You work too hard anyway, Mother."

Deena's gray head peeked around the corner. "Mistress, may I?"

Marah smiled and nodded. No matter what she said, Deena refused to stop wearing the mantle of beloved servant first and Marah's dearest friend second.

"Sit, Mother. We have wonderful news."

Marah looked from her daughter to her friend. "I just got up! Why must I sit?"

"So you don't faint! Sit beside me, Mother."

They knelt on the low bed together. Abigail's voice dropped to a whisper. "We have found her."

Marah knew at once. "Where is she?"

Abigail's story tumbled out. "Well, we haven't quite found her, but we have found two women who know her. The woman returned to Caesarea Phillip where she once lived. But she still has a home here, surely she will return! After she was healed by touching Jesus's robe in the street…" Abigail paused at the wonder of those words, "she left almost at once for Caesarea Philippi. She had not been there for three years, too sick and too poor to travel. Once healed, she left to find her mother the next day."

"Her mother," Marah whispered the words. As she lazed in her bed the last few days, she found herself wondering about her own mother, the woman whose likeness Miriam claimed was the image of Marah and Abigail, the woman standing beside Naaman in the place Abigail alone had seen.

"How did you find this out?"

Deena spoke. "I heard the story from some other women. The two young women are from our synagogue, Mistress. They are the ones who told the woman to seek Jesus, to find him and be healed."

"Do I know them?"

Deena shook her head. "You would recognize them but I do not think you have spoken to them. They are from a different neighborhood than ours."

Marah knew this was Deena's way of saying their families did not keep the company of the family of a synagogue ruler. "We must remedy that at once. Describe them to me."

"I have known them all their lives, since they were children. Their names are Jerusha and Tirzah. Both girls are married, Jerusha with no children and Tirzah with a small daughter and the care of her grandmother. Tirzah is very pretty, tall and thin like you, a quiet woman. I knew the mother of Tirzah very well, she died two years ago."

Marah remembered that day well. She and Jarius were part of a procession of many mourners, a somber train led by the girl Tirzah. Marah didn't even speak to the grieving girl that day. She forced her attention back to Deena.

"Now, Jerusha… She is just the opposite. She is not what people would call beautiful, but something about her… Everyone in Capernaum knows her. People love her and want to be friends with her. She's always laughing, always moving, too. If you watch her for a moment, she's prone to jump up and twirl around on her toes as though she is dancing! She's short, with a round face and big eyes and dimples that shine when she smiles… Dimples like you, Mistress."

Marah nodded, the two girls at once familiar to her. Deena summed up Jerusha perfectly: She looked happy, like someone you would want for a friend. The girl Tirzah was never far from her side.

"I know them. They are always together." She turned to Abigail. "Do you know them?"

"I know who they are, but they are older than me. I have envied how close they seem to be – like sisters."

Marah's heart twisted as she thought about the two girls, about her own sister Miriam. If only she could have given Abigail a brother or sister, too. "Deena, we need to meet these girls."

"Of course, Mistress."

"Mother, Papa will want to go too…"

Marah nodded. "Yes, he will want to speak to the friends of the woman Jesus healed."

It was still Jarius's heartbreak that he was the one to grant the bleeding woman's husband a divorce. "A man I didn't even know," he whispered to Marah night after night. "My pride and envy bettered me. He needed money and a divorce. I wanted the necklace he showed me. I didn't even ask the details of his divorce, and him a stranger! I wanted that necklace for Abigail so much, I ignored my better judgment. I ignored the call to speak with God first, I ignored a story I knew to be full of holes and lies. I only wanted the necklace."

The beautiful diamond and ruby necklace he purchased from the stranger for Abigail's dowry was locked away with the household funds and other items of value in their home. To have purchased a necklace of such value and then learn from Jerusha and Tirzah that its rightful owner was destitute and living in poverty, to learn this sick woman was robbed of her dowry by her devious husband… The story of the bleeding woman's poverty and pain was more than the generous heart of Jarius could bear.

"We will find her and return it," Marah whispered.

"We will find it and return it, but will she forgive me?"

"You did not know. It's not your fault, Jarius."

"I knew everything about him, Marah! I could see it in his eyes. It is my fault. My greed overcame me. I only hope this woman can forgive me." Jarius pulled Marah into his arms and held her tight until sleep overcame her.

Marah turned to Abigail and Deena. "Deena, can you introduce us to these women, in the event the healed woman returns to Capernaum? Or perhaps Jarius will want us to travel to Caesarea Phillip? Either way, we need to meet these women as soon as possible."

"Yes, Mistress."

"And you will please come with us, too? Not as my servant but as my friend, a woman who knows these girls? Please?"

Deena smiled. "Yes, Mistress Marah."

"Fine. Now let me up so I can accomplish something today." Marah stood but at once grabbed Abigail's shoulders as the dizziness returned. She sank down to a crouching position, her head resting on her knees.

"Mother!"

"Deena, the night jar, please." Even Marah was surprised at the calm way she turned from them to once again throw up.

"Mistress!"

"Mother! Are you sick?"

Marah shook her head and scrambled to her feet. "I'm fine. I just need a bit of bread, something to settle my stomach."

Deena cocked her head at Marah. "Mistress, this is not the first time today or this week. I have heard you several times as I have walked by on different days."

Marah colored. Were there no secrets in this house?

"Come to think of it, last night and this morning, you barely touched your food."

"What is wrong with you, Mother?" Marah could hear the alarm in Abigail's voice.

"Nothing at all, daughter. Just nerves and a need for rest."

Deena stared at her with an odd expression, her lips pressed together.

"Mistress, you need a bit to eat. Abigail, please bring your mother a tray of bread and watered wine while I empty the night jar and bring fresh water. Then perhaps you can find your father and tell him the good news about Jerusha and Tirzah?"

"Yes, Deena!" Abigail bounded from the room like a mountain goat, all long legs and skinny arms and shiny black hair.

Deena hefted the night jar in one arm and the water bowl in the other. Before Marah could open her mouth to protest, Deena shook her head. "I'll be right back."

Marah was left alone with her thoughts of the healed woman, the two women who knew her, the ruby and diamond necklace, and, most of all, her rolling stomach.

Deena and Abigail returned at the same time, Abigail with an expression of concern even as she chattered about the two women.

"Are you sure you are all right, Mother?"

"Certainly. Deena is here, anyway. Please go find your father. He will be so glad to hear your news."

"Your mother is fine. I will stay with her. Go." Abigail looked relieved at Deena's nod of approval.

"Really, you two, I am fine! Go find your father, Abigail."

Abigail pecked a kiss on Marah's cheek.

Marah and Deena both smiled at the sight of Abigail's hasty steps from the room. As her footsteps faded away, Deena turned to face Marah. "Sit, Mistress."

"Oh, Deena, I am fine, really…

"Sit."

Marah sat, watching as Deena busied herself. Marah took the damp towel Deena handed her to wipe her face and hands. Deena brought a plate and set it on the floor beside Marah, then lowered herself on the bed, too.

"Mistress, I am reminded of another day many years ago when you when you first arrived in Capernaum. You and I sat here just like this. I heard you crying as though your heart was broken. My dear Jarius lost his temper with you for working in the stables. Do you remember?"

Marah smiled. She hadn't thought of that day for years. She was so happy at Jarius's pleasure with her pregnancy, so lonely for someone to confide in, so haunted by her whisper of fear and doubt. "Remember how Jarius made me stay in bed for seven long months when I was pregnant with Abigail?"

"I remember it well."

"He was so worried." Marah smiled at the memory of her gentle husband flinging the rake against the wall of the barn, spluttering in an anger so unfamiliar to him.

Surely the woman who was healed would understand and forgive Jarius, a man who exemplified forgiveness and grace. It was so important to him.

She heard her stomach grumble its emptiness. Marah gingerly nibbled on a piece of bread, soft and fragrant. It tasted wonderful. She took a big bite.

"Mistress, as I did on that day so long ago, may I please speak freely with you?"

Marah nodded, chewing. Deena always spoke her mind, so the question seemed odd.

"Mistress, I think I know something that you do not yet realize… For the last few days, you have often been ill with vomiting. You take a nap everyday, which was normal for the first few days after Abigail's sickness. But you sleep all the time, which you have never done in all the years we have known each other. Indeed, it's your practice to get up or go to bed at hours no one else can keep!

"One day, you eat next to nothing, picking at your food like a sparrow. The next day, I see you nibbling on olives or bread or figs all day long. You just are not yourself."

Marah was silent, but Deena summed up perfectly what was wrong with Marah. She was not herself... to her own great irritation.

Deena gently took Marah's chin, turning her face to meet Deena's steady gaze. "Mistress, I do not believe you or I have washed out the rags for your monthly courses for at least two months."

A buzz began somewhere in Marah's head. Surely that was not right. Her thoughts raced over the events of the past months, Jarius traveling to Jerusalem, Quintius's illness, Miriam and Asa's visit, that wretched dinner for Zedakiah, Abi's illness...

"Mistress, forgive me for my boldness, but..." Deena pressed one hand against Marah's belly. Marah felt her push against an unfamiliar firm roundness, different from her usual bony flat frame, something she'd noticed but not connected to any opinion of what it might be.

"Mistress..." Deena's voice was a whisper. "Surely you are with child."

The din in her head grew. She pressed her hands to her head as though to silence it. "Perhaps... perhaps I am at the time of life when women change..."

Deena pressed Marah's hard stomach again. "You are far too young for that Mistress... And feel this belly! No, I am certain. You are going to have a baby."

The racket in her head fell silent at once. A baby.

A wide smile spread across Deena's face.

Marah dropped her hands and stared at Deena. "A baby!"

"A baby," Deena echoed.

"A baby," Marah whispered. She closed her eyes. Oh, how great was Jehovah, the God of Naaman and Jarius and Abigail. Her God.

A baby.

Marah's dimples were as deep as the Great Sea.

She thought of her husband. Never once in the years since Abigail's birth did he show a shred of disappointment that Marah only borne him one child. Beautiful Abigail was enough.

Yet, one only had to watch him hold the toddling boys and girls of the synagogue to know he loved children. Jarius would be beside himself with joy. And Abigail! What would her twelve year old daughter think to gain a brother or sister at this age?

Abigail would ecstatic.

"Jarius," Marah whispered.

Deena smiled at the thought of the man she considered her son.

Marah leapt to her feet. "We must find Jarius and Abigail! A baby!"

"Mistress! Shouldn't you–"

"Don't worry, Deena. I am fine! We must tell them at once. Now that I know what is wrong with me, everything is right! How is it possible that God could be so gracious to me? To me, someone so unworthy?"

Deena placed her arm around Marah's shoulders in a tight hug. "You are worthy, Mistress. You are Jehovah's precious daughter, and you are more than worthy. You have always been worthy in Yahweh's eyes."

Marah felt the tears running down her face; her heart was too full for words.

"I will send for Jarius and Abigail." Deena rushed to the door.

Marah nodded. A baby!

A sudden thought interrupted Marah. "Deena, wait! I forgot something important!"

The small woman paused in the doorway.

"The bleeding woman, the woman that Jesus healed… What is her name?"

Deena nodded and the smile returned to her face. "Leah. The woman's name is Leah." She turned and ran from the room.

"Leah," Marah whispered. "Thank you, Lord. Thank you for the life within me, thank you for the life of Abigail, and thank you, thank you Lord… thank you for the life of Leah."

# CHAPTER 33

Abigail and Marah walked with arms linked together, enjoying the cheerful light of early morning. Marah heard Deena humming a few steps behind. Before her lay the aqua-green Galilee, its surface glittering like a million sparkling diamonds shining in the sun. Screeching white gulls wheeled in the brilliant blue sky above.

Marah remembered the day when she and Abigail followed the crowds to Galilee and saw Jesus and his disciples near the boats. Abigail begged to stay and listen, but Marah hurried them away. Jarius was in Jerusalem, summoned by the High Priest.

"We cannot stay," she hissed in Abigail's ear. "Not with your father away!"

That day, Marah thought only to protect her husband and her household from the man called Jesus.

Today, she and her family called that man Lord.

"How are you feeling, Mother?"

"Good." She flashed her dimples at Abigail, a red blush creeping up her face.

"Mother, are you going to be embarrassed for the next six months?" Abigail's voice was teasing. She rubbed her mother's belly. "Soon I will be a big sister! I cannot wait! Get used to everyone hovering over you until this baby makes his or her appearance!"

"You have no idea, daughter. Your father is the worst of all." She had just shared the story of her days of confinement when she was pregnant with Abigail, how worried Jarius was for her and their

326

baby. Abigail crowed with laughter at the story of her busy mother in bed for months, of her sedate father losing his temper, and most of all, of Marah shoveling hay.

Marah smiled at her daughter. "This baby is a blessing, a gift from God for our family. I will take care of myself, yes. Mainly so your father won't fuss! But I am placing the care of this baby in God's hands."

"Papa is coming today?"

"Yes. He is coming to hear Jesus, to speak up if the Pharisees or Sadducees try to shout him down. What he really wants is to meet Leah and ask her forgiveness. But…"

"But first he wants us to meet her, to tell her how sorry he is. I know. We will just tell her everything and ask her to forgive us. After meeting Jerusha and Tirzah, something tells me that Leah will understand. She will forgive us, and Papa, too. I feel it in my heart, Mother."

Marah smiled. She did not know Leah, but for some reason, she felt the same way.

They heard the good news last night, Augustus pounding on their door in the late afternoon. As commander of the century of soldiers stationed here, he always knew things before others.

"He is coming. The Teacher is returning to Capernaum. He and the disciples will stay at Simon Peter's house."

"Then are they leaving Capernaum to go to Jerusalem for the festival? Did Jesus and the disciples go by boat or they will return to Capernaum walking? If they walk to Jerusalem, should we follow them, too? Is Jesus preaching? Will he go to the synagogue or to the sea?"

Only when Abigail stopped for a breath did Augustus tell them that Jesus would be teaching at the Sea of Galilee today.

Then, an hour later, more callers. Jerusha stood in their courtyard dancing on her toes, too excited to stand still, a composed Tirzah behind her with a smile on her face.

"She is here! Leah and her mother are here! They arrived only a few hours ago… They are coming to the Sea of Galilee to hear Jesus tomorrow! I haven't said anything about you yet. But tomorrow, we will introduce you to Leah…"

Jarius ducked his head in shame as Jerusha prattled on, but he did not leave. Marah pulled him into the circle of women that formed in their courtyard, clasping his hands as Abigail uttered a prayer of thanksgiving that Leah had returned to Capernaum.

Jarius could not fall asleep the night before, but Marah slept as deeply as one would expect of a pregnant woman, deep dreams filled with bright hopes for the future.

The Galilee sunshine was warm on Marah's face. She wrapped an arm around her daughter, watching the constant waves. Her heart expanded at the richness of her world. She now counted Jerusha and Tirzah as friends, women who smiled and hugged her when they met. She had never experienced friendship such as this in her life.

Marah loved the serious demeanor of Tirzah, solemn eyes filled with empathy and grace. Everyone referred to Tirzah as the "hard worker." Marah thought it was the highest compliment until she remembered everyone called her a hard worker too... and what had that gotten her?

Instinctively, Marah and Tirzah connected on a deep level.

Tirzah quietly recounted the story of Leah. "The day we met Leah at the well... She was broken and sick and hurting, and yet she refused to give in and cry or beg for help. She was so proud! She did not want the help that Jerusha offered. And yet she was hungry for the good news Jerusha shared, the good news about Jesus I could not yet accept, the story of a man who was a healer and a teacher and a Messiah.

"But Leah listened to Jerusha. Leah believed. Leah made her own way to the Master, to hear him teach and then again to seek his healing touch, alone and on her own, with no one to help her. Oh, to be a strong woman like Leah. Sick for twelve long years, divorced and abandoned by her husband, penniless and alone... And all she wanted was to return to her mother so far away..."

Marah learned that all Tirzah had to do was mention the word "mother" and she would tear up, still mourning the loss of her own mother two years before. Marah reached out an arm to hug her new friend even as she marveled that the gesture was so natural to her.

Tirzah wiped her eyes. "Leah made her way though the crowds and had the courage to reach out and touch Jesus's robes. She had faith that he could heal her. Leah doesn't like to hear anyone say this, but she is an amazing woman of faith. Stronger than me, that's for sure."

Marah remembered Tirzah walking alone, leading her

mother's funeral procession. She hugged Tirzah even tighter. "We are all women of faith, sometimes great and sometimes weak, sometimes steadfast and other times, unsure. Tirzah, I know you are a woman of great faith, too."

"Thank you, Marah." Tirzah whispered.

Jerusha was all everyone said: someone you wanted to count as a friend. Her sharp sense of humor and spirited laughter engaged the entire room, eyes flashing with joy, a wide smile spread across her face. Marah loved her at once. Abigail chattered with her like the sister she never had.

"Without Jerusha, Leah would have never found out about Jesus." Tirzah repeated Jerusha's words Jerusha, urging Leah to find the teacher from Galilee, telling her about the miracle of healing he gave to those who believed. "Jerusha is the one who led Leah to Jesus."

"Leah is a woman of faith and incredible strength. She would have found her way to the Master one way or another," Jerusha responded with an airy wave. "I only did what Jesus tells us all to do, to give to others as he gives to me. 'Give and it will be given to you!' he said. 'A good measure, pressed down, shaken together and running over into your lap!'

"Leah only needed to hear the good news given to me. Her faith sustained her for those twelve long years of sickness – and three years of it on her own, alone and destitute, with only that terrible husband to bring her food once a month. He was so ashamed of her disease, he hid her away for years. He found her necklace, all she had left, stole it and then abandoned her. And still, Leah had faith…"

The women were silent at such great trials and even greater faith.

Jerusha went on. "It was Leah's faith that led her to hear Jesus, to believe that he could heal her. Her faith led her to confess before the Master that she had touched his robe. And Jesus not only healed her, he gave her peace after years of loneliness and shame.

"Leah is the woman of faith, not me. I only listened to the Messiah, believed, and as he commands us, shared the good news with Leah."

Jerusha shrugged off any other comments about her role. "It's God's plan," she smiled. "The good news of Jesus is God's plan for all of us."

The waiting crowds were thick at the edge of the sea. The

news that Jesus and the disciples were returning spread like wildfire.

"Look, Mother! Look, Deena!"

Marah put a hand over her eyes, shielding them from the bright glare of the water, following her daughter's pointing finger. There was the waving figure of Jerusha, standing with a group of women beyond the anchored boats. Her stomach lurched with nerves. Perhaps one of those women was Leah.

"I see Jerusha and Tirzah! And look! I wonder if those women are the ones Jerusha told us about, the ones supporting Jesus with their own money. Some are just believers, but some are like me and Leah, healed by Jesus! Perhaps Jerusha will introduce us to some of those women, too."

"Perhaps she will." Marah tried not to stare. She would like to meet those women, too. She fought off her shyness and followed her daughter, Deena on her heels.

"Hurry, Mother!"

They picked their way through the crowd, some people already sitting, others milling from group to group. Some were clothed in ragged robes, others in the rich linens of the wealthy. Marah glanced down at her own embroidered gown, suddenly self-conscious.

Some sat impassively, perhaps in despair or pain or disbelief, no visible emotion on their faces. Others chattered and laughed, basking in the warm sunshine, seemingly without a care in the world. But everyone, stoic or spirited, wore the same expectant look. Jesus was coming.

"There are all kinds of people here."

"Yes, from all walks of life, it seems."

"Will more come, Mother?"

"I don't know. I only heard Jesus preach in our synagogue, remember?" Marah remembered how when Jesus spoke, her first thoughts were fear for her husband and their way of life. She knew about the miracles of the man from Galilee: young Eri, crippled with legs that no longer held him, the shriveled hand of Old Beker, the paralysis of their own Quintius. She knew about his healings but she did not understand his teachings.

Until Jesus came in to her home to free her daughter from death and into her heart to free her from the bonds of despair, until Jesus released Marah from the whisper of self-hate that threatened to destroy her, until Jesus defeated the demon that nearly cost Marah her life at her own hand… Until Jesus came… Marah had not understood the love and forgiveness of Jehovah.

Jesus gave life to her daughter and restored Marah's heart. The message of Jesus changed her forever.

"Jerusha!" Abigail's shriek of delight pierced the air.

Jerusha twirled around and danced the last few steps towards them, her smile as wide as the horizon. "Marah, Abigail! You're here! Come, there is a place for you right here."

Marah smiled at her new friends. "Hello, Jerusha. Hello, Tirzah."

Two women stood behind Tirzah, different enough in age but alike enough in appearance to be recognized as mother and daughter. Both women had hair streaked through with gray. The daughter's face was drawn and thin, the mother's one of a serene beauty.

Jerusha took Abigail's arm. "Before we sit down, I need for you all to meet." She turned to the younger of the two women near Tirzah. Marah's stomach knotted up. She knew it was too early, but she felt a tiny flutter of movement, as though her unborn child sensed her jitters, too.

"Leah, this is Marah, a woman I have seen in my synagogue for thirteen years – almost all my life! We only became friends a few days ago. She is a very special person who is anxious to meet you."

"Me?" Leah's eyebrows raised in a question.

"Yes, you Leah! And this beautiful young woman is her daughter, Abigail. Marah, Abigail, this is Leah. And this is her mother Talitha, who has traveled from Caesarea Philippi to hear Jesus."

"And to be with my daughter," Talitha added.

Jerusha grinned. "I know. Never to be parted again! Like Naomi and Ruth, that's our Leah and Talitha! Ladies, please meet Marah and Abigail."

When Leah smiled, the traces of what was once a striking beauty shone through. She wore the lines of a fading illness in a face that radiated happiness.

"Oh, such a pretty daughter you have, Marah," Talitha spoke first. "Leah, Abigail reminds me of you when you were thirteen."

Leah flashed a smile at her mother and turned to Marah, looking up to smile at her. "My goodness! You are the tallest woman I have ever met!"

"Leah!"

Marah heard the scolding tone of Talitha and flushed, but at the friendly gaze of Leah, she burst out laughing. "Yes, I am always the tallest woman anyone has ever met. Half the time I am taller than any man they've ever met, too!"

Leah brightened. "Sorry, that just popped out! Besides, I haven't met anyone for so long, I'm glad to know you are really tall and it's not just my imagination! I'm glad to meet you, Marah and Abigail. Friends of Jerusha and Tirzah are friends of mine!"

Tiny in comparison to Marah, Jerusha danced a few steps in her irrepressible excitement, her secret too great to bear much longer.

Marah looked at her and nodded. "Leah and Talitha, it's good to meet you, too. We have been praying for this moment."

"We have been praying to meet you for days and days!" Abigail chimed in.

"Praying to meet me? Why me?"

"We needed to find you. Someone told us Tirzah and Jerusha were your friends, and they told us you would return from Caesarea Philippi to hear Jesus." Abigail bounced on her toes in a fair imitation of Jerusha. "We are so glad you are here at last!"

Marah nodded.

"We had to find to find the bleeding woman!"

"Abigail!" Marah was mortified at her daughter's candor, but Leah nodded as though she had heard the sentiment before.

"Abigail." There was only the tiniest reproach in Marah's voice. "Abigail, please, let Jerusha finish introducing us."

Jerusha laughed and spun around once. "Oh! How I have been waiting to introduce the two of you! I could hardly keep it a secret from you last night, Leah." She took Abigail by one arm, Leah by the other and pulled them close. "Leah, Marah is married to Jarius, the synagogue ruler. Abigail is the synagogue ruler's daughter."

"It's nice to… it's nice…" Leah puffed a stutter of air. Her knees buckled, but Jerusha had a firm grip on her arm.

Tears sprang to Leah's eyes. "You are the girl who died and then… Jesus brought you to life again…"

Abigail nodded. "And you are the bleeding woman who was sick for twelve years and then healed by the touch of the robe of Jesus."

Jerusha spoke up. "Marah and Abigail, Leah is the woman who believed so fervently in Jesus, she knew that just a touch of the Master's robe would heal her from twelve years of bleeding. Leah,

Abigail is the girl who died after three days of illness. Jesus brought Abigail back to life.

"Abigail, Leah was sick, so very sick for twelve long years. But she never stopped believing in Jehovah. After she heard Jesus, her fear was gone. She was not even healed, and yet she believed in the Son of Man.

"Leah, Abigail is her mother's only child, the daughter of Jarius, my synagogue ruler. She is bright and beautiful and faithful, the light of life for her mother and father. Even though the Jewish leaders are denouncing Jesus, even though the Pharisees and Sadducees do not believe in him, her father Jarius believed. He believed despite the reproach of others. He left the synagogue's doctrines behind to ask Jesus to heal his daughter.

"Two miracles, one man. Binding you together forever in your faith."

"Two women, two miracles." Talitha's voice was soft.

Marah cleared her throat. There was something that had to be said before they could go any further. "Leah, we have something that belongs to you." Her voice shook a little. "Before we talk any more, I need to ask you to please forgive my husband Jarius and me."

"Forgive you? Whatever do you mean?" Leah looked confused. "I don't even know you."

Marah prayed for the right words and held out a box to Leah. "My husband purchased this for Abigail. He only thought it would be a beautiful gift for our daughter's dowry. He had no idea the man who sold it was not its rightful owner. Had he known…" she struggled a bit with the words, "had he known of your story, Leah, he would not have helped your husband. Please, forgive my husband Jarius. He truly is a good man. Please, forgive us."

"Forgive him for what?"

"My husband is the ruler of the Capernaum synagogue. He is the one who granted your husband a divorce. And because your husband had no money, my husband Jarius purchased a necklace from him. He thought he was helping, providing money for travel, for more doctors for you. Your husband told Jarius he was taking you home to your mother, and divorcing you so your dowry would be legally yours. He even told Jarius the money would be used to pay for your doctors."

Marah faltered at the look of sorrow on Leah's face. She forced herself to continue. "Jarius feels so guilty that he helped your husband divorce you and abandon you in your illness. But he did not know! Jarius and I are so sorry for what happened. Jarius cannot forgive himself, but he hopes… we hope that you can find forgiveness in your heart."

Leah was silent.

Abigail took the box from Marah and placed it in Leah's hands. "This belongs to you, Leah."

Leah opened the box and looked at its contents for a long moment, the rare jewels brilliant in the bright sun. She touched the ruby and diamond necklace with one lingering finger, and then handed the box to her mother. "It is our necklace, what Reuben stole from me."

Talitha nodded. "The necklace of our family. Generations of women… my grandmother and before, your grandmother, me, you, and someday… this necklace was to have been your daughter's… from mother to daughter, one generation after another.."

"Mother to daughter?" Abigail's voice was weak. She and Marah stared at each other.

Marah forced herself to speak. "Leah… Your husband… told Jarius the necklace was handed down from father to son. He said he loved you and would never remarry. With no son to give the necklace to, he… just wanted to be rid of it and its memories."

Marah bowed her head. "Jarius… did not know. Jarius thought he was helping your husband by purchasing it. We are sorry."

Leah nodded. "Yes, Reuben thought the necklace was his."

"It was never his!" Marah heard the anger in Talitha's voice.

The necklace sparkled in the sun.

Abigail took Marah's hand and as one, both women stood straight and tall, chins high with unwavering gazes. But it was Abigail who spoke.

"Leah? My father is a good, good man. Anyone will tell you so, he is the fairest and kindest person. Papa's heart is broken that he is the one who bought the necklace, the one who gave your husband the divorce. And to think he met you on the street when you reached out for healing from Jesus! He cannot get over this grief he has caused you. Please, we ask for your forgiveness. For my father, for all of us, I beg you to forgive us."

Leah shook her head and sighed.

"The loss of the necklace was a hard thing for me, for my

husband stole it from me even as I was struggling to stay alive. I was so sick at that point. I thought I had hidden it from him. It was all I had left, my safeguard against being destitute if Reuben ever abandoned me. My way back home…

"But more than its value, the necklace was the last thing that tied me to my mother. I should have sold it as soon as Reuben left me here alone, sold it years ago! But to sell it seemed as though I was giving up on all that was precious to me, to give up my last tie to my old life, to my mother…

"After Reuben told me he was divorcing me, I knew I would never see him again. He could not bear the shame of my bleeding, my twelve years of uncleanness and being an outcast from our faith. The time had come. I had to sell the necklace so I could finally try to return home to my mother.

"Once Reuben stole the necklace, it was as though there was nothing left for me, no money, no way home, no tie to my mother, no reason to fight my illness or fight for my life. Nothing. I wanted to die."

Talitha wiped tears away with the corner of her veil.

"But I overheard Jerusha and Tirzah talking about a teacher, a man of miracles. Their kindness to me, a stranger, moved me so. I found what little courage I had left to ask them about this man they called Jesus. Jerusha told me about the power of his healing words, a message that would restore hope to my heart.

"I realized I still had one thing left, one thing that could not be taken away: the faith that Jehovah still cared for me."

She shook her head.

"One morning, I gathered all my strength to come to this very spot, to hear Jesus teach. Except to go to the well, it was the first time I ventured out of my house in three years! I was held captive by my illness and the hatred of my husband.

"It nearly did me in get here… alone, bleeding, an untouchable and so weak I thought I would fall over in the street!! But the message of Jesus is love and forgiveness, and it gave me the courage. Courage to forgive Reuben. Courage to fight for my life.

"Courage to come back another day, to hide in the crowd and then reach out to him with a shred of faith that I might too be healed!

"And he healed me. 'Go in peace, daughter.' Those were the words that Jesus said to me as we stood in that dusty street with the crowds all around us. 'Go in peace.' Abigail, Marah, there is nothing to forgive! For how could you know anything about my troubles? There is nothing, nothing to forgive." Leah took Abigail's hand. "But if there was, I would forgive you just as Jesus forgave me, indeed how the Lord forgives anyone who asks him to save them from their sin."

Marah closed her eyes, remembering Jarius's words that night so long ago "What sort of man can forgive sin, Marah? What sort of man?"

The son of God, she thought. Jesus is the son of God.

Leah took Abigail's hand. "Abigail, I am so honored and so… happy to meet you. For… I must ask you to forgive me for something, too."

"What, Leah?"

"Forgive me for what I did to you. Abigail. When the man ran up to your father… 'Don't bother the Master,' he said, 'for your daughter is dead.' Your father fell over in the street, his grief was terrible to see…"

Marah's eyes filled with tears.

Leah went on, forcing the words. "To think that you… died… at the very moment I was healed from my terrible disease… I was devastated. I was so happy that Jesus healed me, yet my heart broke to hear of your death. A twelve-year-old girl, the daughter of a synagogue ruler, dying died while Jesus stopped to talk to me, an unclean, unworthy bleeding woman! How your father wept in the street. Jesus told me to go in peace, but how could I, when I knew that while Jesus stopped to heal me… you died. If he had not stopped for me, you might not have died. You lost your life even as I gained my own."

Leah took Abigail's other hand and they faced each other. "Yet Jesus was clear in his command to me: 'Go in peace, daughter.' Jesus gave me peace, but I found my joy when I heard that you lived, raised from death by Jesus.

"I have the peace of Jesus. The peace of Jesus is for all of us who believe. I think we can put this behind us and only be bound by our faith. There is no forgiveness between us, only friendship and our love for the Lord. Abigail, I am so glad to meet you, my fellow miracle, my sister in the faith that is the man from Galilee."

Abigail grabbed Leah in an impulsive hug. "I am so glad to meet you, too, Leah."

Leah turned to look at Marah. "Marah, I look forward to meeting Jarius – today, I hope! There are no hard feelings between us, only joy that our lives have crossed and that we stand here today to see Jesus."

There was silence among the women, every pair of eyes filled with tears, watching Leah and Abigail, remembering, reflecting, silently rejoicing, no words for the thanksgiving in their hearts. The air was heavy with emotion, the noise of the crowd a quiet hum, the waves a steady crash on the white sand.

Abigail's cheerful voice broke the silence. "Whew! What an introduction, Jerusha! Now, can we just get down to the business of being friends?"

Everyone burst into laughter.

As a matter of fact, once they started laughing, they could not stop. They laughed until they cried, holding their sides, groaning with joy. Marah, cupping her belly with its small bulge of a baby, laughed so hard she had the hiccups.

Men walked by and shook their heads, glaring at them with sidelong glances. Women! Laughing! Laughing with tears running down their faces, when the man from Galilee might arrive at any moment! The men exchanged knowing looks. Women.

Other women around them looked on, smiling, remembering times they too had laughed until they cried. Oh, such lucky women, to have so few cares in the world, to stand laughing with friends, waiting for Jesus.

They were still laughing as Leah placed a hand on Marah's shoulder. "I'm honored to know you, Marah, to meet you and your beautiful daughter, Abigail. I know we will be friends. Good friends!"

"I hope so," Marah said shyly. She felt Deena's arm around her shoulders.

"Me, too!" Abigail's shining presence could not be denied. The laughter started again.

Talitha spoke softly. "She is clothed with strength and dignity."

"But some of us wear more clothes than others of us. Or maybe we just wear bigger clothes!" Jerusha giggled.

"She can laugh at the days to come." Deena's voice was strong. Marah smiled at her life long friend.

"I know that teaching, Talitha! Papa taught it to me years ago. 'She speaks with wisdom. Faithful instruction is on her tongue.'

That's what Papa said about you, Mother."

Marah flushed red at her daughter's words.

Leah smiled at the mother and daughter and slipped an arm around her own mother's waist. "Her children arise and call her blessed."

Abigail chimed in. "Her husband also. He praises her!" Marah turned even redder.

Tirzah's eyes were sparkling. "Many women do noble things."

The women paused to look at each other. In one voice, they finished Old King Solomon's pronouncement on the worth of women:

"But you surpass them all!" It was practically a shout.

"Look!" Abigail interrupted their laughter.

He came toward the seashore with a purposeful stride, laughing with the group of men around him, bending down to touch the children he passed or nod at those who sat waiting.

Jesus.

As one, the women sat down, waiting for the Master to speak, laughter on their lips and the joy of friendship in their hearts.

An excerpt from the third book in the series
*And Also Some Women*

# Her Heart's Inheritance

## CHAPTER 1

Abigail burst into the room, her veil slipping down to her shoulders. "Hurry, Mother! Everyone will leave without us! Leah and Talitha left this morning! Jerusha and Tirzah are leaving now. We'll be the only ones left!"

Marah did not lift her head from her task at hand. "Abigail, we can always catch up. We cannot go until your father gets here. And we're stopping at Shiloh, anyway. Don't worry so! Help me with the boys' things."

Abigail's twinge of irritation dissolved at the sight of two identical, curly-haired babies on the floor. Twins just starting to totter, they were both hollering gibberish and tugging on Marah's robe, each flashing the deep dimples of their mother and sister.

"Naaman and Ezi! Come! Come to Sissy!" Abigail held out her arms and both boys crawled at once to their sister. "How do you feel, Mother?"

"Good! I feel good. I am thankful we are bringing the cart

340

and several donkeys so I may ride. It would be a long way to walk carrying this load with these two boys tugging on my robe."

Abigail rubbed her mother's bulging belly and grinned. "It would indeed."

"Abi, Abi Abi!" Little Naaman fell with a plop to his bottom, yanking on the hem of Abigail's tunic. When she failed to respond to his urgent demands, he crawled under her tunic instead. Ezi thought this a good idea, but before he could try to commandeer Naaman's secret spot, Abigail bent and picked him up in her arms. They turned at the sound of Jarius' voice, Naaman's little face peeking out from under Abigail's robe.

"Da! Da! Da!" Both boys babbled at the sight of their father.

"Hello! I'm sorry I am late! Come here, Naaman!" Jarius rescued Abigail from her rambunctious brother and kissed his daughter on the cheek. He turned to Marah. "Are we ready? We must be away! Where is Deena? Where is Cook?"

"Cook left with Augustus and Quintius. Deena is… Well, Deena is right here."

The gray-headed friend stood in the doorway. "The only one not ready is you, Master Jarius!"

Jarius laughed, pulled Marah close and kissed her. "I love you, my wife!" Squished by their embrace, little Naaman squirmed to get down even as Ezi tugged to get up.

"Papa! Let's get going."

Jarius grinned at his daughter and turned to place his hand on Marah's burgeoning waistline. "How are you feeling? Are you sure you are up for the trip? It is such a long way to Jerusalem." His black eyebrows drew together. "Another baby! I'm worried. Are you sure, Marah?"

"Of course I am, I feel wonderful! I wouldn't miss this for anything, Jarius. The baby won't come for another few months. How could I could I not be fine with you and Abigail and Deena hovering over me? Plus there's Miriam and my other sisters. And Leah, Talitha, Jerusha, Tirzah…"

"I can't compete with that crowd of women." Jarius threw up his hands. "I'll be lucky to have even a moment of your time!"

Marah dimpled at the thought of her friends, secure in the knowledge that her husband always found time for her. "Once we get these boys to Shiloh out travels will be easy, so many people to help us. Naaman and Ezi will have a great time with their aunts and cousins on the road to Jerusalem."

"And there's much to do in Jerusalem... Meetings, worship in the Temple, seeing our family and our friends, Passover... Is there anything else going on?"

"Papa!"

"Don't tease your daughter, Jarius. It will be a wonderful trip for many reasons."

"Just think, just a few months ago we presented our boys in the Temple." Jarius rubbed Naaman's curly head and then rubbed the baby in his wife's belly, too. "And soon, we'll dedicate this one, too. How God has blessed us!"

Marah smiled, her hand resting the precious baby she carried now for six months.

"Papa! Stop talking and let's leave." Abigail was out of patience. "We don't want to be at the end of the caravan. Hurry! Jesus will be teaching in the Temple this week. Our friends have already left. I don't want to miss a thing. Let's go!"

"You wouldn't be in such a rush because of a certain young man, would you, Abigail?"

"No! Maybe. Papa, please just hurry!" Berry red, Abigail ducked her head in embarrassment.

Jarius and Marah grinned at each other.

Abigail could not wait to get to Jerusalem. Once there, her father would enter into negotiations for her upcoming betrothal. She still could not believe her dream was coming true.

"But he lives so far away," her mother had argued.

"Abi, you could have your pick of any young man in Capernaum," said her father.

Their concerns fell on deaf ears.

Abigail, talkative, confident, exuberant Abigail, stood tongue-tied and bashful when she first met the young man at Aunt Miri's and Uncle Asa's home. She had never met a man quite like him, boisterous, energetic... and very handsome.

But when she learned he was as passionate in his devotion to Jesus Christ as she, when she found out that he sought to meet her and hear first hand her amazing story of life, Abigail found the courage to meet his eyes. And from that moment, she was smitten.

Abigail was in love. And miracle of miracles... John Mark was in love, too... with Abigail, the daughter of the Jarius and Marah.

If you liked THE SIN OF THE MOTHER,
you may enjoy the first book in the series

## *And Also Some Women*

# TWELFTH
# YEAR

### Sherri Sechrist

Beautiful Leah's outwardly privileged life has a dark side, including an arranged marriage to a gruff, silent stranger. But Leah's devotion to her new husband overcomes their differences – until a shameful illness strikes the new bride.

Leah's mother fights for her only daughter, but Leah is cast out by her Jewish community. Abandoned and alone, Leah survives only through her steadfast faith and stubborn will.

One day, Leah overhears two women walking to the well, marveling over the miracles of a stranger in their city. Can the promises of an itinerant teacher possibly be true for a forgotten woman named Leah?

Available on Amazon.com

www.ingramcontent.com/pod-product-compliance
Lightning Source LLC
Chambersburg PA
CBHW060355260626
47160CB00006B/2321